James Hannay

Thrilling Scenes on the Ocean - Or Swell Life at Sea.

A Collection of Nautical Yarns

James Hannay

Thrilling Scenes on the Ocean - Or Swell Life at Sea.
A Collection of Nautical Yarns

ISBN/EAN: 9783337034078

Printed in Europe, USA, Canada, Australia, Japan

Cover: Foto ©Andreas Hilbeck / pixelio.de

More available books at **www.hansebooks.com**

THRILLING SCENES

OR

THE OCEAN:

OR,

SWELL LIFE AT SEA.

A Collection of Nautical Yarns.

———◆———

NEW YORK:

DERBY & JACKSON, 498 BROADWAY,

1860.

PREFACE.

IN presenting the present Volume to the reading public, we have thought that a word or two of preface would not be out of place. We have always believed that all that was necessary to make a Volume of Nautical Tales popular and acceptable, was to get it up in a good shape, and place it properly before the world.

The ocean is a vast store-house, from which Literature can extract as many valuables as Commerce. Sea life abounds so greatly in incidents, that nautical tales ever possess a freshness that no other species of composition can possibly lay claim to. In the course of a single year, a maritime officer will pass over a large portion of the world. He starts from New York or London, and in a few days he finds himself surrounded by the aroma of the tropics. Leaving the tropics, he passes down to Cape Horn—visits the Indian Ocean—looks in upon the Chinese—and the next month, perhaps, directs his prow towards the Arctic Ocean, Russian America, and the dangers and excitements of Behering's Straits and

Hudson's Bay.   At all these places he supplies himself with new ideas, sees mankind under a new aspect, and enriches his common-place book with a thousand facts and fancies, of whose existence the man of conservative habits has no possible idea.

The articles which make up this volume have been selected, with great care, from the writings of some of the best authors of the age; they are of all possible temperaments, from the rollicking adventures of Forbessy to the daring excitements of a Guineaman.

Should the volume of which we are now speaking meet with that success which it so justly deserves, we shall follow it up with others on the same subject—the whole forming a Nautical Library superior to any yet published in America.

CONTENTS.

CRUISE OF A GUINEAMAN.

FROM A

MIDSHIPMAN'S LOG.

BY JOHN W. GOULD, ESQ.

CHAPTER I.

JACK GARNET," quoth Tom Seymour, as we stood upon Pier No. 1, North River, one afternoon in July, 18—, "do you see my brig, yonder? She is a sweet craft—carries twenty long-eighteens, and a long forty-two, besides two twenty-four pound carronades on the poop, and two on the forecastle; two hundred men, who are stationed and quartered as in men-of-war; three officers, whom I call, for fun's sake, second and third lieutenants, and master; and half-a-dozen boys for reefers. Now I want a first lieutenant, and you are the very fellow. Ship with me, and we'll run down to the Trades in ten days, and then—whew! Go away, salt water! She is a Baltimore clipper, sails like the devil, and will put the wind's eye out on a bowline. Give her one point free, and she's off like a shot. Will you go?"

"Thank you," I replied, "I am somewhat ticklish about the neck. I would rather be hung *round the waist.* You are too strong to be honest; and when you are on blue water, you will make some mistake on the subject of pro-

perty ; and then the first man-of-war you fall in with, will
string you all up at her yard-arm, and that's an elevation
for which I am in no wise ambitious.   I would rather die in
my bed when the time comes."

"Well," replied Tom, "I am sorry you are so particular
about your cravats : but will you go on board and take a
look at her?   I hove-short this morning, and shall trip my
anchor in half an hour and go to sea.   Come, I'll leave you
at quarantine."

We jumped into his boat, (a twelve-oared cutter,) and
pulled for the brig.   As we neared it a boatswain's call
"piped the side ;" four side-boys manned the gangway as
we passed over, and we were received upon deck in true
man-o'-war fashion.

"Why, Captain Seymour," said I, "you have a regular
man-of-war brig here."

"Yes," he replied, leading the way to his cabin, "she's
a Johnny War.   Mr. Carline, (second lieutenant,) hoist in
boats, and get ready for weighing anchor, sir."

"Now, Garnet," he continued, as we were drinking wine
in the cabin, "you had better reconsider, and go with me.
You can make your fortune in one cruise on the coast of
Africa, where we are bound."

"Save your breath to cool your porridge, friend Seymour," said I, "for I tell you flatly, I will *not* go ; and you
may as well set your mind at ease on that point, for I have
no more dodge about me than the main-mast."

At this instant, a reefer reported all ready for weighing
anchor.

"Call all hands up anchor, then," said he.   "Garnet,
will you take the trumpet, just to oblige me ?   I have some
writing to do before we leave the port."

I took the deck, accordingly.   The capstan was manned,
the anchor run up, and sail made ; and with a smacking

breeze from the northwest, we dropped down the bay. Just
before we reached the quarantine, Seymour came on deck.

"Captain Seymour," said I, "you will please take command : I wish to be set on shore here. Port, quarter-
master. Boatswain's-mate, call away third-cutters."

"Belay all !" interrupted Seymour. "Lieutenant Garnet,
you are in for it, and shall go with me anyhow."

"Perhaps I shall," said I, dispatching the trumpet at
his head, as I walked forward to the starboard-gangway to
look out for a shore-boat. There was none near, and looking aft, I saw Seymour clear away the end of the main-
royal-halliard, and tie it in a running-bowline. That manœuvre showed me that there was no time to be lost, and
as we were now in the narrows, and within a hundred yards
of the Staten Island shore, I buttoned my roundabout, and
hailing Seymour, "Here goes for the coast of Africa !"
jumped overboard and struck out for the land.

Seymour, however, was as wide awake as I, and as I rose
to strike out the second time, his running-bowline came over
my head, caught me round the body, and I was hauled on
board before I knew what was the matter.

"There," said he, laughing, as he met me at the gangway, "you see I am a bit of a Guacho, and can throw a
lasso on a pinch. You are hung *round the waist*, now, just
as you wished not long since."

My reply to his wit was a blow with my fist, which tumbled him across the deck in fine style ; but before I could
repeat it, I was overpowered, and being taken upon the
poop, was lashed hand and foot to a carronade.

"Now then, Lieutenant Garnet," said Seymour, "when
we get out of sight of land, I'll loose you ; but if I were
to do it sooner, I'm afraid you would be overboard again."

As I could not do battle, I quietly submitted to my fate,
because swearing would do no good. So now behold me,

bound for foreign parts—first lieutenant of a brig-of-war—
anchored *head* and *stern* athwart-ships of a carronade. As
we passed the forts, the first object which met our view was
the frigate Constellation, at anchor in the lower bay.

"The devil !" said Seymour, clapping a spy-glass to his
eye ; "she dropped down yesterday, and had, I supposed,
gone to sea. I remember they looked at me pretty hard as
they passed me at anchor, and now they are waiting to
catch me. I'll weather them yet."

As we neared the frigate, I observed some motion aboard
of her ; and in an instant after, all the ports of the main-
gun-deck, on the starboard side—the side toward us, as she
rode at anchor—were taken out, and the tompions of all
that battery followed.

"Do you see that, Captain Seymour ?" said I, smiling.

"I do, Lieutenant Garnet," was his reply. "Port,
quarter-master."

"Port, sir."

"Mr. Carline," he continued, "take the deck, sir, while I
uniform. Keep her head for the stern of that frigate."

He went into the cabin, and in a moment reappeared, in
the full uniform of the United States' Navy, cocked-hat,
sword, a pair of pistols in his belt, and a cigar in his mouth.
As he came upon the poop, a sheet of red flame glanced
from one of the Constellation's ports, which was followed
by the emphatic report of a thirty-two-pounder. The ball,
by *accident* of course, struck our cut-water, and made us
minus a figure-head.

"The English of that," said Seymour, "is 'come-to, you
rascal.' Since my friend, the commodore, wishes it, I'll do
that thing. Port, quarter-master. Keep her for the bows
of the Constellation. Loose royals and to'gallantsails, for
we've a stiff breeze, and I have no idea of being afraid of
them. Send up our black ensign, signal-quarter-master, at

the peak, fore and main, and *under it* the American flag !
There !" smacking his lips, as that dread banner floated
gayly on the breeze, over the stars and stripes, "that will
do better.   Lieutenant Garnet, what say you ?"

"Go to the devil !" I replied, for I was not in the best of
humor.

"If I do, Lieutenant John Garnet," said he, complacently,
"I have the satisfaction of knowing that you will sail in
company."

"Cast loose both batteries," he continued, "and load
each a round-shot, a stand of grape and canister, and fill
the long forty-two to the muzzle."

When we were about two hundred yards from the frigate,
dashing ahead at ten knots, he ordered the drums to beat
to quarters, took his stand upon the starboard-quarter rail
to cun the brig, and sung out :

"Slack the lee-braces—round-in the weather ones—starboard the helm, hard-a-starboard !" .

We fell off before the wind, and passed abreast the Constellation, as she rode head to the wind, so closely, that the
muzzles of her long main-deckers almost touched our bulwarks.   The captain of the Constellation stood abaft upon
the signal-locker ; and Seymour coolly tossing his cigar upon
her deck, hailed him :

"Brother commodore, if you are short of hands, I'll lend
you a hundred, and take payment in round-shot and
canister."

"Commodore Montague," *I* hailed, "I am detained here
by force.   Compel my release, sir."

"Heave-to, you sir," said Montague to Seymour, "and
send that man aboard of me, instantly."

"I'll see you —— first," was Seymour's resolute reply.

"Heave-to, instantly," repeated Montague, " or I'll sink
you !"

"Do it, and be —— to you," replied Seymour, drawing his cutlass in defence. "Man the starboard-battery! Port, hard-a-port—stand by—mind the weather roll—fire!"

We passed under the Constellation's stern, raking her, as each gun came to bear, dismounting her stern chasers, and clearing her main-gun-deck entirely, for the moment.

"Starboard the helm!" hailed Seymour, firing a pistol at Montague.

We fell off before the wind, and keeping the Constellation's three masts in one, made all sail for the bar, there being no time for chat, as she of course would instantly slip her cable, and bring her broadside to bear. Our fears were groundless, though Seymour's matchless effrontery was all that saved him. While the Constellation's guns actually bore upon us, they were restrained from firing, by their amazement at the impudence of the "little fellow;" and, at this moment, they could not fire if they would. Their cap-stan-bars were shipped, and everything was in readiness for weighing anchor, when we hove in sight; but our strange conduct perplexed Captain Montague, and our raking broadside completely nonplussed him. Our shot unshipped his capstan-bars, cut up his messenger, and totally demol-ished the bitts where the cable was belayed; in consequence of which, the cable ran out until it was brought up by getting foul in the hause-hole, and there it was jammed perfectly fast.

The combination of so many unusual events produced an unwonted result; and for the first time since tar and oakum came into fashion, a United States' ship was in confusion; and before order was restored, we were across the bar, and nearly out of shot, without the loss of a man. Perceiving that I might as well make the best of a bad bargain, I hailed Seymour:

"Cut these lashings, Tom ; I will do as you wish, since I can't avoid it."

"You are a clever fellow, Garnet," said he, complying with my request ; "I like your spunk. You are just the man to be my first lieutenant : will you take that command ?"

"I will," said I, "and I'll be obeyed and respected accordingly."

"It is a bargain," he replied, grasping my hand ; and, turning to his crew, he informed them of my elevation, and commanded their obedience.

"The Constellation has slipped her cable, sir," reported the signal-quarter-master, "and is making all sail in chase."

"Very good," answered Seymour, "she cannot catch us."

"You are wrong there," said I, "she brings the breeze with her, and as it will soon blow a gale, she will have the advantage."

"Night is coming on," said Seymour, "and we'll dodge them. That we can do at any rate."

"You will please remember, Captain Seymour," said I, "that you have a Yankee to deal with ; and, moreover, the fellows whose skins you chafed with grape and cannister will feel rather touchy, and keep a bright look-out."

"Ay," replied he, smiling, "and the commodore, too, will like an opportunity to return my pistol-shot. Take the deck, Garnet, while I work up my reckoning, and make my will."

It was now growing dark, and the array of clouds in the northwest, and the increasing swell of the sea, plainly showed that a gale was coming. It was, therefore, necessary to get all the start we could before it came on to blow ; for in a gale the Constellation, being larger and heavier, could carry sail longer than we, and of course would overtake us. I accordingly gave orders to set fore and main-royals, and fore and main-topmast-studdin'-sails, and as she bore that well, I added to'-gallant-studdin'-sails, boarded the starboard-tacks, and putting her head south-by-west, we were off at twelve knots an hour.

It was now nearly dark, but with our night glasses we could see the Constellation, under sky-sails, and royal-studdin'-sails, steering directly for us, with the speed and the fury of an avalanche.

"Well," said Seymour, watching her with his spy-glass, "unless Montague takes in his sky-sails and royal-studdin'-sails pretty soon, he will have the royal-masts over the side, for the breeze is much fresher with him than with us."

At this moment a heavy squall struck the Constellation : as soon as it cleared up, the signal-quarter-master reported that her sky-sails and royal-studdin'-sails were blown away.

"That's good news," said Seymour, chuckling ; "Garnet, we'll distance them yet."

"She has bent new sky-sails, sir," reported the quarter-master, a moment after.

"The devil she has !" said Tom, stopping short in his walk—" why, she's in earnest.   Set *our* royal-studdin'-sails and sky-sails, Mr. Garnet—we'll pull foot."

I obeyed the order, and away we went, with our studdin'-sail tacks, and royal and skysail back-stays, as taut as bars of iron.

For a while nothing material happened, and each about held her own ; but at two bells in the evening watch, the Constellation's skysails and royal-studdin'-sails blew away, and the skysail masts overboard.

"That is a fair hint," observed Seymour : "Mr. Garnet, we'll save our skysails, and royal-studdin'-sails.   Take them in, sir."

The order was obeyed, and for a moment the brig was

easier—but the wind freshening very much, we were obliged
soon after to furl the royals ; and, shortening sail as it became necessary, at four bells in the evening-watch we were
under main-to'-gallantsail, while the frigate had all three
to'-gallantsails and main-royal standing, coming on "hand
over fist." At six bells she was within range of our long
forty-two—a heavier gun than any she carried. It being
run out at a stern port, Seymour pointed it himself, and
watching the send-forward, fired. The ball struck the
frigate's figure-head, scattering it about in fine style.

"There," said Seymour, laughing, "we are even now.
She knocked my figure-head to pieces in the bay, and now
I have given her as good."

After we had fired a few times, the frigate's bow-chasers
began to give tongue ; and, each hoping to disable the
other, shots were exchanged with great gusto, although it
was too dark to see the effect. But, in spite of everything,
she continued to gain upon us, and at two bells in the mid-
watch was within two miles of us, the wind blowing a gale,
under whole topsails and courses, while we had a reef in
each.

As a last refuge, we bore off before the wind, continuing
to blaze away with our long forty-two, while she, as we kept
her three masts in one, could not fire a shot ; but, although
our shot evidently *told*, they did not do much mischief.

At four bells in the mid-watch, she was within half-a-mile,
and was preparing to give us a broadside, which would have
paid off all scores, when a tremendous squall suddenly came
over, and it became entirely dark.

We hauled our wind instantly, boarded our larboard-
tacks, put out every light, and kept silence fore-and-aft. The
frigate, not aware of that manœuvre, continued her course,
and in five minutes dashed past us, and we were *safe*, being
dead to windward. It continued very dark for half an

hour, and when it finally cleared up a little, the Constellation was nearly hull-down in the southeast. So we escaped her that time, and when we had stood northeast long enough, we squared away, and as the gale moderated, made all sail for the south'ard and east'ard.

A few days after these occurrences, the look-out aloft, one morning, reported a sail ahead crossing our course.

"Keep her away for that vessel, sir," said Seymour to the officer of the deck, "and call all hands to make sail."

Taking the deck, as, according to man-of-war rules, it was my duty to do when all hands were called, I made all sail a trifle quicker than lightning, and then surrendered the trumpet to the officer of the watch.

The stranger, perceiving that we were chasing him, made all sail to avoid us; but it was not so easy to escape, when it put the wind out of breath to keep up with us; and accordingly we were very soon so near that they, in obedience, to our signal-gun, hove to. We hove-to also, and a boat being lowered and manned, Seymour said to me:

"When I wave my handkerchief, Garnet, send up our black ensign at the main, and fire a gun across that fellow's bows;" and jumping into the boat, he boarded the stranger, whom we now perceived was an outward-bound English East-Indiaman. We were so near, that I distinctly saw all his motions. Leaving the crew in the boat, he boarded the Englishman alone, and meeting her captain at the gang-way, he saluted him very politely, and took a turn or two with him upon the deck, as if inquiring the news. Shortly after, however, he apparently made some disagreeable remark, for they both stopped, and began to gesticulate violently, as if their discourse was becoming interesting; and Seymour, drawing his handkerchief from his pocket, carelessly waved it, by way of accenting his discourse. Instantly the sable banner of piracy floated at the mast-head.

and an eighteen-pound shot, travelling across the English-man's fore-foot, put an end to his opposition, and he began to execute Seymour's mandates.   A lot of kegs were shortly after passed into our boat, in a manner which showed that, at the least, they were heavy, and Seymour, courteously bid-ding Captain Bull adieu, pulled aboard.

"Hoist those up carefully, my lads," said he.

"What have you there, Captain Seymour?" I inquired.

"Only a few thousand guineas, Lieutenant Garnet," he replied, "which I *borrowed* from that ship."

"He'll be lucky," said I, "if he ever gets his pay."

Chapter II.

One morning, about forty-five days after we left New-York, we made land in the Gulf of Guinea.   Crowding all sail, we rapidly approached it, and were within five or six miles, when a long, low, black, suspicious-looking schooner, shot out from behind a small island, a short distance ahead, and, without asking any questions, bore down for us.

"Ready-about! ready, ready!" hailed Seymour, with startling quickness, seizing the trumpet.   The helm was put down, and in an instant we were on the other tack, standing out to sea.

"I know her!" ejaculated Seymour—"she is an English man-of-war, and is commanded by one of the sharpest ras-cals that ever drew pay and rations.   He calls his schooner the 'Dare-devil,' and no name was ever so appropriate, for both master and vessel.   He attacks everything, large and small ; laughs at steel and gunpowder, and I do not believe he knows what fear is.   The world is not wide enough to hold both of us, and come what may, there will be one ras-cal less on the seas at sunset.   I have sworn vengeance

against him, and I will take it so amply, that none shall
live to report to the Lords of the Admiralty in what manner one of his Majesty's cruisers went to the devil."

When we were twelve or fifteen miles from the land, we
tacked again, and although the breeze was a stiff one, set
every inch of canvas and stood in for the shore.   The
schooner continued her course, and standing on opposite
tacks, we rapidly neared each other.   Our ports were
closed, and as we made no use of our guns, the English
evidently supposed that what appeared to be long eighteens,
were actually quaker-guns, made of the best of wood—for
show, not use—and that our plan was to cross their hawse,
and run in-shore.

As soon as we were within range, they opened upon us
with a long twenty-four ; and, to do them justice, they
tossed their iron with most terrible exactness and considerable effect ; but as her shot hulled us, they did not interfere
with Seymour's plan.

Ordering the men to lie down upon deck, to avoid the
Englishman's fire, he continued to walk upon the poop as
composedly as if he were ball-proof ; although, as her battery (long-twelves) began to take effect, the shot flew
thick as hail, tearing open our bulwarks, and knocking the
white splinters about in every direction.   As we approached
still nearer, her musketry opened upon us in full volley ;
yet, although he was the target for every shot, he seemed
totally unconscious of danger.   With a flushed cheek, and
an eye flashing fire, he stood proudly erect, and delivered
his orders to the man-at-the-wheel, as composedly as if he
were setting a studdin'-sail.

When our flying-jib-boom was nearly locking with hers,
he suddenly shouted, with a voice like a trumpet-call :
"Starboard the helm !"   We fell off from the wind, and
rising upon a wave, our heavy bows struck the fated vessel

amidships with a tremendous crash. We passed clean over, cutting her completely in two : an unearthly yell arose from a hundred and fifty brave fellows, as they sunk quick to the bottom ; and when we flew aft to catch a glimpse of the wreck, nothing was visible, save the pennant at the main-to'-gallant-mast-head, which for an instant floated upon the surface of the deep, and was then drawn down after the hapless wretches, who had so often shed their blood in its defence !

Having passed the vortex caused by her going down, the brig was hove-to ; as I supposed for the purpose of picking up the survivors, if there were any. But such was not Seymour's plan—and one poor fellow, who, stunned and strangling, rose to the surface, clinging to a spar for dear life, was not even allowed the miserable privilege of floating upon it, until the sharks, or the burning sun of the Equator, should put a period to his agony, but was deliberately shot by Seymour himself, acting upon the stern maxim that " dead men tell no tales." A deed of so dark a hue was never before perpetrated under the azure sky, nor on the deep sea, since the unborn surges slumbered in chaos, and darkness lay upon the face of the deep.

"Mr. Garnet," said Seymour, recovering his rifle as if he had been shooting a duck, " fill the main-topsail, and stand in-shore."

Three times I raised the trumpet to my lips, to give the necessary orders, and as often withdrew it ; and finally, being totally unable to command either my voice or my feelings, I dashed it down upon deck, and walked away without a word.

Seymour looked up at me in surprise, and then, deliberately picking up the trumpet, gave the requisite commands with his usual composure. When we were under-way, standing for the shore, he ordered the boatswain to call " all hands

to splice the main-brace," remarking, that the toast should
be, "Here's wishing the Dare-devils a pleasant passage
to —— !"

"Garnet," said Seymour, when we were about three
miles from the shore, "do you see that head-land yonder,
in the south-east? It is the northern cape of the bay
which we shall enter, and is now sixteen miles distant. I
wish you to observe the course we take to fetch it, and then
say if this coast was not cut out for the express benefit of
the slave-trade."

We continued our course, steering head-on, until within
half a mile of the shore, and then hauled our wind, and put
her head due south, keeping parallel to the beach. About
ten minutes afterward, the look-out, on the fore-topsail
yard, sung out:

"Breakers ahead !"

Seymour was standing upon the poop, looking astern:
he turned short around at this announcement, and hailed:

"Fore-topsail-yard there ! Two points on the starboard
bow, you lubber, distant two miles."

"Captain Seymour," said I, in surprise, "your eye-sight
is better than mine. Those breakers are not visible from
the deck."

"I know it," he replied, "but I am as well acquainted
with every inch of this coast as you are with the pavements
of Broadway. I could sail a line-of-battle-ship through this
channel, in perfect safety, the darkest night old ocean ever
saw, by the lead alone. Straight as you go, quarter-
master."

"Dise, no higher," repeated he at the cun.

"These breakers," continued Seymour, "are caused by a
reef of rocks, running across the mouth of that bay, and
stretching ten miles each way, parallel to the beach, and
distant from it, on the average, half a mile. Inside the

reef we have a clear, safe channel, carrying ten fathom
water, to within a ship's length of the beach, and at both
ends a safe entrance. Now all this is for our particular
benefit; for, in order to enter that bay a vessel must go all
this distance around; and while a man-of-war comes in at
one end, we can slip out at the other. If this does not
prove that Jemmy Flatfoot had a hand in laying out the
coast of Africa, you may call me a marine."

"Pretty good reasoning, friend Seymour," said I:
"you've made it very plain that the Devil is chief cook
and bottle-washer for the slave-trade. I don't wonder it
prospers so well, since he is at the wheel."

We were now inside the reef, and sailing along rapidly,
were within a mile of the entrance to the bay, when a small
canoe shoved off from the shore, and we were boarded by
one of the most hideous-looking black rascals that ever
walked on two feet. Running up the side like a monkey,
he tumbled over the gangway, and accosted Seymour, who
met him there, as an old friend; and after jabbering away
a few minutes in some barbarous lingo, he took a bottle of
rum, which Seymour had ordered for him, rolled into his
canoe, and run it high and dry on the beach. He brought
himself to anchor in the sand, and began to discuss the contents of the said bottle with an earnestness which plainly
showed that they two would not part company, until one
or t'other knocked under.

"Mr. Garnet," said Seymour, walking aft, "my good
friend there has informed me, that there are now two English frigates at anchor in the bay. I must send them both
to sea in twenty minutes after I enter. Do you speak Portuguese?"

"Si, Señhor," said I, "and every other language; excepting, always, the gibberish of that black friend of yours."

"Very good," he replied; "I shall report myself to the

English as Don So-and-so, (with a string of titles as long as the main-to'-bowline,) commander of the Brazilian brig-of-war Achillé, 24, on a cruise ; and will spin them a yarn, which will clear the bay of them as soon as they can up anchor. I have Brazilian uniforms for all the officers and myself, which we will bend now, and walk into the bay under Brazilian colors."

We rigged ourselves accordingly, and mustering upon the poop, sailed into the harbor, with the Brazilian ensign at the peak. It was quite small, and the English frigates were at anchor, near the centre of it, some distance asunder. Gradually shortening sail, we backed our main-top-sail abreast the Commodore's ship, within about two hundred yards ; and when we had lost headway, I roared out in Portuguese—(for their edification :)

"Let go the starboard anchor !" twisting the *n's* and the *o's* and the *r's* about in every direction. We then furled sails, squared the yards by the lifts and braces, hooked the yard-tackles, hoisted our boats, and manning the captain's barge with Portuguese, Seymour pulled aboard the English flag-ship. He was received with the usual honors, and had been on board but a few minutes, when three small flags were run up at the mizen, and a gun fired to awake the other frigate. Not being conversant with the English code of signals, I did not know what to make of this, when an old quarter-master, who had served under Nelson, perceiving my ignorance, informed me that it was, "Hoist in boats, and prepare to weigh."

The English ships were now all alive. Boat after boat was dropped alongside from the guess-warp, and hoisted in, two at a time, (one each side,) decks cleared up, and capstans manned. At this moment Seymour came over the gangway of the flag-ship, and as he shoved off, the Brazilian flag was sent up at the fore, and saluted with eleven guns

We returned the salute—British ensign at the fore, with the. same number—and as they, having weighed anchor, swept past us, making sail, we gave them three cheers, which were duly returned.

"Seymour," said I, when the bustle was over, "what *did* you tell that fellow ?"

"Oh !" said he, recovering breath after a severe fit of laughter, "it was not any of your land-yarns, slack-twisted stuff ; it was an out-and-outer.   When I first boarded her, I began by asking, very coolly, in Portuguese, what were the names of the frigates, where they were from, and where bound, and whom I had the honor of addressing, etc.   The crusty old commodore, having answered my questions in as few words as possible, in Spanish, desired to know the same of me, and asked if I could speak English.   But devil the bit of English could I speak : ' *No intendez Englise, Señor,*' said I, with a face as long as the jib-downhaul, and then proceeded to tell him that my name was ' Don So-and-so ;' that my brig was the Brazilian brig-of-war Achillé on a cruise ; that we fell in, this morning, with a suspicious-looking schooner, mounting eighteen guns, under English colors, and gave her chase ; but as she stood out to sea, and sailed very fast, we had given over the chase, because we had been on short allowance of water for ten days, and had only one day's allowance left, and dared not stand out until we had filled ; that I came in here for a supply, and intended to sail the next day, and catch the slaver if possible, and sling up the rascals at my yard-arm ; and added, by way of clincher, that I wished they would not trouble themselves about her, but leave her for me, as I had set my heart on sending her to the bottom.

" ' That will do for marines,' said the commodore to his first lieutenant, in English ; ' on short allowance of water, indeed !   If he had said short allowance of *courage*, he would have come nearer the truth. He was afraid the slaver would be a Scotch prize to him, if he meddled with her. He will take the best of good care not to chase her again. *He* set his heart on sending them to the bottom, indeed !—ha, ha, ha !' And the old knight laughed loud and long at my bravado. Then, turning to me, he asked in Spanish all about the schooner, when I saw her, the course she was steering, when I lost sight of her, etc., and ended by ordering his first lieutenant to hoist in boats, and prepare to weigh, making signal to the other frigate to do the same. He then talked about matters and things; asked, and told the news; and when I took leave, waited on me to the gangway very politely, expressing his sorrow that he had not time to visit me, but hoped that, as I should sail to-morrow, we should meet on the sea, and perhaps have the pleasure of capturing the pirate together; adding, with a wink to his first lieutenant, which nearly capsized my gravity, that nothing would gratify him more than to fight in such valiant company. So much for so much," continued Seymour, bursting into a roar of laughter, in which all hands heartily joined : " Hurra for John Bull !"

By the time our mirth had subsided, the English frigates were out of sight, having doubled the northern point of the bay. Seymour having satisfied himself of this fact, said to me :

" All hands up anchor ! Mr. Garnet, this bay is no place for us."

After giving the requisite orders in preparation, I desired to know for what purpose he weighed, and whither we were bound.

" We are going up the river, to be sure," he replied, " in order to get our live lumber aboard."

" I see no river," said I, looking carefully around the bay.

"I will show it to you in fifteen minutes," answered Seymour : "so now up anchor, for the wind is fair, and we've no time to lose."

The anchor was soon at the bows, and sail being made, we stood for the head of the bay, which, as I have already said, was quite small—about three miles in length, and one in width at the mouth—narrowing, of course, toward the head. The land around it was considerably elevated, and densely covered with tall mangroves—and nowhere could I see the least indication of a river—the coast of the bay being of a uniform elevation. We went on, however, with all sail set—and as we neared the head of the bay, I observed that the water did not shoal so much as usual, but still I saw nothing of the river. When about a cable's length from the beach, Seymour sung out :

"Man the starboard braces—slack the larboard ones—square away !"

We continued our course an instant longer, and then putting up the helm, doubled a point, and entered an inlet, which stretched inland toward the northeast, while our course from the mouth of the bay had been due east. It was exceedingly narrow—so much so, indeed, that it seemed impossible for two large ships to lie abreast in any part of it, and especially at the entrance. The tide was now coming in, and the wind being fair, we sailed quietly along, and were about half-way through the channel, when the landsman in the chains, who had been lazily reporting five, and four and a half fathom, suddenly came out with "A quarter less three," and an instant after "A half-two."

"Well, Mr. Garnet," said Seymour, smiling at my sudden start caused by this announcement, "do you think we are aground? This channel above us carries fifteen feet water to the bank on both sides, and is perfectly clear. There you see Jemmy Flatfoot again—for a line-of-battle ship

2

could come into it easy enough, but the next thing they
knew, they would be fast in the mud, while we, drawing
less than fifteen feet, slip along unhurt. You had better
keep your eyes about you now, for we may be obliged to
fight our way out of here yet."

For half a mile, the narrow channel was perfectly straight,
but at the end of that distance, it formed an angle of forty-
five degrees—and, on doubling the point, we found ourselves
in a fine, wide river, which stretched away to the eastward
as far as the eye could reach.

"Now, John Garnet," said Seymour, "here is a river for
you, which would not suffer much alongside of the Hudson,
and moreover——Main chains there! What water have
you ?"

The leadsman hove and sung out : " By the mark, five."

"Do you hear that ?" continued Seymour ; "you see
there is no want of water here."

"Yes," I replied, "and I am now convinced that your
friend blocked out this place for your especial benefit."

Shortly after, we came to anchor near the north bank of
the river, and about two miles from the last angle. On this
bank was a collection of miserable mud huts, called a town;
and firing a gun to awake them, we soon had the governor
thereof on board, an unforgotten mortal, who, after con-
fabulating awhile with Seymour, promised him that our
freight should "have quick dispatch," as he had half a cargo
in store, and knew where to catch the rest. Then, being a
large man in his way, he "punished" a quart of half-and-
half, and, undisturbed by the trifling potation, took a ten-
gallon keg, jumped into his canoe, and went on his errand
of love.

About noon of the fourth day after our arrival, as we lay
quietly at anchor waiting our cargo, Seymour, who had been
ashore, returned aboard in great haste, and ordered me to

all all hands up anchor, which being done, we were towed down stream again just above the angle in the river.

"Now then, Mr. Garnet," said Seymour, "get a spring on the cable, and slew us round, so that our starboard battery will command that entrance, for I have just been informed that three English men-of-war (a ship-of-the-line and two frigates) are entering the bay."

"If it be so," said I, "they cannot get more than half way up the narrow channel, as you well know."

"Ay," he replied, "but their boats, my man—their boats can come up."

The spring was accordingly applied to the cable, and our broadside brought to bear upon the entrance of the beforementioned channel. We lay about two hundred yards due east from it, so that anything coming up could not see us until the point was doubled, for the intervening land was high, and thickly wooded. Our guns were then examined, an extra stand of cannister put into each, and the starboard battery depressed and pointed at the angle of the river. We had scarcely finished our preparations, when a six-oared cutter shot out from behind the point, steering up the stream.

"I give you fair warning," shouted Seymour: "'bout ship, or I'll blow you out of water."

"Ay, ay, my fine fellow," said the English lieutenant, coolly—ordering his men to lie on their oars—"of what nation are you? where from—where bound—and what are you doing here?",

"There," said Seymour, pointing to our black flag, which was at this instant run up at the peak—"there is my flag—the rest of me you'll find out if you come so near again. Now I advise you to pull back to your ship, otherwise——All ready, starboard battery!"

"Thank you for the hint, friend," said the English lieu-

tenant, "and, in return, I'll inform you that an English
seventy-four and two frigates are at anchor in the bay."

"I knew all that before," replied Seymour, unconcern
edly.

"Well," said the Englishman, putting his boat about,
"it's my opinion you'll know it again—so, good-bye, so
long;" and his men slowly giving way, he quietly doubled
the point, and pulled down the river.

"Now, Garnet," said Seymour, "we'll have some fighting shortly, for I can't afford to be blocked up here, and
must and will be at sea in eight-and-forty hours, come what
may."

"That's easier said than done," I replied; "for that
liner's broadside would be no child's play."

"Poh!" said he, contemptuously, "I see you don't understand all the tricks of the trade, yet. Take our third-cutter,
and pull down that channel as far as is safe, keeping close
in shore, and then take to the bushes, and find out what
those Englishmen are doing, and return quickly. Meanwhile, I will send ashore for my slaves."

I pulled down stream accordingly, but seeing nothing, I
left the boat in care of the crew, and went on through the
forest alone, down to the hill overlooking the bay. I then
saw that the frigates were the same we had sent to sea after
the pirate, and the liner was a heavy one, carrying a hundred guns. They had anchored, at first, in the centre of the
bay, but now all had weighed again. The frigates stood
down the bay, and anchored, one on each side of the mouth,
athwart-ships of the channel outside, while the line-of-
battle sailed up to the head of the bay, put her helm down,
and bringing everything flat aback, shoved herself into the
narrow channel her own length, stern foremost, and then
anchored head and stern in the middle of it.

"Pretty good *seamanship*, Mr. Bull," thought I, as I ob

served this plugging-up manœuvre—for there appeared to be
scarcely room for her boats to pull alongside of her, much
less for a ship to pass—"it will not be easy to run by a
fellow as wide awake as you are."

I had now ascertained all that was needful—so I returned
to my boat, which had lain snug under the bushes, about
half-way down the channel. As the Englishman's guns commanded the whole of it, we were obliged to unship our oars,
and scull up stream, keeping well under the banks—and it
was well we did so, for just before we reached the angle in
the river, we carelessly shot into the middle of the stream,
when, quicker than thought, six thirty-two pound shot whistled over our heads, followed by a roar of genuine English
thunder. We were not desirous of any more such, and
took to our oars : giving way strongly we doubled the point
just as six more round shot kicked up the water astern of
us.

"Pretty good *gunnery*, Mr. Bull," thought I, as I pulled
alongside the brig, and made report to Seymour. "I have
no desire to play at short bowls with you."

I had scarcely gained the vessel, when the Englishman
began to fire his stern-chasers, one a minute, up the channel,
and the thirty-two pound shot skipped along over the water,
and dashed through the forest, knocking trees and earth
about in every direction—and, of course, completely commanding the whole length of the channel. We were at first
at a loss for the reason of this firing, but when night came
on, and a palpable darkness fell upon us, and the Englishman commenced a rapid fire of round-shot, grape and cannister, we knew at once that his object was to prevent our
playing any "Yankee shine" upon him. He had obtained
the proper range before dark, and as his shot swept the
eastern channel, we were glad to keep very clear of it.

About midnight, however, Seymour determined to try his

hand at the game, and ordered me to take fifty men, armed
with cutlasses, pistols and muskets, and go down through
the woods as near to the Englishman as was prudent, and
then sweep his decks with musketry. Being landed on the
left bank of the river, we silently wound our way through
the forest, and approached to within half-musket shot of
him unheard, and each taking a tree for a screen, according
to old Kentuck principles, we opened upon him in fine style,
directed by the flash of his stern-chasers, with which he was
still sweeping the channel. Although the Englishman was
evidently surprised by our sudden attack, he took it very
coolly, and without knocking off from his stern-chasers a
moment, the marines and small-arm-men were summoned to
their stations, according to the regular routine of nautical
war, and in five minutes his ship was one entire blaze of
musketry, fore and aft. Here, however, we had all the
advantage, being considerably elevated, and entirely protected by the trees ; the flashes of our guns (their only
guide) were of course small, but the broad sheets of flame
from her stern-chasers completely illuminated her deck,
affording us every facility for accurate shooting.

The Englishman soon found that this method of proce-
dure would not *do*, but from our peculiar situation it was
somewhat difficult to tell what *would* do. The banks of
the channel were quite bold, rising at an angle of sixty degrees, and the place we occupied was so much elevated, that
the guns of her larboard battery could not be brought to
bear upon us at all. While I was congratulating myself on
the advantage we evidently had over them, their fire of musketry, which had been unintermitted, suddenly ceased—and
the next instant a lot of thirty-two pound shot were tossed
at us, informing us that John Bull had slewed round his
starboard spar-deck battery. This, however, did not annoy
me at all—for carronades are clumsy things, and their shot

never hit "once in a place," and moreover, are thrown with so little force, that a fellow with stout ribs may laugh at them.   Finding that this did not trouble us, they changed to grape and cannister—but we, still protected by our trees, kept up our fire, not being so easily scared.

When the failure of this experiment became apparent, the increased bustle on the Englishman's decks showed that now he was going about flogging us according to science—and a few minutes after, his stern-chasers, which till now had been steadily sweeping the channel, suddenly ceased firing.   Thinking that something new was coming, I gave orders to change ground ; and the word being silently passed from one to another, we moved a couple of hundred yards to the eastward—and it was well we did so, for the next instant, fire-balls were thrown by the dozens into our former ground, followed by a shower of round, grape and cannister, from the long thirty-two pound stern-chasers, which kicked up a row among the trees in fine style.   An instant after, a few dozen of Congreve rockets were thrown into the bushes in every direction, and some of them chancing to alight in our vicinity, dispelled my doubts as to the propriety of a retreat ; so, instantly tacking ship, we were off at ten knots an hour.

"Well, Mr. Garnet," said Seymour, when I had reported progress on board, "it is very plain that this Englishman won't budge tack nor sheet for all we can do : so, since he won't go away, we must.   I shall go to sea to-day in spite of everything—therefore make your will, and holy-stone your conscience—for though I shall certainly succeed, who will live to tell of it, is another question.   We must get the rest of our cargo elsewhere, for we are not more than two-thirds full."

I admired Seymour's resolution ; but although he had heretofore been astonishingly successful, I did not think

that this plan was among the possibilities, and began to
cudgel invention for a yarn to spin in case of a capture.
Now, for the first time, I began to have some compunctious
visitings as to the lawfulness of my present employment, and
I began to debate with myself how far my forcible entry
into the trade would excuse my remaining in it—and finally
came to the conclusion, as most men would, to stand by and
see what would turn up.

When the day dawned, the English ceased firing, and
were evidently waiting for some of their small craft to arrive,
so that they could come up and attack us on terms of equal-
ity—knowing full well that to attempt to carry us in boats
would be madness.   All the morning, business went on as
usual, and, except receiving slaves on board, we made no
apparent preparation for sea, lest the English should learn
it from the natives, who we well knew always served the
strongest party.   But in reality, every preparation was made,
and by four bells in the forenoon watch we were completely
ready for sea.

At seven bells, (half-past eleven,) Seymour, who had been
ashore, deliberately returned aboard.

"Mr. Carline," said he to the second lieutenant, "jump
into that canoe alongside, with a couple of men, and pull to
the turn in the river.   Wave your handkerchief when the
English liner pipes to dinner, and then pull for us.   Mr.
Garnet, hoist in all the boats, and stow the quarter-boats
amid-ships in the launch, instead of running them up the
davits."

"Now, sir," said Seymour, "pipe down hammocks."

"Down hammocks, indeed," thought I, as I repeated the
order ; "pretty well done for seven bells, A. M.   Captain
Seymour," said I, "it strikes me you are getting sleepy."

"You will find I am wide awake, I *guess*," replied Seymour.   "Now then, John Garnet, unshackle the cable abaft

the bitts, and stand by to slip it. Loose all sail, and hoist away everything. Brace up sharp on the larboard tack. Man sheets and tacks, and stand by to sheet home. Clear away both batteries, and run them in,"—the guns were double shotted with grape and cannister—"and now, Mr. Garnet, we are ready to *run by them.*"

"*The-e-e devil!*" said I, as I walked away, thunderstruck at the madness of his plan; "hark you, Captain Seymour, if that's your scheme, we are candidates for immortality as true as I am a sinner."

"Mr. Garnet," said Seymour, angrily, "I beg you will remember that I command this vessel."

"Ay," said I, "and you will please to remember that I am a pressed man. But this is no time for quarrelling, so we'll be friends for the present. By and by, I promise myself the gratification of shooting you at ten paces."

"Do," he replied, coolly.

The wind was now blowing fresh from the northeast—the tide was running down at four knots—and we rode head to the wind by the larboard-bower, with a kedge astern. Seymour stood upon the poop, watch in hand.

"It keeps English time," said he, "for I set it by their bell this morning. It now wants one minute of twelve. Mr. Garnet, slip the chain-cable—we'll ride by the kedge."

It was slipped accordingly, and the brig swinging around, was brought up by the kedge, though it seemed as if the hawser would part with the strain. A carpenter's mate stood by, axe in hand, ready to cut, and Seymour watched Carline for the signal. An instant after, he waved his handkerchief, and struck out for us.

"Sheet home!—cut away!" shouted Seymour.

It was done—in an instant we were under way—and Carline and his men jumped aboard, leaving the canoe adrift.

"Now," said Seymour, "go below, every man of you,
except those at the wheel, and stay there till you are called.
I will shoot the first man that puts his head above the
combings of the hatches. Mr. Garnet, you had better go
below, too—you can do nothing on deck."

"I am greatly obliged to you, sir," said I, " but I'll stay
on deck and see the fun."

. We shortly doubled the point, and with wind and tide,
shot rapidly down the stream. We were not observed, and
approached nearer and nearer to the liner, undiscovered,
until our flying jib-boom was nearly over her taffrail.

" Port !" whispered Seymour.

The helm was shifted accordingly, and we passed the
starboard side of the seventy-four so closely, that her main-
deck battery swept our larboard-hammock-netting off clear,
while our starboard bulwarks almost touched the bank of
the river. Knocking the ashes from the cigar which was
accidentally in my mouth, I fired the aftermost gun of the
larboard battery plump into the liner, just as her crew,
aroused by the collision, dropped their cans—it being grog-
time—manned their starboard battery, and let drive.
They were a little behind time, however, for we had that
instant shot past them, and all their guns threw their iron
harmlessly astern of us, while we, doubling the point, were
soon out of their reach.

"All hands make sail !" shouted Seymour; "round in
the larboard-braces. Stand by the starboard studdin'-
sails."

With such government, we were under all sail in less than
no time, and with studdin'-sails, and sky-sails, the wind on
the starboard-quarter, we dashed down the bay.

"Pretty well done, Captain Seymour," said I; " but you
are not safe yet. Do you hear that ?"

The English frigates, awakened by the liner's broadside,

were beating to quarters, and as they lay across the channel, on each side of the mouth of the bay, I thought our
final escape was yet a question. Not so, Seymour—for,
rubbing his hands in irrepressible glee, he walked about the
poop, giving his orders, almost beside himself with joy.

"Hillo, signal-quartermaster !" said he—we won't mince
matters ! send up our black ensign at the main. We'll
give Johnny Bull a target for his shot."

The words were scarcely out of his mouth, when a storm
of iron rushed past us, and looking astern, we saw that the
liner, having slipped her cables and fired a broadside, was
coming after us, making all sail.

"Very good oysters," said Seymour, with a grimace that
a baboon might have envied : "Mr. Garnet, poke at him
with our stern-chasers, and make him a 'candidate for
immortality,' while I try my hand at *guessing* with these
fellows ahead."

We acccordingly blazed away with our stern-chasers, to
injure him if possible, and to cover ourselves with smoke.
We soon reached the mouth of the bay, and just before we
passed the points which would bring us within range of the
frigates, Seymour sang out :

"Man both batteries ! Straight as you go, quarter-
master."

We passed the capes, steering right on for the reef,
which, as I have already mentioned, ran across the mouth
of the bay—and as soon as our guns came to bear, we gave
each frigate a broadside, and our aim being true, and the
guns double-shotted, they made a crashing. They reserved
their fire, thinking that we should be obliged to pass near
one or the other, and they would then give it to us solidly.

We continued our fire ; and Seymour, standing upon
the poop, began to cun the brig himself ; and although
the smoke was so dense that we could not see a fathom,

gave his orders as promptly as if it were clear day and plain channel.

"Blaze away, my lads," said he, "we'll *do* Johnny Bull, all we can."

An instant after he sung out:

"Knock off firing! Hold on, everybody!"

The order was obeyed, and the next moment we struck heavily on the reef.

"Very good," said Seymour; "once more, you beauty."

We struck again, and then slipped over the reef into deep water.

"All hands cheer ship!" he shouted. We sent up the English ensign at the fore, gave it three cheers, and went on our course under all sail. The English could not follow us over the reef, as they drew too much water; but they slipped their cables, fired their broadsides at us in spite, and then stood through the channel; but before they were clear of it, we were hull-down in the southwest.

Take it as a whole, our escape was really a masterpiece of daring and nautical skill. It required the mind of a *man* to conceive the plan of running past a line-of-battle-ship in broad daylight and in such a channel, and indomitable reso lution to put that plan into effect; for had we been discov cred *two minutes* sooner, one broadside would have totally annihilated us. The attempt was made when the English piped to dinner and grog, because they would naturally be remiss in their look-out at this time—thinking more of the grog-tub than of us. Hammocks were piped down, because Seymour knew that the liner's main deckers would just sweep the netting. Yards were braced sharp, because, if square, they would lock in the Englishman's rigging. Boats were stowed amidships, because there was no room for them on the quarter. Guns were run in for the same reason; and, after crossing the bay, he steered over the reef, knowing that there was one place where we should tonch-and-go without injury. Such seamanship deserved success—whatever were the cause—and obtained it; for at sunset we were clear of land, and the English fleet was out of sight astern.

"Mr. Garnet," said Seymour, as soon as it was dark, "we'll haul our wind, and stand southeast for the land, because I have no idea of going to Brazil half-loaded."

We altered our course accordingly, and stood for the shore. The former part of the night was quite dark, but about four bells in the mid-watch it cleared up a little. I was accidentally on deck at the time, and, sweeping the horizon with my night-glass, I discovered a strange sail on the starboard bow, distant about three miles. Reporting it to Seymour, I received orders to give chase, and putting up the helm, and crowding all sail, we were after her as fast as a six-knot breeze would carry us. The stranger, perceiving us, made all sail to escape, but it was in vain—for at daylight, we were within half a mile. She was evidently a Guineaman, being a long, low, suspicious-looking schooner, and we ranged up within pistol-shot without firing a gun, so that we could not break any of her *crockery*, and ordered her captain to come on board. He came accordingly, and Seymour, receiving him on the quarter-deck, being moved by virtuous indignation no doubt, began to read him a furious lecture on the enormities of the slave-trade.

"Why," said he in astonishment, pointing to the woolly pates lying about our decks, "you are a slaver, too."

But Seymour only lectured the harder, and wound up as regular-built a preachment as any chaplain ever spun, by ordering him, at his peril, to send all his slaves on board of us instantly. He did not dare to disobey; and, when the transfer was completed, Seymour quietly said to him:

"Now, sir, you may go back to Africa, and get as many

more as you like, for these just complete my cargo. There,
Mr. Garnet," he continued, as we filled and stood away to
the westward, " that's what we slavers call *borrowing*."

Having nothing now to detain us, we cracked away merrily for the south'ard and west'ard, and about noon of the
eighteenth day after leaving the coast of Guinea, the look-
out aloft reported a sail on the starboard bow. The wind
being the south-east trade, and blowing fresh, we instantly
up-helm, made all sail, and gave chase, and by four bells in
the afternoon watch, we could see with our glasses that she
was a large ship on the larboard tack, heading west, and
sailing lazily along under topsails and coursers. One thing
was very plain : the stranger was in no kind of haste, and
being led by this fact to examine her more closely, I became
convinced she was a man-of-war, and accordingly remarked
to Seymour, that perhaps she would be a Scotch prize.

But he replied, that having the weather-gage, we could
sail as near as we liked with perfect safefy, and therefore
cracked away. As we sailed very fast, we were within four
or five miles of her at seven bells in the afternoon watch,
and then saw plainly that she was a frigate. She showed
English colors, and fired a gun to attract our observation ;
but we took no notice of either.

"Mr. Garnet," said Seymour, " I believe that is one of
he English frigates we choused so neatly a fortnight since,
and we'll run down to them, so that we may know them,
and they us."

We accordingly approached within two miles of her,
keeping well to windward, and then fired our long forty-two
at her, and sent up our black flag at the main. That
rather provoked Mr. Bull, the shot happening to hit him ;
and he let drive at us the whole of his larboard battery,
hauled close on the wind on the larboard tack, and, as
quick as thought was under all sail. His shot did us no

essential harm, and giving him our starboard battery in return, we changed our course from west to southwest, crowded everything and ran across his fore-foot unhurt. He instantly up-helm and gave chase, and the breeze being a stiff one, we were both off at a fine rate. For two hours he lost considerably, but about sunset it began to breeze up and threaten a gale.

"Now, Captain Seymour," said I, "you understand we shall catch a gale of wind shortly, and the English being the heaviest, will catch *us*."

"Don't chuckle too soon, Lieutenat Garnet," he replied, "we'll escape this fellow easy enough."

"That remains to be seen," was my brief rejoinder, as I squinted to windward.

The wind now increased rapidly—so much so, indeed, that at eight bells in the second dog-watch, we were obliged to take in all our studdin'-sails—but the Englishman kept his fast, and, although eight or nine miles astern, evidently gained on us. Seymour, however, was not at all disturbed, but gave orders and cracked jokes as cheerfully as ever. With the gale, clouds came on, and it grew quite dark; not so much so, however, as to prevent our seeing each other, while we cracked on, shortening sail only when absolutely necessary, as the English gained upon us slowly, but surely.

About midnight, Seymour, who had been coolly walking about the poop, suddenly stopped, and after thinking a moment, ordered a reefer to call the master.

"Mr. Quadrant," said Seymour, as soon as he came upon deck, "work up your reckoning, and tell me where we are now, and bear a hand about it."

Quadrant dived, and in an instant returning, said :

"By dead reckoning. sir, we are now in latitude 208 25 N., longitude 289 12 W., standing west-by-south."

". Bring me the chart," said Seymour. It was brought, and after studying it a moment, he threw it by, and said to me :

" Mr. Garnet, we are not far from Martin Vas and Trini-dad. Take your post, sir, on the to'-gallant forecastle, and keep a bright look-out ahead. If you see *anything* or *think* you see anything, sing out to the wheel, and men whom I shall station along the gangway will pass the word."

I took my place, accordingly, and " gazed into dim futu-rity." Martin Vas and Trinidad are two small islands in the South Atlantic, not far from the coast of Brazil, which rise precipitously from the sea to the height of three or four hundred feet, nearly or totally inaccessible. They are both quite small—the larger not exceeding five hundred yards across—and this fact, added to their abrupt sides, has entirely preserved them from the polluting tread of man. Here, in the solemn solitudes of the ocean, they silently sit, uninhabited and alone. Ages upon ages. have rolled over them, and they are still the same as on that day when the morning stars sang together, and the sons of God shouted for joy in view of the fair handiwork of the Almighty. The ocean, lashed into fury by ten thousand tempests, has dashed against their rocky bulwarks in impotent wrath— for they stand "steadfast and sure :" far removed from the noise and turmoil of man, clothed in quietness, they slum-ber on, lulled by the murmurs of the deep. Confident in their rocky foundations, they laugh at the roar of the storms. Though the waters of the troubled sea chafe their sides, their summits are visited only by the pure radiance of the luminaries of heaven.

The water does not shoal as you approach them, and being composed of dark rock, there is nothing about them to warn the careless mariner of his danger. Hence our unusual caution.

"How far astern are the English now?" I inquired, about four bells in the mid-watch. The man passed aft, and returning, said—"About a mile, sir."

As the wind now blew a gale, this was as I expected—and shrugging my shoulders at the prospect astern, I turned my attention to the prospects ahead. It had become quite dark; I could scarcely see at all, and was about to relinquish my look-out as useless, when I saw ahead the dim outline of an object resembling a large ship before the wind.

"Mr. Jones," said I to a reefer near me, "go aft, sir, and report to Captain Seymour a sail right ahead, and be quiet about it."

Seymour came forward, and after looking a moment, said:

"Mr. Garnet, that is not a sail; it is the bluff which rises from the sea half-way between Martin Vas and Trinidad. It is nearly two hundred feet in height, entirely precipitous on every side, not more than a hundred feet in diameter at the base, and slightly conical. That is what you suppose to be a ship, and in the dark it might readily be mistaken for one; and, if we manœuvre rightly, it will insure our escape, and put a stop to our pursuers."

He then proceeded to give me my orders, and returned to his station upon the poop.

"Starboard a little!" was my first hail to the wheel. It was obeyed, and produced just enough alteration in our course to bring the bluff one point on our starboard-bow, which, wishing to screen it from the view of the English, was just what was wanted. When very near the island—distant, say, two hundred yards, just as I had repeated my order to the wheel—the English frigate, being only a quarter of a mile astern, fell off a point or two from the wind, and a thirty-two pound shot, from her bow-chaser, carried away our main-topmast. This accident, apparently so disastrous, was our salvation

" Starboard a little," I repeated.

· We were now about a ship's length from the island, and the English not more than three or four astern. At this instant they fired at us again. The shot raked us fore and aft, but it was their destruction. Their vision was obscured by its smoke, which caused them to mistake the island for us, and a loud voice from the Englishman's forecastle, which we knew to be that of her first-lieutenant, hailed :

" Port the helm ! We'll run her down !"

We slipped past the pillar-island so closely, that our starboard main-yard-arm grazed its precipitous side, and the next instant the Englishman's flying-jib-boom, jib-boom and bowsprit successively struck. against the immovable rock, and were driven in upon the hull by the violence of the collision. A moment more, and the hull itself dashed against the fatal barrier, crushing her bulwarks and making a fearful breach for the entering waves. A frigate, however, is too substantial a craft to be destroyed by, perhaps, any one blow that she can receive ; and, in this instance, the strength of her bows sufficed to resist instantaneous destruction. She recoiled, accordingly, a few fathoms, and her first-lieutenant, in terror, shouted :

" Starboard-the-helm !—hard-a-starboard !"

It was too late ! Recovering from the recoil of the first shock, the frigate struck again so violently, that her bow was totally demolished. Meanwhile we had hove to, and now could hear the water rush into our antagonist with a roar, which plainly showed that her last hour was come. She rolled heavily to windward once, and then went down ; and her crew heard, amid the roar of the tempest, the cheers which Seymour, with his usual cold-blooded ferocity, ordered our crew to give them, sounding in their ears like the laugh of the fiends of hell !

Chapter III.

The gale had now abated, and we, having repaired damages, and rigged new spars aloft, crowded all sail for the west'ard and south'ard, and at noon of the fourth day, with Spanish colors at the peak, we entered the harbor of Rio Janeiro.

As we neared the anchorage of men-of-war, I observed among them the United States frigate Constellation, (the one with which we had a brush in leaving New-York,) and perceiving, as we approached, that her quarter-deck was crowded with officers, Seymour altered our course so as to pass across her stern—as we were now in a neutral port, and had nothing to fear from her.   Commodore Montague was standing upon the signal-locker, and as we passed under her stern, Seymour, pointing to the slaves who were lying about our decks, hailed him with :

"Friend Montague, I'll pick out a dozen of the prettiest, and send them aboard of you, shortly, for your own peculiar."

It was beneath the dignity of a Captain of the United States Navy to bandy defiances, or deal in blackguardism, with a slaver—and, accordingly, Montague pretended not to hear what Seymour said—but the blood mounting in his face, showed plainly that the taunt *was* heard, and felt.   To carry out his system of bravado, Seymour ordered to let go the anchor, about three hundred yards from the Constellation, and veering away cable, we lay precisely parallel to her, broadside to broadside.   The weather now being awfully hot, we were of course desirous to land our slaves as quickly as possible, and having made the necessary arrangements with the authorities of the port, we commenced discharging cargo at four p.m., and used such dispatch, that before seven that evening, not one remained on board. This operation being completed, Seymour turned his attention to his small warfare with the Constellation, and mustering our band—a strong one by the way—upon the poop, he saluted Montague's ears with "Hail Columbia" and "Yankee Doodle"—and when eight-bells came, it was "made" in true man-o'-war style—two eighteen-pounders, and a full band, announcing to all in port in general, and the Constellation in particular, that our watch was set.

The next morning, about ten o'clock, having performed my usual duties, I went down into the ward-room, and shortly reappeared on deck in the same dress I wore the day we left New York.

"What now, Mr. Garnet?" said Seymour, in surprise, as I walked aft upon the poop.

"I come, sir, to request a boat," I replied.

"As first lieutenant of this vessel, sir," answered Seymour, still more surprised, "you need not ask that as a favor. It is your right."

"I hold rank here no longer, sir," said I; "I was kidnapped by you, and have participated in your infamous atrocities thus long, only because I have had no opportunity to leave you. While you were in danger and difficulty, I scorned to quit you: it would have seemed like fear, to which I am a stranger. But now, assuring you that a viler scoundrel than yourself never crossed my hawse, I inform you that I am about to surrender myself to Commodore Montague aboard the Constellation."

"My respects and a pleasant voyage to you, sir," said Seymour—for he saw it was useless to remonstrate, and his pride was mortally piqued at my unexpected personal denunciation—"boatswain's-mate, call away the first-cutter. I hope, sir, you will do me the favor to take your pay, due

for services rendered.   Sam, (to his steward,) bring me a
bag of guineas."

Not being disposed to prolong the interview, or accept
his offer, I walked to the starboard gangway without reply,
and entering the first-cutter, pulled for the Constellation.
The moment I reached her deck, I ordered the boat to
shove off and return to the brig, and then walked aft to
meet the commodore.

I proceeded at once to detail my adventures, so far as was
necessary to explain my appearance in his vessel, and concluded by surrendering myself a prisoner.   He heard me
through, patiently and courteously, and then, pursuing his
own investigation, inquired the particulars of Seymour's
conduct and cruise.   When I had finished a brief sketch of
the same, he abruptly asked if all her slaves were then
ashore, and all hands, and Seymour, aboard.   I told him
they were.

"Mr. Roberts," said he, to his fourth lieutenant, "take
ten men, and board the ship which has just anchored between us and the slaver : she has a long range of cable out :
present my respects to her commander, and request him to
heave-short ; assist him with your men, and remain on board
of her till recalled.   Mr. Thompson, (first lieutenant,) clear
away and man the starboard-battery—load with round,
grape and cannister, and order the gunner to open the
magazine, and stand by to pass up powder."

By the time these orders were obeyed, the merchantman
had hove-short, and the brig lay exposed to view.

"Take good aim, my lads," said Montague, "*at the slaver.*
All ready.   Fire !"

At the word, the whole of the Constellation's starboard
broadside was poured into the brig, tearing open her bulwarks, and dismounting her guns.   For five minutes, the

frigate continued a most terrible battery, and Montague then perceiving that the brig was a total wreck, ceased firing, and ordered the boats to be manned to board her. As the men were jumping into the boats, I observed that the brig was evidently beginning to sink, and was communicating that fact to an officer near me, when an explosion, louder than thunder, rent the heavens, and the slaver, blown into ten thousand fragments, flew into the air. For an instant, there was a dead silence, which was followed by the falling of the shattered masts, spars and planks of the brig, mingled with the dead bodies of her men. And thus, *as it ought*, ends the " Cruise of a Guineaman."

FITZ-GUBIN,

OR,

THE ADMIRAL'S PET.

BY THE AUTHOR OF "SINGLETON FONTENOY," ETC.

CHAPTER I.

WHEN Mogglestonleugh got the Thunderbolt, (for col lecting evidence on the continent about Lady ——, which proved highly serviceable in the divorce case,) his first youngster was Lord Alfred Fitz-Gubin. The Thunderbolt was flag-ship on the South American station. They excused Fitz-G. from the mizen-top because he was young, and from night watch because he was delicate, and from boat duty because there were other youngsters to attend to the jolly boat without troubling *him*. The assistant surgeon reported him ill at Lisbon, and the surgeon recommended a week at Cintra for him. The minister had a party to meet him. The chaplain gave him a Bible, the "gift of his well-wisher, the Rev. T. Jenks," as the fly-leaf proclaimed. Fellows in the mess wrote home to "Dear papa,"—"We have a pleasant set of messmates here; young Lord Alfred Fitz-Gubin is one of my most intimate friends among them." Smoggbuckle overdid his share of it, for he lent him fifty pounds, which was soon after returned by his mother (through the captain) in a letter, in which Smoggbuckle

was called a "designing person." When he shot a bull
belonging to the beef contractor, the captain blew up the
beef contractor, and paid for the bull. Lord Alfred walked
upon velvet through the service.

The Thunderbolt being paid off, the Admiralty deliberated as to what was the best ship—and sent him to China,
because they foresaw active service there, and wished to
give him a chance of distinguishing himself. . He showed
such gallantry—(against a junk with a wooden gun in it)—
that Captain Tournspit felt it his *duty* (indeed, could not
have rested in his bed quietly had he neglected it) to mention him with praise in a despatch. The Chinese War
becoming a mere bore, in due time Lord Alfred came home,
(by the overland route,) and soon after "passed" for lieutenant, and went out to the Mediterranean. This was convenient, for some relations of the family were going to yacht
there. The yacht Giselle was in preparation for an august
party at the time Fitz-Gubin sailed in the Cocytus to Malta.
They arrived there at a period which naval men will remember as that when Roribel became flag-lieutenant. A sketchy
paragraph on Roribel's reception of the news of the vacancy
may not be amiss. "It requires," said he, "a particular
class of man to be flag-lieutenant. He should be gentlemanly, (here he looked at his boots;) handsome, (here he
pulled up his shirt-collar;) of good abilities, (here he smiled
with self-complacency;) and generally popular!" (here he
bowed and rubbed his hands, as much as to say, "Now you
have him!") Roribel was made flag-lieutenant, *vice* Maunderson, who had taken advantage of the position to make
up to a great wine-merchant's daughter, (whom the wags
of the squadron had christened the Countess of Bucellas,)
and had retired from the service into matrimony, accordingly.

The Cocytus broke down off Pantellaria; why, nobody

seems ever to have found out. As there was scarcely any wind, she was in an awkward plight. She signalled to the old Bloater, *Mrs.* Pappleton commanding, (such was Adair's joke, though the newspapers never so described the corvette, to my knowledge.) The Bloater was jogging along as usual, returning to Malta from a cruise, and Forbessy was in charge of the morning watch. He at once proceeded to the cabin to report the event to Pappleton, who left the society of youth and beauty (this was the phrase of the gallant and polished Mules, the clerk; I must tell you he meant Mrs. P., which you would never have guessed) at the stern call of duty—in fact, came on deck to see what was the matter. A boat, of course, had to be sent to the Cocytus, and Forbessy went in her to the steamer.

A ladder was lowered as he came alongside. He found Captain Hostibus storming and raging about the deck, and all the engineers under arrest; out of which, however, they were constantly called, every now and then, to see if nothing could be done. Forbessy was walking about the deck, waiting the return of Hostibus from another visit to the engine-room, when he heard a low, languid voice—a voice of blended effeminacy and indifference, saying—"Provoking! and before breakfast, too! very irritating to our friend Hostibus, all this must be. Confounded engineering fellows!"

Forbessy turned, and saw the speaker before him—a long youth, with light hair, and big, watery blue eyes, whose dress bespoke him naval, though it was by no means punctiliously fashioned after the regulations. He looked at Forbessy, and said, lazily, "You are from the corvette, I suppose?"

"I am."

"By Jove! I hardly see my way. I suppose Hostibus

3

must do something, or you do something for Hostibus. But
I was thinking—let me see—yours is a rather large boat?
. . . I have it."

Here Hostibus re-appeared, and came aft. "Nothing
for it—the corvette must send her pinnace on to Malta,
and ask for a steamer for us! She must take on the
mails, too."

The youth spoke again. "But, Capt. Hostibus, couldn't
she (the captain paused for the suggestion or advice) . . . .
couldn't she . . . so very slow, this—— couldn't *she take
me in* ?"

"Lord Alfred Fitz-Gubin," said Hostibus, "the service
must be attended to !" Hostibus turned on his heel.

This was the first glimpse Forbessy ever got of Lord
Fitz-Gubin. It was characteristic. It would not be too
much to say, that it exhibited his naval views altogether.
He had been so dandled and pampered during his career,
that he expected obstacles to fly before him—like strag-
glers out of the path of a Roman Consul. They say that
when the "Lotos" was lost by the genius of Mooner, Lord
Alfred thought his chest the paramount object to be saved.

We will not trouble ourselves further with the Cocytus,
except to say that, by dint of a fair wind, she reached
Malta in safety. Next morning after her arrival, a gun-
case made its appearance on board the flag-ship, followed
by a couple of pointers. Sensation in the Sovereign ! These
were succeeded by a chest of more than ordinary dimensions. Increased curiosity! A fishing rod and beautiful
dressing-case next arrived. ("This is a gentleman !" exclaimed Cuckles, with decision.) But what was the feeling
when an object came which was almost immediately recognised as a tent ? ("A person of consideration," exclaimed
Cuckles.) Lord Fitz-Gubin himself reported his "joining"
to Commander Mutter, in the course of the day. The com-

mander, one of the serious school, (who are often of the most aristocratic principles—looking on "dignities" as parts of the "great scheme," and truckling accordingly,) received him with *empressement*, and introduced him to Cuckles. Cuckles deliberated as to who were the most eligible men in their mess whom he could form a little "set" out of, for his "noble friend."

In the Sovereign, as in most large messes of any pretensions, there is a "red-book" section of men, who, somehow or other, fancy themselves, or make themselves, or are tacitly allowed to be, what our old friend Jenkins would call the *crême*. It is the same in provincial towns, and in fact in every sphere where a moderate number of people live together. But it is by no means easy to say *how* the arrangement takes place, or distinctly to point out *what* the laws are which divide the sets, or form the upper set. As scientific men are not agreed how fairy rings are produced, (though I believe it is certain that toad-stools and such *fungi* have something to do with it,) so "circles" of society are as difficult to account for;—whatever, too, we may allow to the "fungus" influence in their case! It is not only birth, or only money, or only brains, or only manners;—these are all powers in their way, but any one of them will sometimes make a hit, and I have known hits made by people who possessed none of them. Generally, the blending of various advantages in moderate proportions is the staplé of success, and the having a pursuit in common, the great bond of union. Cuckles then, who was upper-deck-mate of the Sovereign—who had in that position the Commander's ear, and was, so far, of consequence—who further was a senior mate, and a very shrewd, worldly person, was one of the swell *clique* of the Sovereign; Tom Riddel, with the largest income in the mess, and a free, daring way about him, was another; Siddlington again, by

dint of great respectability and careful manners, and an
orthodox way of looking at everything, was a third.   These
and others gave the tone to the mess, which was a sumptuous and stately establishment, beyond the dreams of Benbow.   About one in the day, a knot of fellows were usually
to be found in a main-deck cabin, which one of the lieutenants allowed to be made a lounging-place of.   The Sovereign at this time lay habitually in Malta, more like an immovable castle in the harbor there—stately, and utterly
calm—than a ship.   The captain, of course, lived on shore ;
you might see him any day, trudging along Strada Treale,
as his children were dragged down the street in a pony
chaise, by his side.   As for the Admiral, he was seldom
seen, though perhaps oftener heard of than people wished.

To the cabin in question, supplied with a comfortable
sofa and chairs, and adorned with a picture of a brigand
and his daughter, Cuckles led Fitz-Gubin.   The knot were
there, consuming ices brought on board by an old Frenchman daily, about whom the legend went that he came to
Malta originally as the son of a noble, banished by the
Revolution.

Fitz-G. was duly introduced, and found the conversation
busy with the old topics—the Admiral, the Captain, the
Sovereign, the Court-martial on P——, (not held *really* because he neglected so-and-so, you know, but because he
jilted old Froggan's niece.)   A new anecdote of Mr. Adair
was added to the day's stock by Tawney, who dropped
down, after copying an "order," to have a chat.   It seems
that, after Mr. Adair left the Bloater, for the Preposterous,
("where," said Tawney, "Ricks swears he'll finish him,")
he was crossing the harbor in one of the cutters, when who
should pass but Mrs. Pappleton in her husband's gig.   Mr.
Adair made the crew of his boat toss their oars, *as to a
Captain*—an audacious professional jest indeed !

Lord Alfred Fitz-Gubin, our new messmate; Mr. Riddel, Mr. Siddlington," said Cuckles.

"Been in the Mediterranean before, Lord Fitz-Gubin?"
asked Siddlington.

"No. I've come out here to look about me a little now,
though. I was in China; I was in South America." He
said this languidly, as usual, and then paused, as if he had
ceased to take any interest in the subject. Have you ever
seen a sluggish compass? (But of course, if a naval man,
you have.) The quartermaster must jerk it with the string
to keep its mystic force alive and active. Fitz-Gubin often
seemed to resemble it.

Old Polonai came in with some ices. "Good morning,
old Polonai," said Riddel, (one of your sanguineous-looking
fellows, close-cropped, red up to the ears, bare-necked, and
bursting with animal spirits.)

"Good morn, Signor Riddel," said the old man, with a
meek smile.

> " Glace je fais,
> On ne me paye,
> Je suis le Sire de Polonai!"

said Riddel, jumping up from his sofa to seize his ice.

"That's rather good," said Lord Alfred, looking at Rid
del.

"Oh, I made that, some mornings ago—about Polonai.
'Gad, he's descended from the Coucys, for aught I know.
. . . . . I say, Polonai, pick up the spoon, like a
good fellow!"

The old man stooped, as he was bid, and gave the spoon
to Riddel. (Have you ever wondered, reader, what sort of
fellow you would have been, by this time, if you had been
turned adrift at eight years of age?)

"I'll take an ice," said Fitz-Gubin. The ancient Frenchman brought his tub to the cabin-door to supply him

Polonai, junior, (for our friend had married a Maltese in due time, and was now naturalized as a Maltese, almost—though he occasionally disappeared from the island—" to France," people said)—a handsome boy with those intensely black eyes which the Maltese have—carried it for his father.

"Well, younker," began Riddel, who had "chaff" ready for all comers—"you're the rising hope of the Polonai family, eh?"   "Yes, *Signor*," said the boy.

"But, by the toe of St. Peter—where did you get that cap worked for you?"

"That, *Signor*," the youngster answered, with some reserve, " was my sister's making."

Old Polonai spoke to his boy in Maltese—and he went away. The gentlemen of the cabin looked at each other.

Polonai looked up, with his meek smile and subdued manner—"Anything more to-day?" The world had—by long passing him through its hands, and rubbing him to and fro—smoothened and flattened him like an out-worn sixpence ;—all the stamp and impress was gone. The world treats unlucky fellows like one of those defaced sixpences one sometimes comes across. They pass, to be sure, (for what little they exchange for,) but you can see that they have everywhere had the ill-luck to be suspected—bit—pinched—blackened all along.

"I think—no more, to-day. And, Polonai, I owe you something, and here it is," said Riddel, producing a dollar or two.

" Thank you, *Signor*."

" And, Polonai—but no—no matter! Good day, Monsieur de Polonai."

With his meek smile and subdued way, the old Frenchman shambled off.

" Oh ! never mind him, my lord—old mate, of the name of Manton," whispered Cuckles—as an interpreter might render to you the sayings of a Cherokee.

In a little while the party were ready to go on shore. When they went on deck, Cuckles was there—seeing the bitts blacked, and the paint washed—the work which has to be done in Malta harbor, and which must be carefully done, too.

As Riddel was at the side, calling a shore-boat, Fitz-Gubin, who by this time had acquired a wonderful knack of knowing the men liable to his influence—and whom he generally contrived, in every ship, to win and use—chatted very affably with Cuckles. " Mr. Cuckles had been very courteous ; would he—might he, Fitz-G., hope he would—just see about his hammock and hammock-man, and—he supposed a good marine was unengaged—but really he was ashamed." Cuckles, civil at every pore to rank—the pet of the commander—undertook everything, and discharged what he promised, like the faithful fellow he was. In the meantime, Mr. Riddel hailed the mess-boat, which you might have known anywhere by its flag—bearing the mess-arms, (a donkey *rampant*,) and in it the party seated themselves. There was a scandalous report, by-the-by, about this time, that some youngsters had so destroyed the confidence, which is the basis of all commercial credit, that you could not get a casual shore-boat without difficulty. But this was, probably—like a rumor about Lieutenant Bulrush (commanding the Roarer, 10) and his *calèche*—a mere idle invention—one of that copious crop of rumors which every season at Malta brings forth. We cannot be expected to waste our time upon these !

We may now—for, by the magic of fiction, we have landed our party in Mula's *Café*—skipping past Strada St. Giovanni and its shops—(I say skipping past its shops—

and if you will put an evil construction upon our smartness
in passing Darba's—why you must!) consider Lord Alfred
as having *begun* his naval career in the Mediterranean. For
isn't the shore the predominant, the important scene of
such career? Whom do you dress to please in the Mediterranean?—somebody on shore. Where did Riddel keep his
pony? Where did Siddlington buy his jewelry? Where
did Montemart display his waltzing?

"This is pleasant enough," said Fitz-Gubin, lounging in
the cool halls of Mula. He paused. "I like Malta, I
think. I think it's as well though, to be here, *in a ship.*"

"To be here, in a ship?" Riddel repeated, somewhat
puzzled.

"Why, you know, you sleep out in the sea-air."

"So you do," said Riddel, thoughtfully. "Gad, that's
a new point in the profession."

"I like the profession," said Lord Alfred Fitz-Gubin.

I am not going, at this time, to take our friends into those
circles of beauty and fascination, which waited Fitz-Gubin's
pleasure. That the Admiral knows of his arrival and will
probably produce something *drinkable* when he asks *him* to
dinner—an event to which the gallant officer's nieces, also,
look with an interest of their own ; that other houses, with
that regard for the peerage, which is a characteristic of the
island, intend to show a proper attention to the "descendant of an ancient family in Picardy," we may, of course,
presume. But this evening, I ask your company to dinner
in the Sovereign, and invoke the shade of Benbow to be
present at the board !

Our party has returned to that stately line-of-battle ship,
and twilight is wrapping itself round the white island—twilight of a faint blue, through which the hulls and spars of
the vessels in harbor rise dark and solemn. As it deepens,
the bells of Valetta are ringing, vexing the languid air with

their silver clang, clang, to the which answer the bells of
Burmola, meeting them half-way on the harbor waters, and
ringing a half-mournful melancholy note over the marriage
of summer and sea. There is a momentary thrill of coolness that almost chills, as the breeze comes noiselessly from
the outside ocean, and air, and waters, and bell-notes mingle
together. Deepening yet, though the bells jingle as if they
would fain frighten the darkness away. In the distance, a
light glides across the harbor—like a corpse-light gliding to
show you where a funeral's path shall be. It is a boat,
reader, taking Brown of the Ganges to dine with Smith of
the Bustard. Let us leave the harbor alone. Have we not
three hundred and sixty-four twilights to look at in the
year, and are we not going to dinner?

The mess-dinner of the Sovereign is laid out. Some
twenty-five fellows sit down. The steward (elaborately
attired) bows as he sees Fitz-Gubin seat himself with the
knot at the head of the table—Riddel, Corbicton, Siddlington, &c. His satisfied eye welcomes the mild, familiar glass
of china, and silver, and the pleasant gleam of the huge
decanters of iced wine. The dinner is the object of constant admiration, and Cuckles daily jokes on its splendor,
as compared with that which he supposes to be the habitual
fare of the mess (except, of course, those of our degree)
at home. (Pleasant Cuckles—thou man of fine heart and
fine taste !)

The steward, with a profound bow, now hands to Lord
Fitz-Gubin, the *carte*. I say distinctly, the *carte*. Shade
of Lord Collingwood—(to whose descendants in the female
line, a grateful Government would *not* continue the title*)

---

* And this—though COLLINGWOOD, besides boasting such services, and
such a mind and character as were his, was a man of distinguished family !
If we *will* plebeianize our peerage, let us, at least, cease to sneer at our
plebeians.—ED.

shade of Benbow, wag your ghostly pig-tail, and let us look
at the items of the *carte.* (The cook of the Sovereign was
a man of genius, and will probably die a baronet.):—"*Cote-
lettes à la Trafalgar ; Fricassée de Gibier en pigtail antique ;
Vol au vent, au maintop ; Brimbousky marine, &c., &c.*"

These were the leading features of the entertainment that
day, with sufficient substantials, of course ; which, by-the-
by, were highly necessary to the youngsters, who could not
always, if we are to believe some people, get any of the
finer specimens of the *cuisine.* Bung, the master's assistant,
made a democratic agitation on the subject, by bawling to
the servants after some of the "*ong pigtail hontick,*" but the
roar of laughter (which his pronunciation justly raised)
soon caused him to subside into silence and boiled beef.
What was worse, he never heard the last of the matter
You don't, indeed, often hear the last of a joke in the service, and many a fellow who has got himself a nickname in
his first week, retains it for life, carries it over the whole
globe, and through every grade of rank, and dies in it.
Accordingly, the youngsters were perpetually at Bung—
"Bung, any *hontick* to-day ?" &c., &c.

"Lord Alfred, a glass of wine," said Cuckles, ordering
champagne ; a luxury in which, to do him justice, he did
not often indulge. They drank.

"I like the dinner," said Fitz-Gubin, with his usual deliberation. "The cook is really not bad. *He ranks, of course,
as a petty officer ?*"

Here, I think, I may close a chapter, and leave the reader
to his meditations !

CHAPTER II.

THE mere mention of the cockpit—such as it once existed—justly excites a fastidious sneer. The reading public has to be disabused of several notions about Her Majesty's navy. The blockheads who believe that a midshipman "shivers his timbers," are, of course, hopeless, and with them I decline to communicate. But a better informed class may still be ignorant, that on board the Sovereign, Brummell might have attired his person with all the care which it demanded. Again Fitz-Gubin expressed his satisfaction, when he found the comfortable and spacious place for his chest; where a judicious array of curtains made up a cabin, and where his marine had prepared everything for him. Cuckles, whose apparatus was not far off, was busy about the place, keeping the lavatory arrangements of the youngsters within proper bounds. Siddlington, again, in a corner, was devoting to his whiskers that intense and absorbing attention which auburn whiskers demand. How different the leisure and space here, to the absurd difficulties of the Bloater, where the wretched Mules wore out his heart in endeavoring to keep up his appearance !

The *toilette* hour in one of your big ships is always a lively one. How properly, in one sense, was the table where the many (for they could not all have curtains and seclusion) washed, called the *amputation table!* How were reputations lopped, and dissected, and pruned, and trimmed, over those pewter basins ! What pleasantries about Ricks, about the commander, the notabilities of Malta, and the news of the squadron ! What chuckles when Manton, the old mate, could not find his wig ! What roars when the DON penetrated (which he had no business to do, for why the deuce did Jack Treloony, who had the morning watch, let him on

board ?) to these haunts ! There was a laugh, indeed, when
Saijan, when Nathan, or Darba came groping along among
half-lashed-up hammocks. The Dun in your place like Malta,
becomes quite naval. He knows when the Intolerable is
going to get her orders ; that the Viper is to be sent home,
because she's overmasted ; he hears, as soon as the squadron does, that Captain Ransacker has lost all that money
at blind-hookey ; and he wonders, as everybody wonders,
what the devil Ransacker *will* do this time.

That laughter from the youngsters, when the Dun makes
his morning call, is to the philosophic ear, a melancholy
sound. What a number of us have joined in it at sixteen,
and sighed at it at six-and-twenty ! This association of
humor with the serious events of life (as the apparition of
the Dun eventually becomes) is very strange. We joke in
youth about dunning, about matrimony, and about hanging,
I believe, more than any other subjects. Yet, infallibly,
the time comes when we pay—we marry—and if we don't
hang, (as is to be hoped,) yet we think with seriousness on
that catastrophe, and life generally. That morning, the
prophetic eye, beholding Livingstone the youngster giving a
huge order to Darba, might have seen through the vista of
years a vision such as Livingstone would have shrunk from,
could *he* have foreseen it. Horace's *Cura* sticks not more
closely than the fatality of the Dun—*Post equitem sedet*.
Here he is behind you on the hack you have hired, and on
which you are trotting—from Valetta to Citta Vecchia—or
by-and-by, along the pleasant shores of Baiæ, or the rocky
brown hills of Greece, or the heath-lands of Troy, or the
rich green fields of Smyrna. He mounts the "trireme,"
viz., the pinnace of the Bellerophon, which you command ;
and the boat at Richmond wherein you pull, years after.
When you are starring it, I say, in London, or shooting
red-legs in Brittany, there is one fellow who knows your

movements as well as any of your family.   It is DARBA of
Strada Reale !   Awful thought !   He will write in time to
your venerable parent, and request him to pay the inclosed
bill " out of your son's patrimony "—(suggestive Darba !)
Something will ultimately have to be done about that man's
bill.   . . . But in the interim, here is Livingstone, young
and downy-cheeked, light-hearted and light-tongued, giving
Darba a large order.   For a year, Darba will make no mention of the matter, and Livingstone will. spend his ready
money in forgetfulness of the man—whom he dimly intends
to pay some day—when (as it will turn out) neither his
cheek nor his heart are as fresh and unworn as they are now.
The age requires two treatises—the philosophy of dissipation,
and the philosophy of Duns !

   The day began in the Sovereign with the crossing of the
topgallant-yards, after which, the hammocks having been
tortured into perfect smoothness of outline, a party of two
were sent to potter about the dockyards, or elsewhere, and.
the huge vessel lay still as the waters which reflected her
glowing copper, or her gleaming hull.   Awnings spread and
yards squared, she was as quiet as the island itself in the
sea.   You might lounge on the poop, and watch the bright
green and yellow boats glitter across the harbor, like dragon-
flies—gaudy as lizards ; or the town almost misty with the
intense sunshine, and fancy the days of the Order of St.
John back again, and the Podgerses and Rodgerses still in
their chilly northern homes.   A whole day, nothing would
break your reverie, but the shrill pipe of the dinner-hour,
when the fruit boats swarmed alongside, and when poor old
Polonai the meek, with his boy and the ice-can, came sham-
bling over the ship's side, bowing to the officer of the
watch—modest before the sentry—civil to everybody.

   Fitz-Gubin was loitering about the upper deck at noon,
and had just thrust into his pocket the Admiral's invitation

to dinner, (that morning arrived,) as the veteran Polonai
came on board.   Fitz-Gubin gave a little hasty glance round
the deck ; Cuckles was away ; his messmates of the watch
were far aft on the poop, sitting (there is no good denying
it) in perfect idleness on the spanker-boom.   Fitz-Gubin
came up to the gangway.   I have mentioned his solemn,
determined manner.   I have to add that concealment was a
strong feature in the young gentleman's character.   He
rarely let anybody know what he had in his thoughts ; still
less in his intentions.

"Hee ! Polonai.   *Glace.*"

The old man was about to descend the main hatchway.
He turned back.

" Monsieur no take it in the cabin ?"

"Non.   No.   Here, Polonai !"

The veteran complied.   It was a sight to see Fitz-Gubin
leaning against the bitts, and with perfect deliberation, consuming the lemon-ice.   He put some money in his hand,
with the glass, and was turning away.

"*Mais, Monsieur, c'est* too much," said old Polonai, eagerly;
" you not have so much to pay as this, Monsieur."

" *Fitz-Gubin.   Lord* Fitz-Gubin—Polonai ! . . . Never
mind, Polonai.   Quelque jour, je vous ferai une visite, peut-
etre, et donc."

"Milor Fitz-Gubin.   Prenez le money, if you please !"
And the old fellow, with many bows, and a slight color over
his withered old face, forced it upon him.

Fitz-Gubin walked aft in meditation.   Riddel and one or
two of the men had just come up the companion-ladder.

"I say, Lord Fitz-Gubin, we've been wondering what's
become of old Polonai to-day ?"

"Have you?   Why, *I* saw him a little ago knocking
about," said the youth.

" Fox, of the Queen, has seen his daughter ; so he said,

last night, at dinner. He swore she's an angel,"·Riddel observed.

"Ah, well, perhaps she is. How hot the day is !" said Lord Alfred Fitz-Gubin.

Whereupon, Lord Alfred (who, bless you, could not be occupying his mind with the family of an itinerant vender of ices) edged away. A moment afterwards, he was in the cabin of the Commander, and asking leave to go on shore, "to dine with the Admiral."

"I should not be likely to refuse you leave on general grounds," said the Commander, with a Christian smile, becoming a serious man ; "on the present special one I grant it with pleasure ! You will find that household, indeed, a charming one. Beauty, with genius and gentleness—these are,.I say it on the authority of my personal observation, its characteristics."

And the Commander smiled, as if addressing the compliment to the persons themselves—as indeed he would have liked to have done, I dare say ; perhaps he thought something of the sort might reach them from him, through Fitz Gubin.

To make matters still more agreeable to our friend, he gave him a seat in the cutter, then on the point of landing·a parcel for Mrs. ——, his wife, under the charge of a mid· shipman ! The cutter was cushioned, gilt, varnished, and adorned with a tiller that would have been an ornament to a drawing-room table, at the cost of said midshipman, Leslie Clare, (lost last year, I observe, poor fellow, jumping after a negro who tumbled overboard, and would have caught cold, if an English gentleman had not risked himself, and so lost his life, in picking him up.) Leslie Clare was the only midshipman who had a successful contest with Cuckles. Cuckles had wished to send him in this cutter, which he commanded, and just after he had had the first touch put

to it, to bring the beef on`board. Clare appealed to the
Commander; the Commander decided that the jolly-boat
should go. He was a joyous youth; his family were rich :
all went well with him, till he met the ill-omened nigger,
who proved the agent of his fate.

You are not to suppose that Fitz-Gubin dressed himself
in full fig before landing at this time. . This would not have
been becoming one so essentially a member of the "swell"
naval world, with which we have at present to deal. He
carried a carpet-bag. He patronized the Mitre Hotel.
Riddel had his horse there. Siddlington put up at the
Mediterranee. Corbieton preferred the Royal Princess's.

As the boat landed, Lord Alfred turned to Clare, with
whom he had scarcely exchanged a word, (he associated
with none out of a clique in any ship,)—"Will you allow
one of the men to carry my carpet-bag to the Mitre, Mr.
Clare ?"

Clare was so surprised that he involuntarily said, "Yes."
Fitz-Gubin bowed, and set off. The seaman followed ; and
in due order they reached the house, where the obsequious
landlord received his Lordship with all proper deference.
Of course, Snacks had seen the appointment, which had
been copied into a special paragraph by itself, in the *Malta
Dip.*, for the benefit of the aristocratic "sympathizers," (to
use a Yankeeism,) who are plentiful in Malta.

Fitz-Gubin never long required aid in finding his way
about a place. Already an introduction or two put the
threads in his hand. He knew the art—which you may
have observed, characterizes the knowing of the English
great world, abroad—the art of comporting himself in
mixed society ; I don't mean, of course, the obvious art of
behaving himself in company (which is within the range of
an idiot—and for ordinary purposes a common-place affair
to anybody not decidedly cursed with the *air bourgeois*)—

but a higher art than that. I mean an art like that of the
fellows who dive in the wreck of the Royal George, and
who retain their self-composure, eye-sight, and individuality,
among strange fish, monstrous timber, and mud. In a word,
the art of mingling in society conventionally inferior to your
own, (yet the only society of the place you are in,) without
committing yourself to it in the slightest degree ! Did the
fashionable Poodle scouring the Mediterranean in 184— use
up the services, the dinners, horses, evening parties (everything that could keep his great soul from perishing in its
own exhausted receiver of emptiness)—pic-nics, of every
society from the pillars of Hercules to the Golden Horn?
Yes. Did he form a tie of decent grateful friendship with
one man or family? When Branton, junior, (of the Maltese
firm,) was in town some time ago, (awakening Government
to the importance of the Gozo traffic in Peas-pods,) did
Poodle show him any attention? No ! Yet, wherever
you had met Poodle in the Mediterranean, you would have
thought him domesticated in its circles. That was Poodle's
art—the merit of which is not to be denied to him. A
similar art enabled our own Fitz-Gubin to play off Cuckles
for his utility, another man or two for their sociability, and
so on ; while he knew precisely the worth of each according
to his ultimate standard of social appeal. Be wise, my good
reader, in your generation, and remember to do with your
Cuckleses, &c., as you would with foreign money :—piastres
are very useful in the East, drachmas in Greece, and dollars
in Malta—you are not expected to take them and pass them
in England !

All this time the afternoon has been, of course, wearing
away; by half-past six, the Admiral's door began to give
forth a series of thunderings, after each of which it rained
in a visitor. Roribel, the flag-lieutenant, was an object of
serene brilliance ; Sir Ajax Thorp, dignified ; Lady Thorp,

magnificent; Captain and Mrs. Plimmer and Miss Plimmer,
truly imposing. Of Fitz-Gubin's fresh, sumptuous, and
languid appearance; I can only say this, that he looked
(can you fancy so charming a figure?) like Narcissus after
a Turkish bath!

"How do thoo do, Lord Fitth-Gubin?. My nieces——
How'th your father, Lord Fitth-Gubin?" said the extremely
aged Admiral, in his peculiar way. These established
questions over, (and Lord Alfred, remember, though an
aristocrat, was only a "mate,") the Admiral left him to
make his way with the nieces.

"How do thoo do, Mr. Clarendon? How'th your
father, Mithter Clarendon?"

So was dismissed Mr. Clarendon, a lieutenant, cousin to
the First Lord. And the Admiral, a minute afterwards,
was wagging his old gray head, alongside Sir Ajax Thorp,
in close confab.

Roribel and Fitz-Gubin fraternized; they had known
each other in South America, and Riddel Roribel was a
swell.

"Who are we waiting for?" asked Fitz-Gubin, in a quiet
corner with Roribel. He told him.

"I wish he'd come."

"So do I. By Jove, Sir! we are to tap some of the
good claret, to-day," said Roribel, in an impressive tone.
"You know our excellent friend is considered rather a
screw. In fact, between ourselves, there was no keeping
up the *entente cordiale* over the stuff he used to produce
here! 'Gad, the services could not act in harmony; and
the Island was falling into anarchy. They say Ricks gave
him a hint!"

"The deuce!" said Fitz-Gubin.

The laggard having arrived, Fitz-Gubin moved in his
order, with Miss Plimmer, to dinner; and found himself

between that young lady and the Admiral's youngest niece.
Miss Plimmer, knowing that Fitz-G. was a lord, kindly
overlooked the fact that he was only a mate. In ordinary
cases (papa being a captain, you know) she could not have
been expected to take much notice of anybody under a lieutenant. As a lover of discipline, I cannot but admire the
discipline which in these places arranges such matters. It
would puzzle Garter King of Arms (an official for whom I
have an unaffected respect) to discriminate and arrange
precedence in some societies I have known. A captain is a
captain we know, (and a very strange gentleman he is,
sometimes,) and that Mrs. Captain Plimmer should take
the lead of Mrs. Lieutenant Jenks, is natural enough; but
what if Mrs. Jenks' father the alderman be a knight? Is
the youngest daughter of a captain in command superior to
the eldest daughter of a captain on half-pay? Again, a
midshipman is nobody, we know; but what if he is the only
son of a man with five thousand a-year?

Would Rosa Plimmer have made an exception in his
favor in such a case? It may be so. Rosa was pretty
affable now; for the third year of the commission of the
Unsaleable was now wearing away; and in a few months
Captain Plimmer and his family must retire into private life.
It is, indeed, a touching sight to see one of those veterans,
whose eye, the other day, carried terror in every glance,
moving about a seaport town, in a blue overcoat—a merely
private man; they linger in these towns, I think, as a
mourner lingers by a churchyard, musing over the memory
of defunct power—meditating on the glory of past
greatness.

The ladies departed.

"Lord Fitth-Gubin, I hope thoo like the Sovereign;
Mithter Clarendon, I thrust thoo are comfortable in the
Spitfire?"

The duties of hospitality being so far performed to these gentlemen, and the "*good* claret" set moving, the conversation of the evening went on with its usual decorum on such state occasions—taking the initiative from the Admiral, and Sir Ajax Thorp—and moving (like a state elephant at an Indian festival) in a heavy manner about. Naval news was said little of—indeed, naval talk about that period was half made up of growls about the Admiral himself (which you could scarcely expect to hear at his own table); politics were, of course, tabooed; and, finally, you could only wonder, as Fitz-Gubin mentally did, what the dinners were like on the "*bad*-claret days."

In the drawing-room, where, in due time, (but not before Fitz-Gubin's light, delicate complexion testified, by a tinge of faint color, to the "sanitary reform" which had been lately made in the Admiral's dinner arrangements,) they adjourned, Fitz-Gubin found the ladies talking about "conversion"—the conversion of the Maltese.

"Can you convert a Maltese?" asked Fitz-Gubin.

"Why," said the eldest Miss Wyoming, smiling, "we have not had much success, hitherto. A system which so weds itself to the imagination of the devotees, you know—attracting through the senses, as our minister in St. Kilderkin—Mr. Fatton—says—having no such attractions to offer—"

"No attractions about Mr. Fatton, you mean, Miss Wyoming," said the genial Roribel, smiling.

"Mr. Roribel is a wit, you know, Lord Fitz-Gubin, and we must excuse him. But you understand me, the absence of all that splendid ornament—"

"Those heavenly little crosses," said Miss Plimmer. "I declare the altar at St. John's—you might fancy it was an emperor's side-board."

"We know *whom* it is but too calculated to please, dear

Emma, as Mr. Fatton says," went on Miss Wyoming mysteriously. "But I *do* feel an enthusiastic wish to save—to
win—*one* beautiful lamb to the true fold. I should like,
shouldn't you, Mary, to convert little Marie Polonai ?"

"Little Marie Polonai," replied Fitz-Gubin, mechani-
cally.

"Marie Polonai; do you know the name ?"

"I know there is one Polonai, an old man, who sells ices
to the mess. At least, I think that's the name."

"The same man," Miss Wyoming went on, warmed by
her own eloquence ; "they live in a little house in the Strada
St. Orsola, with a green gate."

("A little house in the Strada St. Orsola, with a green
gate," mentally repeated Lord Alfred.)

"And a kind of court-yard, where there is an orange-
tree."

("A kind of court-yard, where there is an orange-tree,"
continued mentally Fitz-G.)

"There is a dried-up fountain, with broken sides—so
romantic."

("A dried-up fountain," his lordship went on.)

"Lord Fitth-Goobin, I with you a good night. Mithter
Clarendon, I with you a good evening." So saying, the
Admiral, whose load of years made it require no apology
for him to withdraw early, toddled off to bed.

Not long after, the party broke up. The girls were
quite pleased with the interest Fitz-Gubin had shown in
their talk. A hint about a pic-nic to Bosketto had been
thrown out, and joyfully hailed.

"A very pleasing face," said Miss Wyoming to her sister,
as they were going to bed. "Quite the look of the old
blood, my dear."

"Quite, indeed," was the innocent reply.

It was a lovely night, of the whitest moonlight, as Fitz

Gubin strolled away. Here and there he caught a glimpse,
through a street, of the sea, which was all alive with light.
The air was cool, yet there was scarcely wind enough to
disturb the blossoms on an almond tree.

Need I say, that in Mula's Café, whose hospitable door
was open to the night, there was a large party of naval
men? Fitz-Gubin strolled in, bent on the cooling lemonade; and found the usual smoking, supping, refreshment,
and conversation going on.

"Yes, sir, Smithett will get the vacancy. You'll see,"
said a mate.

"Vacancy!" whispered a midshipman to my friend, Pug
Welby, "he's always running on vacancies, that Moggles."

"Yes," said Pug, "he has always a vacancy—in his
head!"

Fitz-Gubin sat down at one of the little marble tables by
himself, and lolled in tranquil meditation. He felt the
lemonade thrill him with a pleasant coolness, and there was
present to his mind's eye—a little house in the Strada St.
Orsola, with a green gate, and a kind of court-yard, with
an orange-tree in it.

I could tell you stories about Fitz-Gubin's South American adventures (only they have nothing to do with our
present scenes), which would show you that it was no
wonder that he sallied forth after finishing his lemonade on
the present occasion. In his most indifferent manner, he
inquired for Strada St. Orsola, of the waiter of the hotel
where he changed his clothes. It was not long before he
found himself in a narrow and steep, hilly street, of which
many of the houses were high, but lank and meagre-looking.
Nothing was stirring; his own shadow in the moonlight
was all he saw, as he walked quietly along, keeping close
on one side. Sleep soundly, old Polonai! Come out and
look at the moonlight, young Marie!

Fitz-Gubin presently paused, and reconnoitred. "Tall houses," he thinks; "high windows." But a friendly bottle with the boatswain, and a few dollars to some forecastle men—and a *Jacob's ladder* would be made which would dangle as lightly as a cobweb from the highest window in Malta! A *Jacob's ladder*, whereon evil figures (unlike those of the dream of the patriarch) might ascend and descend; know we not such objects? thinks Fitz-Gubin. The boatswain of the "Coromandel" might have told you stories about *Jacob's ladders*. They say, Harry Bulstrode was all but caught with one at a lofty enough window (in all senses), somewhere in the Mediterranean; and that the Admiralty promoted him out of the way.

But it was *not* a tall window, nor a high house this, as our hero almost immediately found. It lay back from the street, inside this kind of a court-yard; and here is the adventurer at the gate. Looking in, he sees a figure with its back towards him—sitting, leaning over the dried-up fountain.

The house itself was all dark. With the gentlest of movements Fitz-Gubin moved the gate, and entered the court-yard, with a beating heart. The figure instantly started; back flew a mantilla, and the moonlight fell in a *douche* on one of the prettiest faces—one of the sweetest girl's faces—he had ever seen.

"Hush," said the youth, "I am ill. I am fainting. I come to ask you for a glass of water."

Putting his hand on his heart, he knelt, and lay on his side on the grass. The girl's face showed that she believed him, and she went inside and brought a cup. As she stooped to put it to his lips, the whole beauty of her face and neck—a neck that the sun had not been allowed to spoil, and beside which you would have thought pearls vulgar—revealed itself to him. Darker eyes—fuller of

4

sweetness and light—never held truth in the bottom of their deep wells.*

"I am better ; thank you, in the name of the Blessed Lady," said our friend. (This apostasy he found service-able in Catholic countries.) "By what name shall I remember you ?"

"My name is Marie."

"Then, thank you, Marie. I am better and must go. You live here ?"

"This is my father's."

"I must be going. You have a pretty place here, Marie."

"It is quiet, and we are quiet—are you now well ?" inquired the girl.

He rose. "Thanks to you, I am—and I must go home. What a smell of flowers ! I must send you a jewel for your kindness, Marie."

"Good night, Signor," said the girl, in a very serious manner.

He bowed, and hurried away into the street. He strolled down it with a firm stride. There was a step behind him, and a Maltese voice eager and hoarse, said—

"Signor, where you been ?"

He turned sharp round, and saw a young and brawny Maltese before him, who retreated a stride, and kept a black and glowing eye upon his face.

"Where have I been, you infernal rascal of a *smytch*, what's that to you ?"

"Curse you all ! that's the way of you all, with your 'fernal ways and 'fernal tongues. By G—d, a knife the only thing for you ! If I think you play your impudent tricks with Signora Marie, I put knife in you, by G—d, Signor.

---

* *Verbatim* from Forbessy's papers.—ED.

You go make love to your English lady; leave Maltese
lady alone!"

As Fitz-Gubin afterwards told his friends, the closing
sentence of this "rascal's" speech was enough to make anybody laugh:

"You impudent scoundrel, take yourself off," he said.
"I'll have you hanged, sir, if you talk to me!"

"You been see Signora Marie?"

"How dare you, sir?" said Fitz-Gubin, sincerely indignant at the fellow's impudence.

"Antonio!" cried the Maltese. A figure started behind
Lord Alfred. He started, too, to meet it—but a blow from
behind fell with a heavy force upon his head, and he sank to
the ground.

Let us return to Mula's *café*.

A man entered the café, late, whom some of the party
there knew—a man belonging to the Vixen.

"Any of the Sovereign's fellows here?" said he, moisten-
ing a cigar in his mouth, very quietly, and sitting down.

"Yes," answered Riddel. "Yes," answered Siddling-
on.

"Because," said he, "there's one of your fellows lying
bleeding in a street near the Lasçares. I advise you to
look after him."

"The devil there is!" said the two gentlemen, suddenly
starting up.

When Lord Fitz-Gubin came to himself, he found himself lying in his hammock, on board the Sovereign, with a
wet cloth on his head.

CHAPTER III

FITZ-GUBIN's head (for reasons which I need not enlarge upon) did not suffer any permanent injury, or, indeed, any serious hurt on this unfortunate occasion. He was a little puzzled when he came to himself at first, and found a sentry near him, who immediately reported his recovery to the assistant-surgeon. That officer, MacStirk, was instantly at his side to see how the case was going on, and to administer a draught. Next morning Fitz-Gubin was, of course, reported in the sick list ;—"Contusion—a little fever—quiet," said the surgeon. So the patient took up his abode in that cabin on the main-deck which we are already acquainted with—decidedly pale and seedy, and with an awkward clot in his hair, testifying to the smartness of the tap on his skull, but not in any danger. Here he spent his time in bed all day, near the cool port-hole, and opposite the engraving of the brigand and his daughter—an object of interest and sympathy to his friends.

What had happened?—that was the question, as people justly remarked. He had been dining at the Admiral's : "Couldn't have had too much to drink *there !*" remarked Pug Welby, satirically, when he heard the story. "A row with the police," said others, as if that were a matter-of-course affair, which it ought not to be in a well-regulated squadron. "Fell from his horse," Cuckles reported, apparently by authority. The surgeon, no doubt, knew whether the contusion was such as a fall from a horse would cause. MacStirk, with his usual ignorance of the world, must needs blurt out, when the Commander put it carelessly to him and the Surgeon together (for Cuckles had been chatting with the Commander just before), "whether Lord Fitz-Gubin had hurt himself by a fall?"—that it was "more of the

nature of a varra severe bruise, such as a maan with a
'rung——He beg-ged pardon, he meant a stick !"—but the
Surgeon cut this bore short, and left the Commander to
take his own view of it. So the Commander did ; and a
charming little narrative, investing the accident 'with the
hues of imagination, reached the Admiral's house. Poor
Lord Alfred had had a severe fall (these Maltese streets
are notoriously dangerous to one unused to them), and the
Misses Wyomings sent him works to read when convales·
cent, including tracts, which found their way to the gun·
room, and excited wonder and admiration there. The
"Mariner Rescued" (2d) was one of these, and an effort
was made to bring its influence to bear on Bung, the master's assistant—of course without any success—by the
midshipmen. But, indeed, there is no want of works calculated to awaken the nautical mind among those supplied by
Government, if they are brought up from the hold—a preliminary which I have known to be neglected in some of
Her Majesty's ships and vessels of war.   •

It is to be supposed that Riddel and that set guessed more
accurately than the multitude the nature of Fitz-Gubin's
misfortune. Cuckles was with him the very next morning
when he had moved into the main-deck cabin, and Fitz-
Gubin then said, with a feeble voice, "You won't let me be
disturbed, Cuckles ?—Don't let us have the fellows eating
ice, and joking that old French Maltese in here, like a good
fellow !" Cuckles promised faithfully that he would see that
nothing of the sort happened. In a few days, when he was
better, and some of the set were sitting with him, be began
to talk a little more freely of his accident. He " had *met* a
girl, and, by Jove, he was talking to her——"

" Whereabouts ?" asked Siddlington.

" Oh, why, you know I don't know Valetta well. But I
had—somewhere near the market, I fancy—met her ; and

she had just gone, when this confounded cad—by Jove, I
never read of such insolence—must needs accost me : and
what do you think he said?—'Go make love to English
lady ; leave Maltese lady alone !"

Riddel and Siddlington roared with laughter, and the
speech of the *smytch* was pronounced one of the most characteristic lately produced by the island.   Fitz-Gubin leaned
back, and grinned at the reminiscence.   "I was so taken
aback by the extraordinary insolence of the fellow," he continued, "that I did not notice a man who must have been
lurking in the neighborhood, and who suddenly gave me a
blow——"

"Ice to-day, *Messieurs* ?" said a voice at the door ; and
there appeared the meek but not vulgar head of old
Polonai.

Cuckles was going to expel the speaker, in spite of his
age and reputed nobility of extraction, summarily ; but
Fitz-Gubin, coloring slightly as he saw him, called him in.

"Ah, the Sieur de Polonai !" said Riddel.   "Well, Polonai, musing on the downfall of the *noblesse*, eh? An ice,
Polonai.   When Henri returns, we shall have Polonai on
his legs again."

The old fellow, seasoned to chaff, having been trained like
a war-horse to stand that fire, by the experience of innumerable ships on board which he had carried the ice-can, went
on filling the glass with perfect composure.

"Thanks, Seigneur de Polonai ! *Merci!* You know,
Polonai, your order brought their exile on themselves by
their infernal tyranny," went on the lively Riddel.   "I can
just fancy old Polonai wopping a vassal !"

Polonai grinned in his mild manner.

"An ice for me," said Fitz-Gubin.

Polonai worked away with the spoon in the crimson mass,

pleasant to the eye as to the tongue, and handed one to him. As Fitz-Gubin raised himself—

"You ill, *Signor*?" Polonai said, glancing at his bound-up head. Fitz-Gubin colored a little, and nodded. Polonai looked at him; you would have been surprised to see so much interest in that tame old face. He had a soft and even refined *empressement* (don't sneer, Tompkins, please!) in his manner, as he bowed at the side of the sofa, and presented Fitz-Gubin with the ice. When he drew back, and stood modestly beside his can, you might have noticed that his eye rested rather frequently on Fitz-Gubin. '

The side was piped. The Captain was coming on board to hear complaints, which had accumulated since his last visit from his house on shore. The Commander had summoned all culprits, and the regular old routine was being gone through; a marine who had polished off a corporal—a seaman or two who have got drunk, and told the officer of the watch they would see him d——d first, are waiting judgment. But the gun-room mess are summoned to an interview with the Captain in the Admiral's cabin, regarding the carrying of an instrument, known as a "colt," which has been applied to a meagre and pallid youngster, who has complained of the same. So away go the cabin-party; old Polonai has glided out; Fitz-Gubin has just composed himself for a *siesta*, with a handkerchief over his eyes, when the door is very gently opened.

He drew the handkerchief off and looked up, and he saw, entering with extreme quietness, and closing the door behind him, old Polonai.

"Lord Fitz-Gubin," the old fellow said in a low voice, "you got that wound in your head in Strada St. Orsola. Hush, *milor*, I am a very old man. I bear you no ill-will, and I respect your nation. One word, only, Lord Fitz-

Gubin, take care! Not what I might do I threaten you with. No, I am a poor old devil, and no matter. But, my lord, be a brave man and respect all men's rights!"

Fitz-Gubin felt his throat dry as he was going to speak, and before he quite recovered from that effect, and from a confusion which somehow came over him, the old man disappeared. Fitz-Gubin lay there, and wondered over the speech—dozed and woke up, fancying he heard him at his ear, then slept deeper and found himself in Strada St. Orsola. There he was at the fountain, and Marie sitting near him—her eyes on some object on the opposite side—and never looking at him, and the fountain seemed to fill up with water suddenly, and out of it came somebody who was his father and old Polonai in one, in some unaccountable manner. Then he was at Castellan, at home, and wandering round the old mausoleum where the Castellans used to be buried in the olden time, and *he* was going to be buried there, and thought it very odd that he should know anything about it; and just as the Miss Wyomings were putting a nosegay into his coffin, and Marie taking it away to keep as a *souvenir*, he awoke. The ship's bell was striking, and *not* the bell of Castellan church tower, and the afternoon was far advanced. The dream impressed him a great deal—and even in these anti-superstitious days a dream will impress people. (Manchester, to be sure, expounds the vision of Jacob, by supposing him to have taken too much meat for supper; it is a great blessing to live in an enlightened age!) He found it necessary to cheer himself up with a little soda-water and curaçoa, and the word being passed for Hobb, that marine soon brought the refreshment from the gun-room—where, by this time, the cloth was laid for dinner, and the steward had broken off the composition of a sonnet to his mistress, to indite the *carte* for the day. The fragrant and crisp beverage revived Fitz-Gubin, and dinner following—

(at which Cuckles took good care to send a faithful attendant with plenty of the *Brimbousky marine* to the cabin)—he
soon only remembered the dream as "deuced odd," and the
speech of old Polonai as that of a "queer old fellow." As
his head mended, he lay there and meditated on little Marie, and on the necessary precautions to be taken for the
future, against violent "cads." For indeed, he habitually
considered a "cad" who rivalled him in these affairs, much
as a kind of poacher—one who interfered with the rights
of the lord of the manor.

In a short time news came to Malta—brought by a young
fellow of the name of Forbessy—that the "Bloater" had
been "lost" on the coast of Spain! This was the cause
of the arrival of Scrymgeour Forbessy, Esq., in Malta, and
his subsequent apparition in the gun-room of the "Sovereign" one fine morning. Open flew the door, and in stalked,
to the astonishment of the fellows there) including the con-
valescent Fitz-Gubin), a long youth in a picturesque but
seedy garb, decidedly resembling that of a Spanish privateer.

"Why, hillo—who's this?" asked old Manton.

"Don't you know me? You do, Siddlington—Forbessy
of the 'Bloater?'"

"The devil! so it is, why, what's the meaning of this
rig?"

"The 'Bloater's' lost, Sir," cried Forbessy, flinging
himself on a chair. "Not a rag of my traps saved; the
officers and company are to be sent for, and the admiral
must send a craft too, to bring away the lower masts and
rudder."

"Bring a bottle of porter!" cried Siddlington, with professional zeal; "and you—how the deuce came you here?"

"Pappleton sent me on, in a Spanish merchant schooner,
and, 'gad, I had to borrow a rig from the skipper, and I
figure for the present as Antonio Perez."

4*

"Pappleton's smashed then, by Jove," said a midshipman
"Nay; they'll try Mrs. Pappleton, my dear fellow," Pug
Welby said.

"Well, I'm d—d," old Manton began; "they can't keep
a ship in the service, now, by the blazes they can't. That's
the third ship there's been lost since the beginning of the
commission. I don't know what the service is coming to.
There won't be a ship left to do the work of the station,
soon. I'll be hanged if the men that are appointed now-a-
days know how to keep a ship afloat. The service is changed
since I joined, I'm hanged if it ain't! There was Tails; he
had the Fizgig in the Baltic in 1814, and he took her off a
lee shore—blowing; by the Lord, it did blow in those days!
and, by Jove, I say Tails—he brought the Fizgig safe and
sound home to Spithead. Why, they knew how to do it in
1814; but, now, the longer I live, the worse the service gets."

That Manton could have continued in this strain all day
long, anybody who remembers the venerable mate, will at
once agree; the key-note (that is, the few simple words
which begin the harangue) once struck—off he went; and
instantly, Siddlington winked at Riddel—Pug nudged Latimer—the youngsters playfully capered behind his chair, and
various exhibitions of comic delight began. When he stopped, everybody felt that a familiar bit of fun had terminated:
and then old Manton, wagging his broad coat tails, disappeared; Fitz-Gubin watching his movements as a *dillettante*
stares at the ribs of some fossil ante-diluvian. "Bravo,
Manton," Latimer cried; and as the door closed behind
the veteran, Beaulieu looked up (having heard the oration,
with his eyes fixed on the page of a novel,) ejaculated—
"Rum old cock!" and returned to his favorite writer!

"Go on, Forbessy," Siddlington said. "Capital porter
that—I think? We haven't room for above fifty dozen of
it—without displacing the Madeira!"

"I'll go on, my dear fellow; but I feel a barbarian in this garb. I shall have to borrow a rig from you—we're just about a size—till Darba can make me something. I've forwarded Pappleton's despatches on to the Admiral, and he will likely send for me, to examine me about the matter in person; you know it won't do.to appear before him as Antonio Perez."

"That's true; come on to the cock-pit," said the good-natured Siddlington.

"This will be a serious matter for Darba!" said Pug Welby, with gravity.

"Gad, I don't know. Except Forbessy—none of the 'Bloaters' look like Christians," observed Riddel.

A quarter of an hour's lapse brought Mr. Forbessy, looking like the professional Forbessy of every-day life, to the gun-room again. It was about lunch-time, and a hot lunch was not tardy in coming, accordingly.

"You won't be sorry to get a beefsteak, or a quail on toast, again, Forbessy?" said Siddlington.

"Not I—though quails were never common in the Bloater.'"

"No quails?" Riddel said.

"No quails," replied Forbessy, gravely. "But a steak, after the wretched oily messes of my friend Perez, won't be amiss."

So saying, Mr. Forbessy seated himself at a table, and seized a knife and fork with the glorious inspiration of sea air, since 4 A. M., stirring in him. The languid youths, who had been three months in harbor, envied him that ogre-like appetite.

"I should like an ice," a youngster said, discontentedly; "but there's no getting an ice to-day, unless you send a man on shore on purpose! Old Polonai is gone."

Fitz-Gubin looked up. It was the first moment he had

exhibited any animation for an hour-and-a-half. Perhaps
he felt bored by seeing a stranger attract so much attention
as Forbessy had been doing ; perhaps he was amused, and
not bored, by the county paper from home, which he was
lounging over.   Even the family of which Fitz-Gubin is a
member, must tire of that paper, I think ; though it every
other week or so has "Rejoicings at Castellan—dinner of
the noble landlord's tenants—Mr. Kiss in the chair—the cloth
being removed, and the usual toasts, &c., &c., the chairman
gave the Noble The, &c., &c., (tremendous cheers,) the young
Lord Evremond, (great cheering,) the Infant Plantagenet,
(renewed and enthusiastic cheering,") and so on, on goodness knows what, and how many occasions, *per ann.*   Even
they, I remark, must tire of that print, and its sycophancy ;
and probably they despise it, too. But this is a digression.

Fitz-Gubin, I repeat, looked up.   "What did you say
about Polonai, youngster ?".

"What did I say?   I said he was gone to Marseilles,
somebody said."   The youngster was as curt and saucy as
a youngster in the "Sovereign" dared to be ; for, "confound the fellow and his title," (the youngster afterwards
observed to a brother juvenile, during a smoke "on the sly,"
at the main-deck bow-port,) "he never takes any notice of
your existence, except just at his own convenience ;" and,
true enough, several people did make some such complaint
about our friend Fitz-G.   He lived with you, breathed the
same air with you, yet seemed to discover you as if you
had just dropped from the moon, some day, suddenly—when
you could be made useful !

"Now for the loss of 'The Bloater,'" said Siddlington, as
the cloth was removed.   "Let me give you a drop of curaçoa—just a globule, if you like—and give us the story."

There were not many men left in the mess, and Forbessy
stretched his legs out, and was just beginning, when Lord

Alfred rose, begged pardon, and passed out. "Hem!"
ejaculated our friend Forbessy—who was an off-hand, open
sort of fellow—"I've been *boring* that young gentleman, I
fear. I've seen him before, somewhere, too. To be sure—
I remember—he was in the 'Cocytus,' when she broke.
down some time ago, before our last cruise. Would you
believe it, he wanted himself and his traps brought in, in
our pinnace, before the mails, if I remember right?"

Siddlington smiled, rather faintly. "Oh, I dare say he
was *gaté* as a youngster, you know. We—ah"—he looked
at Riddel—"we find him a good enough sort of a fellow
here." Which moderate speech, and mild appeal to Riddel,
meant that—that, in fact—we *were* of rather aristocratic
tastes in the "Sovereign," but that we were *not* tuft-hunt-
ers! Siddlington's father was a fashionable physician—so
his family had lived within ear-shot, and within the *parfum*
of the great world, at all events, and had been accustomed
to reverence it from infancy.

"Lord Alfred Fitz-Gubin is a young man of great promise, a great family, own half ——shire," said Cuckles, with
emphasis.

"——shire, eh?" said Forbessy. Then he relapsed into
thought for a moment, and presently laughed, and said,
"Oh, I know who he is, then! But, however, to my tale;
I won't detain you long.

"You know the 'Bloater' was sent some time ago to Barcelona. Mrs. Pappleton had never seen Spain, and justly
believing it to be one of the most romantic countries in
Europe, why she was curious to visit it! Accordingly,
one day in Dockyard Creek, when I was in charge of the
watch, I received a note, which I afterwards preserved as a
curiosity, and which, I fear, must have perished with my
kit. It was addressed to '*The Officer of the Watch, Bloater,*'
and ran thus:—'*Mrs. Pappleton requests that the Officer of* .

the Watch will send the Pinnace on shore, with the mast out.
I always obey orders; so I did send the pinnace, and it
returned with a cargo of bandboxes and bundles, and a
message from Madame, by the coxswain, that we were to
bend the studding-sail gear! I at once saw that we were
off, and soon afterwards the commander and his wife came
on board, and we got under weigh.   Time at sea in the
Bloater went slowly enough; Pappleton and his relations
(by which I mean nearly all the officers in the ship) seemed
to enjoy themselves; but for a private gentleman, uncon-
nected with the 'Family,' a 'Family Ship' is at best a dull
residence.   I was duly asked to dinner, to be sure; but I
do *not* take any special interest in the social news of Pleb-
Biddlecumb, which was the staple subject of conversation.
Once in a way, the social intrigues of a second-rate county
town—how the respectabilities there try to keep *in* with the
county gentry, and to keep *out* retired tradesmen and
farmers—may be curious.   Habitually, such topics seem
(to me at least) rather stupid.

"We left Barcelona, when it came on to blow.   I had
the middle watch, and it was freshening towards morning,
(as is the wind's way in the Mediterranean,) when I was
relieved by Joe Bluffett, the master, who always kept the
morning watch.   Joe had just joined us, before we left—a
bandy-legged, silent man, of heavy aspect.   He took the
telescope from you, glanced at the compass, 'Hum, Nor'
and by West,' lays her course—hum—and devil a word of
'good morning,' or 'fresh breeze,' or anything approaching
to human communion.   He called Mrs. Pappleton, 'Marm,'
and kept out of her way, or if she spoke to him he touched
his cap and answered the question, and sheered off.   She
called him, in private, 'the bear,' and Pappleton took a
dislike to him.

·   "Well, this morning that I am speaking of, Bluffett came

up, as heavy and as silent as ever, and did not seem to think
it was blowing a bit. Some fellows think it never blows in
the Mediterranean, (if they had been on the coast of Syria
in the winter of 1840, they would have found out·their mistake,) and I dare say Bluffett, who has knocked about the
planet since he was four feet high, did not expect much from
a bit of a breeze, where we were. He took the glass with
the customary grunt, and I went off to my hammock, tired
enough. When we were routed out at five bells, I found,
as I had expected, the breeze much higher, and then began
the comforts of a gale in a small craft—hammocks below—
such an atmosphere and such a deck—hatches battened
down—smoke filling the lower deck—black and white Pappleton prostrate in the berth—the mess-boy crawling aft
with some coffee and ship's biscuit in a tin pot; and, when
you'd quitted all this with disgust, the moment you shot
your head up among tarpaulins, through the companion-
way, slash went the spray in your face—you found the deck
wet fore and aft, and were deafened by the roar and shriek
of the wind through the gaunt and dripping rigging and
bare-looking masts.

"The first day the wind was hot and unrefreshing—
always an unpleasant feature; and at sunset there was
thunder brewing. The horizon was black, streaked by flying masses of gray, and the darkness was settling well down,
when a window seemed suddenly opened in the horizon's
wall—you know that look the black sky has—a lid seems
to rise and quiver for an instant, disclosing a whole region
of shuddering fire—then shuts, and the thick, sonorous roll
of the thunder hurries along. The close-reefed main topsail
gleams white against the sky with intensity for a minute;
then a pause and more wind, and the heavy clatter of rain.
The lightning showed the yellow jaws of Pappleton looking
ghastly indeed, I can assure you, that evening. I had the

first watch, and Pappleton stuck pretty close to me. 'Bac
night, Mr. Forbessy! I hope Mr. Bluffett is alive to the
importance of looking out.' At eleven, being near his ladder, I heard a faint sound, which proved to be the cabin
bell. Mrs. Pappleton was in want of mulled wine! Men
were moving to and fro, and to old Bluffett's inquiry what
was the matter, I heard this answer given. For two hours
that veteran had not opened his mouth; he ejaculated
d—n!

"Next day passed, and the third day of the gale arrived,
when the question was, 'where were we?' 'Mr. Bluffett;
where's Mr. Bluffett?' was perpetually in the mouth of
Pappleton. A wag among the crew picked up the expression, and as I was passing forward—and as a huge roll of
the ship capsized half-a-dozen basins, out of which the men
were taking their pea-soup—I heard one of them cry, ' O
Lord! where's Mr. Bluffett?' and the laugh that followed.
Pappleton, meanwhile, kept descending to the cabin tc
pacify Mrs. P., and coming on deck to see the master
Then he would look up to the masts, as if he understood al!
about it, (which he didn't,) and then go and fiddle about
the binnacle—having a notion that there was something
wrong with the compasses.

"At noon it was whispered about—and reached the ears
of Mules, who brought it to our dog-hole of a berth (you
should have seen the berth by this time)—that there was a
difference of opinion between the master and Pappleton.
The master said we were off Los Murnos, and Pappleton
declared we were fifty miles south of the Reschio Palado.
The boatswain, Crabb, communicated his opinion to me,
gratuitously, that they 'was neither of them right, or he'd
be d—d,' and indulged in the gloomiest prophecies. When
I went up to keep the 4 to 6, I found old Bluffett and Pap
pleton's controversy coming to a crisis.

" 'Mr. Bluffett, I'll wear and keep her W.S.W; there's an error in the compass of——'

" 'It's my opinion, Capt. Pappleton, that you are mistaken. I beg distinctly to recommend——'

" 'Wear ship, Mr. Forbessy,' said Pappleton.

" 'Then, Captain Pappleton, I must beg to give up charge,' says the master.

" 'Eh ? Here. Stop, Mr. Forbessy,' and again he was undecided. (You know we had a talent for losing our way in the 'Bloater.' I have known her dodge round and round Malta, without finding it, before now.) He then consulted Hackles, the First Lieutenant, and it seems that *he* agreed with him, for when I was swallowing some tea about seven, I heard, ' Wear ship !' The last thing I heard before turning in, was that the wind had abated, and sea too, and that we were running before it.

It was about eleven at night when I awoke with a start, and fancied somebody was tugging at my hammock. By Jove ! we had STRUCK. A man who has felt that sensation, that peculiar electric vibration which a ship gives at that moment, will not readily forget it. *'Hands save ship !'* a voice bawled out close to my ear ; one spring into my trousers and jacket, and I was up. The watch below were crowding to the forecastle ladder, and in that press, ' O Lord ! where's Mr. Bluffett ?' was again heard from a wag. The ship had heeled over, and there she lay, head on to a black-looking coast, and thump, thumping as the sea rolled in.

Hackles was giving orders when I got to the quarter-deck ; but Pappleton was in an abject condition—as well the poor fellow might be, with Mrs. Pappleton to look after. She, however, proved the trump of the occasion, for she girded herself up to meet it ; and while P. was yel-low, and in that confounded state of indecision, which is his habitual plight, she backed up Hackles with might and main, and urged him on. But the 'Bloater' will never swim again !"

Forbessy paused for breath, and just as he did so, the head of a quartermaster showed itself inside the gun-room door. "Mr. Forbessy, sir, the Commander wants you." Up jumped Forbessy, and when he reached that officer, found that he was required to attend *instanter* at the Admiral's, to be ready to answer any questions about the "Bloater" which might be put to him.

"This is a very serious business, sir," says the Commander, shaking his head.

Indeed, it was so. The service had lost a corvette, and--and—the devil of it was that a relation of the Admiral's commanded her ! I tremble for Bluffett, the master, though !

CHAPTER IV.

FORBESSY paces along the street, *en route* to the Admiral's. You have had a glimpse of him before, I think ? He is tall, has a lounging walk rather, and a somewhat careless, if not absent, manner in ordinary ; but gather up those cords of manhood when OCCASION comes, and you have a sinewy force of a man ! A certain easy refinement hangs loose about him, and is not less effective for being unconscious. He has the Northern head, and Northern eyes of gray blue—such as you may see (planted on a body well able to take care of the same) any day that you choose to ramble among the hills and dales of the Nith, or in the valleys of Cumberland. He has, likewise, an under-lying seriousness, (not of the tract species, but human and

natural,) becoming a man who wishes to do something in
the world, and in an age which seems inclined to break
loose from all hereditary and traditional ideas—to preserve,
at all events, a vigorous personality. ·

Forbessy gained the house. The brilliant Roribel received him, and showed him into a waiting-room—justly so
called, as he presently found. Nobody, of course, had any
attentions to show to our friend, who was scarcely known
in the squadron or the island—a mere midshipman of the
"Bloater," in fact! The door opened, and a servant
looked in, and went out again; came in once more and
locked up something—the Marsala perhaps! Half-an-hour
afterwards, a cat began to scratch at the outside of the
door, which was, at least, an incident. A quarter of an
hour passed, and a light laugh was heard on the stair, of
which his imagination might make the most. Then Miss
Wyoming and a sister came in with a mighty jingling of
keys, and taking no more notice of our friend than if he
had been an arm-chair, retreated again with the aforesaid
Marsala—a fact which, combined with the distant odor of
roast mutton, seemed to show that it was now dinner time.
At last, Roribel bounced in suddenly, "This way, Mr.,"
(he had forgotten the name already,) and Forbessy was
shown in to the Admiral, who was poring with aged eyes
over papers.

"Thit down, thir."

Forbessy sat down, while the old man stared at the paper, and in a few moments, "Tho, it theems, the 'Bloater'
ith lost? Sthand up, thir!"

Forbessy stood up.

"How did you leave them?"—Forbessy replied.

"Who wath in charge of the watch when she struck?
You, thir?"

"No, Sir B——" and he told him. It was one of "the

Family," unfortunately. I wonder if the Admiral wished
it had been Forbessy ?

"Hem." The Admiral fumbled a little with the papers,
turned his faint and dim eyes up and rubbed them, asked
another question or two, and dismissed Mr. Forbessy, who
was to be borne on the books of the "Sovereign," till Captain Pappleton and his gallant crew arrived in Malta for
trial. Thus was Forbessy brought within Fitz-Gubin's
sphere of action, but for which circumstance the public
might never have heard of the career of that great aristocrat.

* * * * * *

Fitz-Gubin was now recovered from the effects of his
accident, and showed himself (one often wondered why he
made no charge for the exhibition) on deck, and on shore,
in his usual health. His head-quarters on shore continued
to be the Mitre, and there, if he was not inclined to go off
to dinner, he dined. He had a running account at the
Mitre. He had a running account with Squirrel for horses.
He played a good deal at billiards. He also played a good
deal at the Café Verdanti :—not at your absurd and stupid
dominoes, but, up stairs, in *the* room—in the private room,
in fact, where only a select party assembled, and where
there was some excitement to be had. Roribel and others
met others, and it was four in the morning before they
supped and broke up, so that Fitz-Gubin sometimes reached
the "Sovereign," just as the hands were turned up, to exercise loosing sails. On these occasions, he popped on blanket
trousers, a jacket, and cap, and attended to his duty ;—
sleeping all day afterwards as you may easily believe. The
advantage of sleeping all day obviously is, that you are
lively at night time ; and thus, when the excellent *cuisine*
of the gun-room had set him up, he was just in the humor
to go on shore again. There was a good deal of luxury

and idleness going on about this time; and several times had the Admiral launched "general orders" on the subject. These compositions are the "Bulls" of the navy. They were favorite compositions with the Admiral, who, in the consciousness of great literary talent, (and upon my word any literary man might envy an author who had the power to *make* people read him!) always proluded at great length, and with a magnificence of language worthy of a better cause. To be sure his eloquence was a trifle wasted on some fellows, but what can you expect? Here, the mess are lounging about the gun-room in the forenoon. Looking through the stern port, Clare observes answering pendants flying up, and knows the "Sovereign" is signalling. Presently boats shoot out from under the great sides of the line-of-battle ships, and midshipmen come on board to copy a

General Order.

"The maintenance of that unsullied excellence of discipline, which, whatever form it may assume, is the chief characteristic of advanced perfection in a squadron of His Majesty's ships, is not compatible with a high scale of personal extravagance on the part of junior officers.

"The Commander-in-Chief, Sir B. B., K. C. T., G. G. H., has observed with regret, that this salutary knowledge—if that can be called knowledge, which is obviously imperfectly apprehended by those whom it most beheoves to *know* it—is not diffused in the squadron under his command, or if diffused, has not penetrated to the consciousness of officers, or if it has penetrated to the consciousness, has not yet availed to govern the conduct of officers; he therefore is compelled again to address some observations on this important subject to the officers under his command.

"The Commander-in-Chief, Sir B. B., K. C. T., G. G. H., therefore proceeds to propound——"

But, bless you, our venerable friend could go on in this style to any extent, as might be proved, did we choose to avail ourselves of a collection of his documents—very kindly placed at our disposal by a butterman. Suffice it, that the old gentleman made various efforts to control the exuberance of the youth under his command—with what success people acquainted with the subject know.

One of these great lucubrations reached the "Sovereign" one day about noon from the Admiral's office, and with it a private note from Roribel to Fitz-Gubin, of very elegant appearance, and perfumed, so that it justly excited the scorn of Bung, whom Cuckles sent below with it, and from whom Fitz-Gubin received it. His formal "Thank you, Mr. Bung," made Bung secretly writhe; but we must not be detained by Bung, who, indeed, has returned to the main-deck, to see the spirits served out, as becomes his rank.

"DEAR FITZ-GUBIN—It is complained that you never call here, and you know what Chesterfield says*—'Women make no allowance for business or laziness.' I think this fine day ought to tempt you; we can have a ride, afterwards, somewhere; and unless you are in a hurry 'off' at night, we can give Pump his revenge. Bolus is boring the dock-yard people, so don't be afraid of him.—Ever,

"R. R."

Fitz-Gubin seemed to approve of the suggestion, for he was seen, half-an-hour afterwards, strolling along the Strada Reale.

Fitz-Gubin was one of those fellows who are never, what you might really and truly call, *intimate* with anybody—not even with a mistress. Any decent intimacy of heart and

---

* Fitz-Gubin did not know that Chesterfield had made that remark · but Roribel knew it would please him to be *thought* to know it.—ED.

cordiality was unknown to his nature; but for all that he could be friendly and easy enough. To please himself, he could be handsomely liberal at times; and if he sometimes took even elaborate pains to win a pretty girl, whom, after all, he had nothing worthy the name of a passion for, he could be generous and lavish of everything but heart! He was cold; but then there are different sorts of coldness. The coldness of marble one can admire; but there is a coldness which affects others with dulness, while the being itself has a liveliness and warmth for its own purposes. The eel is cold; but how active its vital principle—how it can enjoy its mud.

I know not why I broke into this paragraph so suddenly; but it may be useful; let it stand. Yet, do not fancy that I would have you picture young Fitz-Gubin as one of your absurd, unnatural abstractions of calculating coldness, only; his look might, perhaps, make you think better of him than my words have. Here he is—there is a fresh, soft look about him, and his big blue eyes seem harmless, as he knocks at the Admiral's door.

Miss Wyoming was glad to see him looking well, still, and so was Adeline Wyoming, who had a most innocent admiration of aristocracy, and thought that every "lord" was necessarily the direct descendant of William the Conqueror. And so both chatted away, of course not forgetting the poor old "Bloater."

"So provoking," said Miss Wyoming.

"I always thought Mrs. Pappleton could have saved the ship if needful," said Adeline, with facetiousness. "But she must have been sleeping on the watch, as, I hear, all you sailors do."

"That depends on whether we have anybody to think of," said the polite Roribel, who, by-the-by, thought of very few people indeed. They said that he was attached to

Miss Wyoming, and then that it was to Adeline, and then that it was to Lilias, but nobody knew ; and Roribel loved himself better than all three put together.

"I wish people would not lose ships," said Miss Wyoming; "it puts uncle out so much. I am sure these horrid Courts-Martial might be done without, if people would take care. Everything would go on happily,—and poor Captain Pappleton is invaluable at a pic-nic."

"He is the best mixer of salads I know," said Roribel, deliberately.

"He is a kind of relation of ours," Adeline remarks. (He was indeed.) "A most good-natured man, Lord Fitz-Gubin. I'm afraid he'll be reprimanded. So unpleasant."

"If it doesn't all turn out to be the master's fault," said Roribel, good-naturedly, and withdrew on business. So the conversation ran on, on other topics, among the three.

"I hope your sister is very well?" Fitz-Gubin, recollecting that there was one absent, suddenly said.

Miss Wyoming looked a little serious. "Lilias is employed on a little task of *duty* to-day. By-the-by, Adeline dear, perhaps she is tired, and would like some lunch."

"You know we endeavor to aid, as far as we can, our friend, Mr. Fatton, in his endeavors to enlighten the poor people here. We ought not to spare any trouble in such a task, and I am sure this poor beautiful child—"

The door opened, and Lilias Wyoming came briskly in, all unconscious of a visitor, accompanied by MARIE!

The color came very suddenly to our friend Fitz-Gubin's face this time, you may be sure. "Bless me, Lil—," Miss Wyoming was going to have exclaimed, but she checked herself, and, rising up, with the best air of ladylike superiority and Christian patronage, she said to Marie, in Italian, "I hope you are well, child, and have attended to Lilias. This is our little *protégée*, Lord Fitz-Gubin !"

Marie's large and solemn dark eyes lighted full upon him, and Fitz-Gubin bowed. He wondered whether she remembered him. He was silent, and Marie, with an inclination of her head, looked very simply up, and said, "I have seen you, *Signor*, before. Are you well now?"

"What?" says Miss Wyoming, looking no little surprised.

"Oh, I can explain that," Fitz-Gubin said. "I thought I remembered the face! The day of my accident, you know, Miss Wyoming, I was ill, and, passing near your friend's house—at least, I suppose it is her house—I asked for water, and—and—*she* brought it!"

Marie stood and looked at him, and said nothing—keeping her quiet magnetic eyes on his face.

"Ah," said Miss Wyoming, slowly; and in a moment young Marie was spirited away by the other sisters. Upon which Fitz-Gubin began to talk, with great vivacity, on the subject interrupted by her arrival, to convince Miss Wyoming he was no way startled by the incident; and having prolonged his visit to the furthest verge of politeness, he took his leave.

"What a pretty girl she is, to be sure!" he soliloquized as he strolled along. "I only saw her by moonlight, but she's quite as lovely by daylight too. And what an innocent goose to say she had seen me before there! But it was knowing of her, to say nothing when I gave *my* version of the business, too. She's a little knowing devil, I believe, after all. 'Gad, that is it! I never took such a fancy to a girl."

After this fashion mused Fitz-Gubin, till he almost tumbled against Riddel, who was sauntering along the street.

"Why, you're in a brown study," said Riddel. (He might have said, more accurately, a *black* one!)

5

"So I was, indeed." They joined arms, and walked on together.

"That's a pretty ring of yours, Riddel; where did you buy it?"

"Oh! in Malta here—at Greenstone's."

"I wish you would introduce me."

"With the greatest pleasure, let us go at once!"

Mr. Greenstone had, not very long before, opened a jewelry establishment, and he had a highly promising business. He was the most enterprising of tradesmen; he added a charm to his gems by the way in which he handled them to show them, and would have laughed at the notion of ready money. Mr. Greenstone was much encouraged in Malta!

When Mr. Greenstone found that Lord Fitz-Gubin, of the "Sovereign," was the gentleman who proposed to glance over his collection, he glided about like a gnome in a mine. Gold, and silver, and jewels, and that fine filagree, which is as delicate as hoar-frost, fell under happy lights, and glittered like live things. Fitz-Gubin and Riddel peered, and admired, and compared. Riddel's taste was gross rather; he loved much gold work, and bore sometimes in front of him an elaborate barbarism representing a battle-axe grasped by a mailed hand.

Fitz-Gubin selected for himself a ring, and then seemed doubtful what to do. He fidgetted and paused: but presently Riddel happened to go to the door.

"Mr. Greenstone," said Fitz-Gubin, "send that bracelet to me at the Mitre Hotel, early to-morrow." He moved to the door. "Ready, Riddel." "All right." "Come along then." And away they went; Riddel remaining ignorant of the purchase which his friend had just made, and to make which was the object of that gentleman's visit. This was just his mysterious way. In South America, men who thought him an ordinary *roué*, were surprised to find out every now and then, that he had been carrying on an under-current of plot : he got wounded ; or a consul came on board storming with a complaint ; or an anonymous letter threw his captain into fits ; or he lost five times what he could afford at play, and the "family," as usual, had to do something. Yet happen what might, he was ever, out-wardly, the same indifferent, every-day, mawkish Fitz-Gubin, and carried into the scenery of romance the person of an every-day worldling. He sought beauty as pertinaciously as a caterpillar does flowers, and with scarcely a finer feel-ing than its dull greed. But enough of description for the present.

Fitz-Gubin, then, and Riddel having dined, proceeded to the opera and stationed themselves in the pit. Up rose the curtain on the eternal old mediæval castle of the establish-ment, and enter the Baron in the same court-dress obviously worn by his ancestor in the thirty years' war ! The second act was wearing away, when Fitz-Gubin gave a start, and muttered something. Riddel turned to see what was the matter.

" Why, Riddel, do you see that d——d huntsman in the green coat !"

" I do."

"That's the scoundrel that I told you of, who was so insolent that night."

" Is it ?" says Riddel, with animation. " Bravo. Now I'll tell you what I'll do. I'll go out and raise the fel-lows in the cafés, and by the toe of St. Peter, we'll duck him ! We'll pin him at the stage door, and bring him off !"

" Hush, man !—no, no ! Everything will come out. Sit down, Riddel, do !"

With an ill grace Riddel (who had a superfluous amount of champagne in his veins) composed himself. The truth

was, that Fitz-Gubin instantly divined that Marie might be
in the house. He turned cautiously round, and everywhere
sought the dark eyes—the eyes compared with which, Fitz-
Gubin, thy soul was dull ! From box to box—from row to
row, his vague, eager look went. Yet he missed one face he
knew. Miss Wyoming was there, and saw him ; and she
watched him, too, and had thought of the scene with Marie,
and of the possible interpretations of it, oftener than he
imagined. As soon as she saw his inquiring look, she took
care to avoid it, and keep back, but not without a watch
upon him.

Fitz-Gubin again turned to the play, but disappointed.
The music rolled over him like mere meaningless noise. He
looked with a calm, dull hate and scorn at the Maltese who
had brought the wound upon him, and thought that the
beautiful Marie could never surely love *that* poor beast !

Meanwhile, Mr. Riddel, of whom a fixed idea had taken
possession, (and the tenacity of one idea is a common phenomenon among the results of too much wine,) had glided
away from Fitz-Gubin's side. He passed quietly through
the pit, and when he saw a man he knew, he telegraphed
him to come out. Forbessy, who was sitting by himself in
a corner, unobserved, saw individuals here and there whose
faces he knew as naval men, stealing away to the doors.
But Forbessy was entranced by an object which he had
just seen a quarter of an hour before, and that object was
one that long afterwards recurred to his vision among the
soul-and-body-oppressing heats of African Bights, and elsewhere. The dull vision of Fitz-Gubin had passed over
Marie, after all. Forbessy was near her, and if ever accident but let a glimpse of her face be seen, his eyes lighted
upon it, and watched it with the most perfect admiration
which a face had ever excited in him. Vague sadness and
still worship took possession of him, and he lingered,

resolved to know who could be so beautiful in that dull place, where his heart had no home.

The opera was over, and there was a great rush and crowd in the narrow street, where *calèches* were crowding to the doors, and people swarming out. Mr. Riddel had been seen during the past half hour at Mula's, at Micallef's, at Ricardo's; and a whisper had gone abroad that a "lark" was in preparation. A party had gathered under his auspices, and was gathered together near the scene of action.

"Miss Wyoming's carriage!" bawls out a servant, and off rumbles the *calèche* of the Admiral.—"Sir John Sumper's carriage!" "This way, Sir John." "Good night! Home!" Next carriage—doors slammed. "Out of the way, *Smytch*, d—n you!" "Beg pardon, *sar!*" "Drive on!" Such was the Babel of sounds with which the little opera emptied itself; and, amidst the confusion, Riddel and his party had assembled rather lower down the street.

Out of the press, in deepest mantilla, shrouded, passed a figure which Forbessy had already learned to know; and Marie, with quick, small steps, moved away along the street. "Shall I follow her?" he thought. "I have no right to follow her! No! I won't destroy the picture she has left in my imagination, by knowing anything of her but that she is perfectly fair."

But before she was out of sight, she paused and stood still.

"Somebody is to take her home," Forbessy thought. "Poor child!—Her father, I hope. I would not like to know that she had a lover. I will pass by her, and see her face once more!"

The crowd was now thin, and the street becoming deserted. Riddel's eye was on all doors. Out came a Maltese from one.

"Hah !" says Riddel, "I know his face !—Good *Signor Smytch,* a word with you," says Riddel to the young Maltese.

"With me !   What you want with me ?"

"Why," says Riddel, mimicking him with the most intense contempt, "I want duck you for d—d impudence to English officer some weeks ago ! You and your friend hurt English officer ; we go duck you !"

With a waive of the hand, out came a knife. Riddel rushed at him, and seized his arm with a gripe of iron ; with his other hand he seized him by the throat, and squeezed him ; the Maltese's struggles were awful ! Down came the knife on the pavement with a ring. "Bravo !" was the cry. Riddel kicked away the knife with his foot, and a moment afterwards, down they both went, Riddel uppermost. "Police !" was called out ; windows flew open ; rattles were sprung.

"Now I've got him !" Riddel muttered. "Give us the lashing."

In a few instants of fiery excitement they bound and gagged the unfortunate fellow. He was hoisted aloft by the determined band, who carried him bodily, along unfrequented streets, to the harbor, and to a boat.

It is not, I trust, without a due feeling of indignation that I record the fact, that the breaking light of the next morning found that Maltese exposed on the *fair-way buoy !*

Chapter V.

Cuckles, the artful and worldly, came on deck next morning early, and set the crew to work at the holystoning and other processes in good time. For that useful mate had not been on shore, or dissipating the previous evening. He had taken a weak glass of Marsala and water, with his cigar, on the main deck (edging in his chair, unobtrusively and modestly, near the lieutenant's smoking party, so that he was asked to join them, and did his best to be agreeable)—after which he got his desk out and pottered over his accounts till half-past ten, when he went to bed, cool, calm, and with a conscience at rest. *He* was not a rake, nor a spendthrift, nor any such bad man; but was only a hypocrite, and toady, and worldling, and schemer, and very much respected !

Cuckles walks about the deck, while the sleepy fellows huddle up the hatchways with their hammocks. The gray morning fills the harbor with its gradual light, and the houses of Valetta loom through it, looking gray too.

The quartermaster—steady Marshall—turns his glass on objects far and wide, and has never his eyes away for many minutes from the flag-staff of the palace. An object attracts that glass towards the harbor's mouth—and again—and once again.

Marshall glided down the starboard poop-ladder as quickly and quietly as the fairy in a burlesque—what man moves like a sailor? He reached Mr. Cuckles' side. " Mr. Cuckles, sir. Fair-way buoy, sir ! Man on it, I think !"

Cuckles took the glass from him, without speaking; looked, and said, "Yes, there is. Call away the first cutter ; and Marshall go for Mr. Leslie Clare."

Away went the quartermaster. The youngsters who were puddling about the deck, barefooted, (at the express command of Commander Mutter, a sworn foe to goloshes— on youngsters,) brightened up at the excitement of the news. In five minutes the blanket trowsers of Leslie Clare, Esq., appeared on deck, that young gentleman looking very sleepy and glossy, having been just disturbed in a dream, in which partridge shooting and lunch were the principal features. Clare and Cuckles never wasted words on each other ; and Clare simply marched into his boat to obey orders. "Take that man off the buoy, and land him," said Cuckles ; and Clare shoved off to do it.

"Give way," said Clare, and off started the boat.

Here was a spectacle ! The cutter's crew were tittering, fore and aft, as they drew near the buoy. It bobbed up and down in the water, and astride on it, with a leg on each side of the huge ring—and lashed to that ring—was the unfortunate Maltese. The paleness of the night's rage and watching was visible through the brown tints of his face ; his black eyes were glittering with fire. The cutter circled round, and presently sided on to the buoy.

"Why, how the devil did you get here ?" said Clare, who had been on board all the evening, and knew nothing of its events. The Maltese made no answer ; fumbled in his side a minute.

"Take care, sir," said the coxswain ; "he's feeling for a knife !"

Clare's hand fell on his sword hilt—"Is he ?" said he— but he took it away again, as the Maltese raised *his* empty, for we know how he had lost his knife.

"Come, jump in," said Clare, who was a good-natured fellow, and pitied the unfortunate man's plight. Not one word came from the Maltese. The men cast him loose, he came into the boat, and still he never spoke. The boat steered

to the usual landing-place, and there Clare landed him ;
keeping dead silence, and preserving the same, as, without
bow or ceremony of any sort, he sprang upon his native
rock and strode away.

"There's murder in that chap's eyes, sir, or I'm a liar,"
said the coxswain, from his perch behind, taking off his hat,
and getting a "chew" out of it.

"I dare say," said Clare, and the boat shot along
towards the "Sovereign."

"Landed the man," said Clare to Cuckles, briefly, when
he got on deck.

"Very well," replied Cuckles.   On which Clare returned
to the cockpit to finish his sleep, and Cuckles proceeded
with the morning's work, the monotony of which he relieved
by sending a youngster to the mizen-top, barefooted, (to
make him hardy,) and by caning a second-class boy.
Easy, gentlemanly employments, congenial to Cuckles'
mind, and the practice of which had gained him some
repute as a "disciplinarian."   For there are grades in
disciplinarianism, as in everything else ; and links to be
traced—as, from a Bacon to a baboon, so from a Sir
Charles Napier to a Cuckles, or a beadle.

It was observed in the cockpit of the "Sovereign," at
dressing time that morning, that there was an unusual demand for soda water ; and Bung complained of the peril in
which he was placed by the flying corks.   Stories were
afloat about the adventures of the previous evening—about
serenades astern of various ships in harbor, and suppers at
Joe's ; and several gentlemen were observed to be sunk in
languor at breakfast time, and there was a frequent request
for something devilled at that meal.   On such mornings
there is a coolness about a yellow melon which cannot be
too highly praised, and more than one fellow was up to his
ears in a huge slice of that fruit, which was going to "great

5*

lengths," you will admit ! Presently Cuckles descends to
his morning meal.

"Rasper," says Cuckles, "my omelette—sharp." And
down he sits.

"Omelette ?" says Fitz-Gubin, speaking for the first time
that morning ; "I'd like an omelette !"

"I fear," says the faithful Rasper, "there wasn't only·
heggs enough for the one you ordered, Mr. Cuckles, sir."

Cuckles had ordered that omelette over night ; the thought
of it had cheered his morning watch : he felt a tremor run
through·him ; could he—should he offer it to Fitz-Gubin?
Fitz-Gubin maintained a dead silence, as much as to imply,
"Here am I, wanting an omelette; let an omelette be
brought. What the deuce is to become of English Institutions, if I can't get an omelette?"

"Oh," says Cuckles, with a grin—which looked damnably
uneasy to a knowing eye—"have mine, Lord Fitz-Gubin, I·
don't care about it !"

"Eh ? You're very good, really," Fitz-Gubin replies, in
a cold-blooded, matter-of-fact manner. "As you don't
care about it, why—"

"You don't mind garlic, of course," said Cuckles.

"Oh, d—n it ; I hate garlic, like poison. Never mind,
thank you, Cuckles."

Rasper showed signs of being about to interpose a remark,
but Cuckles' eye checked him. He brought the dish, and
Cuckles devoured it—though, between ourselves, it was as
perfectly free from garlic as the veins of Fitz-Gubin from
the blood of the gentleman of Picardy. By such little
strokes of ready cunning as this, Cuckles somewhat justified
a belief which he entertained of his diplomatic talents. He
deserved to enjoy the dish, and apparently he did so, for no
word did he utter until his plate was clear. Then, he open·

ed the subject of tha Maltese who had been found on the
fair-way buoy.

"Fair-way buoy," said Fitz-Gubin, spreading marmalade
slowly. "Was there a cad on the fair-way buoy ?"

"Yes," Cuckles answered, looking over at him to see if
he was only pretending ignorance, and ready to give a pleasant leer should such prove to be the case. But Fitz-Gubin
was quite serious.

"Rather a cool berth for a cad," said Fitz-Gubin. "Did
he appear to enjoy it ?"

"I can tell you about that," said Leslie Clare, from the
lockers. "He looked, when I cast him off and landed him,
as if he'd like to cut my throat. He's a black fellow with
a mark over his eyebrow ; it's my opinion he'll lie in wait
some night for some of us, and will cut our throats."

Fitz-Gubin looked grave. "Why, Riddel, is it our
friend of the opera ?"

"I'm afraid it is," answered Riddel. "Serve him right,
too."

"But," said Fitz-Gubin, "did you not feel you might
compromise *me*?"

Fitz-Gubin rose in a dignified manner after he had uttered
this characteristic speech, and left the gun-room. Riddel
had a head-ache, and lay down on the lockers without making any remark ; Cuckles assumed a serious air ; Siddlington
whispered to Beaulieu that "he thought Lord Fitz-Gubin
took too serious a view of the matter"—like the polite
fellow that he was ; old Manton, who had just taken down
a battered old cocked-hat box (in which he kept his cigars)
from the place where it lodged, immediately began—

"Well, I'm d—d ; I don't think discipline can last in this
squadron. I don't see how ! When I entered the service,
a youngster would have been flogged for half the tricks

there has been played in this harbor within the last three
weeks." And so he ran on for a few minutes, *more suo*, to
the general amusement, till he had run himself out. I have
known stagers of the old school, who were both wise men
and good examples, and proper givers of advice ; but there
are others who differ from the moderns just as an old Dutch
clock does from a new watch—make more noise in telling
you the time of day, but keep it no better than the last
dandy invention.

At noon, or not long after, down came a midshipman
from Commander-Mutter, with a bit of news and a message.
" Commander wants the names of all the fellows who were
on shore last night, and the time they came on board !"
What a sensation !

" When, the deuce, did he give the order ?" said Beaulieu.

" This minute. The information's required from every
ship in the harbor," said the midshipman.

" That means mischief," remarked Riddel. " I see Sir
B—'s hand in that suggestion. Well, put down Riddel,
Esq., Two A. M."

" It was nearer Three, I fear," said Beaulieu.

" Was it ? Why, what time was it when we had the
brandy after floating the *smytch* ?"

" Why, not much after One ! But you forget we had a
game of billiards after that. And then, you know, we
knocked up Joe Sprogaleff, and his wife put her head out
of the window ; and we went to Boyetrel's, and they
wouldn't let us in, and you kicked the door in, and refused
to leave the house till they brought some supper—"

Riddel groaned.

"—And the waiter came in with a ham and some bread
and butter, and you would have a bottle of champagne and
a lobster, and Boyetrel was going to send for the police,

and you made him sit down, and we wouldn't leave till they brought some more brandy. Then you wanted a cigar, and, don't you remember, we met Wallop, of the Jupiter, and he was drunk, and wanted to fight the marker at Mula's ; and you went into a police-office to get a light, and insisted on being locked up, till we dragged you away ;—"

.Riddel gave another piteous groan.

"Whereupon, Wallop began a song about a cavalier, and we all came down to the harbor, *without* serenading Ricks, as you finally proposed."

"Riddel, Esq., Four A. M., I fear must be the entry," said Riddel.

The midshipman wrote it down, and added the names of Beaulieu, Corbieton, and others. "Anybody else ?"

"Yes," said Forbessy, "I must be put down."

"Why, Forbessy, this is the first time I've heard your voice this morning."

"So it is," said Forbessy ; "I am dull, I suppose."

"Anybody else ?" was once more asked, after the entry of Forbessy's name and hour. At that moment Fitz-Gubin entered, and was informed of the inquiry in progress. He seemed rather annoyed ; and the mess were surprised as he dictated—"*Lord Fitz-Gubin, Five A. M.*"

Why did Forbessy feel chilled as he happened to look up at the speaker ? Who knows? Have you ever felt in the presence of a man that he had an element in him which was repugnant to your spiritual nature? He is a dunce, perhaps, but *his* sneer will wound *you*. He has a disagreeable relation to you—you don't know how. Out of some such sentiment came the notion of the evil eye, of the evil genius, of the fascination of witchcraft. You can call it, if you please, a "natural antipathy," but you do not *explain* it. A touch of this ran through Forbessy at that moment, and he thought, as he looked at Fitz-Gubin. Was it your cold, hol-

low voice that startled me only ?   Why do I shrink from
it ?   Or what, in the name of mystery, is the destiny that
binds together you and me ?

Fitz-Gubin's announcement, I say, surprised those who
remembered that he had not joined the party of the previous
night.   They were, indeed, beginning to find out that he
was not a very communicative fellow.   Here, indeed, was
a man who lived with you, was familiar with you, and the
rest of it, and who carried his heart locked up, and the key
in his pocket ; who travelled in your company in life, (as an
iceberg travels in company with a ship,) yet would part with
you for ever to-morrow with a nod and a good bye !   You
wondered what the deuce his notions about existence were,
or his object in life at all.   But, to be sure, what business
on earth many men have might puzzle us ; they dress, and
dine, and die, and never seem to think it odd that they
should exist for these purposes.

The midshipman wrote down the entry, which showed
Fitz-Gubin to have been the latest of all arrivals on the
previous night ; Riddel turned round on the lockers, and
composed himself to sleep ; Forbessy leaned back in his
chair, and mused.

Fitz-Gubin turned languidly over the pages of a novel—
seeming to think it strange that nobody did anything to
amuse him.   Then he strolled out, and proceeded to the
cock-pit to dress himself ; for he ceremoniously went through
the various toilettes of the day, and soon a yellow glare in
the fore-part of that place showed that he was busy.
Commander Mutter observed that Fitz-Gubin did not ask
leave to go on shore, till he had dressed himself for that
purpose ; whereas it would have been a little more modest
to have postponed his adornment, and not to have looked
quite so confident of obtaining permission.   This might
have irritated a less Christian mind than that of Mutter,

but he remembered "what St. Paul had said," (to use a favorite expression of his,) and did not altogether forget the—last edition of the Peerage.

When Fitz-Gubin reached the Mitre Hotel, where, as we know, he had his head-quarters on shore, (and where notes were left for him from Roribel, from his tradesmen, from fellows in the regiments, &c.,) he had a neat little parcel handed to him by the polite and dignified landlord.

The landlord was one who boasted that he had an eye for a gentleman, or indeed "know'd a gentleman when he see'd him," if you prefer his own expression. A gentleman in fact (whose steward he had been) had placed Sproggs in the Mitre—endowing him with a wife, by way of further kindness, and (you don't know how people talk in places like Malta) with a child to begin with! Mrs. Sproggs was a buxom, dressy, lively mortal, who never allowed her husband to show himself too much, justly believing that she was far more likely to be agreeable to strangers than he was. But to-day she was out, and it was Sproggs himself who gave to Fitz-Gubin the parcel, which (we know before he opens it) contained the bracelet from Mr. Greenstone. Sproggs had pried into it, and afterwards told a friend he knew "what Lord Alfred was after," and remarked what a sly gentleman he was.

As he opened it, the light broke from the magic stones; he had none but a sensual feeling for the beautiful, but that he had keenly, and he was pleased with the glitter. How the bracelet would become Marie's arm! If he could only get an opportunity of putting it on? Or—should he send it, and whom could he employ? Who was this knave of the opera? Would it not be as well to buy him out of hand, and not have a ridiculous controversy with him? If that man could have been—I don't say murdered before Fitz-Gubin's eyes in any cruel manner—but sunk into fifty

fathoms water with 68 pounders, quietly and effectually—
he, Fitz-G., not seeing it, and no questions asked, he would
have decidedly liked it—authorized it.   Men's hearts are
as bad as ever they were, as anybody ought to know from
his own ; we are more effeminate than our ancestors, and
bloodshed shocks our nerves more ! but that is all.   What
matters it that your skin is a little thinner ?   Just reflect a
moment, good reader ;—Claudius does not carry off his
tradesman's daughter by force now—but bless you, he tells
her lies, and gives her jewelry, and a brougham, and a
box at the theatre, and gets old Virginius a place in the
Rag-bag office !   Is he any better than the ancient patrician ?   In the same way, we do not fight with each other,
and pay fines for maiming—why ?—because we want to stay
at home, and make money !

    Fitz-G. was still gazing musingly on the bracelet, when
he heard a step on the stairs, and just as he whipped the
ornament into its case, and the case into his pocket, Roribel entered.   The face, the whiskers, the air of that elegant
creature, were as light and as cheerful as ever.

    " Fitz-Gubin, have you forgotten where we dine to-
day ?"

    " Dine ! are we engaged ?"

    " Then you *have* forgotten.   This is Mr. Bulder's dinner-
party, and go you must."   Fitz-Gubin acquiesced ; he had
a very vague recollection of Bulder's invitation, and no particularly vivid one of his person ; nevertheless, he looked
on dinners as scenes that must be gone through, some dull,
some lively, some good, some bad ; and on Bulder's dinner
to-day, as a *routine* dinner to be eaten.   And he instantly
rang his bell, and when he emerged from his bed-room, he
looked, I am bound to say, a worthy companion for Roribel
They were a pair of deities in the eyes of certain circles in

Malta ; the Castor and Pollux of the Service, twin children of the Latona of aristocracy !

Shall I give you, good reader, a letter of introduction to my friend, Mr. Bulder, of Strada Polentoni ?   I shall be very happy.

"My Dear Sir—You will oblige me by showing any attention in your power to young Mr. Brown of the 'Auricula.' He is the son of the late Captain Brown, who distinguished himself so much in the last war, (his invention, you will remember, was twenty years under the consideration of the Admiralty,) and I am interested in his success, for he is a youth of parts, and I fear my poor friend Brown did not leave his family too well provided for.

"I am, my dear Sir, &c. &c."

Perhaps this is not the kind of introduction which would do much for you ?   Indeed, I fear my friend Bulder would ask you to meet young Galipotti, the docter's son ; give you a dinner ingeniously compounded of the *reliquiæ* of his last dinner-party, and go to sleep after it, leaving you to employ yourself on some watery claret.   Let us try another.

"My Dear Sir—This will be presented to you by a young friend of mine, Mawker Pemmison, just appointed to the 'Vestal.' You are familiar with the name of his father, Mawker Pemmison, M. P., the well-known member for the wealthy town of Strikeham, of whom every man of business has heard.   I dined with him yesterday, and Lady Alicia expressed her hope that Mawker would meet with friends in the country to which he is going.

"My dear Sir, yours, &c., &c."

Suffice it to say, that this was a "Pemmison" day, and, as a man of the world, (which, of course, it is your ambi

tion, as a young man, to be,) you will agree it was the
best day Fitz-Gubin could have had for dining with Bulder.

They have, I believe, in Malta, a hundred copies of
Debrett. (Mr. Muir of Strada Reale may correct me if I
am wrong.) The Bulders had looked out Fitz-Gubin, of
course, in their copy, and gloated over the account of the
grandeur of houses in Picardy. Bulder respected aristocracy as most people do, that is, he did not so much respect
the thing itself, as respect the respect for the thing! Do
you understand? And the Bulders enjoyed, by being abroad,
the advantage of entertaining far greater people than they
could have hoped to entertain in England. When Lord
Troubadour's yacht arrives at Bombakea, Lord Troubadour must dine with the consul, or mope on board, and
know nothing about the place. When the Countess of
Ostrich's yacht is in want of repairs, and is laid up in Malta
for the purpose, she must have a corvette to go to Naples
in, and she and her party must dine with Prodger. These
are great considerations, and worthy of all acceptance by
the middle classes, who think of settling abroad. They
should make up their minds to enjoy the advantage while
the opportunities last; a day comes when the Wyomings
retire to Harley-street or Tyburnia, and are potentates no
more; a day comes when the ship is paid off—when a
Cuckles departs to lodgings near Charing-cross, and a Fitz-
Gubin to Grosvenor square.

Young Bulder cultivated a moustache and affected military society, but was damped early that day by Fitz-Gubin's
asking him what regiment he belonged to. The cool, stolid
manner of Fitz-Gubin gave no possible hint that he intended
a sarcasm; and of course young Bulder looked all the more
annoyed for the moment. His father enjoyed Fitz-G.'s
mistake, having observed with regret the increasing aliena-
tion from business of his son's tastes. For the youth made

off, every evening, when he could, to the *cafés* and the billiard-rooms, where Ludder of the Marines, Hunibleston of
the —th, and other gentlemen, occupied themselves with
cigars and pool, and (old Bulder's dinners being famous)
were civil to him. There seemed, indeed, every hope that
this youthful Bulder, so far from turning out an awkward,
reserved, prosperous man of business, would become an
elegant and agreeable young fellow, fit for—nothing at all,
and throw a lustre on the family.

Bulder, had he told the truth, would probably have con-
fessed that he found Fitz-Gubin slow. But he could not
have complained of his manners, for Fitz-Gubin (though
his fancy was ever wandering to another part of Valetta)
was ever attentive, self-possessed, and satisfied with everything. When the business of the island was talked of, he
was mild and reasonable, and knowing next to nothing
about it, said that next to nothing cheerfully. Did they
talk of the churches, antiquities, people, he was the same
composed individual. No advantage more prominently dis-
tinguishes our modern man of quality than this. He is,
perhaps, at a public dinner: the occasion important; the
crowd immense; he has to speak and expound his views;
he has no views, and nothing of the least consequence to
say. Does *he* blush and stutter like a *roturier*? Not he!
He rises, and with the best air in the world, says his
nothing, and charms the assembly.

The saloons of Mr. Bulder (for, at a certain stage of
a man's prosperity, his rooms become saloons, by their own
right) were thrown open that evening to a numerous assembly. Our friends, the Misses Wyoming, were there;
Captain and Mrs. and Miss Plimmer; Sir John Sumper
and "party," and Sir John Lumper and his party; the
Kingfishers, the Crawsters, the Popanells, and many others
And the sea-breeze is so famous for its healthiness, that you

may observe it quite revives and brightens up even a reputation sometimes ; so that at the houses of the Bulders and others, notabilities from England, of a certain rank, glide about quite blooming, and free from all traces of naughtiness ! Fitz-Gubin and Roribel knew these cases of moral convalescence perfectly well, and whispered together, as two figures passed in the distance, about whom stories could be told.   It was fine to see these two potentates, on occasions like the present, when they were the " swells" of the navy present, or at all events of the junior navy ; for we must not forget professional rank, which, of course, takes the *pas*, and has been remarked at times to supply the place of manners, wit, birth, and all that classifies mankind !

"Fitz-Gubin, let us come and speak to the Wyomings, and you ask Miss Wyoming to dance," said Roribel.   It was Roribel's duty to see proper attention paid to these ladies, as became a flag-lieutenant ; and an attentive, graceful officer he was, performing all offices of chivalry, duly— not entangling his heart, however, as he told Fitz-Gubin, with a sigh.   " Charming girls," said that mirror of courtesy, with his very best sadness.   " Beautiful creatures ! but I am but a younger son, Fitz-Gubin."   Fitz-G. smiled languidly, and thought it very good-natured of his friend to sigh on the subject, and perhaps a little affected of him to sigh to *him*. . . . . And so they approached the ladies in question.   Some of the prettiest girls in Malta looked with admiration at the two gentlemen, and envied the Wyomings.

" Do you see those two infernal idiots?" said Mr. Jigger, of the brig " Bustard," to Mr. Wheeler, of the brig " Racer."

" I do.   That's the flag-lieutenant, the oldest one," responded Mr. Wheeler, " the other fellow's a Lord Fitz-Gubin, or some such name."

"They'll promote him to lieutenant *instanter*, and send him to the Royal Yacht, you'll see," said Jigger bitterly.

"Oh, of course. This is confoundedly slow," said Mr. Wheeler, looking round savagely. "Hillo! here's Mott-ford of us. Who asked you here, Mottford?"

"Who do you suppose? Bulder, of course. My father banks with his brother; and they always ask me to two balls and a dinner every year."

"Is there any brandy in the refreshment room?" inquired Mr. Jigger, with a business-like air.

"I fear not," Wheeler answered. "Gad, I'd rather have a quiet tumbler at Mula's, than go to any evening party in Christendom."

"Why did you come, then?" said a mild young gentle-man of their acquaintance, who affected "society."

"Because Kiddleton wouldn't have given me leave to come on shore, except to come here; and if I hadn't come, there's Weavel, our purser, in the rooms, and he would have told Kiddleton. Now do you see?" The mild young gentleman was silenced.

"You have heard of the general order, of course," Jigger said. "It was sent out this afternoon, and gives one hun-dred and fifty-five reasons why putting a Maltese on the fair-way buoy is at variance with sound discipline."

"I wish they had kept the fellow on the buoy till eight o'clock, and then we would all have seen him," Wheeler remarked. "Is there going to be an inquiry?"

"Goodness' knows. Probably, as everybody seems to have heard that some flag-ship fellows did it, we of the small craft will have our leave stopped," said the sardonic Jigger.

In the meantime Lord Fitz-Gubin had been dancing with Miss Wyoming.

"Did you like the new *buffo* last night?" she asked

"Yes," answered Fitz-Gubin; "but you were not there, Miss Wyoming."

"I was."

"Strange that I should not have seen your party then," he observed. "I looked to see if there were any faces I know in the house too," said the quiet youth. Miss Wyoming was silent.

When the dance was over, the Miss Wyomings, Roribel, and Fitz-Gubin fell into a group. Roribel began to talk of a pic-nic to Bosketto, which had for some time been meditated in the polite circles of the island. Who does not remember the sloping valley of strawberry gardens, the deserted old house with yet a certain air of old feudal gentility about it—the stalactic cavern, with the fresh fountain bubbling up among its carved and moist stones? That pic-nic was determined on..

As Roribel and Fitz-Gubin were walking together after the party, the subject of the Maltese and the adventure of the previous night came up in their conversation. Fitz-Gubin was regretting that he should have been out so late, and should have figured in the list so very conspicuously. "You in the list!" says Roribel—"you were not in the list!" Fitz-Gubin was astonished, and no little pleased; but puzzled to account for the lucky circumstance. "I shan't complain, however," he said, with a pleased chuckle. They speculated on the subject, and reflecting whose hands the paper had passed through, concluded that the attentive Cuckles had taken care of the omission, as, indeed, Cuckles had; and the chapter may end as it opened—with a mention of his honored name.

Chapter VI.

One fine day of that autumn, some excitement prevailed in the squadron ; it was the day of the pic-nic. They say that the " Sovereign's" launch was once sent on a cruise with wine and other luxuries on board to regale a party at St. Paul's Bay, who had made a pilgrimage to the place where the apostle landed, to drink Moselle, and eat chicken pie. It may be so. It may be that the ships, and ships' boats, and flags, and men, are, every now and then, employed in the service of all kinds of agreeable men and women, and that we are a luxurious, money-spending, debt-contracting generation. " Here's a pretty fellow," exclaims Tomkins, indignantly, " to be sneering at his old profession ! Pray, sir, have you never shown your approval of pic-nics, or the ' Sovereign's' Madeira ?" " Tomkins, I like Madeira, and I have been a jolly fellow in my time, but I don't know that that much affects the question at issue." Let us proceed with our sketches of swell life at sea, and make the most of this fine day.

Squirrell, the livery-stable keeper of Strada Borni, found his stock of animals in much request this morning. It will be admitted that naval men ride much better than Commodore Trunnion, in our day ; that in Malta we can produce a man or two with credit at the races, though much remains to be done yet, as anybody who has seen Jigger galloping past the royal carriage at Naples, with his trousers split across the knee, knows. But the constant employment of the horses of Squirrell, about this time, was improving the practice of youngsters. Squirrell's horses, in fact, exhibit every variety of peculiar disposition. "Joseph " invariably backs against a stone wall ; the " Governor" is famous for his efforts to seize the horseman next him by the leg, and so on. By selecting them by turns, one learns to combat different tricks. By long habit, all these noble animals make a dead stop at the " Dairy," that well-known way-side hostelry, where generation after generation of fellows have paused, and have consumed rum and milk. The policemen about the gates were quite excited this morning, as the conveyances of the party rolled by, and after them, at a canter, with gold-laced caps glittering, the naval men came. Fitz-Gubin and Roribel were the best mounted men there. They were both in plain clothes, and both indignant at Jigger, (who belonged to the party, nobody quite knew how,) who kept shooting ahead at a gallop, and whose trousers, escaping from the thraldom of straps, were constantly approaching his knees. Cuckles was not present, invariably avoiding festivities accompanied by expense, if possible. Commander Mutter was one of the party, being a paternal kind of man, and, from general harmlessness, serving well as a he-duenna. The Commander had had all his pluck taken out of him in the course of a long and severe matrimonial training. He was just the fellow to be paternal among young girls and young fellows on these occasions; exercising a kind of restraint, yet not in the way; overflowing with small talk and heavy goodness; moderate in wine himself, but never forgetting the corkscrew. A most useful man ! Mounted on a mule, Mutter trotted alongside, first one carriage of the cavalcade, and then another; paying attention to the wives and daughters of the influential people. How is it (as I so often remark) that the serious and saintly party are such worshippers of the authorities ? Yet, on these holiday occasions, Mutter would be easy and lively with a youngster now and then, having a certain fund of good-nature in him, which the consciousness of rank did not altogether keep down. Indeed, how many a worthy man is there in this world, who is spoiled by the big-wig or cocked-hat power, and who, divested of these symbols, would be universally respected and popular !

The landscape which lies before you as you ride out from Valetta to the country—if country it can be called—is not cheerful to the eye. A white or brown stony surface, intersected by white or brown walls, bounding scraggy and dreary fields, cannot be very much enlivened even by the brightest sunshine. Your gaze wanders to the low-lying horizon and loves the thought of the sea. Yet there are spots of interest and attraction, both to mind and eye, as you let your fancy and your bridle go pretty loosely, and leave the harbor and the fortifications behind. There are hints and gleams of the beautiful in the stony waste, as in ordinary life. St. Antonio, with its palace and gardens, is a little islet of joy, where the heart warms to the glitter of the sweet and cool orange trees. A little village, quaint but lively, is before you at one turn, with a fantastic chapel, and gaudy and picturesque images basking in corners in the sun ; where the gay-colored attire of the brown-skinned and black-eyed people, is characteristic of their Eastern descent.

Or, you slacken at a rather long though not steep hill, and the boom of the cathedral bell through the quiet air meets you on the way. Yes ; the genius of romance is , alive still in that island. And, are you a sentimentalist, as well as a humorist ? then pass Mr. Balder's dinner parties— leave Roribel in the burning street . . . . turn into the old building dedicated to St. John—cool, venerable, and with the thick incense-smell lingering about it, and loiter a little over the flag-stones bearing the coat-armor of the Knights ! The " enlightened " individual (I allude to —— Bagman, Esq., the distinguished traveller, who judges of every place by its ability to produce cotton) will tell you stories about their misdeeds ; when their day as an Order was over, and

6

their great purpose had spent itself ——— : but they were
pious, brave, high-hearted gentlemen in their time ; and let
us beg the distinguished Bagman to allow their ashes to
rest !

When our party drew near Citta Vecchia, the population
were all astir. Frank came out, cap in hand, from his hostelry, to offer his services ; the beggars (of whom Malta is
productive, and who rush into unbounded luxury if they
secure two-pence) swarmed around ; a knot of poor little
sucking priests, in black knee-breeches, and stockings, pale-
faced and meagre lads, stared from a respectful distance
tranquilly, and perhaps (poor fellows) envied the rosy and
fiery Jigger who galloped Squirrel's horse. " Shampoo" up
and down the place at full speed. It was a fine sunshiny
noon. The party came to a temporary halt ; some of them
went to see the curiosities of the place—the church or the
catecombs ; others lounged about where some trees afforded
a shade.

" Well," said Roribel, to a section of the party, who by
natural gravity had approached each other, " what shall we
do ? There's the catecombs, to be sure, but—"

Miss Wyoming said, " they were places of great interest,
but—"

Captain Plimmer said, " Oh, highly, highly, you know.
But—"

In fact, nobody liked to say what everybody felt, that
the catecombs would be a bore. Roribel thought it due to
his reputation to come brilliantly out of the difficulty.

" Well, we've all seen catecombs, somewhere ; and really,
because previous generations chose to bury themselves in
such a style, I do not see that we should bury ourselves
too ! I confess," continued Roribel, with rather a wicked
smile levelled at Commander Mutter, " I confess that I am
a cheerful Christian."

So that notion was lightly disposed of ; and for the present they moved into a garden, where seats were placed under an awning for them. Meanwhile, the attendants were defiling along towards the Bosketto, with the preparations for lunch ; and in their rear trotted on his pony, jolly little Lieutenant Bulbous, bent on seeing that the wine was properly put in a cool place, and everything in train. His sunny red face shone as he jogged along. He had not come to see anything, or to enjoy anybody's company, but simply to lunch with an appetite, which indeed, is, after all, the vital part of a pic-nic. Roribel directed attention to the retreating figure of Bulbous, and hoped that young Jigger would not get loose among the bottles too early in the day ; and was otherwise very lively.

An hour's pause, and they proceeded on their journey to Bosketto. The old country house above mentioned, with its yellow old walls, looked empty and forlorn as usual. Some faint and seedy vestige of what was once gay painting adorns rooms which were once rooms of banquet ; a few words of Latin straggling across the door by which you enter, invite you to festivity. Do the ghosts accept that old-fashioned invitation in the lonely moonlight nights there, and make merry with each other? One could fancy so. Altogether, it is a dreary, empty, seedy, picturesque old den. It stands there as poverty-stricken in its pride as a poor old Jacobite Scotch peer of the last age. Curiosity made Roribel and some others look in, and they gazed silently about the rooms. Adeline Wyoming, whose pensive love of aristocratic memories we have remarked, bewailed the desolation, and thought Fitz-Gubin must feel .quite a brotherly interest in the place.

" How interesting !" said Adeline.

" Yes !" said Fitz-Gubin, in his happy indifference ; " but very small. In —shire we have ruins enough. There are, really I forget how many, old castles within some miles of us. We do what we can to preserve them—prevent people carrying off the stones, and all that."

"What wickedness," said Adeline, "of them to think of such a thing! But I think the English respect old ruins, and old—old—families."

"They ought," Fitz-Gubin said; "if they don't, why, what guarantee have we for preserving—for anything, in fact?"

"Very true," said Roribel, wishing to persuade Fitz-Gubin he had made an intelligent observation; but flattery was not very potent with that swell! And why? Because he thought so well of himself that *your* opinion could add nothing to it!

"Is there anything more to see?" inquired Miss Wyoming.

"Why, there's the wall outside, but that's *modern;* in fact, a few years' old," said Roribel, pointing to a stone wall in the neighborhood. This flash of pleasantry made everybody titter; and they left the melancholy old house and proceeded to the garden.

"Lord Fitz-Gubin is very silent to-day," whispered Miss Wyoming to Roribel.

"I don't know that he is ever very lively," replied Roribel drily. But looking at him again, he observed that he *was* abstracted more than usual. His arm hung loose, so that Adeline could scarcely hold it properly.

"Can it be," said Roribel to Miss Wyoming, "that he is in love?"

Miss Wyoming looked very grave. Roribel was puzzled. "She cannot," thought he, "possibly imagine that *that* is a marrying man." Miss Wyoming was not such a fool, but, indeed, knew both Fitz-Gubin and Roribel better than they supposed. Roribel was much the more lively and genial of

the two men, bnt in heart, probably, they were on a par—
just as a pound of feathers is as heavy as a pound of lead.
Mrs. Plimmer, who was presiding in the capacity of mater-
nal guardian on this occasion, knew the truth, likewise—an
experienced dame, who had that acquaintance with match-
making which is nowhere attained in such perfection as in
garrison society.

The day of strawberries was over; but the pool of fresh-
est water in the stalactic cavern was as cool as ever, gleaming calm and cool in the centre of the fretted stone-work—
fluted, graven into fantastic forms with fairy icicles of rock,
adorned and pointed—speaking of immeasurable time and
eternal moisture. Here the summer sun never saw his face
reflected; here, like Diana's nymphs bathing, the pleasant
claret bottles kept their fine natures most beautifully cool.
There was not a drop of romantic blood in the old carcase
of Lieutenant Bulbous, yet had he here achieved a spectacle
of poetry!

The lunch proceeded in due time. Pop goes a champagne
bottle; maddened by the confinement in such weather, the
eager wine leaped out to meet the summer and the air, foam-
ed triumphantly into a glass, and died happily, meeting the
lips of pretty Rosa Plimmer! Not a cloud was in the
Mediterranean heaven. The almond tree revelled in the
heat.

"I miss one face," said Roribel, with tenderness. "I miss
Captain Pappleton!—Let us drink his health."

"Poor Captain Pappleton!" said Adeline; "he would
have been happy here!"

"He mixed salad better than any man in Europe!" said
Roribel, with a gush of fondness. "Ladies and Gentlemen!
Captain Pappleton has recently had a—slight accident
Let us wish him an honorable acquittal!"

Roribel drank. The company joined.

"After all," said Roribel, overflowing with brotherly
kindness, "after all, Miss Wyoming, it is my opinion, as a
professional man, that the unhappy loss of the 'Bloater'
will all prove to be the fault of—I don't wish to impeach
anybody—Bluffett, the master!"

In this cheerful manner the lunch opened. Jigger drank
any health, anybody proposed; "health, sir : the devil's
health in this wine!" said Jigger. "Silence, youngster,"
said Bulbous, who overheard him. Fitz-Gubin was at that
moment observed to look round in a bland and brotherly
manner; and presently he said, "Oblige me by preparing ,
your glasses, I am about to give you a toast. Ladies and
Gentlemen ! ("what a great manner," thought Adeline;
"d——d puppy," thought Jigger,) the distinguished officer
whose flag we have the honor to serve under, ("I ought to
have proposed this," thought Captain Plimmer, with some
pique,) deserves the homage of our attention to-day. Himself one of the greatest men whom our naval history has
produced, and represented here to-day (Fitz-Gubin threw
into his voice a touch of gallantry) by the lustre of beauty,
he commands our reverence, and enchants our hearts. I
propose, with all the honors, our Commander-in-Chief !"
(Great enthusiasm.) Of course, the health was most cordially responded to. Mr. Thimbleston, Ensign of the —th,
observing, however, to a neighbor, that "the army ought
to have taken precedence ; by Jove, sir, why the deuce
didn't the army take precedence ?" and so forth.

By degrees, people strolled away from the lunching-
ground, and lounged about in the gardens, and chatted.
Adeline Wyoming went again to look at the old country-
house ; and as she returned, she passed quickly down the
garden walk, and she put her arm through her elder sister's
and drew her away till they were quite by themselves.

"What's the matter, Adeline?" said Miss Wyoming, "you look quite frightened. What is it, dear?"

"I have been in that old house again, and in the room where we were—"

"You saw a ghost, you silly thing!" interrupted Miss Wyoming.

"No," Adeline said, "but I have found this."

And she drew out a small ornament. It was a thin chain of very fine gold, and suspended to it was a locket, on which was engraved the word "Marie." The two girls paused, and kept dead silence a moment. Then Miss Wyoming (who had turned quite pale) said, "Run and put it back, you foolish child, why did you touch it?"

"I was so surprised, I—I—did not know what I was doing." The tears came to the girl's eyes.

"Give it me," her sister said. It needed no long thought to tell her *who* had lost it; and like a glimpse through the dark, she saw now something of Fitz-Gubin's character. The mystery of iniquity which underlies our social life, and which we ignore so determinedly, *does* now and then cast a shadow, where only the sunshine of purity should be. Hints and chills (like those thrills of cold which we feel and cannot account for) tremble through the frame of society in its garb of safety, and refinement, and purity; telling of something unhealthy and unholy in the air.

Miss Wyoming moved quickly up the garden. Adeline remained behind; she had allowed herself to fancy Fitz-Gubin was one who could be loved, goodness knows why; don't we see that a bird will sit on a stone, if it be only decently like an egg? and don't women give their heart-warmth away, in this unprofitable manner, constantly? The eldest, I say, moved quickly up the garden. She would put the locket in the room again, and Fitz-Gubin would be sure to seek it there if he missed it; and then—

why she would try and not think of it any more; or she
would save the poor little girl from—She was full of anxiety and painful feeling when she approached the house, but
her heart grew cold as she saw Fitz-Gubin enter it before
her. He had gone, plainly enough, to look for the lost
locket; she felt frightened to think that he might come out
and meet her.

In the meantime, the party were growing dull, and beginning to think of moving. Roribel was on the move, and
crying "to horse," with his accustomed liveliness. He
walked up the garden-path, and the whole group broke up,
and spread themselves out into knots. Roribel reached the
head of the garden just as Fitz-Gubin came out of the
house with a shade of annoyance on his brow. Miss
Wyoming was turning the other way to rejoin her sisters.

"To horse!" says Roribel. "Why, Fitz-Gubin, what's
the matter?"

"Oh, nothing; I've been in that old house again, that's
all."

"Well, did you meet the ghosts of your ancestors, or
what? By Jove, I know people in very good society, who
would be startled if they could see their ancestors," said
Roribel. They approached each other nearer; Miss Wyoming had meanwhile moved quite away.

"But, hillo!" said Roribel again, stooping suddenly to
the ground, and picking up something, "what's this? a
chain and a locket with 'Marie' on it; treasure-trove, by
Jove!"

Fitz-Gubin started. "Give it to me, Roribel!"

Roribel was in his most champagne mood.

"Marie! eh," cried he, holding it behind him, to prevent
Fitz-Gubin seizing it, "we must exhibit this."

"Roribel, don't be a fool," said Fitz-Gubin, angrily, and
very much frightened that the Wyomings would see it.

Roribel gave the locket to him, seeing him so serious. Fitz-Gubin was delighted to recover it ; thought he must have dropped it coming down the garden, &c.

But the journey home was one of the dullest ever known. When one is carrying on any wickedness, one is unusually suspicious, and the manner of the two Wyomings sufficiently disturbed Fitz-Gubin. He suspected Miss Wyoming had seen the locket lying on the ground ; he well knew how it would startle her, and in conjunction with previous circumstances, it would alarm and shock her. He cursed his carelessness as he went on board, and reproached himself for being a "fool," yet never suspected that he was anything worse.

CHAPTER VII.

IT is twilight time, and the bells of Malta are jingling away as if they wished to welcome the night in enthusiastically. English Malta is going to dinner. Malta proper has dined long since, and is airing or resting itself, and happy in the enjoyment of a breeze which is cool from leagues of blue sea. Malta proper is right to dine early. For delicious above all of Nature's delights is twilight in the South. Nature's highest function is to pacify the spirit and elevate the heart of man. In warm climates you feel more a part of nature than elsewhere. Hence from these climates come Pantheistic religions ; in the North you have " frost-giants" and the like—hard impersonations of nature, which is severe there, and has to be fought against. The South merges you in the universal : the North sharpens your individuality. The South produces despots, emblems of the universal : the North aristocracies, embodiments of great individualities. And so might we go on to contrast and compare, but that our duty calls us to the personages of our story, and to the events which we have in hand.

We are in the twilight, I say, of the autumn, when all these events of ours happened. The harbor is alive with boats, for the court-martial on Captain Pappleton and his officers for losing the *Bloater* is just over—the second day has concluded the matter; and at every dinner in the harbor the SENTENCE is discussed. Was it fair to Bluffett, the master? Who knows Bluffett? Are not all these Pappletons notorious gabies? How did Hackles give his evidence? Had Captain Bobbles a right to sit? Huge subjects of discussion, which accompany (but do not retard) the discussion of the *Brimbousky marine* and other luxuries; and on the whole, perhaps, give a stimulus to the consumption of the iced wine, so grateful in that climate. There can be no great harm in gliding into the gun-room of the *Sovereign*, and just learning a little about the particulars of the trial. For our friend Forbessy is cast loose on the service again by the dispersion of the *Bloater's* officers and crew, which is decided on; and Forbessy is to figure before the reader in various pages yet, before we have done with him, whatever may become of our Fitz-Gubins and others.

"Have not had such a trial for a long time," says Siddlington; "not since Terryton was tried for insubordination."

"There is a piquancy about an insubordination trial which you don't have in a mere loss of a ship case, though," says Beaulieu, talking of the affair as hunters do of a "run."

"Yes," Riddel said, "Ricks was good. His telling the timid witness that he had a head like a scupper-nail was calculated to calm the poor fellow."

"Ah, ha! and I thought it excellent when he asked where the midshipmen were, and looked so sulky when nothing whatever appeared against them!"

"Did you see Pappleton shed a manly tear during the defence?" inquired a midshipman, in rather an unfeeling tone. (Cuckles made a mental note about *him*.)

"Very good defence, too ; Hookins's, I suppose?" asked Beaulieu.

"Yes. I know that touch about the 'memory of unfortunate disasters being a punishment in itself.' He got old Stokey off with loss of a year, for being drunk in the middle watch in the *Fandango*, by that one stroke, I believe!"

"I remain of opinion that Mrs. Pappleton should have been tried," said Pug Welby.

"By ——," began old Manton, "when Fowler lost the *Porcupine*—in '18,—off Devil's Head, (by —— not a compass that would work in the ship—there wasn't,) and the sails were all worn, and by —— it blew as it never blew on the coast of Spain—he didn't come off so cheap I can tell you! 'Reprimanded,' indeed! They reprimanded you with a d—d good breaking, and if need be, brought a youngster to the gun, &c., &c." I cut short Manton, as indeed the mess did, by the various laughs and exclamations which he produced. Poor old gentleman! He was one of a breed gone by now, of whom the last will soon be laid by the side of the pigtails of the dead generation.

This speech of old Manton has revealed to you the result of the trial to Pappleton. He was "reprimanded;" but Bluffett, the master, was "reprimanded *severely*," and was not to be employed for a year. Everybody else was acquitted. What then remained to do in the case of the *Bloater*, but what good housewives do with domestic breakages—viz., to pick up the pieces? For that purpose, a ship was sent to the scene of the wreck, which brought away the lower masts and rudder in tow ; and (the head authorities at Malta regretting that Mrs. Pappleton had lost her wardrobe) there the matter ended! Captain Pap-

pleton was "hereby reprimanded accordingly"—which did
not spoil his dinner—and after much sympathy from the
good-natured Wyomings, he and Mrs. P. went to England
luxuriously, in one of the "Peninsular and Oriental" boats.
He has been employed since, too, (as you will be glad to
hear, and as we all ought to be proud to know,) and I believe Mrs. Pappleton will often talk over the loss of the
Bloater in her nautical way, and tell you that if they had
"worn" at 6 P. M., or kept W. and by S. after 3, or otherwise done something which they did not do, the *Bloater*
would not have been lost.   ·

The talk about the "sentence" having flagged, while the
mess were still at their wine, Beaulieu looked round; and
observing that many of the fellows, who were not in the
best set, had gone out of the gun-room, said quietly, "I
did not tell you my adventure last night!"   ·

Men pricked up their ears. "I don't think the affair of
any consequence, to be sure," continued Beaulieu, carelessly. "But I was passing along an obscure street, and a
fellow tried to stab me!"—Beaulieu sipped some wine.

Fitz-Gubin looked up. Forbessy looked up. The eyes
of these young men seemed to meet naturally, somehow,
and having met, to turn away again, rather hurriedly.
Forbessy looked especially serious, and there was trouble
in the expression of his gray eyes.

"The deuce he did!" Riddel said. "How do you account for it?"

"Nay; who knows? He must have taken me for somebody else. In warding off the blow, I showed him my face;
the man made no other attempt, and vanished!"

"'Gad, Riddel says. "There are not many of your
inches, either! Stand up, Beaulieu, and show us how you
were walking."

Beaulieu smiled, and stood up. Truly, he was a goodly

length of a man, Beaulieu. He was the son of an Admiral
Beaulieu ; but he and his father bore a likeness to a family
more illustrious than any known under *that* gentile appellation. Who knows the exact truth? Yet, few who were
up to high scandals, doubted whence father and son inherit-
ed the high manner, the royal air. Their personal qualities
had not suffered, as their escutcheon had, from the brand
of the bastard's bar !

"There's not so tall a man in the mess, and consequently
not in the squadron," said Riddel. "We whop the squadron in everything, in horses, in Madeira, in Palestine soup,
in exercising sails." (He classified, you observe, in a characteristic order.

"Forbessy is two inches less," said Siddlington.

"I am," said Forbessy, quietly.

"Lord Fitz-Gubin, I think, is as tall, though," said Cuckles. (Foolish Cuckles, he didn't know what he was about.)

"Ah, Fitz-Gubin, measure !"* Riddel said.

Fitz-Gubin was sulky that evening ; but he rose, and
stood up back to back with Beaulieu. Their heights were,
indeed, much the same. A joke or two was made on the
point, and on Beaulieu's story, but Fitz-Gubin was quite out
of his usual, cool, indifferent tone of manner. He was icy
and fretful—prickly with icicles of manner, if I may be
permitted such a figure. The party broke up somewhat
abruptly ; the men went to smoke on the main deck, or to
get ready to go on shore, or to whatever else they designed
for the evening's employment. And among the smoking
party, Riddel drew his chair alongside Beaulieu's, and
opened a chat with him. First of all, Riddel told the
handsome Beaulieu, that there was no doubt that he had
been taken for Fitz-Gubin, and that he certainly would be
stabbed instead of him if he didn't take care. He reminded
him of Fitz-Gubin's previous adventure.

"He is such a deuced mysterious fellow!" continued Rid-del. "If he would tell one what he was about, one might be warned. But there is no knowing all that fellow's mys-teries. . . . . By Jove, there he goes on shore now, in plain clothes!"

Sure enough, the long figure of Fitz-Gubin was seen gliding up the companion ladder, and in a few minutes the young men saw through an open port a boat shooting away towards the landing-place.

Beaulieu had much of the shrewdness and elegance, and much of the personal tastes of his father the admiral, and his grandfather, the admiral's Parent. (Let us dignify the great progenitor of the Beaulieus with a capital, at all events.)

"Well," said Beaulieu, "it is very convenient to make love personally, and get stabbed for it—by proxy!"

"Do you know," said Riddel—who was a trifle feather-headed, and flew backwards and forwards between facts, as a bird does between trees, undecided where to light—" the case must stand thus :—Your assailant was the cad of the fair-way buoy, who . . . . . but then *you* were not of that party. But, stop. He wanted to get at Fitz-Gubin ; and I suppose he is the brother of some girl that Fitz-Gubin has been making love to."

"And I am to be sacrificed to her, like a lamb to Venus!" said Mr. Beaulieu.

" He will get himself into some terrible scrape," Riddel went on. "For my part, I hate your adventures, and watchings, and knives, and rope-ladders, in such matters."

"You are of Horace's opinion," said Beaulieu, who thought that a " gentleman " ought to know Horace, and only studied certain authors whom he thought a " gentle-man" ought to know, besides him: "*Amo Venerem facilem,'* &c.

"I am glad Horace and I agree," said Riddel. "But, by Jove, too, (he went on expounding the half-moral code, which he and many other young fellows hold in our day,)— by Jove, I say, it is not fair to be always following up a chase of this kind like a red Indian on a track. Hang it, if an apple drops into one's mouth, well and good; but don't go sneaking like a burglar over the orchard wall." Whereupon, Riddel, thinking he had made an ethical hit, sucked some sherry-and-water, and hugged himself as a good fellow.

· "There is a great deal of sound English feeling about that sentiment," said Beaulieu, with a grin. "Let's take a turn on deck."

They left the main deck and found the night lovely. They mounted to the poop, and commenced a pleasant turn there. The stars were out in the heaven, and the winds loose upon the sea.

"Who's that on the other side?" asked Riddel. He spoke of a figure which was leaning over the side of the bulwarks, and looking towards the shore.

Riddel strolled over to see. The figure did not move. He returned, and told Beaulieu :. it was Forbessy.

"Ah, a quiet, and rather melancholy fellow," Beaulieu remarked, as they leaned over the bulwarks of their side. "Never saw him, till he joined a few weeks ago. Seems of a good family, and not rich; affectionate, but without chums; earnest, with no particular beliefs; and clever, without having decided what he will make his cleverness do!"

"Why, Beaulieu, what an infernal observer you are," Riddel said, with an astonished air. "I scarcely ever saw you speak to Forbessy."

Beaulieu laughed, looked down at the water, and said nothing.

" I tell you what I remark," Riddel went on, sharpened
by Beaulieu's example, "Forbessy and Fitz-Gubin never
speak to each other, now I think of it."

" Let us come over and see what Forbessy's about," said
Beaulieu. " Do you know that ' attempted assassination,'
as the papers would call it, has made me curious about one
or two things."

They moved across the poop, as he suggested. Forbessy
was leaning in the same place still, and watching the line of
shore. In the tranquillity of the night, the harbor and the
town, seen from the *Sovereign's* high poop, seemed to hang
like a curtain spangled with lights. Lights shifted to and
fro, and played in and out—from houses, along the water's
edge—from boats. It was the picture, perhaps, that Forbessy was so interested in ; the picture .of that stillness
pierced by those lights, under such a sweet sky, and full of
so many associations.

Forbessy turned as the young men joined him. ".What
a fine night it is," he said.

" You seem interested in the look of the town to-night,"
said Beaulieu, good-naturedly.

" I was looking at—at. the town, in fact," replied our
friend rather vaguely. " What's the time, I wonder ?
About nine, I suppose ; and this is the fourteenth."

" This is the fourteenth," Riddel answered, " I believe.
1 hope I shall hear from my aunt by next mail ! And now
I think of it, I shall go on shore this evening." So saying,
Mr. Riddel (whose ideas had been set into a new train by
the sudden reminiscence of his aunt) departed.

" Mr. Beaulieu," said Forbessy, turning round briskly
to that gentleman, with whom he was now left alone, " I
listened with interest to your story in the gun-room. Permit me to tell you that there *is* danger to be apprehended

by you—as I clearly see from the circumstances which you recounted ; as, in fact, I may say, I *know*."

" Indeed," Beaulieu said, in a quiet and composed way ; "really there seems an unwonted degree of mystery and an unusual atmosphere of romance pervading H. M. S. *Sovereign* and Malta, just now."

" There is always more of both, everywhere, than people readily believe," Forbessy said. " But, Mr. Beaulieu," he continued, " I will open myself to you more frankly. We have not been long in company in the ship ; nevertheless, I have seen enough of you to know that you are melancholy for want of definite convictions about life ; friendly, without having confidants ; and—but the rest might sound like flattery—suffice it to say that the rest gives interest to the other phenomena I have observed !"

" Why," said Beaulieu, " you echo the very remarks which I made, not half an hour ago, about yourself."

" Nature, then, intended us to be friends," said Forbessy.
" So be it," said Beaulieu.

As they walked together for half an hour in the moon-light, arm and arm, Forbessy told Beaulieu a story which interested him a good deal. What is needful for us to know of it, we shall know at the proper time. Meanwhile, I would just say, *apropos* of the eternal question of the age and its reforms—might we not, considering the many editions of the *De Amicitia* which we possess ; and by way of doing a little instalment towards reform of a more profound sort, than giving expression to the enlightened wisdom of " £10 householders ;" might we not, I say, achieve a little stroke of " reform " by privately worshipping and recognizing, more than we do, the antique sacredness of the sentiment of friendship ?

CHAPTER VIII.

THERE was a rumor spread about the circles of the *Sove-reign* (for is not a line-of-battle ship a kind of town, and with as many degrees and circles in it as any town of them all ?) that Lord Fitz-Gubin had "got leave," and was go-ing over to Sicily to shoot. He encouraged, however, no curiosity that anybody might feel on the subject. In fact, he withdrew himself, more than ever, from society in the *Sovereign.* He kept his watch, dined—when he did not dine on shore—at mess, and kept up, to be sure, an ac-quaintance with Riddel, Siddlington, and others, and used Cuckles, but slight was the intimacy which any of them at-tained with him. If Siddlington had ever formed a vision of himself as a guest at Castellan, and a successful wooer of a Lady Eleanora there, Siddlington must, by the time at which we have now arrived, have seen that it was a vision indeed. Other Jacobs, whose dreams had revealed to them ladders up to high life, had awakened too. The impenetrable, selfish easiness, and mysterious and solitary, yet common-place nature of Fitz-Gubin, kept everybody off. Nay, a party actually formed to quiz him ! One or two men used to try to draw him out by hypocritical devices, encouraging the immense latent pride of the man to show itself ; teasing him as you might tease a tortoise, and, per-haps, by a sudden turn, toppling him over on his back, and leaving him helpless ! For one of these conventional gen-tlemen, once out of the protection of social convention, rudely brought in contact with nature, is as helpless as a tortoise in that position. Jigger once, seeing him with a collar of unrivalled finish and stiffness, exclaimed, in his fine bluff way, " Well, d—n it, Fitz-Gubin, nothing *does* so take in the public as an imposing gill !" Fitz-Gubin turned as pale as death ! Another time the conversation was led to the subject of expensive living in messes. Fitz-Gubin wondered, after some careful drawing-out from our wicked clique, "how the deuce some fellows managed to live in the service, now-a-days." By-and-by, in a moment of farther encouragement, he said that "he would⋅ be worse off with two hundred a-year than others with a third of it, having his rank to keep up," and so forth. But he was very knowing in his way, and had once or twice seen glances pass between men which he did not like. Beaulieu, (the villain,) who was "up" to the facts about the connection of the Fitz-Gubins with P———, showed an inclination to hint at *that* old story one day, and it was all Forbessy could do to keep him off the dangerous ground. Latterly, however, Forbessy and Beaulieu, still more together than ever, put themselves less and less in Fitz-Gubin's way. Such was the state of things when the above-mentioned rumor about his shooting expedition got wind. ⋅

The intimacy between Forbessy and Beaulieu caused a good deal of curiosity among the gentlemen of the *Sovereign*. What would a mess be without those⋅ combinations and antipathies, those personal likes and dislikes which divide its society, and give piquancy to its daily life ! A large mess is like a town, and its society includes as many conflicting elements. Often there is an intrigue going forward—a mystery slowly evolving itself—of which numbers of those who breakfast and dine together, day after day, never have a suspicion. Poor Charley Wremond dies, and we learn that he had run away with a ward in Chancery, and had a family of little ones of whose existence we never dreamed. No wonder Charley was wont to be serious at times when we were piqued at his being "slow⋅!" Jack Montacute is going to fight a duel with Sandwich the next port we come to ; but they must dine together meanwhile.

and nobody must guess that there is anything of the kind meditated between them. What made Bellomont so friendly with Tangueray? He wás his natural brother, my dear sir; hence the peculiar felicity of Bung's constant joke about the likeness between them! Yes, romance underlies us everywhere in society, as the mystery of life underlies the fair city and country life we mingle in, and the existence we enjoy; to both, however, the fool (to his gain, and also to his loss) is blind and deaf.

Forbessy and Beaulieu are sitting at the stern ports of the gun-room early in the morning. It is near the hour for taking a shore-boat to Bighi Bay to bathe. A marine is cleaning Fitz-Gubin's gun; an operation watched with interest by one or two men who happened to be up as early as our friends. He performs the operation in their presence, and in the mess-room; for, of course, they must take an interest in anything belonging to so notable a man.

Latimer watches the process; remarks that he thinks Fitz-Gubin will have a fine time of it; and, by-the-by, where is he going to shoot? Is he going to Sicily, or where?

Forbessy looked at Beaulieu in that d——d mysterious way (I borrow this expression from Latimer) in which these gentlemen occasionally interchanged glances. They rose presently, and made for the door.

"Going to bathe?" Latimer called out. Beaulieu waved a towel in his hand, by way of answer; and in a minute they were in a shore-boat. Out glided the heavy green and yellow boat, with awning spread, from the *Sovereign's* side towards the harbor's mouth—the faithful Maltese (for the Maltese is among the most devoted and obedient of mankind, when kindly treated) rising and falling as he plied the oars, industrious and contented. "Bighi, sir?" he asks. "Yes, Jocko," says Beaulieu, good-naturedly enough, (for B. is a gentleman in all ways,) but with the same kindness with which he would give an apple to a monkey; for B. is an Englishman, dealing with a subject of another race.

Forbessy and Beaulieu said little at first. The morning was opening up into a fine day. They were content to see the forts relieve with their deep hues the blue monotony of the sea—the life spreading itself along the harbor's edges—the stately masts of the few men-of-war in harbor tapering away into the sky—and to let the picture sink into their minds in peace. The boat with a heavy motion drew farther and farther out, and the Maltese brushed away his curly hair, and paused a moment.

" That's her !" said Forbessy, suddenly.

Beaulieu looked up, and saw in the line of the pointed finger a merchant-brig lying. There was nothing peculiar in her appearance to distinguish her from any *Annie Jane* or *Isabella Briggs* sent out by our country.

" Row to the brig," said Beaulieu to their boatman, pointing to her. The Maltese obeyed, and soon brought them close to her. A head popped over the side with no very welcome expression, and said, " What d'ye want, master ?"

" Go alongside," said Forbessy to the Maltese, and without giving the head any answer, up jumped Beaulieu, up jumped Forbessy, and stood on the brig's deck. The head—which was no less a head than a skipper's—was set on a short little carcase. The skipper was no-way pleased to see his visitors, but, with hands in pockets, looked up at them, inquiringly

" You take passengers," said Beaulieu, glancing round with a cool air of observation.

" There you're wrong," said the short skipper, briefly.

" You never take passengers, eh ?" asked Beaulieu.

" There you're wrong again," said the little skipper.

" Your ears are longer than your tongue, I think, my good man," said Beaulieu, ineffably cool, and with the

"great air" which he knew how to put on. "But waiving
any attempts at epigram, which are ludicrously unsuited to
your social position, suppose you show us your cabin?"

"We come from the *Sovereign,* I may mention," put in
Forbessy, carelessly

"Oh!" The little skipper began looking round, and
assuming a very knowing expression—"Friends of Lord
Fitz-Gubin's, I see!"

The eyes of our friends met instanter.

"So far so good," said Beaulieu, enigmatically. "Let
us see the cabin, then."

The skipper paused. "Did you say friends of Lord Fitz-
Gubin's, sir?" asked the skipper.

"Skipper!" said Beaulieu, "I did not say so. Permit
me, however, to make it plain that we must see your cabin.
Why, I ought not to explain: I may want a passage. If
you wish me to say more, I have more to say; but I will
be content with a look-at your cabin."

The skipper hesitated, but he yielded. They followed
him down his cabin ladder.

"There, now, gentlemen, Lord Fitz-Gubin's taken that
berth; that I s'pose you know."

There was nothing specially curious about the place destined to receive Fitz-Gubin. It was not so luxurious as
one would suppose Fitz-Gubin would wish it to be. They
looked at it and paused. The skipper seemed puzzled and
uneasy, and watched them.

"When do you sail?" asked Beaulieu abruptly.

"I think to-night."

"Well," said Beaulieu, suddenly becoming quite free-and-
easy in his manner, "I dare say Fitz-Gubin will have a
nice passage of it. A devilish pleasant cabin you have.
He dines with you, no doubt—finds his own wine—takes
the run of your prog—and will have a fowl occasionally, if

the hen-coops are not washed overboard. We need not wait, I think," said Beaulieu, with a twinkle of his eye at Forbessy.

The skipper brightened up, and a weight seemed taken off his mind.

"Skipper !" said Beaulieu, fixing his eyes upon him with a look like a rapier thrust, "where do you stow lady pas sengers ?"

The little man gave a start back. He was so manifestly upset that there was no concealing it. "Who are you sir ?" he said, "and what do you want with me? That's what I want to know."

"My good man, I am an officer in her Majesty's service, who takes some interest in the brig *Victor*. You must have seen that I know what I am about, and am not to be trifled with. First, you must show me the cabin taken for a young lady some weeks ago ; second, you had better say nothing about this visit ; third, you had better sail at your appointed time, and not mind about all your passengers being on board : you know whom you expect first !"

The skipper made no resistance nor remonstrance. He showed them into the cabin. Forbessy came with Beaulieu to the door of it. Truly it was a snug little nest—with a snow-white little crib—wherein a fairy might nestle, and be lulled by the murmur of the sea. Forbessy peeped in in silence, and turned away with a sigh. Beaulieu moved away, drawing the skipper by the arm; in that instant Forbessy slipped a letter under the pillow.

As they got on deck, Beaulieu gave his card to the skipper, and said, "Some day I may do you a turn if you behave yourself ; meanwhile, good morning !" But the little man expressed no cordial wish that they should ever meet again ; they saw his head at the gangway as they were rowed away, watching them, unmoved, till it dwindled to a speck.

Meanwhile, breakfast was laid in the gun-room. Up from the cockpit came the fellows of the mess. Here was lively Riddel, polite Siddlington, artful Cuckles, Latimer the simple, and Manton the gruff, with many more. Rasper, the steward's assistant, brings endless eggs ; Riddel, the extravagant, orders wine. Now is the hour for reminiscences of last night, and endless varieties of squadron news. Now glide away, with various expressions of face, the infinite varieties also of the *genus* Dun. Pallid but pertinacious Tosta, eager and pimpled Sarjan, humorous but inflexible Baldero, you have been dodging about the cockpit the last hour ; it is now time for you to go. Most implicitly do I believe you when you say you will call to-morrow !

The eggs, the squadron, the duns are discussed together. "Gad ! I dreamed last night I paid Baldero !" said a youngster, chipping his egg.

"You fellows *affect* duns," said Riddel. "You think it fine to be dunned. Mark me, lads, the day will come when the fun will vanish out of these bills, and leave a balance you won't like !"

Everybody is impressed, for everybody feels that the speaker ought to know.

But at this moment—enter Fitz-Gubin. Forbessy and Beaulieu both look at him. You might see Forbessy's lip quiver if you cared to watch him. Fitz-Gubin is in mufti—bran-new semi-sporting rig. He is a little pale, but this may be our fancy, who have been peeping at his secrets ; yes, he *is* a litte pale, and has a more serious expression than usual. He takes his usual seat up among the leading seniors, with the usual quiet mechanical air of superiority, and the steward (whose aristocratic predilections are well known) attends to him in person. Fitz-Gubin eats an egg, consumes toast, drinks a cup of tea ; then remarks, that the day seems fine, and wonders whether the breeze will hold.

Fitz-Gubin threw out a remark occasionally to an audience, as one scatters crumbs to birds, with a careless good-
nature that seemed to say, " Eat, and be filled." Cuckles
hastened to observe, that the day was fine, and to hope that
the breeze would hold.

"Think of going to-day?" called out Beaulieu. Fitz-
Gubin did not hear him. Beaulieu kept his eye fixed in a
somewhat impressive manner on him ; so Cuckles, fearing
mischief, called his attention to Beaulieu.

" I beg your pardon, Mr. Beaulieu?" Fitz-Gubin's manner was, indeed, tremendous in its politeness. Bung was
awed, and tried to imitate the style, afterwards, at the grog
tub.

" Are you going to-day ?" repeated Beaulieu.

" Perhaps so. My intentions are not quite definite."
Bung was lost in admiration ; Cuckles felt himself elevated.

Beaulieu said no more at that moment, and Cuckles and
others doubted not that he felt himself rebuked. And so
breakfast passed off, and men dispersed.

Breakfast once well over, our friends Forbessy and Beaulieu disappeared. We, however, who know what they are
about, will follow them on shore. They march briskly
through several streets, and pause at a place where horses
are to be had. All the way along, Forbessy has been serious, not to say gloomy. He has carried on a kind of mon-
ologue, to which Beaulieu has listened with the faithful
patience of a friend.

" There," says Forbessy, " there was the street. That
was the church. A church, by-the-by, which is an emblem
of all Europe ; for over the graves of dead earnestness and
greatness, populace gather, and boobies prate. (I saw
Bagman, Esq., there, with a party one morning, making
notes for an anti-superstitious harangue, and grinning in

7·

pitiable idiocy, and with perfect ignorance, over the graves
of the knights.) Some day I may tell you all that has
passed in my head and heart, since I took part in this little
drama, of which the catastrophe approaches. Beaulieu,
my dear fellow, you shall see her to-day!"

CHAPTER IX.

THEY were now cantering through the gates, past the
fortifications, with their green turf and their solid stone,
which form the hem of the garment of that sea-damsel, Valetta. Before them lies the stony landscape, which we
described the other day, basking in mild autumn hues.
They turn into a narrow road, and make for an unfrequented village. A dog barks; some children rush out; a crone,
reposing under the shadow of a chapel, wakes up, and
stares, and grasps her crutch. But, in a moment, she
slumbers again, as quietly as the dry and dusty trees which
front a small row of little white houses; as quaintly, too,
as yonder wooden saint, perched up in a box with glass
windows at the corner.

"Why, the whole village is asleep," exclaimed Forbessy.
Indeed, it looked like it. But Forbessy, riding close up to
the windows of a house, tapped with the butt-end of his
whip at them. A sleepy and also woolly head appeared
there, staring as if still in a dream, then vanished, and out
from the door appeared a Maltese, and proceeded to offer
his services to hold the horses. They dismounted. Beaulieu took Forbessy's arm, resigning himself to his command,
and they strolled through the little place enjoying the afternoon air. The houses forming the village were grouped
together so fantastically, and without order ; trees shooting
up amongst them ; bits of garden dividing them, with an

effect so careless and unsystematic, that you might fancy
that the whole had been scattered by the hand of a flying
deity *en route* to Greece. The chapel had somehow got
planted in the centre, and seemed to hold itself up as an ensign for the houses to rally round. There *was* a time when
the chapel was that everywhere.

"This village," said Forbessy, taking a firmer clasp of
his friend's arm, " enjoyed some patronage during the days
of the Order. The knights came out here occasionally as
a change; some of them had houses here. In this little
place, for instance, I recognize the relics of a gentleman's
dwelling."

So saying, Forbessy opened a garden gate, and followed
by his friend, marched in. The house stood apart from the
village, and had, indeed, an air, even in decay, of former
better fortune. The garden still boasted trees of orange
and of almond. · And among the wild grass, which sprang
up rank over the ruins of a wall, there were fragments of
stone of which the carved and shapely proportions indicated
that they had formed part of structures, when the occupiers
loved beauty.

" By Annabel!" said Beaulieu, rather affectedly, "a
pleasant place enough! One sometimes fancies one could
live in such places, and be very very virtuous and romantic;
but one comes back to civilization and milk punch."

" Yes," said Forbessy, "couldn't òne lie on the grass
with a pipe in one's mouth, and hear the *Castle of Indolence*
read by—somebody? But here she comes!"

As he spoke, the door opened; the porch, overgrown
with roses, which were waving and falling in heaps, vibrated.
A little boy came skipping out, ran up to Forbessy with
perfect familiarity, and hailed him as "Missa Forbessy,'
most intimately.

Forbessy lifted him up, and played with him, to the im-

mense amusement of Beaulieu. "Marie come directly,"
said the youngster.

"Who asked you about Marie, *enfant terrible?*" Forbessy said. Beaulieu smiled, and admired the fatherly air
of Forbessy, who made himself at home, and produced from
his pocket certain *dulciaria* for the juvenile, quite like a
veteran.

The door opened again. This time, there appeared in
the garden a little thin old man in black, with a skull cap
on. What linen was visible on the old gentleman was not
very clean, and time had played havoc with his teeth. But
his head was good ; his-face was the peasant face, tempered
by the priestly position, and by drilling since boyhood, the
common priest-face of Malta.

"Father Simola, my friend Mr. Beaulieu," said Forbessy.

Father Simola was very polite. Father Simoia had acquired English. He looked at Beaulieu, and then he said,
rubbing his hands together, "Is your friend from Lancashire
like yourself?"

"No," said Forbessy. "No, Father Simola. He wants
to know if you are one of the——but never mind," he continued rather abruptly. Forbessy treated the Father with
a great deal of good-natured courtesy, though the old gentleman made but a small figure in conversation ; was, indeed,
the ordinary, unromantic priest of the lower orders, and up
to the calibre of the little chapel.

More arrivals—two or three more younkers, among
whom at last sailed out our young friend, Marie Polonai.
Beaulieu was all eyes ; he had never seen her before, and
when he first found her one of their group, and standing
tranquilly before Forbessy and the Father, he scarcely knew
what to say—she was so much more beautiful—so very
superior in all ways to his anticipations. Forbessy, who

had shaken hands with her in a brotherly manner, when she first appeared in the garden, presented Beaulieu to her. Beaulieu was struck by nothing so much (not even by her eyes, which were miraculous, and which I should despair of describing) as by the utter naturalness of her manner. This was what delighted all competent observers in Marie Polonai. She was as natural as a rose, if I may be permitted such a comparison ; that is, she was always equally delightful ; equally in her place, singing, talking, running, dancing ; all her actions flowed from a central beauty of which they partook, and while you wondered at her perfection, and strove to account for it, you found criticism to merge at last into mere assent, and were contented with the fact without puzzling yourself with the " why."

The youngsters brought seats. They sat down and tranquilly basked in the afternoon, of which Forbessy seemed to cherish every passing moment. The wind blew a few rose-leaves from the mass at the porch, which scattered themselves all over Marie, and fell about her.

"Oh ! that wind," said Forbessy. "I hate the wind ! It carries away good fellows like Beaulieu and me from all we love—sailors are its slaves. It does the evil work of autumn, for it carries the flowers and leaves away long before autumn has altogether ruined them, and while they are first tinged with a new beauty by it. It is going to take Marie away, as it has just done the roses !"

"Yes, but the wind that takes me can, by and by, bring you," said Marie in a low voice.

Forbessy looked up at her, but said nothing.

"How glad your father will be to see you, Marie," said Father Simola, simply.

"He will. He is to take me to Naples. I am to learn to sing. The ladies Wyoming say that I already sing like an angel."

"These ladies," said Father Simola, alluding with severity
to their plans of conversion, "are not good ladies."

"They are very kind. They wished me to begin a new
worship, it is true. I told them worship is worship, and be-
longs to the heart. I cannot argue, but, already, if I am
good, I know how to pray. Every day, after I have seen
them, I have seen Father Simola ; he can argue ; and I
have known him since a little girl ; but the ladies Wyoming
will not see Father Simola !"

Beaulieu smiled. "You are a good girl," said Father
Simola.

The little boy came running up, laughing and shouting.
Something new was evidently about to begin ; and Beaulieu looking up, saw a party of Maltese approaching.
Forbessy and the others were ready to receive them. Forbessy shook hands with one or two, and Beaulieu observed
that they all treated him with great respect, and seemed to
know him quite well. Beaulieu felt the scene new, and as
he strolled about the garden, fancied himself a *seigneur*
presiding at the festival of his peasantry.

"But, my good fellow," said Beaulieu, recognizing a face
which he had seen before, "surely you and I have met
somewhere ? If I mistake not, it was on an occasion when
you wanted me to taste your knife !"

The Maltese smiled and bowed very low. "Pardon me,
sar—I think it was !" Then, again taking off his cap and
bowing very low indeed, he twisted round and shot away to
another part of the garden.

Beaulieu stood watching them. Father Simola, who
drew near, said, "They all adore Marie !—she is the pride
of their whole neighborhood, she is so kind and good—she
is so modest and gifted ; they would kill any one who they
thought would insult her." And so the old *padre* rattled
on about the gifts and graces of the girl, and the worship

of her by the Maltese. Some of them had formed a band
of worshippers, and were pledged to guard her—and so
forth.

But the afternoon was wearing away. The pale rose-
colored fire was already spreading itself over the west. It
was time to go. Beaulieu was conducted with many de-
monstrations of politeness to his horse; Forbessy lingered
a few minutes, and then followed. Waving his whip to
Beaulieu, he motioned him to follow at a gallop; and for
many minutes they clattered on in silence. At last Forbessy pulled up and began to talk before any questions were
asked him.

"A strange episode—eh? You observed how much
alone I was, and how much occupied by unshared thoughts,
till you and I *discovered* each other, as I may justly call it?
Accident threw me in the way of that charming being. I
made acquaintance with her family, chiefly by favor of that
old priest, whom—but no matter at present about my relation to him. I was interested by her genius—for it is genius
which gives that air of superiority to her manner, and which
raises it above her birth. She will be a great artist; and
I hope the world will never spoil her. Well, I almost immediately discovered the designs of our gentleman from
—shire, and for weeks I have amused myself by counter-
acting them—keeping him from possibly coming in contact
with her, just as a gardener would keep a slug or caterpillar
from his flowers. The gentleman from —shire, (by Jove!
I could give you a capital history of the Fitz-Gubins. Ours
was one of the families which their patriarch Gubbins managed to manœuvre out of ——shire) saw Marie once at
night, in Valetta, and once at the Wyomings, who patronized her as a barn-door fowl might patronize a nightingale.
He puts *you* in danger by haunting her dwelling at all
hours; but never saw her again. He sent her letters,

which she handed over to old Simola, who used to burn
them with much ceremony, and cross himself afterwards.
And (here Forbessy laughed) he employed what he calls
'a cad' to convey those epistles, who, by the way of keeping up a lucrative employment, got somebody to write an-
swers ; and Fitz-Gubin lived in the conviction that he was
encouraged.   He sent her bracelets and a locket; and I
am sorry to say that old Simola sent these off yesterday to
the Wyomings, for their friend the ' Lord Fizzgubbing" as
he calls him.   This I did not know in time to prevent
it, which I would have done for their sakes.   The final
step you already know—viz., that having learned the how
and when of the girl's departure, he got leave to go for a
trip, and took a cabin in the *Victor*—a fact of which she has
no knowledge—intending to give her a delightful surprise,
and have a pleasant cruise as the irresistible Fitz-Gubin !"

"Upon my word, a devilish pleasant programme !" said
Beaulieu.   .

"A word of this notable scheme would have caused some
friends of Marie's to do what would have stopped Fitz-
Gubin's career, perhaps, finally ; but then the service is to
be considered.   No ; we must stop him ourselves.   I owe
that 'great family' a grudge, and shan't be sorry to punish
him."

Little does the solid BULDER think what plots are being
plotted, what a secret life is transacting itself under the
brilliant surface of his lighted saloons this autumn night !
Let us be thankful that we do not see society as the microscope shows us a bright drop of water, with ugly objects
preying on each other in its heart !   Let us be thankful for
its apparent brightness and purity, and topple it off *without*
applying the microscope ; at least, without applying it always.   Pass on, stout Mr. Bulder ; thou art a good-natured,
hospitable old gentleman, happy among thy guests, not de-

voured by secret anxieties, nor bored by those whom thou
entertainest.   Glance at Lady Ostrich the beautiful; is
she not happy?   Is not everybody happy here?   Listen to
the music—the embodiment of luxury and romance—is it
produced by a band who hate the party for taking them
away from their pipes at the canteen?   Has the apparent
happiness a secret fact lurking under its production, like
that fact about the music?   It may be so.   But *carpe diem.*
Wine will give you a headache; but, if you do not take
wine, you may yet have a headache to-morrow.

Beaulieu and Forbessy were both dancing.   Beaulieu
always danced; it pleased the people of the house, and,
after all,-did not bore him much.   But regularly as each
quadrille was over, he and Forbessy glided together.   Never, for any length of time, did they lose sight of Fitz-Gubin.
The Wyomings were there; but Fitz-Gubin did not dance,
and avoided them.   His eyes once met Forbessy's, but no
sign of recognition passed; but Forbessy and Beaulieu remarked how easily he carried himself—how well he hid
under his calm exterior the secret excitement which must
have been at his heart.

Forbessy grew restless.   Beaulieu again and again sooth-
ed him.   So long as Fitz-Gubin remained in the room, (as
he urged,) all was well.   Presently, Beaulieu approached
Forbessy, and whispered to him, " Come."

When they stood outside on the landing place, Beaulieu
said, "A man of the —— gives a supper at the hotel ——.
Fitz-Gubin is to be there.   I have got myself and you
asked, at the last moment.   Fitz-Gubin is evidently to start
from there.   I met Siddlington, just now, and drew from
him carelessly, that he had formally begun his leave, and
left the *Sovereign.*   So let us off to the hotel, and manage
the affair as quietly as we can."

They were the last arrivals.   The party consisted of some

7*

fifteen men. As they entered the room, Fitz-Gubin was
talking away; and, though we know that he had himself
under tolerable control, he did not look pleased when he
saw our friends enter. They were the only men of the
Sovereign present, and just the two men of the *Sovereign*
whom he least knew, or least cared to meet.

"Mr. Beaulieu, and Mr. Forbessy," said the good-natured
host, "messmates of Fitz-Gubin's, I think? This way!
Will you begin with a quail? What wine, Beaulieu?
Fitz-Gubin, you don't drink!"

They sat down; some gentlemen had begun to drink evidently pretty early. Wine of the best sorts was plentiful
enough: the supper comprised all that Malta can afford;
and Malta is not poor in that department. Bones from the
funeral pyres of gallant turkeys (*ossa perusta*, a Latin poet
would call them) came up in quick relays; the pleasant
quail on his bed of toast; the piquant becafico, who nou-
rishes his fine soul on the romantic fig, awaited the appetite
and excited to wine ; while for the mere sentimental dawdler,
fruit and liqueurs offered their voluptuous charms. When
you had exhausted every sense of the palate, you could still
seek coolness and forgetfulness in some iced punch--punch
as attractive and exciting as the eyes of houris.

There was a great deal of drinking. Two or three fellows early babbled, and became merely bores. Forbessy
drank, too ; but the pre-occupation of his mind kept him
from being overcome ; wine only strung up and sharpened
his faculties, and intensified his sense of past, present, and
future. The conversation (when the two or three babblers
fell asleep) became fixed among a few, and the rest listened.

"But come, Fitz-Gubin—come; about this last adventure, you know! You were shaying?" began a young
gentleman, whose hair was fast getting into his eyes.

" Fitz-Gubin, you don't drink ?" said the host.

" Your last, what d'ye call it, ye know ?" continued the speaker.

" Oh, nothing very extraordinary !" said Fitz-Gubin, with an intolerably conceited manner. " I'm an old stager. When I was in South America—ah, never mind ! Poor little Madeline !"

" Wouldn't she have you, then ?" called out Beaulieu.

Fitz-Gubin did not take any notice of him. Beaulieu, who was drinking pretty hard, poured some moselle into his tumbler, and drank it off.

" About Madeline ?" called out Beaulieu, very loudly.

" No—no ; about the new one. I say, Fitz-Gubin, let us hear about her. Are her eyes blue ?" asked the first speaker, with a determined and most serious air.

" No ; charming dark eyes ; nice as the Spanish girls."

" Sit down, Forbessy, for God's sake ! and wait a little !" whispered Beaulieu, for Forbessy was turning pale and very serious.

" Oh, hang dark eyes ; give me blue eyes !" said the aforesaid young gentleman, looking round with an imbecile expression.

" Fitz-Gubin, you don't drink ?" said the host, once more.

" I mustn't drink : I'm going to sail at daylight."

" Sail at daylight ?" inquired somebody.

" Gentlemen," cried Beaulieu, " fill your glasses."

The roar with which he said this, accompanied by a thump which made all the glasses ring, startled the whole table. Wine, punch, all conceivable liquors were poured out—sherry by some, into champagne—and brandy by some, into sherry—as the mad genius of the hour dictated. Beaulieu stood up, with a tumbler full to the brim of wine, balancing himself with a slight lurch. " Gentlemen, I propose

a toast. I propose one of the most beautiful and innocent
creatures God ever made!" Here there was an immense
noise, with wild outcries and the crashing of glass. "The
man who does not drink it, shall rue the hour. Gentlemen,
Marie Polonai ! Forbessy, return thanks!"

"Marie Polonai !" screamed a dozen voices, and again
there was a noise which shook the room. "Who is she?"
called out several men. "Forbessy!" roared others.

Fitz-Gubin had started to his feet, like a man shot in the
heart, and stood up speechless and pale with surprise.
Forbessy had done the same, and, as the noise died away,
the two stood there facing each other ; men, sober enough
to judge, saw that in the look of the two faces, as they met,
there was deadly mischief.

"Do you drink that toast, Lord Fitz-Gubin?" Forbessy
asked.

"I drink it ! You surprise me, sir, by asking me about
any proceeding of mine. Capt. Bechamel—thank you for
your hospitality : it is late and I must bid you good night."

"Lord Fitz-Gubin, you leave not this room to sail in the
Victor : mark me, to sail in the *Victor,* I say ! If you are
such a craven as——"

This was the one thing needed to make the scene complete.· Like a handful of powder falling on a fire, the room
went into a blaze. Noises of every kind caused a scene of
extreme confusion. Fitz-Gubin lost himself in spite of his
caution ; there were fatal words, and a scuffle.

"Now," said Captain Bechamel, "nothing remains but
to separate for the evening, and postpone all necessary
ulterior proceedings till the proper time. After what has
passed, of course, Lord Fitz-Gubin will see the propriety
of remaining in Malta, till the matter has come to its pro
per termination."

*   *   *   *   *   *

The next day after this scene, the mail from England arrived, with (among other novelties) Fitz-Gubin's promotion to the rank of lieutenant.   This brought a new element into the matter.   Explanations—memoranda—notes—recapitulations, and botherations of all kinds passed between the parties in the quarrel and their representatives.   Finally, everybody was "satisfied."   But to this hour it is the opinion of Fitz-Gubin that Malta is a d—d hole !

CRUISE OF THE IDA.

FROM COLBURN'S UNITED SERVICE MAGAZINE FOR APRIL.

CHAPTER I.

HOME.

I LOOK upon money," said my father, filling out for himself a glass of port wine, and pushing the decanter towards me, " to be the root of all evil."

" The love of it, you mean ?" said my mother, with that meek, inquiring smile with which she was wont to question the paradoxes put forth by her better half.

" The want of it, by Jove, Sir, 'the *res angusta domi,*' is unquestionably far more prolific of real misfortune," interrupted I, with all the pertness of a youngster.

"Make money honestly, if you can, my boy," replied my father. " If you can't, I would not recommend the ' *quocunque modo.*' It will be quite the same to you, a hundred years from this day, whether you were clothed in purple and fine linen, and drove down in your carriage to ' the House,' listened to a few drowsy speeches, and returned to a sumptuous banquet in Belgravia ; or whether you swept a crossing for sixpence a day, and dined off broken victuals, the tenant in common of a lodging in St. Giles'. You won't fare a bit the worse in the next world because you are poor in this."

" Ah !" said my mother, "that is all very well, once we get *there;* but does it not make some difference while we are *here?* You would not be sitting in that comfortable arm-chair, beside that cheerful fire, and beside me, if you had nothing but a crossing to sweep."

" I think, Sir, it is Lord Bacon who says : ·'There can be no stronger proof of the slender value which Providence sets upon money, than the sort of people he gives it to ;' but at the same time, I am rather inclined to agree with my mother, that a deficiency in the commodity is a much worse thing than too much of it."

"Pish !" replied my father, cracking a filbert, and adjusting his napkin across his knees, "the subject is one not unworthy of grave discussion ; much can be said on both sides. The influence money has upon the destinies of man-kind—whether in the individual or the abstract—is all-important. A scrutiny into the pecuniary dealings of any one person, from the cradle to the grave, would not only be a complete history of his life, but when we come to con-sider the vices and the virtues with which it is connected—dishonesty, extravagance, intemperance, profligacy, frugal-ity, and self-denial,—the corruption that follows upon the love of it, the industry which is sweetened by its acquisi-tion, the vicissitudes that follow in its train—there can be no doubt that such an investigation would hold a perfect mirror up to nature, and exhibit the man as he really is behind the scenes, not as he moves and plays his part before the public, on the great stage of human life."

My mother looked upon her lord with an admiring eye, as he refreshed his eloquence with another glass of the generous liquid, gave a preparatory "*hem,*" and continued—

"'Blessed is the rich that is found without blemish, and hath not gone after gold.' There are few who come within the range of this benediction ; a thousand temptations—a thousand snares—beset his path who is born to opulence ; wealth will alter his mind—the desire of gain grows by

what it feeds on—it is seldom associated with nobler
objects; and I look upon the mercantile spirit of the age,
I mean the mere investment of money, for the sake of repro-
duction, to be one of the strongest and most fatal signs of
the utter degeneracy of the times. Therefore, my son, I
think it is just as well for you, whether as regards your
temporal or your eternal welfare, that you will not inherit
anything from me; the best patrimony I can leave you, is
a true heart, a good education, and a strong will. Let these
temper the edge of that sword with which you will carve
your way through the battle of life. You will find the
road open to you, as easily as the oyster of ancient Pistol,
or this filbert which I split with my knife."

Having thus concluded his discourse, my father carefully
raked the under-bar of the fire, upon which he threw a fresh
faggot of log-firs, and having crossed his legs and folded up
the napkin that lay on his knee, he leaned back in his easy
chair, and went off into a gentle slumber.

Let us take a glance at him, reader, as he is enjoying his
post-prandial nap. There are no candles upon the square,
small, old-fashioned table, with its quaintly carved legs,
which stands upon the hearth-rug. Nor is there any other
light in the room, save that emitted from the ample fire,
whose flashing rays, dancing up the chimney, threw out in
strong relief the outlines of the form reposing in the old
arm-chair. It was that of a large, powerfully-built, and
handsome man, in the decline of life; a few thin silver
hairs were all that remained around the temples, and the
features, even in repose, seemed strongly marked by the
traces of care as well as of years—well might they—but
with the vicissitudes of his life, these pages have little
to do.

I have set down the conversation just recorded, in order
to show my father's nature; it will be sufficient to demou-

strate that slender regard he attached to those objects for
which the generality of men so eagerly strive. Of a careless, frank, and confiding nature, his easiness of temper had
been his besetting sin. Having allowed himself to become
involved as surety for some distant relations, he was left to
pay the penalty of his imprudence; and, although of our
family property a sufficient margin still remained to afford
even the comforts of life, his income was reduced to little
more than half of what it originally had been. My eldest
brother had been brought up to the bar, where he was
slowly but surely wending his way to independence.

I had been educated at home, under the eye of my father,
who, although a simple-minded man in some respects, was a
ripe and elegant scholar. Being of a contemplative nature,
I had long brooded over the difficulties in which my family
were involved, and I had meditated endeavoring to push
my fortunes in some mysterious way, as the tales and histo-
ries with which I was familiar had taught me people did in
the olden time. My passion for reading was intense, and ·
plays, voyages, and travels, were my principal studies ; and
I had almost by heart, Captain Bligh's narrative of his voyage to the South Sea Islands, and his account of the mutiny
of the crew. Our library was a tolerably extensive one,
and afforded ample materials for the indulgence of my favorite taste. But in time I had exhausted these—and, so insa-
tiable was my appetite, that I seized upon every occasion
for borrowing and collecting other books, and every leisure
moment for reading them. Those in which our library was
deficient I generally procured at Silverthorne, where one of
my mother's sisters resided, whose husband, Sir William
Herbert, a distinguished officer, had amassed a considerable
fortune in the East Indies. They had only one child ; my
cousin, Lucy, had been my constant associate almost as
long as I can remember. She was a beautiful creature,

with large blue eyes, and the sweetest smile it is possible to
conceive. If childhood could have found a voice to reveal
its dawning passions, the feelings I from the first entertained
for my cousin, would have been called love ; but, as it was,
our intimacy was only regarded by most of the members of
our respective families as the natural result of our near re-
lationship. Thus my early youth glided on, happy and
undisturbed, save by the family cares at which I have
already hinted. Of my father, save in the mornings and
evenings, I saw but little ; he passed his whole days surrounded by his books. But Lucy and I were inseparable ;
we had lived through and were now past that epoch of
our lives when it had been necessary to watch over us with
unremitting attention. Our great delight was to wander
together, at earliest dawn, through the woods and gardens
surrounding the old hall. We have often, hand-in-hand,
beheld the rising of the sun—we have watched rejoicing
nature reviving under its influence. Those early hours
•were so many additional ones that we could add to our
accustomed periods of recreation ; and although we had
now arrived at an age when such a constant intimacy might
have been considered objectionable to our respective relatives, no exception was ever taken, nor did I fully compre-
hend then the smiles of peculiar meaning with which my
mother would regard us, when she saw us returning hand-
in-hand from some of our pleasant woodland rambles. Of
her I must say a few words.

At fifty years of age, my mother still retained many
traces of that beauty by which she was pre-eminently distinguished. She was slight and delicate, with large dark
eyes and a fair brow, over which her hair parted, which
had prematurely become gray. The quiet self-possession
and easy grace of her manner, as she sat intrenched beside
her little work-table, occupied with some of those little

nameless employments that tend to the dissipation of female leisure, would have, at a glance, convinced the most care-less spectator that she was of gentle breeding. Descended from a family, the various members of which had, in their day, done the state good service, she had brought my father little save the charm of her beauty and the affectionate soli-citude which had lightened many a sorrow and relieved the darkest and most cloudy days. She was, indeed, the gen-tlest of beings. My mother's relatives had occupied distin-guished posts, some of them were still high in office, and such interest as they possessed had been from time to time enlisted in my favor. But whether the army, the navy, or the foreign office, was to be my destination, remained a mystery, which had yet to be decided. This brief retro-spect will be sufficient to acquaint my readers with a suffi-cient portion of my previous history to enable them to un-derstand the posture of affairs, as they stood when I intro-duced myself to their notice.

Redburn Hall, where we resided, was an old-fashioned house with many gables. It stood in the centre of an am-phitheatre of hills, open to the south, where it commanded an extensive view of rich woodland scenery. The lawn, which lay to one side, terminated in terraced flower gar-dens, which had once been extensive and trimly kept, but were now reduced to half their original dimensions by the encroachment of the woods, which seem to have been allowed to grow in upon them. The lawn was almost swept by the hanging branches of the oak and laburnum. And among the flowers of the parterre, the wild rose and anemone mingled, with a profusion which afforded abundant evidence that the care of the gardener was not now restrict-ed to the legitimate objects of his jurisdiction.

From the further extremity of this piece of pleasure ground, walks branched away through the woods, some leading to the village which was distant about a mile, others to the farm, and others, more dark and shady, through glades overgrown with tangled brushwood, which, in summer, were fragrant with the clematis and woodbine— far away into the hills of the upper park which lay in the distance.

Times had changed, and with them the hall, but it was a comfortable old-fashioned English residence, still keeping up to the rest, of a rather slender ability, its former reputation for hospitality. It had for several hundred years been the hereditary residence of our family, of which my father was now the representative. I was called Charles, after a great uncle, by my mother's side. Of my childish life, the little I remember, it is not necessary to recapitulate here, more than I have already done. I had been carefully educated under the eye parental, and the course of reading which I have already described, had stored my mind with a species of knowledge very different from the ordinary run of information possessed by boys of my own age. Of my brother, George, I know but little; being many years older than myself, he was at school when I was still in the nursery, and during the vacations he occasionally passed at the hall, I was frequently absent on visits at my uncle's residence.

It was a crisp, bracing morning, in early autumn, and we were all seated in the library, awaiting the advent of my father, ere we sat down to breakfast—for it was a rule in our household, that the morning meal should invariably be enjoyed together. The urn was hissing upon the table, my mother sat behind the tea-cups, looking towards the door, and I was occupied in airing at the fire the county paper, when my father made his appearance with an open letter in his hand.

"News, my dear," he said, as he took his accustomed seat near the fire

" From George ?" inquired my mother.

" No," said my father, " you are all astray."

" From Silverthorne, then ?"

" You must guess again," my father said, with rather a portentous expression of countenance.

" Good heavens ! then I hope there is nothing wrong ;" for the momentary shadow, as it flitted past, had not escaped my mother's anxious eye.

" There is nothing wrong ; give me my tea, and you shall hear all about it."

His cup of bohea having been handed to him, my father pushed the letter across the table. No sooner had the tea-maker perused the document than her countenance fell. That letter contained my future fate. It conveyed an inti-mation that I was appointed to a frigate, then fitting out at Portsmouth for foreign service.

" It cannot be possible," my mother said, taking off her spectacles, which had somehow, all of a sudden, grown very dim.

" Possible ! It is true. Charley, you are now Her Ma-jesty's property. Remember my precepts, boy ; and when I am occupying an humble tenement, you may perhaps sleep in Westminster Abbey."

" I'd rather have him at home, in the old blue room. Why, he's a child, quite a child;" my mother said, now bursting fairly into tears.

" Pish !" said my father ; "nonsense, the boy will do his duty ; won't you, Charley ?"

" I will try, sir," I said, with a gulp intended to keep down a lump which seemed rising in my throat—it was the buttered toast—I didn't feel sorry then—the deuce a bit.

" There is no time to be lost ; the vessel sails within a fortnight, and you must be rigged out from top to toe," my father said, rubbing his hands ; for any little excitement always sent the old gentleman into a perfect fever of spirits, and so long as there was anything to be bought, or any expense to be incurred, he was perfectly happy ; but when the time arrived for payment, his spirits were by no means so good.

"God's will be done. But the blow is a sudden one," my mother said, drying her tears, and impressing a kiss upon my curly head, which made that accursed toast rise in my throat once more.

The notice was indeed somewhat of the shortest, and it is quite possible I should have given way a little, had I not, a few days previously, been engaged in an animated discussion with my cousin, during which she expressed her admiration of naval heroism, in a manner that inspired me with the strongest determination to be a Nelson, at the very least ; but now that the die was irrevocably cast, in which the fate of my future life was to be moulded—now that I was about to go away from the old familiar scenes among which my youth had been past—I felt my ambition to become a hero begin, like the courage of Bob Acres, to ooze gradually out of my fingers' ends.

No period of time in my life, perhaps, ever passed so rapidly as that which intervened between the arrival of the portentous letter and my departure from home. We were busily engaged, morning, noon, and night, in the necessary preparations. The whole house was turned topsy-turvy, and we had scarcely even time for our meals. There was a country town in the neighborhood which supplied some of the articles which were requisite ; but the greater proportion had, of course, to be fetched from London ; and, what with the arrival of packing-cases and the opening of them, the inspection of portmanteaus, the making of shirts, the superintendence of stockings and other kinds of fleecy hosiery, all parties concerned found active occupation, and managed almost to forget in the evening, devoted to their respective tasks, the approaching event that had caused this commotion. Lucy, too,·had come over from Silverthorne, and flitted to and fro like a fairy. She made me a huge pincushion, with pink rosettes at the corners, which I have got to this day, but which was rather an unnecessary appendage at that time. She laughed and cried by turns, and made herself, in a small way, as busy as the rest, until the setting of the last sun which shone upon my boyish career at the old hall.

Until the final moment for departure was so nearly at hand I could scarcely realize to myself the idea that I was about to leave all those things to which I was attached by so many ties of affection. As we were returning from our last stroll through one of those well-known glades, Lucy and I wept along in silence. There, underneath an old oak tree, my cousin threw her arms around my neck, and promised me, for the first time, her faithful, fond, and unalterable love. She had never before, during the long term of our happy intercourse, thus spoken to me, and yet, even then, an unknown feeling of doubt and desponding—a strange, unaccountable foreboding—struck a sudden chill upon me, as I clasped her to my heart. "Ah! Lucy," I said, "I shall soon be far away; when I am gone, and you are surrounded by others, you will soon cease to think of me." "Never!" she said. "I have never known, I have never loved any but you; it is only now that we are about to part, I have discovered how exceedingly dear you are. When you come back, I shall be a woman; but my heart can know no change to you." I kissed her in silence, and her head rested on my heart as she murmured, "You can have no fortune, but mine will be more than enough for us. When you come—if you love me—then you have but to claim me, and I will be yours for ever." ·

With the thrill of unutterable happiness which I felt at
these words, there mingled once more the same strange
foreboding.

"Will you write to me sometimes, Lucy? Will you only
remember that it will make me so happy?"

"I will; take this little ring, wear it always for my sake,
and when you look at it, you will always remember me."

With all the ardor of boyish passion I pressed her to my
heart, and we returned for the last time to the hall. That
was our farewell meeting.

Cʜᴀᴘᴛᴇʀ II.

Pᴏʀᴛsᴍᴏᴜᴛʜ.

Tʜᴇ George Hotel was full of life and bustle as the post-
chaise, containing my father and me, drove up to the door.
The activity which pervaded that well-known establishment,
the sunshine and the happy looks of men, contrasted
strangely with the oppressive feeling which had, at times,
weighed heavily upon my spirits during the journey. I
have purposely passed over all the farewell scenes, not that
I am unable to describe them, for they come back upon my
memory now as clearly and as full of distinctness as any
incidents in my whole career, but because I do not wish to
trouble my readers with what can have but little bearing
upon the course of my history. Dinner was ordered, of
which, when it appeared, I partook with a hearty appetite,
notwithstanding my sorrows. In this I followed the example of my father, although he affected to belong to that
school of philosophy which is above being disturbed by
trifles. I had observation enough to perceive he was not
unmoved by our approaching separation. How well I

remember that dinner. Whether it was because I had
never dined in a hotel before or not, I am unable to say,
but there was not a single dish appeared which at this
moment I could not enumerate. I imagined everything,
too, had a sort of maritime look about it. The waiter suggested to me the idea of a retired seaman, which for aught
I can tell he may have been ; and the whole establishment,
excellent as it was of its kind, smacked somewhat of that
pursuit in which I was so soon to engage, I thought. We
dined in the coffee-room, of which, at first, we were the only
occupants ; but the cloth had not long been removed, and
we were sitting with a decanter of port—the best that the
George could produce—on a table before us, when four
gentlemen entered and took their seats at a table which
had apparently been prepared for their reception.

"Did you put the champagne in ice, as I bid you,
Joseph ?" said the youngest of the party, who might be
some two years older than myself.

" Yes, sir," with deferential politeness, said the waiter,
who seemed old enough, at the very least, to be the father
of the querist.

"Dinner, then, as soon as possible. '

While my father was finishing his, bottle of port, I occupied myself by scrutinizing the strangers. However erro-
neous may have been the opinion I had entertained about
the waiter, as to the new comers there could be no mistake
of any kind. They were certainly of the naval profession,
and, for aught I could tell, they might be men of considerable eminence, although the manner in which they spoke of
the dinner tended by no means to impress me with an elevated idea of the estimation in which they held it.

" Did you dine with the Port Admiral on Thursday,
Staunton ?" said the youth who had evinced his anxiety
about the champagne.

8

"No; his feeds are bad—everything cold but the wine, and that's as hot as the devil," was Mr. Staunton's rejoinder.

"Can't be worse than we are on board," said the first speaker, as he tossed off a bumper of wine.

"What can a youngster like you know about the matter? You can't tell a good feed from a bad one, Ellis."

"Can't I, though? I like this better than cold pork, and I prefer champagne to three-finger grog," replied Mr. Ellis, in the tone of a deeply injured man.

"The service is going to the devil; give me another slice of that mackerel," said one of the party, who had not before spoken. He was a mild-looking youth, with curly hair and light-blue eyes.

"That it is," replied Mr. Staunton.

"You seem fond of mackerel," said another of the party.

"Very," responded the gentleman thus addressed, who, I was shocked to perceive, used his knife upon the occasion.

"Take my advice, then, and try the tail."

"I will," said the youngster, "if you'll have the kindness to hand it over."

"Not that way," said the connoisseur in fish; "don't cut the tail off. So—pass your knife under and slide it gently up to the head."

"Oh," said Staunton, "that's the way, is it? Here goes then."

"Now, before you go any farther, let me give you a second piece of advice."

"What's that?"

"The next time, don't be green enough to let any one persuade you you don't know how to eat a mackerel; go on, I wish you a good appetite."

The young fellow thus addressed, feeling that he was "sold," laid down his knife and fork, and staring at the speaker, exclaimed—"For half a farthing I'd make you eat it, and begin at the head; mind your own business, can't you, and leave me to mind mine?"

"Take a glass of wine with me, my boy, and don't put yourself in a passion about nothing."

Such is an average specimen of the conversation which took place at the adjoining table; jokes of a like nature seemed the order of the day, and each moment the merriment of the party waxed louder and more boisterous. My father and I exchanged glances, and sat silent, but not unobservant spectators.

"We are bound for the east, I believe?" the gentleman said who was named Staunton.

"So I hear," responded Ellis.

"Well, we shall have only one more dinner on shore, so let's make the most of our time."

"The deuce, when do we sail then?" inquired the mackerel-eater.

"You may sail when you please, but the Ida sails on Tuesday," said Staunton sententiously.

The dinner, which had been protracted through its various stages, was at last concluded, the cloth was removed, a plentiful supply of claret, with a handsome dessert, was placed upon the table, and the party drank and laughed and "chaffed" each other with the most boisterous good humor. Staunton told droll stories, sang droll songs, and pushed the bottle backwards and forwards, making noise enough for a half dozen; so, what with laughing, and talking, and drinking, the scene grew too noisy to afford any farther amusement, and we prepared to retire to our respective apartments.

"Charley, my boy," my father said, as we proceeded up stairs, "what do you think of your shipmates?"

"A noisy set of fellows enough, sir," I said.

"I hope the first time you dine together, you will let
them see you know the head of a mackerel from the tail,"
my father said, with an air of quiet raillery, as he bade me
good night.

The next morning we waited on the captain, to show we
had a letter of introduction from my uncle. My father sent
up his card, and was at once admitted. Captain Deadeye
was a fat man, with a red face, broad shoulders, and, what
is vulgarly called, a paunch. He had a tight look about
him, as if all the blood in his body was squeezed up into his
head, which appearance was probably produced by a stiff
military stock he wore ; he was attired in a somewhat faded
uniform ; he was unbuttoned, and his trousers seemed very
much too wide for him. He received us with great cordiality, and begged us to be seated.

"You have come in good time ; we sail the day after to-
morrow."

"Indeed," said my father. "Allow me to introduce my
son to you."

Captain Deadeye then shook hands with me. "1 hope
the youngster will do you credit," he said, with a grim
smile ; "if he only makes as good a sailor as his uncle, he'll
do." This was encouragement ; and I expressed my ac-
knowledgments by a blush, which I endeavored in vain to
repress.

"This being your last day, we shall not occupy your
time further, Captain Deadeye ; I wished only to make the
boy known to you before he went on board," my father said,
preparing to take his leave.

"Not a bit ; I never put off things to the last moment,
so I've got plenty of time on hand ; but if you'll dine with
me here at seven, I shall be delighted ; your son will then
have an opportunity of becoming acquainted with some of
his messmates."

My father promised his assent, and we withdrew from the great man's presence, rather favorably impressed by the result of our interview.

We passed the remainder of the morning in wandering about the town, and inspecting such lions as the place contained. We visited the dock-yard, walked down to the pier, and saw the steamers, which plied to and fro to Ryde, whose white houses, ranged tier above tier, sparkled in the autumn sunshine. To me, however, the most interesting object of contemplation was the old "Victory," about which I had heard and read so much ; there she lay, a sheer hulk ; that old vessel, which had carried the thunders of England through so many a storm of fight. How tremendous she must have been once. How helpless she looks now, for the shirts and other garments, which were hung upon lines to dry, fluttered in the breeze, and gave the gallant old ship more the appearance of a floating laundry than anything else.

Having inspected the docks and the neighborhood, we strolled until it was time to go and dress for dinner. The captain, upon our arrival, received us with a cordial welcome, and introduced us to such of the company as had already assembled ; among them were two of the young gentlemen who had dined in the coffee-room of the George upon the previous day, to whom I was gravely introduced. "I like to make my officers acquainted with each other, if I can, before they go on board ; you'll see some more of them by and by." I was then presented to Mrs. Deadeye, and afterwards to her daughter ; and the remainder of the guests soon arriving, dinner was announced, and, marshalled in due order, we proceeded down a flight of somewhat narrow stairs, which led to the place of entertainment.

With the exception of a gentleman in a white tie and a suit of unexceptionable sables, whom I rightly conjectured to be a clergyman, the remainder of the male portion of the party, my father, of course, also excluded, were of the sea-faring order. Captain Deadeye was in high feather, and though he struck me as being deficient in that polish which I should have expected a man of his rank to possess, he seemed very good-natured ; and for so great a man, (for at that time I would have regarded a prime-minister with a good deal less awe,) I thought him affable and condescend-ing to a degree. His better half was a buxom woman of forty-five or thereabouts ; and of their daughter Julia, all that I can say is, that any comparison between her and my fair cousin would have been infinitely to the disadvantage of the former.

When we were fairly seated at the table, and the first clatter of plates, knives, and glasses had subsided, the soup being removed, and the sherry handed round, I had more time to observe the company who were then and there as-sembled.

The first lieutenant sat nearly opposite to me : he was a bluff weather-beaten person, verging upon forty, with a cast of countenance which expressed, as strongly as a face can, the strong resolution and determination of his nature. In person, he was short and thick set ; and having suffered se-verely from the small-pox during his infancy, Mr. Morris was not, by any means, what could be called a handsome man.

The second lieutenant impressed me less favorably than his senior : he was rather better-looking, but he had a pee-vish and irascible air about him ; his voice was singularly harsh and forbidding, and his tone dictatorial enough for an admiral, at the least.

In the persons of two other guests I recognized, as I have already said, members of the dinner-party at the George on the preceding day, and with them, ladies, whose names I could not learn, and my father and myself—such was our party.

The conversation turned chiefly upon nautical matters, and the second lieutenant monopolized the conversation, I thought, rather more than was consistent with my ideas of good breeding. The midshipmen paid delicate attentions to the young ladies, and drank as much wine as they could get hold of without attracting public observation.

Of the captain's conversation I could not hear much; it was shared for the most part between my father, who sat on one side of him, and an elderly gentlewoman, splendidly arrayed in green satin, who sat upon the other.

Upon the whole I was not sorry when the banquet, which appeared to me to be protracted to an unusual extent, had terminated; and it was with unfeigned satisfaction that I found myself again in the drawing-room, when the captain's lady took kindly notice of my forlorn condition, and inquired after my mother, asked if I had any sisters, and whether I liked the idea of going to sea.

When I sought my pillow that night and fell asleep, what a confused train of disjointed images tumbled as it were through my brain. I thought of Lucy—then she suddenly changed into Mrs. Deadeye—with whom I thought I was on the eve of something like matrimony, in the village church near the old hall; while a post-chaise with four horses was waiting to convey us on a hymeneal expedition into North Wales. This dream was so awful that I wakened suddenly, but it was only to fall asleep again, and dream of things still more strange and appalling, which I shall not stay and set down here.

Chapter III.

The Ida.

There was a heavy drizzling rain falling, and it blew a stiffish breeze, when at the appointed hour we set out in the captain's barge for the ship, which was lying at some distance. My father would see the last of me, he said, so he accompanied me on board, when we parted. To describe the feeling of desolation which came over me, when I saw him re-enter the boat, would be impossible ; a melancholy foreboding was on my mind that I should see the old man no more; and, as I leaned over the side of the gigantic vessel, to watch the boat now rapidly receding in the distance, I felt that ere long I would vainly sigh for the tranquil scene of my early years, and regret the hour when I had been tempted to forsake them. I never felt more deeply the strength of the ties which bound my heart to my old home than I did at that moment, but it was too late for regret. The past was beyond recall. All that remained for me to do was to endeavor to profit by those lessons of wisdom, which had so often been impressed upon my mind ; and something like the feeling came at last to my mind, that even should I utterly fail in my duty, it would not be for any want of energetic determination on my·part to fulfil it.

When I looked about me, the uproar and confusion which prevailed upon deck were beyond anything I could have imagined ; officers were thundering forth their orders to a confused crowd of seamen, in a language which seemed to me utterly unintelligible. The men were rushing to and fro, tumbling about in all directions, and cursing vociferously. A number of strangers and women, who, having received permission to come on board to see their relations, were still lingering, seemed in everybody's way.

I spoke to some of the people near me, but they were too busily engaged to pay attention, nor did they even seem to understand what I was saying; and during the greater part of the forenoon I remained in this forlon condition, until at last I succeeded in discovering a quiet corner where I could rest my aching head, and recover the possession of my wandering senses.

After some hours of active exertion, the officer in command at last succeeded in getting things in some degree to rights. The deck was cleared of the strangers who had come on board, and the boats from shore, in a perfect flotilla, by which the Ida had been surrounded, gradually disappeared towards evening. The captain came on board, attired in full uniform; he was received by the two senior officers, and in a short time afterwards orders were given to weigh anchor. I was cheered in some degree by the lively sound of the fife, and the animation of the active sailors—who worked at the windlass, and were springing about the rigging—was not without its effect in recovering my spirits. The wind was fresh and fair; the evening cleared; and the Ida glided from her moorings, saluted from the shore and from the ships we passed, by loud cheers, which were repaid with interest by our crew.

It is a rare sight, and no novice has ever seen it for the first time without emotion, to witness the departure of one of these great bulwarks of our national glory, thus setting forth upon her adventurous career; a thousand hearts, ready to brave the battle-fire or the wreck, are beating within her, and look upon their native land, may be, for the last time. They go forth in the pride of hope, they dream but little of the fury of the storm, the crash of battle, or

the home which may await them in the unfathomed caverns
of the great deep. Their hearts beat high with confidence
and with joy ; and of the two, the feelings of those on
shore are perhaps less to be envied than the adventurous
sailors.   •

Occupied by reflections such as these, it was some time
before I mustered up resolution to inspect the quarters
which had been allotted to me.   Having at length found a
sailor who appeared sufficiently unoccupied to warrant me
in requesting his guidance, I was shown the way down a
ladder into a dark region between decks, where, in the fore-
part of the vessel, the midshipmen's berth was situated
The domain at first sight seemed by no means an agreeable
residence, nor did a further inspection tend to increase its
attractions.   The greater portion of the room was taken up
by a deal table, above which was suspended a lamp.   The
table-cloth was spread as if for supper, and the clatter of
plates somewhere in the neighborhood indicated that preparations were on foot for that repast.   My allotted seat being
pointed out to me, I saw nothing better to do than to sit
down and occupy it—which I did accordingly, marvelling
much at the miserable accommodation which her gracious ⸗
Majesty was pleased to afford to the officers in her service.

I do not remember ever feeling more profoundly miserable than I did at that moment.   The spot I occupied, from
the culinary preparations which were going forward, began
soon to be invaded by a combination of savory odors, which,
in that close atmosphere, was very far from agreeable.   To
eat, I felt, would be quite out of the question ; had 1 known,
then, the comfort to be derived from tobacco, I should, in
all probability, have solaced myself with a pipe ; but that
was an anodyne as yet unknown to me.   I felt a dejection
of spirits and a sense of misery it would be impossible to

describe.   I wished heartily I had never left home, and I
felt so entirely down on my luck, that I would have willingly exchanged situations with old Joe Harvey, my father's
gardener.   I was soon, however, aroused from my dreamy
reflections by the appearance of supper, simultaneously with
which my new associates came tumbling in—with some of
whom the reader is already acquainted.   They were eight
in number, and, when seated, were quite sufficient to fill the
room. . I was introduced in succession to each of them, by
my friends of the preceding day, and we soon became on
excellent terms.   I was let into all the secrets of the mess,
down even to the rogueries of the purser.   The peculiar
idiosyncrasies of the captain, as well as of the first lieutenant, were explained to me in a few graphic touches.

My companions addressed themselves at first so vigorously to the evening repast, that they found but little leisure for the exercise of their conversational powers.   The
viands disappeared with a celerity which seemed marvellous.
The empty dishes were cleared away, the allowance of grog
was placed on the festive board, and at length, with one
consent, the tongues of the company were unloosed.

" I say, old fellow," said a messmate, whom they called
Hamilton, " why do they keep secret where we are bound
for such a deuce of a mystery ?"

" It's no mystery at all.   We are to cruise awhile in the
Indian Ocean."

" Why did Deadeye look so d—d important, then, when
we talked about it the other day at dinner ?"

" That's not it ; I'm in the secret," said the little mackerel-eater, whose name was Ashton.

" Holloo, let us hear what the boy has to say.   Now then,
Ashton, out with it !"

" He knows no more than Adam," broke in Hamilton.

" Not half so much, perhaps," said Ellis.

" Do you think old Deadeye knows himself ?" suggested another.

" I tell you, I know," persisted Ashton.

" Why the devil don't you tell it, then·?"

"Stop his grog until he does," shouted Ellis ; and the glass which contained that liquor, whereof Ashton was drinking, was seized upon forthwith.

" Now then, out with it, as Mrs. Brówn said to her son when he swallowed a farthing," thundered Arbuthnǫt, who was the wit of the midshipman's ward.

" We're going to hunt down the Malay pirates," said Ashton, compelled by this powerful process to reveal his secret.

" Who told you that, Spooney ?"

" My uncle heard it from a friend, who has a connection with the Admiralty."

"The Admiralty be d—d ; give him back his grog ; he knows nothing about it."

" I thought I heard Captain Deadeye whispering to my father somerhing about China," mildly suggested I, breaking silence for the first time.

" That's nearer the mark, somewhat," said Hamilton.

" What's the difference between the Chinese and the Malays, I should like to know ?" said the little mackerel eater, who, having swallowed at a single draught the entire of his grog, had now regained his confidence.

" Ashton, were you ever at school ?"

" To be sure I was."

" Were you ever flogged ?"

" Generally speaking, about once a week."

"Then they should have done it once a day, and you might have known something ; as it is, Heaven help you! you are little better than a donkey."

" Poor devil ! don't bully him so infernally," Hamilton said, smiling kindly on the benighted midshipman.

"What sort of a fellow is Morris, the first lieutenant—does any one know anything about him?" inquired one of my messmates.

"Don't speak so loud, or he may happen to hear you. He's on deck with òld Deadeye, looking out for squalls: I saw him as I came down."

"I don't know, I never saw him in my life before until I met him at dinner; he seems a very good-natured sort of muff.".

"He's a Scotchman," said Hamilton.

"The deuce he is; I don't like that; I sailed with a Sawney once, and he was next door to a brute."

"Morris looks like a tartar."

"So does his wife—she dined at Deadeye's."

"Wife! what business has a lieutenant with a wife? I should like to be informed of that."

"She had red hair, and eyes like a ferret, and put me altogether in mind of a dose of Epsom salts."

A roar of laughter followed this sally, in the midst of which the door opened, and the fortunate proprietor of this exquisite object of wedded endearment put his head into the room.

"Less noise if you please, gentlemen; Captain Deadeye is extremely surprised at such a disturbance."

"Has he heard us, do you think?" whispered Hamilton, as the door closed upon the first lieutenant.

"Of course he has; he is easy in his mind, at any rate, in one respect."

"And what may that be?"

"Why, that you are not in love with his wife."

"No; my affections are unalterably plighted to another."

"Who may she be?"

"I'll tell you if you won't try to cut me out."

" Certainly not."

" I'm afraid of you."

" What, is the fair creature on board ?"

" I wish she was."

" How, then, can I interfere with your prospects, most cautious Paddy ?"

" It's Julia Deadeye."

" What ! the little girl who squints ?"

" She doesn't squint, and she'll have ten thousand pounds. I'll marry her when I return—retire from the service, and keep a pack of hounds."

" You had better learn to sail first ; do you remember our excursion to Hampstead ?"

" What happened ?" inquired Ellis.

" He rode over a respectable elderly lady, and he shortly afterwards broke the horse's knees."

I have recorded this conversation, not from any exaggerated notion of its importance, but because it affords an average sample of our daily topics of discussion. Of my messmates, the only one for whom I felt, upon putting a question, I could conceive any feeling akin to regard, was Hamilton. His appearance was singularly prepossessing. He was tall and rather strongly built ; his chiselled features, flowing, light brown hair, and graceful figure, would of themselves have arrested my attention ; but what made the greatest impression upon me, was a good-humored and genial expression, which indicated the kindness of his nature. We spent the evening pleasantly enough together, but I was not sorry when bed-time arrived. Hamilton showed me how to get into my hammock, and laughed heartily when he saw me rolling round and tumble out on the other side ; by his assistance I contrived to regain my position, when sleep soon came to steal away my wretchedness ; and I wakened the next morning, thinking I was still at Heathfield Hall. When I went on deck, I found the weather thick and squally, and through the cold, miserable haze of a November day, I saw the Needle Rocks, the high cliffs at the back of the Isle of Wight, far in the distance, and receding gradually until they became a mere outline : all the noise and hurry of departure had subsided into the reality of a trackless expanse of sea.

From that time forth I began to pay strict attention to learning the details of my duty. I studied drawing and navigation, and read eagerly everything I could lay my hands on, that had any bearing on my profession. I soon acquired the favor of the first lieutenant, before I had been many weeks on board, by the strict attention I paid to the little duties he gave me to perform. I had been put into a watch and stationed in the foretop, and quartered at the foremost guns on the main deck. Although I had been told by the youngsters that Mr. Morris was a bearish, surly, and villainous Scotchman, I never experienced anything but kindness from him ; his manners, even when under the strongest excitement, were uniformly those of a gentleman, and he was always ready to impart to me such information as he possessed upon such affairs. With the second in command, however, I was not so fortunate ; his sole delight appeared to be in inflicting every possible species of annoyance upon those who were so unfortunate as to be placed under his control. He was of a nature naturally mean, and although he had bowed and fawned himself into the good graces of the captain, boy as I was, I had little difficulty in perceiving that neither with my messmates, nor with the crew, was he by any means a favorite.

CHAPTER IV.

MY FIRST ADVENTURE.

I MUST leave to the imagination of my readers the suffer-ings which, for the first few days, I underwent. It was a considerable period before I obtained the use of what are technically called my sea legs ; and as to eating, Lord bless me ! the recollection of my endeavors to swallow the salt beef and potatoes haunts me to this day. Long after the first terrible sensation had passed, my aversion to food still continued. Whether it was the earliness of the hour, or the disagreeable sights and smells by which I was assailed, which usually act as a check upon all appetites fresh from shore, I shall not pause to determine ; but it was not with-out great difficulty I at last prevailed upon myself to swal-low a morsel. The beverage was not less unpalatable than the food ; the black-strap, an awful mixture, tasting like sloe-juice and logwood, was only worse than the grog ; and whilst my messmates were imbibing their potations, I re-flected upon my new situation, not without considerable re-gret. I remember well how, notwithstanding all my enthu-siasm, and the aspirations after fame and adventure which had warmed my early life, my heart failed me as I contrast-ed my position with that which I had renounced. When I remembered the old house, with its light and pleasant aspect, the summer woods waving round it, and the perfume of the fresh flowers coming in through the open windows, and con-trasted those scenes with the gloomy hole in which I was cabined, cribbed and confined with the rough uneducated men, whose very language was a new dialect to me—with my noisy companions uttering their opinions upon all man-ner of subjects, of which I knew nothing ; when I con-

trasted all this with my old home, and my former associates, I must confess I felt a faintness of heart which was
most oppressive. Since these days, years have rolled away,
yet my early sufferings are still fresh in my memory ; nor
have the varied scenes through which I have passed oblite-
rated my recollection of them in the very least. I made
up my mind, however, and nerved myself, as well as I could,
for endurance. A midshipman's berth is about the last
place on earth suited to the indulgence of vain regrets. I
spent much of my time on deck. Scenes of adventure began once more to come back upon my mind ; and now that
we were on the broad bosom of the ocean, the regret for all
I had left behind, and the doubts and misgivings as to my
chances of success in the life I had entered upon, began to
give place to brighter.hopes. Our life was, for some time,
unvaried in its daily routine. In time I got accustomed to
the night watch, which at first I found rather a severe trial.
Gentlemen, who live at home at ease, and never leave their
comfortable beds, can have very little notion of the immense
discomfort in having to leave one's hammock at midnight,
to shiver for four mortal hours on deck in the wet and cold.
To this, however, like the rest, I soon became inured by
practice. The weather, after some time, set in very stormy.
A stiff south-wester was blowing, and as I paced the deck,
during the night watch, my reveries were interrupted by a
sudden splash, and a cry of "man overboard."

"Down with the buoy, and pipe the cutter away," sang
out the second lieutenant.

The order thus given was promptly executed. The cutter was lowered, and I jumped into it ; not a moment was
lost in getting out the oars, and lighted by the buoy, whose
lurid glare fell upon the heaving water, we pulled rapidly
towards the object of our search ; but, notwithstanding all
our exertions, so great had been the way upon the ship,

that some time elapsed before we could come up with our
beacon light. We shouted out the man's name, but all was
silent. "Is he a good swimmer?" I inquired.

"Lord love ye, sir, Bob Smith can swim like a duck, no
fear of him."

I thought I heard a faint cry·some distance to windward.
"Give way, my lads, I hear him on the starboard," sung
out the quartermaster, whose ear had caught the same
sound.

"Hark, sir! that is the captain's voice; I hear him hailing us."

"Have you found him?" sung out Captain Deadeye,
who, it would appear, had been roused by the tumult.

"No, sir!"

"You have got too far, I hear him on the larboard—pull
now with a will."

The boat's crew pulled like devils towards the spot indicated—we rested to listen, but not the faintest sound, save
the plashing of the waves and the drip of the oars, could be
distinguished.

"Hist!" exclaimed every one almost simultaneously, as a
faint wailing moan came floating on the waters from a spot
apparently quite close at hand. We strained every nerve and
soon reached it; but we could discover nothing. Again
we rested, and floated over the surface of the waves, whose
dark ridges, tipped with foam, shone like silver in the moonlight; at one moment we thought we heard the same cry,
but it proved to be only the wind whistling off the blade
of one of our upturned oars.

"By jingo! there he is," sung out the coxswain. And
there—no mistake this time, we heard a sound like some
one swimming.

"Call him by name," I said, my anxiety roused to the
very uttermost.

"Smith! Bob Smith! hilloa, my boy, hilloa!" sang out the coxswain, with the voice of a Stentor.

There was no reply.

"It is all up," the mate said, resting on his oars; "had we not better make for the ship?"

"Hark! there it is again."

"It is, by G— !" said the man who pulled the stroke oar.

"I hear nothing," said the coxswain.

"No more do I," said the stroke oar.

Whether it was fancy or not I am unable to say, but the voice of the last speaker seemed to my unpractised ear tremulous with some suppressed emotion. I looked at his resolute face, tanned by exposure to the sun and wind, but could detect nothing in its expression more than usual. It flashed upon me then—all that I had heard of the superstition of sailors; and I thought some nonsense of this kind might be weighing on the man's mind.

"Now, for another pull;" I said, "we may do better this time."

"You ain't a going to spend the night floating about here, sir, I hope," said the coxswain, touching his hat.

"Afraid of Bogy, are you?" replied the stroke oar, who was a native of the Emerald Isle.

"Obey your orders; we won't lose a chance, so long as I think one remains; put her head round and try to windward; if the man is so good a swimmer as you say, we shall have time yet."

The men bent to their oars, but, it was quite evident, no longer with the same inclination as heretofore; some mysterious influence, likely one superior to mine, was at work upon them.

"Here he is at last, I see him, close under the bow;" and, in my anxiety to clutch at what seemed the object of our search, I nearly tumbled overboard.

8*

Alas! it was only the poor fellow's hat, which, upon being lifted into the boat, was found to contain nothing but an old handkerchief, stuffed tightly into the crown.

We had not more than sufficient time to examine the contents of the hat, when our attention was attracted by what, beyond all question, seemed to be the missing seaman swimming rapidly towards us.

" Cheer up, my brave fellow, we'll have you on board in an instant !" pushing an oar towards him, as I thought.

Suddenly, however, the sound of swimming ceased, and the oar which I had extended no sooner touched the water than we were covered with a dash of spray which nearly swamped us ; the boat vibrated from stem to stern, and for an instant I thought it was going to pieces.

Not a soul spoke ; the men clutched eagerly at the sides, as if to steady the cutter, as she rocked to and fro ; their eyes were staring with terror ; big drops of perspiration were standing out like beads upon their corded foreheads.

" God of Heaven ! that accounts for poor Bob Smith," said the coxswain.

" What is it ?" I inquired, as I looked.

" A shark !—look, there he goes ;" and as I looked, I saw a dark object going rapidly through the water, near the surface, in a direction parallel to ours.

I gave an involuntary shudder, and enjoined silence to the men, whose fears seemed to have got the better of their reason.

" Ah ! no ; we must pull for our lives now, if we would ever reach the ship," said one of them.

" D—n her eyes !—where is she ? if she ha'n't left us in the lurch, after all, my name's not Brown," said the coxswain.

I jumped up and looked around ; but there, far as the eye could reach, lay one wide, trackless expanse of sea, broken only by the crests of the waves, as they gleamed in the wan moonlight; not a mast nor a sail, for miles around, was visible against the horizon.

"Now, then, for it, my men, with a will; unless you choose to spend the night here, you must pull for it."

"Ay, indeed," broke in the coxswain, "for there's a lubber down there will make acquaintance with some of us before very long."

I looked, as the man pointed, and it was with difficulty I refrained from an exclamation of horror, as I saw moving slowly beside us, just under the surface of the water, the same dark object—a long track of phosphorescent light followed like a gleaming meteor in its wake. Gracious Heaven, it was a shark!

At this crisis, the wind, which had blown in fitful gusts, began to fall; the moon, too, was overcast, and to add to our embarrassment, the men seemed by no means inclined to obey the orders of one whom they evidently considered a greenhorn, whose rashness had led them into their present peril.

"Silence!" I shouted; "pull steadily and together, or I'll report every man of you, when I get on board."

"And when 'll that be, I should like to know? We'll be aboard of Davy Jones's locker, afore long, I'm thinking," said the stroke oar in a surly tone.

Scarcely were the words out of his mouth, when a sudden jet of light streamed forth in the distance, followed by a loud report, which came booming heavily across the waters.

"Hurrah, the ship!" burst forth with a hearty cheer from the boat's crew—recalling them to their duty in an instant—the men pulled steadily for a considerable period, in the direction whence the sound proceeded; but although our exertions were indefatigable, and we were actually streaming with perspiration, we seemed to approach no

nearer to the object of our pursuit ; nothing was to be seen
but an apparently trackless expanse of sea and sky. Suddenly, another loud, rushing noise, like the roar of a cata-
ract, was heard to windward.

"Another gun," thought I ; but the water, which had
hitherto been so smooth, began to undulate with a sudden
motion, and a terrific hurricane, driving before it a sheet of
foam, came driving after us. There was little need for the
oars now ; we were swept before the tempest as you see a
withered leaf blown about in autumn. There was nothing
to be done but submit quietly to whatever end Fate had in
store for us. The spray was dashed in clouds of foam thick
enough to obscure anything around. The ocean appeared
to seethe like a boiling cauldron, while the heavens overhead loomed darkly down in one thick impenetrable pall.
The boat was already half full of water, which it required
incessant exertion to keep baling out. I fully expected
that we should go to the bottom every instant. This state
of painful suspense was too agonizing to endure much longer, and I felt it would soon be terminated one way or other.
I looked from the roaring water to the gloomy sky, and as
I thought of the foe who was following in our lee, like the
sailor in the Tempest, I would have sacrificed all my hopes
of future glory for an acre of barren heath and safety. The
faces of the crew, who had braved a hundred times battle
and wreck, were haggard with fear ; each man seemed certain that his hour was come ; and as for myself, I am not
ashamed to own, that in that terrible moment I breathed a
silent ejaculation to Heaven for mercy. The clouds, which
had been so long dashing down upon us, now burst ; a peal
of thunder, that was absolutely deafening, followed ; the
very flood-gates of heaven appeared to open ; the rain fell
in torrents ; the wind abated, and from the clouds, as they
were rent asunder, far up in the serene sky, the moon shone

forth in dazzling brilliancy, pouring a flood of serene light upon this scene of terror. No poet or musing lover ever welcomed that glorious light with more heartfelt joy and gratitude, for it revealed a sight for which we were little prepared. About half a mile distant, with studding sails set, and her canvas gleaming, like silver, in the moonlight, the Ida was rapidly bearing down upon us. A flash broke from her bows, and a loud report came booming over the waves. The boat's crew replied with a hearty cheer ; and I felt then, for the first time, that the bitterness of death was indeed past.

Chapter V.

An Enemy.

I pass over a considerable interval of time, which slipped by, unruffled by any incident save the monotonous routine of daily duty, to which I gradually became accustomed. After a most stormy voyage of several weeks, which strained the ship considerably, and entailed upon us the loss of some spars and sails, we found ourselves in the Indian Sea.. Our destination was no longer a secret ; we were to join the squadron engaged in hostile operations against China. We were passing through the Straits of Sunda, with a favorable breeze, when, just as the sun was going down, we caught sight of two small sails in the horizon. A thick fog coming on shortly afterwards, no more was thought of the matter. I had the middle watch. A light, drizzling rain was falling, and the ship was close-hauled, carrying royals. The men had made up their minds for a quiet night, during which reefing or furling would be unnecessary. Most of them were asleep wherever they could stow themselves away, and, I am sorry to confess,

⁎ ᴀs following their bad example, and dreaming, if I remem-
·er aright, of old scenes which I might never, perhaps, re-
visit any more, when I was suddenly disturbed by a sound
like the creaking of oars. ·I was awake in an instant, but
so entirely had my mind been occupied on other scenes that
for some time, I was under the impression that the soun?
had been an illusion. I thought, however, I might as well
look about me, and standing bolt upright, I peered forth.
It was time I did so, for nearly under our weather-bow,
about a cable's length distant, I saw two small sails, which
had evidently no business there, so I called out as loud as I
could bawl :

"Sail ho, close aboard !"

The first lieutenant was beside me in an instant; with
the practised eye of a seaman he saw at once what was to
hand.

"Keep the ship away ; keep her head off," he shouted to
the man at the wheel.

Round went the ship, and seizing a speaking-trumpet, he
shouted—

"All hands on deck—look alive !—the pirates are close
aboard us."

Every one was soon in motion. It is a remarkable fact
how wide-awake an English sailor becomes when he finds
there is any prospect of a row. The men came tumbling
up, most of them with nothing on but their shirts and trousers. We were going full before the wind ; and Captain
Deadeye's voice was soon heard, ordering the braces to be
laid aft, and the deck cleared for action.

Meantime, the strangers were no longer visible. I
thought we had distanced them, but soon I heard the
voice of Staunton exclaiming, with an oath, that they were
close under our weather-beam. Orders were given to ease
ship, which probably saved us from being boarded at this

moment. Meanwhile, everything was in readiness. The
guns had been shotted and run forward, loaded with grape
and canister. I saw a knot of men busy with the second
gun primed, and could hear the voice of Deadeye, as he ordered how it was to be pointed.

"There can be no mistake, I think, Mr. ——," he said;
"we'll give them a warmer reception than they bargained
for."

"Mistake! by G—," growled Morris, "you might blaze
into any craft on these seas, and never hurt a respectable
man," was the reply.

All the men were now at their quarters, and all was still
but the rushing sound of the vessel going through the
water, and of the rising gale amongst the rigging.

"Now, men, mind your aim," said the captain. "I will
join the ship, and as the guns come to bear upon the boats
nearest to you, slap it right into them."

"Starboard your helm, and bring her round to the wind,
my man."

As she came slowly round, bang! went a carronade right
into the nearest of the proas, driving it into staves, and
scattering the crew in the water. A howl arose, like that
of a thousand demons.

A breathless stillness ensued. Orders were given to
open the arm-chest, and distribute cutlasses and pistols.
Everything looked ominous; I began to think we should
have a desperate engagement, and all our throats cut afterwards.

By this time the ship was on a wind, steering full, while
the two remaining proas had closed under our quarter, so
as to avoid the possibility of our having another slap at
them. Deadeye evidently knew what they were at, and
with the view of out-manœuvring them, he ordered the
helmsman to tack. Round went the ship; but the cursed

9

proas, lying as they did nearer to the wind than we, were
still so close under our lee-bow, that to fire upon them was
out of the question. Such was the pleasant aspect of
affairs ; we did not know the instant we might be boarded.

"I say, young 'un, you ain't funking, are you ?" said
Hamilton, who, I perceived, had a drawn cutlass in his
hand and a leather belt round his waist, stuck full of
pistols.

"Not a bit," said I, for I was in truth too much interested in what was going on around me to have any other
feeling.

The pirates were now close under our beam, and just as·
a carronade was brought to bear upon them, a grapnel was
cast from the nearest of them with admirable precision ; it
caught, however, only by a ratlip, which a sailor, who stood
near, severed instantly with his cutlass. This was just at
the moment when they had risen to haul up alongside ; so
quick was the release that about half-a-dozen who were
coming up our sides tumbled into the sea, and the Ida
passed ahead, leaving the assailants in her wake. No
sooner had we got clear of them than the helm was put
down and the ship came into the wind in a minute. As we
passed, each of our guns as it was brought to bear was
discharged in succession, but without effect. They doubled
on us, however, before we had time to load again, and were
soon close on our wake.   •

"Persevering fellows those," said old Deadeye to the
first lieutenant. "We'll have a visit from them shortly, I
expect."

"Be ready, men, to receive boarders."

"Here they come, by jingo," I said, as the foremost
ranging close alongside poured its horde of miscreants upon
our deck. Up to this moment all had been silent ; a yell
now arose, which seemed to rend the very heavens, as a

close hand-to-hand encounter ensued. Such an infernal scene I never expect to witness again. The pirates had stripped themselves almost naked, and cursing and yelling, each of them in a fashion of his own, fought with the most desperate courage. Our men behaved with the most admirable coolness, and it was apparent even to my inexperienced eye that our assailants had not even the ghost of a chance; indeed, the very desperation of their fighting showed it. The second of the boats had succeeded in effecting a lodgment of her crew also. They were in the act of getting over the netting when a volley of fire arms was fired which sent four of them to their account. The rest succeeded in gaining the deck, and proved a most formidable accession. They were led on by a swarthy fellow, of herculean proportions, with whom Morris was soon engaged in a hand-to-hand encounter. It did not last long, for the experienced swordsman, turning aside a thrust, at a blow clove his assailant to the chine. Hamilton was close beside me, laying about him furiously, and our men were fighting with all the gallantry inherent to British sailors. For an instant, so terrible was the onslaught, the issue of the fight seemed dubious, but our antagonists at length gave way, and we were driving them towards the mast of the ship, when a sudden reinforcement appeared in the shape of about twenty naked savages, who, armed to the teeth, suddenly climbed over the nettings, and came to the rescue of their companions. I imagined all was lost. Our people, with the exception of old Deadeye and the first lieutenant, for a moment held back. The pirates rallied and fought with renewed courage; it was now not for conquest but for dear life, as retreat was rendered impossible in consequence of the parting of the grapplings, which had fastened their craft alongside of ours; escape was therefore out of the question.

"Now, then, men, follow me and drive the savages over board!"' shouted the first lieutenant, flourishing his cutlass and jumping down into the waist of the vessel.

So furious, however, was the onset made upon him that he was thrown back with the foremost of those who followed him, and about twenty of the pirates leaped after him, yelling like demons.

"By G—, this will never do, we must bring one of the guns to bear upon them," said Deadeye.

"Round with a carronade, my boys, and pitch slap into them;" but the order was unnecessary, for, on seeing the first lieutenant go down, Hamilton, with a party of marines, had rushed to his assistance. He was fortunately unhurt, and was up again in an instant, laying about him with a hearty good will, and setting an example which was followed with such effect that the ruffians began to give way; nearly one-half of them were cut to pieces on the deck where they stood, and the remainder leaped overboard, where those who did not perish in the sea gained a temporary safety by swimming to their boats, which had already drifted to some distance.

The events I have thus been endeavoring to describe, took place in the course of a few minutes. The bodies of the slain were thrown overboard, the guns were secured, and when day at last broke, it dawned upon decks which were slippery with human gore. The wind and sea abated considerably; and when the crew were mustered, it was found that, although there had been no loss of life, eleven of them were so severely wounded as to require surgical assistance.

Such was my first adventure, causing me at the time many profound reflections which I cannot now stay to enumerate. Eight bells in the morning watch had struck when we piped to breakfast, to which we did ample justice.

The first lieutenant, shortly after we were seated, made his appearance with his arm in a sling.

"Hallo! old fellow, what's the matter?" inquired Hamilton, on seeing him enter.

"Only a mere scratch—nothing more—been having some sticking-plaster put upon it."

"Well, the impudence of these fellows is beyond everything—to attempt to board a British man-of-war is a cool trick certainly, ain't it?"

"Old Deadeye is blaspheming awfully; he has got a bullet hole slap through the crown of his hat," Morris said.

"The devil he has! pity his coat tails hadn't been shot away into the bargain," said a midshipman.

"They certainly did fight like devils. I wish we had taken a prisoner or two."

"My eye, if we had! wouldn't Deadeye have given them a high hanging?" said the middy.

"He'd have flogged him first and hanged him afterwards."

"Would his blood be the same color as his skin, I wonder?" inquired the middy, who seemed to have a turn for philosophical investigations.

The whole of the party burst out into a loud roar of laughter at this sally.

"I should like to have had a cast of that black ruffian's head who was the leader of the gang; he seemed one of the finest animals I ever saw," said Dr. Colocynth, who had just entered and taken his seat at the breakfast-table.

"Why, you look fagged—and little wonder," he added.

"My arm is still painful," replied the first lieutenant.

"Take some breakfast, then, and turn in; I'll make you a cooling lotion to put upon it. No fever, eh?" said the medico, slightly touching with his forefinger the wrist of the first lieutenant.

"Not a bit of fever—as hot as the devil though; some

fellow gave me a confounded crack on the head when I was down."

"Oh, wasn't it nearly all up with you then?" said Staunton, who was a bit of a wag in his way.

"I took good care of you with my marines, didn't I, my boy?" said Hamilton. "By Jove! the daring of these fellows surprises me."

"They took us for a merchantman at first, and thought they would easily run aboard of us; then, when we showed our teeth, their blood was up, and they wouldn't draw off."

"Well, not many of them have lived to tell the story."

"I rather imagine not," replied Staunton.

"Do they often try that sort of thing in these latitudes?"

"Yes; frequently upon merchant vessels and cruisers, when they have a chance of success in shot."

"But seldom or never upon men-of-war."

"There have been instances, but they are of rare occurrence."

Having dispatched my breakfast, I went on deck. It was one of those days when a general lassitude prevails. The ocean calmly sleeps, as if it were wearied—its broad expanse reflecting the heaven above, from which it receives its intensity of blue. The turtle rolls lazily along; and the sea is undisturbed by even a breath of air, the surface looking like a smooth and varnished mirror. The decks had been cleared and set to rights, and the men were lounging about or chatting, in twos and threes, upon the subject of our recent encounter. A light breeze at last sprung up from the eastward; once more a ripple disturbed the face of the ocean; and, creeping from her enthralment, the Ida got into the sea breeze and swept with crowded canvas towards her destination.

"Sail ahoy!" was the cry from the fore-top-mast-head of H.M.S Ida, on the early morning of what promised to turn out a remarkably fine day. The signal midshipman, having brought his glass to bear upon the object which hove in sight, was struck with admiration. The vessel which approached us was a splendid one; and a square blue flag, which flew at her fore-top-gallant-mast-head, indicated she had the admiral on board. We exchanged the salutes usual on such occasions, and proceeded to follow the movements of our superior in command. The weather was misty, and it began to blow from the south-west as we bowled along; towards evening it settled down into a species of weather which was decidedly uncomfortable—the wind, to use the phrase of one of the sailors, having been engaged in knocking in heaps about the deck, so that nearly every ten minutes we were obliged to turn the sails to some light air from a fresh direction.

"Why," said the first lieutenant, "the wind seems to be blowing from all points of the compass at once; a man might be many a year at sea, and never meet with the like of this."

"Oh!" replied the master, "that's nothing to a gale I encountered off the coast of France, when I was in the brig Niobe. It had been as bright a summer's day as ever shone, when about four bells in the afternoon watch, a breeze sprung up from thirty points of the compass all at once; you may be surprised, but it is as true as gospel, they lifted us all nearly out of the water; some of us thought we were going up to heaven, and perhaps a few were nearer it at that time than they have ever been, either before or since, but we were astray in our reckoning, enough of the Niobe remained afloat to hold on by, and off we went at the rate of twenty miles through the water."

"Why, Mr. Scott," said I, "you don't mean to assert that to be a fact?"

"He is the most infernal liar that ever was born," whispered Morris, in my ear.

"Fact, I will take my oath to it this blessed moment, by —— I will," replied the master, who had a shrewd idea that the whisper meant to impugn the accuracy of his statement.

"Boy, bring my Bible," he said, turning to the cabin boy who stood near.

"You have been tearing it up to light cigars with, sir, for the last three weeks."

"You d—d ass, can't you bring any one else's Bible and say it's mine?"

The boy having departed on his errand, soon returned to say, that he had searched everywhere in vain, a fact which did not speak very highly for the piety of H.M.S. Ida and her crew.

I was absurd enough, at this moment, to suggest, that if he pleased I could lend him mine ; however, my offer was met by such an unusual shout of laughter as did not encourage me to repeat it.

"Do you really think he'd mind an oath a single button, or that his swearing so fast would make it one bit the more veracious ?" said Hamilton, as we walked away together.

Having cast anchor off the coast, which we neared in the course of the afternoon, a boat was manned and dispatched to the Admiral, which returned, having letter bags, and sundry packages of newspapers, &c., with dispatches for the captain.

I received some letters from home, which gave satisfactory accounts of my friends ; having read them, I returned to the ward-room, where I found the officer who had arrived on board with the dispatches. He had a decanter of wine before him from which he was regaling himself by copious libations, while a little crowd of my messmates had flocked round, and were literally devouring him with questions.

"Who have you on board ; any of the old set ?"

"Yes, Skysail and Mildmay."

"Ah ! Mildmay is afloat again, is he ? how does he get on ?"

"Ah, much better after his flogging."

"What do you mean ?" said Hamilton ; "flog a midshipman ! I never heard of such a thing."

"Why, not exactly that either," replied the dispatch bearer ; "only he was near it, which comes pretty near to the same thing after all."

"How did it happen? give us the particulars."

"Why, Mildmay was always rather too fond of cheek, and in his last ship, the captain, always a tartar, would stand no more of his impertinence, so one day he was ordered up to the mast-head to cool himself.

"'Mast-head, sir ! what, you surely don't mean that ?' said Mildmay.

"'Yes I do, though,' replied the captain, 'and stay there too until you have my permission to come down again.'

"'Why, sir, upon my soul, that's too hard, now.'

"'Another word, and you remain there all night.'

"'Well, now, what a cursed tyrant,' whispered Mildmay, as he reluctantly ascended the rigging, which was to conduct him to his destination. The captain, meanwhile, went to his dinner ; an hour elapsed, then another ; at the end of the third, Mildmay thought the captain had forgotten him, and feeling tired of his uncomfortable situation, he descended, and stowed himself away somewhere, thinking he was safe until morning.

"When the captain had dined, and drank his allowance of claret, for there was a party that day, he requested the first lieutenant to see to the culprit, and allow him to come down.

"The first lieutenant having departed to execute his commission, soon made his appearance, with the astounding

9*

intelligence, that Mr. Mildmay was not to be found, and hinted the probability that he might have fallen asleep on his perch and dropped overboard.

"'The infernal young villain, no! he's too wide awake,' said Captain G—; 'have the ship searched, and fetch him here the instant he's found.'

"It was not long before the first lieutenant returned, bringing with him the object of his search, who looked not one whit abashed by the enormity of his conduct.

"'How dare you, sir, come down without my permission?'

"'I have had a severe cold for some days upon me, and I really thought that further exposure would endanger my life,' replied Mildmay, with unabashed effrontery.

"'By G—, I'll warm you. Howard, desire the boatswain's mate to fetch his cat here, and a quarter-master to bring the seizings.'

"Mildmay was in a devil of a funk; the stern countenance of the captain showed he was not in a humor to be trifled with—so he held his tongue, and looked at the company assembled at table, hoping that some of them (for his ready wit had made him a great favorite) would interfere in his behalf.

"The ministers of justice made their appearance; the boatswain's mate carried a red bag, in which was the instrument of justice, and the quarter-master carried the seizings.

"'Fasten this young gentleman to the breach of the gun, quarter-master.'

"'Will you be good enough to let me know one thing, sir,' said Mildmay, 'before you punish me.'

"'Yes, sir; what is it? No more impertinence, or I'll flog the seven senses out of you.'

"'Are you justified in punishing an officer in this way without a court-martial?'

" 'Tie him up, quarter-master,' roared the captain, in a voice of thunder.

" Mildmay was now tied up, and every arrangement made preparatory to punishment.

" 'Sir,' said he, 'I wish to say one word to you before you begin.'

" 'What have you to say?'

" 'Only this : that I consider your conduct ungentle-manly in the extreme.'

" 'Do your duty, boatswain's mate,' said the captain ; 'give him a dozen to begin with.'

" The boatswain's mate, a brawny fellow, with thews and sinews like a giant, gave one swoop with his cat, and down it came, with a ringing crack, upon the poor midshipman.

" 'Now, sir,' said the captain, 'what do you think of it? are you sorry for your conduct?'

" 'Yes, sir, extremely sorry,' whimpered the culprit.

" 'Will you pledge me your honor, as an officer and a gentleman, that you'll obey orders in future, and be guilty of no further impertinence ?'

" 'I will, sir ; I pledge my honor.'

" 'On that condition, then, I'll let you off,' said the captain ; 'but, remember, I'm not to be trifled with. Cast him off, quarter-master—and mind, sir, let me see your face as seldom as possible for some time to come.'

" 'No, nor any other part of me, if I can help,' replied Mildmay, buttoning up his dress and retreating with considerable precipitation.'

" Confound the fellow ! now I call that really too bad," said Hamilton ; "I hope we've not got him out here."

" No, I believe he did some other things, which did not bring him into the list of advance at the Admiralty ; so they have let him lie by for a little ; at all events, he has no command in this expedition."

" The devil mend him! I should not like to sail with such a beast."

" What sort of a fellow is old Deadeye ?"

" Oh ! a regular trump, but one of the old school—bores you a little—he's so d—d particular."

"I hate your particular people; but I must be off now. Will you see if there's anything for me to take back ?" said the envoy, who, with a little assistance, had finished nearly the whole of a decanter of sherry.

When I went on deck, it had come on to blow, the courses were clewed up, and the men were aloft furling the top-gallant sails. The wind, which had shifted several points to the northward, was rapidly rising to a gale, and the sea had risen. A little band of my messmates I found discussing the news, and talking of the story they had just heard. But it is time for me to turn from these private and unimportant squabbles, to those in which nations were engaged.

CHAPTER VI.

.CHINA.

IT was, as all the world I suppose is aware, in consequence of the unjustifiable conduct of Commissioner Lin, the imprisonment of Her Majesty's Plenipotentiary, and other English subjects, with many acts of violence by which his reign was marked, that called for stringent measures on our part. The Court of Directors of the East India Company, as well as the British Government, had a common object to protect our trade and our subjects in China, as well as to demand reparation for the insults offered to the person of our representative. I don't pretend to an accu-

rate knowledge of the particulars of the original dispute.
The quarrel, as it stood, was a very pretty one—and the
expedition of which we formed part, had been fitted out for
the purpose of bringing the Chinamen to their senses.   Sir
W. Parker commanded it, and Sir Henry Pottinger went
as Plenipotentiary, with full power to negotiate any satisfactory arrangement that could be adopted, so as to avoid,
if possible, the commencement of hostilities.   But as it was
not expected, from the temper and tone of recent commu-
nications, that a pacific arrangement would be practicable,
and the scene of operations would necessarily be in rivers
and along the coasts, attention had been directed to the
fitting out of armed vessels especially adapted for that particular branch of the service.   The practicability of using
iron as a material for ship-building had long been evident;
the opportunity was considered a favorable one for testing
its superiority in the species of service upon which we were
engaged; and, although some frigates and sail of the line
formed a portion of the expedition, it was for the most part
composed of strong-built iron steamers, constructed with
reference to their employment in river navigation.   In
fitting them out adequately for this peculiar service, no
expense had been spared.   The line had never yet been
crossed by an iron steamer.   There was much doubt, therefore, as to their capability of weathering the rough sea
about southern Africa.   A variety of questions respecting
the effect of lightning, the errors of the compass in or upon
vessels of this description, as well as the other great phenomena of nature which are incident to voyages in tropical
climates, had been satisfactorily solved by the perfect success of the expedition.   It now only remained to be seen
how the steamers would stand the river service.   The Nemesis, although commanded principally by officers of the
Royal Navy, had been sent to sea as a merchant steamer—

and so profound a secret had her equipment and destination, as well as those of the remainder of her companions,
been kept, that it was not, as I have already intimated,
until very recently, that the whole extent of our mission had
transpired.

The Nemesis, which was destined to play a conspicuous
part in the subsequent events, was about seven hundred
tons in burthen. She was one hundred and eighty-four feet
in length, and in breadth about twenty-nine feet; her en-
gines were of one hundred and twenty horse power; she had
twelve days' supply of coals, with water and provisions for
four months, and stores of all descriptions, together with a
duplicate set of machinery in case any accident should
occur. Her ordinary draught of water was little more than
six feet, but commonly in actual service she did not draw
more than five. She had no keel and was perfectly flat-
bottomed, but for the purpose of obviating as far as it was
possible these disadvantages of her construction, she had
two movable keels, capable of being raised or lowered to
the depth of five feet below the bottom of the vessel. Each
of these was about seven feet in length, one placed before
and the other after the engine room. They were inclosed
in a narrow case a foot wide, which, being open underneath,
allowed the water to rise to the level of the sea on the outside. The entire length of the vessel was divided into seven
compartments, which were water-tight, by means of iron
bulk-heads, so that in case of any accident, such as striking
upon a rock, or a shot hole, the effect upon the compart-
ment where it should occur would not be attended with
any dangerous result to the remainder of the vessel. I
have thus been particular in the description of the vessel, as
it may serve to illustrate the tenor of her subsequent operations.

The weather for some days proved boisterous and squally,

but at length we arrived at Hong-Kong, and from that time every possible exertion was made for sailing northward. Many of the ships had troops on board. After knocking about the harbor for some days, we were delighted to see the Nemesis hoist the signal for starting. It was a welcome one to us. We should otherwise have been long in getting to our position in the fleet, whereas in a few hours we were towed up on their left to make the best of our way. A signal made Chappel Island our place of rendezvous. The breeze was fine and favorable, and we ran into the harbor of Amoy on the evening of the 25th of August, in the year of our Lord 1841. Several shots were fired at us from the batteries as we entered, none of which, however, did the smallest mischief. The fleet was formed into three divisions ; the centre being under the command of Captain Herbert, in the Blenheim, assisted by Commander Clarke of the Columbine ; the starboard division was under Captain Bourabier of the Blonde, assisted by the Cruiser ; while the second division was placed under the direction of Captain Smith of the Druid, assisted by Commander Anson of the Pylades. It was directed that a boat should be in constant readiness on board of each transport, for the purpose of towing the ships clear of each other in case of a calm, and orders were given, that no boat should be permitted to pass from one ship to another, without permission from the senior in command of the division.

The whole armament was composed of thirty-six sail, and, unless I am greatly mistaken, the very sight must have caused the Chinamen to quake in their little wooden shoes. There were two line-of-battle ships and seven other ships of war, namely, the Modeste, the Druid, the Columbine, Blonde, Pylades, Cruiser, and Algerine. There was the Rattlesnake troop ship and the Bentinck surveying vessel ; four steamers, belonging to the East India Company, the

Queen, the Phlegethon, the Nemesis, and the Sesostris, besides twenty-one hired transports and store-ships, most of them of large size, many of considerably more than a thousand tons burthen; while the force stationed in the vicinity of the Canton river was composed of six vessels of war, including the Herald and Alligator, the whole under the direction of that able seaman and efficient officer Captain Nias.

The sun had risen in bright unclouded splendor as we entered the harbor. It was a proud sight. The wooden walls of England, which had braved so many a year the battle fire and wreck, were here in all their glory, so many thousand miles away from home, ready to strike terror into the heart of the foe. The bright clear sea speaking freshness to the heart was just rippled by a gentle breeze. At a short distance beneath our weather-beam, with the early beams of morning glinting from her bristling sides, her lofty masts and superb hull, sailed the magnificent Blenheim, like a lion moving in all the majesty of conscious power. The batteries frowned upon us with awful sternness, but as yet their iron mouths were silent. Before, however, I go further, dear reader, I must inflict upon you a little bit of description, which is absolutely necessary to enable you to understand the difficulties surrounding the scene of action. The harbor which we were entering is situated in the southeastern district of the island of Amoy, which, with another known by the barbarous appellation of Quency, occupy a considerable portion of a large bay studded with many similar islands. The most remarkable of these, as having direct reference to the subject of my description, is Kolingso, which is only divided from Amoy by a narrow passage leading directly up to the harbor. This island is, as it were, the key to the whole position. The scenery by which the town was surrounded is very striking—high mountains, some of them wooded, slope away in the distance, and large rivers coming from the heart of the country, discharge their waters into the bay. The town appeared about ten miles in circumference ; it is concealed by fortified heights. The suburbs, which were extensive, appeared separated from the inner town by a line of rocky hills, which extended trans- versely down to the sea along the face of the outer town, or what may. be called the outer harbor, which extended along the front and formed a large estuary that ran deep into the island across· its centre, and skirted the northern side· of the city. The whole front of the city is there washed by the sea ; the walls appeared strongly built and castellated at the top. Immense forts and field-works had been erected on the heights which commanded the town, as well as upon the smaller islands. by which the harbor is studded. We could see at a glance that extensive prepa- rations had been made to give us a warm reception ; a line of guns for nearly a mile in length bristled from a long stone battery, faced with turf, which stretched right in front of the town.

The small island of Koliugso, which stood directly in our course, the passage between it and the town being not more than six hundred yards across, seemed likely to op- pose a formidable impediment. It was literally bristling with heavy cannon.

Such was the position of affairs when we sailed into the harbor under the influence of a favorable wind. Every- thing was in readiness. The captains, who had gone on board of the Admiral for instructions, had returned to their respective ships. The gigantic Nemesis, with her smoky companions, were engaged in letting off their super- fluous steam, and every soul on board was anxiously await-

ing the expected signal for the commencement of operations,
when a small boat was observed putting off from the shore
bearing a flag of truce.

"I'm blowed if they ain't a-going to strike sail after all,"
said an old quarter-master who stood near me.

"We shall have all our trouble for nothing then, that's
all about it," said Hamilton.

"It's the old story of the King of France with his sixty
thousand men," interrupted Staunton, who was looked upon,
as I have already intimated, as the wit of the mess.

"Watch old Deadeye, how he's twitching his empty
sleeve about." (I forget whether I mentioned that our
captain had lost his left arm at the battle of Trafalgar.)

"Maybe he's not angry; he thinks there's going to be
no fighting after all."

By this time the boat containing the flag of truce had
gone on board of the Admiral, and it soon became known
that the object of the embassage was simply to inquire
what were the intentions of our squadron. It soon transpired, also, that an answer had been returned, which was
calculated to allay the apprehensions of all fire-eaters. In
the name of her Majesty, it was requested that certain very
stringent demands which, in the preceding year, had been
made by Captain Elliott, should, without further delay, be
complied with; or that, in case of refusal, hostilities would
instantly commence; but as the commanders of the expedition would willingly spare the effusion of blood, which otherwise must necessarily ensue, they were willing to allow all
the troops in the town to retire with their arms and bag-
gage, on condition that the fortifications should at once be
abandoned, and the town of Amoy delivered over into the
possession of the British troops. In case this very reasonable demand was not complied with, the refusal on the part
of the Chinese authorities, it was politely requested, should

be notified by the erection of a white flag upon the citadel.

The morning was oppressively warm as we lay for two
mortal hours exposed to the full glare of a meridian sun,
waiting to see whether the Chinese would make up their
minds to be cannonaded or not. At length, more than two
mortal hours having elapsed, during which the men exhibited symptoms of the greatest impatience, we observed the
Admiral hoist the signal for the commencement of the attack. It was a magnificent sight to see how beautifully
the ships stood in defying the batteries which frowned so
awfully upon them. The Sesostris led the van, the Wellesley and the Blenheim followed, but did not fire a shot until
they were within less than four hundred yards from the
principal battery; but as the attack deserves a chapter for
itself, I shall reserve my description for the next.

Chapter VII.

The Battle of Amoy.

In the course of a few minutes the Ida had taken up her
appointed station. The Blonde, Druid and Modeste came
to—close by the works of Kolingso; and we were soon hotly
engaged. The roar of the artillery was tremendous. The
Chinese worked their guns well, but not expecting in all
probability we would come quite so near to them, the range
was too high, and the shot for some time flew harmlessly
over us, hurting nothing more than a spar or a sail; this
error was, however, soon rectified.

"Hallo, Bill! we want more shot here," shouted one of
the men who was working a gun.

"Ay, ay, you shall have it."

"D—n it, let them have it," shouted Hamilton, who was standing near.

"Mr. Hamilton," said the first lieutenant, with a solemn visage, "this is no place for swearing; if this lasts much longer, you may be in another world soon."

"Hurrah! then, go it, my boys, have at 'em with a will," shouted my valiant messmate, as Bill came tumbling up the hatchway with two large canvas bags filled with rusty iron, cannon balls, and wads. Most of my messmates had taken off their neckcloths, which were tied round their waists; some helped the men to work the guns. As for myself, seeing there was nothing for me to do, I stood with my hands in my pockets—a spectator whose only concern at that moment, I must confess, was, whether any one would soon be shot, coupled with an ardent aspiration that the unfortunate individual might be any other than myself. As yet there had been no harm done, and I was beginning to congratulate myself that the damage was likely to be all on one side.

Having observed some men, who were stationed on the forecastle, cheering heartily to their comrades below, I walked in the direction to see what was going on. Nine men were stationed there with the first lieutenant at their head. They seemed, like myself, to be merely lookers-on. The long guns, which belonged more properly to this part of the deck, had in consequence of their extensive range been removed to another position which afforded more space to work them.

These men, I soon discovered, were stationed at their post in order to watch and repair any temporary damages. They had as yet nothing to do except look on and shout, which they seemed doing to the very utmost of their ability. They were equally exposed with the rest of us, and in the absence of the excitement attendant upon physical exertion

and hard firing, they were endeavoring to amuse themselves
by encouraging their comrades.

"Hurrah! my hearties, pitch it into them," said one.

"A little bit lower ; now for it! there goes a gun knocked
to eternal smash!" shouted another.

It was an elderly seaman who spoke, and just as he had
uttered the words a round shot came tearing along; the
men all dodged on one side with the exception of the last
speaker, whose attention had been so much occupied by seeing the Chinese gun knocked to eternal smash that he was
placed in that predicament himself.   That was the first
blood I saw drawn, and I must confess that when I saw
the form which a minute ago had been all life and animation, stretched on the deck a lifeless mass of clay, I did feel
what Mrs. Harris, had that worthy lady been present,
would have called a turn ; however, the rest of the men
took no notice and went on with their cheering as heartily
as ever.

I walked away and rejoined Hamilton, who was standing
by the bulwark with one of the ropes in his hand, superintending the working of a gun.   I had scarcely come up
when a round shot came whistling through the sides, knocking bolts, planks, and everything else before it.   When the
crash was over I saw Hamilton was down ; I ran towards
him, but he was unhurt ; the rope upon which he had been
leaning was cut in two at a little distance from his hand,
and he was merely knocked down and a little stunned by
the wind of the shot.

"Close shave that, by Jove!" said he, rising from his
recumbent posture.

The firing was now tremendous ; such an infernal din I
certainly never heard before, nor do I expect to hear the
like again.   Our guns were, however, doing their work,
while the batteries to which we were opposed were rapidly

becoming dismantled ; and the men gave a hearty cheer as they saw each of them rendered *hors de combat.* In the meantime the Blonde and Druid had not been idle. The three principal batteries on the island of Kolingso were now completely silent, and a party of marines had been landed and had taken possession of the forts.

"They say poor little Mr. ―― is killed, sir," said one of the men, coming up with rather a rueful expression of coun-tenance ; "and two others besides. I have just come up from below. The surgeon says there's no chance, but I can't quite learn the rights of it yet."

At this moment Shaw came walking forward along the gangway, when a round shot from the batteries struck the hammock netting, tearing out the feathers and blankets, and hitting Shaw upon that portion of the human form which for some wise reason it is considered alike indecorous to turn to a friend or to an enemy. Over went the short gentleman like a ninepin, but the force of the ball had been nearly expended when it reached the ship, and the yielding nature of the fabric through which it had to pass had taken away any of its remaining power for mischief.

"Well, I never was hit there in my time before," said Shaw, getting up and rubbing the part affected.

"If the Chinamen had put a little more powder into that 'ere gun I'd have felt obliged to them," growled a seaman near me whom Shaw had ordered to be punished a few days previously.

When I returned to my post on the quarter-deck, I found some of my messmates who had supplied the place of the wounded men and were busily engaged in working a gun. Old Deadeye was all alive and kicking, superintending the operations and working his empty sleeve about as if it was under the operation of galvanism.

"D—n them, they'll soon have had enough of it; raise the gun a little, there. Why the devil don't you work, sir?" he said, turning upon me like a savage.

"So I will, sir, but I can find nothing to do."

"Here, then, you had better help Hamilton and Ellis with that gun."

"Ha!" said Ellis, "I'm glad to find you alive and hearty, my buck, kicking, sir, like a cover on a copper tea-kettle. What the devil have you been about all this time? So there, a little aloft," he said, looking along the sight of the gun he was pointing.

The trigger line was in his hand, which he was just about to pull, when crash came a round shot; in an instant every man of us was floored, the port hole had been carried away, the tackles shivered to pieces, and splinters knocked about in all directions. One of them had hit Ellis in both arms, another knocked Hamilton over, while I received a nasty bruise on the hip from a fragment of one of the bolts.

"Any of you killed, boys?" said old Deadeye.

"Not so bad as that, sir," replied Hamilton; "only a little frightened, that's all."

"Up and at 'em again; fire out the gun; we'll have the place set to rights presently."

While I was stooping in the endeavor to execute these orders, I heard the whiz and crash of a shot overhead; it only carried away one of the stanchions, and went plump into the mast, where it stood out like an enormous pea.

The unpleasant reflection then occurred to me, and it was doubly disagreeable to remember, that had I been standing upright, the shot must have gone straight through me. I felt my courage begin to ooze a little through my fingers' ends, but the glance of the old captain, as I looked up, revived me.

"Every bullet has its billet, you son of a sea cook!" he said; "that was meant for the main mast, and there it is, you see."

"Hurrah, hurrah, my boys! they strike, they strike!" shouted a dozen seamen all at once, as forth from the canopy of smoke which shrouded the batteries, out of which red livid glares of light had been darting, arose into the calm, bright summer air a small white flag. We gave three hearty cheers at the welcome sight, and paused to rest from our labors.

I should not pass over in silence the military operations by which our men had been so admirably seconded; it will be enough briefly to dwell upon them.

The Phlegethon and Nemesis had been brought up close alongside the shore, with the troops on board, and a number of boats ready for their disembarkation. Under cover of our fire they were safely landed, under the inspection of Commander Gifford, of the Cruiser; a small outwork upon a hill near the beach having been escaladed, the British flag was placed on its summit, and the troops then advanced to attack the town. To the Eighteenth Royal Irish was assigned the honorable duty of escalading the castellated walls by which the principal battery was guarded, which ran along the hill-side at right angles to the march. The Forty-ninth Regiment were ordered to move in a parallel direction towards the lower angle, and storm its embrasures.

As the parties advanced, each upon their respective objects of attack, a heavy matchlock fire was opened upon them, which, in consequence of the exposed nature of their situation, did considerable mischief. Nothing daunted, however, they advanced, with three hearty cheers, to the attack. Having arrived at the wall, the scanty scaling ladders were found a serious drawback. They were obliged, in the face of a heavy fire, to mount on each other's shoulders to gain the top of the wall. Captain Hall was the first to make good his footing, and having cut down the Chinese who opposed him in single combat, he coolly took out of his pocket a small flag, which he had carried for the occasion, and waved it in token of triumph ; but this exhibition was a little premature. The Chinese still continued to make a stout resistance, but the storming party being joined by the Eighteenth Royal Irish and the Forty-ninth, who had also forced their way through the embrasures, formed a force which carried everything before it.

The most difficult portion had, however, yet to be carried. This was a steep range of sentry heights which commanded the city. Had this been stoutly defended, the loss of the attacking party would have been most severe. It was here that two Chinese officers of high rank, mounted on horseback, made a determined resistance. The leader of the storming party, conceiving it would be a fine opportunity for making a prisoner of distinction, made a dash at the foremost, but he was instantly surrounded by the bodyguard of the mandarin. A few of our soldiers contrived to penetrate, and now a hand-to-hand encounter took place of the most desperate description. The Chinese officer, who wore the white button, was a tall and remarkably athletic man. Captain Hall singled him out, and after a sword fight which lasted several minutes, the mandarin fell, severely wounded in the arm. His sword was taken from him, together with his other badges of distinction. A vigorous attempt at his rescue was made by the Chinese. Our party were surrounded and nearly cut down before further aid could arrive. Thus, the object of the assailants was not so much the defeat of the enemy as the rescue of their prisoner, which they succeeded at last in accomplishing ; and the mandarin, who, from his being the subject of such great

10

competition, must evidently have been a person of great consequence, was borne off in triumph.

The attack had now succeeded; the Chinese were in full flight in every direction, closely followed by a body of our men, which had, in the meantime, been thrown ashore from the Wellesley, under Commander Fletcher. Upon going within the battery, many of the Chinese were found dead, but the wounded had nearly all contrived to make their escape. In a cavern in the rocks were collected a great number of old men, women, and children, who had fled there for shelter from the shot. They set up a piteous yelling, being, I suppose, in the full expectation of having their throats cut from ear to ear, as it is the policy of the Chinese to represent us in the most unfavorable light, as cruel persecutors and savages. Many Chinese officers of the highest rank had fallen during this eventful day—some of them, it was said, by their own hands. The Chinese commander, seeing all was lost, walked quietly into the water until it covered his head, and remained there until he died. Such was the battle of Amoy.

Chapter VIII.

The Day after the Battle.

By half-past five o'clock the action was at an end. Partial firing still went on in different parts of the navy for some hours, but the general cannonade had ceased; and Captain Deadeye, after seeing that every precaution had been taken for the safety of the ship, made it his business to visit the wounded in order to see that proper attention was paid to them.

I went down below, to try if I could get a little snooze, as I felt greatly fatigued and exhausted from long exposure to the sun ; a drowsiness came over me which I could hardly call sleep. Visions of the battle floated before me, and phantoms full of conflagrations and uproar, mingled with apparitions of young ladies, filled my overheated imagination ; then the scene would change, and I would find myself once more among the pleasant glades and green fields of my own country. No one, perhaps, who has not mingled in the excitement and din of warfare, can imagine the feeling of gentleness and tranquillity which is connected with every vision or recollection of home. I had spent a couple of hours or so in this species of somnolent indulgence, when I was awoke by the noise on deck caused by the operations of the men who were engaged in clearing away the devastation occasioned by the Chinese guns, and in executing the necessary repairs.

I went on the deck, pausing in my way to visit the cockpit, which was filled with wounded men ; there the surgeon was hard at work, with his coat off and his shirt sleeves rolled up to his elbows. He looked like a butcher in the shambles. I felt a sickness of heart and a sensation of faintness come over me which were quite overpowering, but as I turned to go, I heard a voice feebly articulate my name ; it was that of the old coxswain, who had been badly wounded.

" Ah, Pipes, my poor fellow, is that you ? How are you ?"

" It's all up with me, sir ; I'm bound for Davy Jones this time."

" Cheer up, my boy, you'll get all right again."

" No, sir, no," the old man said, " I'm settled at last ; Death's hard aboard of me. My top-light is growing dim ; I'll never cross the line no more. Let me have your hand for a moment, sir."

I gave him my hand, and as I looked at his uneasy and sunburnt features, over which the salt tears were rolling, I felt greatly affected.

"I han't known you long, sir; this is our first cruise together, but I have a small favor which, as you look a kindly gentleman, I hope you'll not refuse me."

"What is it, Pipes? I'll do anything you want, depend upon me."

· "See, sir, if you please, that the d—d old gunner don't make me chew more baccy than my allowance when I'm shoved off."

"I'll take care of that for you, Pipes;" although for the life of me I could not, at that time, make out what the poor fellow meant.

"I've just an old 'oman, sir, too, as lives near Portslade, in John Street, No. 10; if you should ever happen to be down that way, and inquire if she's got my pay and all that, I'd thank you."

"You may depend upon me, Pipes, I'll do it."

"Thank'ee, sir; I expected it from your kindly face. Here I'm a sheer hulk, my spar gone, never to answer to my helm no more. I'll never see Portslade again, nor make auld Beachy in a misty morning; but it's all the same, we must go when our time comes."

As the poor fellow uttered these words, his grasp tightened, then relaxed; a film came over his eyes; his frame was agitated by a momentary convulsion: all was over. The spirit of the sailor had drifted off, from the troubled sea of human misery to a harbor where no unquiet waters ever come.

The Chinese batteries still continued to burn, and the discharge at intervals of their heated guns sounded like mournful minute guns lamenting the devastation which had been committed during the day; while, as the night drew on, a gentle breeze arose, which, whistling through our torn rigging, seemed to sound as it were a fitting requiem for the spirit which had passed away.

When daylight appeared on the following morning, all hands were turned up to clear away the wreck. Our loss had been very inconsiderable ; and we were being engaged in knotting, splicing, cutting, getting up new rope, and storing away the remnants of the old rigging, when a voice was heard summoning all hands on deck ; there we found old Deadeye with the other officers collected in a cluster around him. He addressed us in a short speech, praising our conduct, and complimenting the master in high terms for the admirable manner in which he had brought the ship alongside the battery. Our names were then called over, and we piped all hands to breakfast.·

After getting our vessel refitted, in about eight days we sailed out of the harbor ; the rendezvous appointed for the fleet being a promontory, called the Buffalo's Nose, which is situated near to the entrance of the Chusan group of islands. Our progress was at first rather slow in consequence of a heavy ground-swell accompanied by light winds, but we kept pretty close in-shore, and so continued to work our way notwithstanding the combination of adverse circumstances.

When we cleared the harbor it had been fine weather, but towards noon it began to blow. We were coasting along about musket-shot from the white beach, with the clear bright green sea on our right, and beyond it the dark waters of the blue and stormy ocean, and the snow-white waving surf on our left hand, as we wore to the breeze. There was the beach almost level with the water, the land was covered with beautiful white sand and shells, which glittered transparently along the surface. The north-east monsoon now began to set in, making its appearance rather

earlier than usual, and accompanied by heavy squalls and a
thick spray, which caused the separation of our squadron.
At the commencement of this change of weather, old Deadeye had been in unusual good-humor. He was gratified at
the conspicuous position the Ida had occupied in the recent
action, and pleased beyond measure at his name having been
honorably mentioned in the dispatches. Some injuries having, however, been sustained by the spars, which had occurred in consequence of the carelessness of one or two of
the men, the captain lost his temper, and swore an oath, too
awful to be set down here, that upon the next occasion that
such an accident occurred, he would make a severe example
of the offender. Now, Deadeye was by no means the manner of man to be trifled with, as John Handlead soon found
to his cost. Handlead was a careless, contumacious sort
of fellow, fond of discourse, as well as of more grog than
was quite good for him, and having been found guilty of
repeated acts of carelessness and disobedience of orders, he
was ordered up for punishment. It was upon a certain
Thursday—a black Thursday—the men were mustered at
dinner ; the carpenters having been previously ordered to
rig the gratings, which were accordingly in readiness. The
culprit stands upon one of them, to which his feet are fastened, and he leans against the other, to which his hands are
tied. The officers are assembled in gala dress—all the marines drawn up under arms, and the whole of the ship's company mustered on the opposite side of the deck. The master stood near the gratings, with his sword in his hand. I
marvelled much at this wonderful display when I considered
the occasion of it, and I expressed my wonderment to a
messmate who stood near, when the only reply I could elicit
was that of—

" How jolly green you are !"

Green, indeed, I may have been, but I soon turned white.

The arrangements having been completed, the first lieutenant went below to report to the captain, who speedily made his appearance on deck. All was silent. I must confess I felt a more anxious trembling about the nerves in the region of the heart than I did when we were going into action.

"John Handlead, stand forward."

Old Deadeye, in his calmest of moods, was seldom free from a species of nervous agitation, nor had nature gifted him with eloquence. He was now performing a duty which he evidently did not like nearly so much as blazing away at the Chusan batteries.

"John Handlead," he said, "I am really sorry to see you brought up here. You have been guilty of repeated acts of disobedience to orders. You have neglected your duties—neglected them shamefully. You are likely to become a disgrace to the profession of a British seaman. Discipline is the life of the service—it must be maintained; and I should be neglecting my duty if I did not punish you as you deserve, as an example to the rest of the ship's company. Strip, sir."

John Handlead turned a quid of tobacco which he had in his mouth, coolly squirted the juice on the deck, and began deliberately to *peel* himself.

"Seize him up," said the captain.

The hands of the prisoner were then tied to the upper grating, and his feet lashed firmly to that underneath.

A master-at-arms then threw a covering over his shoulders, while the clerk read aloud the articles of war relative to the punishment of any seaman who should be found guilty of negligence of duty.

This being done, we all put on our hats, which had been taken off during the performance of this portion of the drama.

"Give him a dozen," said the captain.

The boatswain's mate, a large athletic fellow, with thews and sinews like a giant, seized his cat. The handle was about two feet in length, covered with red cloth. The tails of this weapon were nine in number, each of them about the size of the cord used for fastening a portmanteau.

The mate, who handled this instrument with the air of an adept, looked at it from top to bottom, cleared out all the tails with his fingers, and held out the mere ends in his left hand, as the right was raised to inflict the lash. He then gave his arm and body a sudden swing—the tails whizzed through the air, and as they came down upon the naked creeping flesh, and I saw the long red marks imprinted upon it, a deadly sickness overcame me, and I was obliged to lean against the bulwark for support. When I looked up again, the drops of blood were slowly trickling down the prisoner's back. The first dozen had been finished, and the executioner rested from his labors, looking for further orders from the captain.

"John Handlead," said the latter, "are you sorry for your offences—will you amend in future?"

"D—n you for a lubber," grunted the seaman from between his clenched teeth.

"What does he say?" said old Deadeye; "I can't hear him."

"That he's sorry, I believe," said the first lieutenant, who humanely wished to hide what he knew would be the result.

"I said, d—n you," roared the prisoner.

"Oh, very well! call another boatswain's mate then," said Captain Deadeye.

The new practitioner pulled off his coat, holding his hat in his left hand, and stroking his hair down his forehead with the right.

"Give this man two dozen," said Deadeye, ": and if you favor him, I'll have you put under arrest, and stop your grog."

This gentleman was as large as the last. Having planted himself firmly on his feet, he set to work ; but this fresh application of the lash did not elicit from the prisoner a single exclamation of pain. He bore his punishment in sullen silence, and when the three dozen had been reported as having been inflicted,

"What do you say now, John Handlead, are you sorry ?" inquired the captain.

But unfortunate John Handlead was beyond the expression of regret or despair—in a word, he had fainted away. He was cast loose—restoratives were applied, and he soon came to himself. As for me, it was some time before I could get the scene out of my memory. The punishment is terrible, but I suppose it is a necessary one.

"What ailed you this morning ?" inquired Hamilton, as we were seated round the mess-table at supper.

"I think that scene this morning was most disgusting and painful."

"What would you do with a rebellious rascal like that ?"

"Is there no other mode of punishment that would serve quite as well ?"

"Oh, yes ; there, for instance, is the black list."

"What may the black list be ?"

"It is made up of men who have been found guilty 'of trifling offences, not sufficient to entitle them to be placed on the list of the first prisoners."

"And what is done with them ?"

"Oh, that depends upon the taste of the captain entirely."

"By Jove," interrupted Staunton, "I heard of one who
10*

made the black list men, when the day's work was over, carry about their hammocks, with a musket lashed up in it; at every six feet or so, a rope was placed across the quarter-deck, about three feet from the floor, over which they had to step; it was worse than going up the treadmill."

"That was an ingenious device, indeed."

"I heard of another," replied Hamilton, "who had a fancy that the iron pins about the ship should be polished until they shone like silver; some water the grog; others stop it entirely. There is no end to the fertility of their imaginations. It is nasty, to be sure; but upon the whole, I believe the men themselves like to be flogged better than anything else."

"Now, suppose there was no such thing as flogging, what would be the result?"

"We should go to the bottom like winking, I guess," said Walter.

"There would be loss of masts and of lives, wrecks, fires, and all manner of devilment," said Hamilton; "in short, the service would go entirely to the devil."

"I think it is going there as it is," said Staunton.

"Well, perhaps it may be; but slowly."

"Promotion is infernally slow."

"Are you fit to be promoted?"

"Yes, I am decidedly of that opinion."

"Could you, for instance, bring a ship of ninety guns into action, with all the batteries blazing away at you, as old Hum did the Ida?"

"Why, I'm not so sure of that; in the meantime hand me some more grog."

"It is ten o'clock, gentlemen; please to put out the lights," said the master-at-arms, opening enough of the door to admit his head.

"By all means, master-at-arms; dowse the glims, boys."

said one of the oldsters. Not many minutes had elapsed, during which, it is needless to say, the order had not been attended to, for we were so busily engaged in discussing the question of flogging, with other important nautical affairs, that we forgot all about it.

"Gentlemen, it is past ten," said the quarter-master, opening the door once more. "I really must report you to the first lieutenant."

"Very well, we'll do it in less than no time. Hamilton, send the rum this way ; do you think no one has a mouth but yourself ?"

"That reminds me of a story I heard the last time I was in Ireland," replied Hamilton, who was a native of that country.

"What is it—out with it, whatever it is."

"Why, some Papist gentlemen were dining together during Lent, and although they don't eat meat, they do eat salmon and lobster sauce, or turbot with ditto, as the case may be ; that they call fasting. I was at a party where some one grabbed up rather more of the fish than fell to his share.

"'Hallo, stop that,' said a longing companion, pulling the dish away from him. 'Deuce take you for a gormandizing vagabond ; do you think no one has a soul to be saved but yourself ?'"

Again the master-at-arms made his appearance. "Gentlemen," he said, "I really must go to the first lieutenant—I am very sorry—but you know it's my duty."

"Take a glass of grog, old Weather-the-Mizen," said Hamilton, "before you go."

"I shall be most happy, sir ; your health, gentlemen !" said the master.

"We will put out the lights, and no mistake ; hand that lanthorn here," said Staunton,

The candle was shut up in its tin case accordingly, and the master departed ; but the instant his back was turned, it was taken out again.   At length the noise and uproar of the party rose to such a height, that a messenger came from the first lieutenant, ordering us instantly to repair to our hammocks, whither we went accordingly.

A STRANGE SAIL.

For some days the gale continued—and one morning we had been skipping along the shore, with the land-wind on our beam, at the rate of five or six knots ; but so quietly that I could hear the roar of the surf, as the long, smooth swell broke on the beach, which, from the loudness of the noise, could not be more than a mile to leeward of us.   It was a cloudy morning ; as we rose and fell on the long seas, with our sails flapping and bulk-heads creaking, the black clouds which had lowered along the horizon, spread rapidly, and the weather had all the appearance of becoming rather dirtier than usual.   The breeze was fitful, and came down in sudden irregular gusts or catspaws, as the nautical phrase is, when a strange sail was signalled to be abaft our weather-beam.

The glasses of Captain Deadeye and of the other officers were anxiously pointed in the direction indicated, and in less than half an hour a vessel hove in sight.

"What do you make of her, Mr. Morris?" said the captain to the first lieutenant, as he sat aloft with his glass directed towards the new arrival.

" A large junk, sir, standing right away from the shore."

" What did he say ?" inquired Hamilton, who stood near the gangway.

" A junk, I believe."

"Bravo!" said Hamilton, clapping his hands; " we shall get some prize money at last."

"To be sure we shall ; I'll sell my share of it."

"What will you take?"

"I'll take ten pounds for it—ready money down, though."

"I don't much like speculating; but, if you please, I'll give you half." ·

"What, five pounds for a Chinese junk! laden, perhaps, with Sicee silver; what a greenhorn you must think me: five pounds! Well, I remember now, I'm rather hard up, I will accept your offer; give me the blunt."

"You must trust to my honor. I'll pay you the first port we touch at."

"Ah, that's quite another matter; not that I doubt your honor in the least; but I should much rather have the money."

In the meantime we had rapidly neared the junk, which was, like all vessels of her class, a slow sailer. Perceiving us in pursuit of her, she ran in towards the shore, and at length got into water so shallow as to render any further pursuit of her rather a dangerous venture. Old Deadeye, having run the Ida as close in as the depth of water would permit, within about two miles of her, cast anchor, and ordered out the boats.

The officers and men who were selected for the service were called up and mustered on the quarter-deck; in the meanwhile the wind had fallen, and it was nearly a dead calm. Everything was soon in readiness. The boats received their guns, which were fixed on slides, so as to render it practicable to fire them over the bows, if it was found necessary, without interfering with the operation of the oars. The sailors, with their cutlasses belted round their waists, the marines with their muskets, all stepped in. The order was given to shove off. The crews tossed their oars, and with three hearty cheers, set out on their expedition.

I was in the pinnace, which led the way, and in less than an hour we had arrived within gun-shot of the Chinaman.

"There is a gun from her," said one of the crew, as a long volume of blue smoke came rolling over the water.

"The devil there is! what, she'll show fight, then, will she?" replied the first lieutenant. Slowly the smoke passed away, and a round shot, darting the spray in our faces, went ricochetting over the boat, and disappeared almost half a mile astern.

The boats, which had been pulling in compact order, were now directed to separate, so that there might be less chance of any future shot taking effect.

We continued our advance ; two more guns were fired at us, but as yet without effect.

"There's grape, by Jove !" said the first lieutenant, as the sea near us was ploughed up into a sheet of boiling foam.

"The cutter returns her fire," said the coxswain.

"And there's a jolly rattle from the barge ; we'll soon be alongside. Hurra, my boys," shouted one of the crew.

The firing now became hotter ; gun after gun from the junk was fired at us in quick succession, which we returned as rapidly as we could. We were now close under her stern, keeping up an incessant fire of musketry.

"Ready, men, to board," said the first lieutenant, as we pushed alongside. "I'll open the ball; now lie close in."

"And I'll be your partner," shouted Hamilton, following his chief, as he swung himself on deck.

We clambered up after them as rapidly as we could, and, after a very short conflict, in which none of us were hurt, the junk was our own ; but the expectations of those who had calculated upon prize-money met with a sad disappointment upon searching her ; not an ounce of Sicee silver, which had been calculated upon, was discovered. She was a war-junk, armed from stem to stern.

There was nothing then to be done but to take possession

of her, which we did accordingly, and Captain Deadeye
requiring a pilot, we contrived, through the medium of an
interpreter, to make his wishes known to the Chinese crew.
But not one of them could be found to accept the invidious
office.

It was in vain that old Deadeye offered a reward of ten
dollars to any one of the captured crew who would steer us
safely into the harbor of Chapoo, which we were now approaching.

At length half-a-dozen or so were marshalled on the deck,
and, through the medium of an interpreter, were thus addressed by the captain :

" Will you pilot the vessel safely into the harbor ?"

A unanimous shake of the head was the only reply.

" Fetch a rope," said the captain, " and have the first fellow hanged immediately."

A cord was then fastened round the Chinaman's neck,
and the end passed over the yard-arm of the vessel. The
poor fellow perfectly understood the hint, and began to
evince considerable symptoms of trepidation.

"String him up at once," said the captain.

" I will do what you require," said the Chinese sailor, in
a piteous tone.

"Take him to the wheel ; keep the rope fast round him,
and the instant you think there is any reason to apprehend
he is leading us into danger, hang him," said Captain Deadeye.

The Chinese pilot, under the influence of this gentle species of coercion, did his work to admiration. We rapidly
drew near the entrance of the harbor, and the tide being
favorable we were soon inside, and within reach of two
small forts which had been raised to protect the entrance.
Not a gun, however, was fired from either, and we passed
into full view of the town. In front of it were drawn up a

large number of trading vessels of every description, moored
in parallel lines, and 'protected by a fort which commanded
the harbor as well as the town.

"Now we shall have prize-money, and lots of it too,"
said the first lieutenant with a grin.

"I hope so," replied Staunton ; "but look at these fellows, how they're mustering in the fort: we shall catch it
soon, I reckon."

The Ida now stood in straight for the shore, and took up
a flanking position as close to the fort as it was possible to
bring her.

"Give them a touch with the grape and round-shot,"
said the captain.

The order thus given was promptly executed. Shot,
shell, and cannister were poured in in quick succession ; the
fire from the fort waxed feebler and feebler, until at length
all was silent : but, though vanquished, the fort was not subdued ; a number of well-armed troops were seen rapidly descending the adjacent hills, bringing with them heavy jingals
mounted on triangular stands, which soon opened a smart
fire upon us.

"They are firing musketry, by Jove ! there's one of our
men down," said Hamilton.

"Now, then, forward with the long gun: cram it well
with grape, and let us see how neatly you pitch it at that
column," said Deadeye.

"Steady, my man, steady ! a little higher, now you are
about at it."

"Fire !"

The effect was tremendous : we could see the serried
ranks scattered like a whirl of autumn leaves. Another
shot or so settled the business, and they scampered off as if
the very devil was at their heels.

The boats were then ordered out, and possession was

taken of the fort by a party of marines : four guns, two of
brass and two of iron, were found and spiked. The sheds
and buildings were set on fire, the magazine deluged with
water, and the entire place rendered harmless in regard of
any further offensive or defensive operations.

The men were now piped to dinner. When they had
dined, we took possession of the junks in the harbor, many
of which were found to contain stores of considerable value.
The day's work was a hard one ; but, as it had turned out
so profitable, we were all perfectly satisfied with the result
of our labors, and the Chinese pilot grinned from ear to ear
with delight when, the noose being removed from his neck,
he was dismissed from his employment with ten clinking dollars in his yellow hand.

It was during the operations which I have thus been endeavoring to describe that Morris came out in his true character. He had always been accused of a tyrannical temper,
but until now it had never shown itself save in petty instances. Now, the love of justice inherent in old Deadeye
was such that I do not believe he would have had a soul in
the ship wronged wilfully. But the difficulty was how to
satisfy him. And I believe the incident I am now about to
relate opened his eyes for the first time. It was the duty
of Ellis—having been confined to the deck until two, which
was called the forenoon watch—to superintend any of the
operations which might take place, such as launching of the
boats, &c., when the pinnace was required to take a party
of the marines ashore. Morris, having called the mate, said
to him, "Mr. Ellis, you will take these men on shore in the
pinnace, and return again immediately."

"Very well, sir," replied the youngster, pushing off.

It so chanced that I was on deck. Having nothing better to do, I was amusing myself by watching the men landing. When they were all safe ashore, Ellis stood up and

gave the order to return, when a sergeant of marines came back to the boat for some of his accoutrements, which had been forgotten in the hurry of the moment. Scarcely five minutes elapsed for the whole transaction, and the boat returned to the ship.

"I thought, sir, I had desired you to make no delay?" said Morris, who had been watching the proceeding.

"No more I did, sir ;" and Ellis related the fact as it had occurred.

"I don't care, sir, about the d—d marine, my orders should have been attended to."

"I only delayed a few moments, which were absolutely necessary ; the exigencies of the service required it."

"D—n the exigencies of the service ! what right has a youngster like you to think? You'll stay on the deck for two hours."

"But, sir, you can refer to——"

"Hold your tongue, sir, or I'll report you to the captain ; I'll teach you to obey orders."

Well, thought I, if this be not an ill-conditioned ruffian, I never met one. My messmate had no more intention of disobeying orders, or of acting save for the best, than he had of flying. I therefore availed myself of the opportunity of Morris turning his back to go up and express my opinion of the whole transaction.

"He is a beast !" said Ellis ; "I always thought him so, now I'm sure of it."

"Halloa," said I, "what a lot of fish are swimming about here ; come down into the chains and have a look at them." Now, if the chains are not a part and parcel of the deck I know not what is ; but so it was : we had been there only a few moments when the voice of Morris was heard exclaiming—

"Where is Mr. Ellis?"

" Here I am, sir."

" How dare you leave the deck without my permission !"

" I did not mean to leave it, I assure you, sir.   I thought always the chains were a part of the deck."

" They are not, sir ; by G—d, I'll teach you the difference !"

" I assure you, sir, I had no intention whatever of disobeying orders."

" Hold your mutinous tongue, you young rascal."

" I'm sure I'm——"

" If you utter another word I'll report you to the captain."

" I wish to Heavens you would, sir ; he would not see me so unjustly treated."

" I'll take you at your word ; I will report you, by the Lord ! you'll catch it : in the meantime you shall remain where you are until ten o'clock.   I'll take the temper out of you, you infernal young devil."

Now let us see what was the consequence ; simply this : the poor fellow was obliged to remain, kicking his heels about the deck until eight o'clock, when his turn of duty came to keep the midnight watch.   He was thus exposed for nearly twelve hours without the chance of getting a wink of sleep.   But the persecutor did not escape.   It transpired before long that the whole transaction had reached the ears of the captain, and I have every reason to believe that Mr. Morris got a sharp rap over the knuckles for his misconduct.

We now proceeded to beat up for our destination, but the strength and rapidity of the currents among the Chusan islands, together with the boisterous weather which soon set in, rendered it a task of difficulty to keep time.   We were the first at the appointed rendezvous, however ; but the Admiral did not arrive until many days afterwards.

MORE FIGHTING. ·

I had the morning watch. We were standing in pretty close to the shore. The air was pure and cool; the bright tints, peculiar to all tropical climates, being mellowed with a subdued light, which imparted great beauty to the scene. The thick mists which hung over the shore gave a great apparent extent to the view. The sea looked a transparent blue, while the sky above glowed with a rosy tinge, which gradually increased to gold, as the sun came rolling up above the horizon.

"What a lovely morning it is," I said to Hamilton, who stood near me.

" Yes, only too fine for the work we have to do."

" Why, certainly, bloodshed and war are not pleasant things; but if they must be, the sooner they are over the better. We must do something for our pay."

" Pay, indeed! a nice sum, per diem, to run the chance of being made food for the fishes."

" Well, then, glory is something," I replied, "and fame—"

" D—n glory and fame; they are both humbugs !"

With this sentiment of my companion's, thus forcibly expressed, I was not at that moment disposed to quarrel. I had not received any intelligence from England for a considerable period, and I was beginning, not indeed to feel home-sick, but to entertain some apprehensions that evil of one kind or another might have befallen those whom I loved best upon earth.

It was pretty well known throughout the fleet that our expedition was to be made up one of the great rivers of the country, known by the name of the Yang-tze, provided the attack upon Chapoo, for which active preparations were now being made, turned out successful. As yet our operations had been attended with signal success, and the glory which has hitherto followed in the course of the British flag had not for an instant deserted us.

At the distance of about fifty miles from the great city whose capture had been determined upon, lies the town of Ningpo. It is of considerable commercial importance, being famous throughout the world for the richness and variety of its silks. The town is a much finer one than Amoy, or indeed than any other of the newly-opened ports upon those seas. Junks of large size are built on the river, and the inhabitants, in spite of the prohibition of their government, have always evinced a strong desire to trade upon peaceable terms with other nations.

It was at this place, towards the conclusion of the seventeenth century, that the Portuguese missionaries first commenced their operations in the East. Their influence, for a long time, was unbounded, and high expectations were entertained, as to the results of their labors, as soon as the good seed which they had sown should have time to ripen to maturity. But, alas! missionaries, after all, are but men, and the failings common to humanity seem to have been shared in, to a great extent, by these teachers of Christianity. They omitted no opportunity of aggrandizing themselves at the expense of the unfortunate natives. Repeated instances of this kind, followed up by cruelty, gradually weakened their influence, and at length the Chinese government peremptorily forbade the further teaching of a religion, the inculcation of which was attended by consequences so completely demoralizing. This important city, whose history I have thus briefly sketched, was taken possession of by our troops in the month of May, but it was found impossible to retain possession of so great a place without having in it a larger garrison than we could well afford; a virtue was therefore made of what, in point of fact, was an urgent necessity. The magnates of the town were invited to attend in solemn assembly, where they were addressed by the present Lord Gough, then Sir Hugh. He informed them that her gracious Majesty had been pleased to restore to them their capital, which he hoped, in consideration of this act of clemency, would be used for pacific purposes in future.

The Chinese mandarins looked in much astonishment from one to the other, as if they found it difficult to account for the reason of this extraordinary proceeding; but when the keys of the gates were handed over to the persons appointed to receive them, their joy knew no bounds. They were lavish in expressions of gratitude. As to the origin of the quarrel between the two nations, it is by no means within the scope of my purpose to pause for its investigation. I can only, speaking as I do, from the constant opportunity of a personal investigation, confidently assert that upon our side the contest was carried on with a magnanimity not unworthy of the British prowess.

"Huzza, my boys! I have glorious news to tell you," shouted Hamilton, waving his cap round his head, as he rushed into the gun-room, where we were quietly supping off the remnants of a somewhat frugal dinner.

"Bear a hand, and out with it," we exclaimed simultaneously.

"We are not to wait any longer for the rest of the squadron. Old Deadeye is going to attack the town without them. Hurrah! no more of this coasting work; I'm sick to death of it."

"Wash the cobwebs out of your throat, old boy, and tell us all about it. Here's a glass of three-finger grog for you."

"Well, then, the first lieutenant has just told me, he having had it direct from the skipper, that as the reinforcements have not arrived, instead of waiting for these negoti-

ators, diplomatizers, or any botheration of the sort, he has
made up his mind to sail slick into the harbor and knock
the town about their ears." .

" Amen !" ejaculated Staunton, with a pious fervor which
was infinitely entertaining.

But old Deadeye was not to have all the fun to himself;
and perhaps it was just as well for his ship's company. The
remainder of the squadron were shortly afterwards signalled
in the distance. We waited until they came up, and the
Cornwallis, Blonde, Columbine, and Plover, with troops on
board, soon joined us. We then bore up, sweeping to the
westward ; and about nightfall, just as the range of hills
about Chapoo rose towering above the sea, we cast anchor,
and waited patiently for the dawn.

When the sun rose, we found ourselves nearer to the
shore than we anticipated. The aspect of the country was
beautiful ; the fields seemed well cultivated with a variety
of crops, which were luxuriant. The view, too, was a splendid one. A high range of hills sloped down nearly to the
water's edge. In a nook of these, and close to a small
promontory which ran out to the westward, lay the town.
It appeared well-built and extensive, and afforded promise
of being the most important capture we had yet made. As
we stood in towards the shore, a fishing-boat which was
cruising about the bay was captured, and the crew brought
on board, whom we interrogated as to the defences of the
place we were about to attack.

" How many soldiers are there in the town ?" inquired
Deadeye.

The man bowed to the ground, performing the same species of homage he would to a mandarin, but spoke not.

" Tell him I'll have him flogged, if he don't answer my
questions," said Deadeye to the interpreter

" He won't understand what that means, I fear."

" Well ! bastinadoed, then ; it comes pretty much to the same thing, I believe," replied the captain.

The hint was accordingly conveyed, and the fisherman muttered something which was quite unintelligible.

"I can't make him out, for the life of me," said the interpreter.

" Try another of them, then," said the captain. " Perhaps they are all dumb ; they look as queer a set of fellows, at any rate, as ever I clapped my eyes upon."

Another was then desired to stand forward, but a similar question put to him met with a precisely similar result.

" You must treat him as you did the pilot—that's the only language they understand."

" I'll have you hanged, you ruffian, for daring to trifle with the captain of a man-of-war."

The same ceremony was then gone through ; but when he saw that preparations for stringing him up were all completed, the fisherman found a voice, and stated, in effect, that the batteries were very strong, and that there was a force of several thousand soldiers there for their defence.

" Ha !" said old Deadeye, working his empty sleeve, " we shall have some warm work ;" and the veteran, as he spoke, looked like one smelling the combat from afar.

As we approached nearer, the place looked exceedingly formidable. Breastworks were thrown up along the heights ; they seemed particularly strong in the slopes between the hills. Upon the side nearest to the town there were two batteries, mounting, as well as we could make out, about seven guns each ; and upon a low hill, in front of the suburbs, there was a circular one with fourteen guns. Further on to the westward there was a masked battery, which seemed not yet finished.

The usual soundings were duly taken along the whole extent of the shore. Although we had run close in, not a

shot had as yet been fired upon us. We could distinctly
see, through our glasses, mandarins dispatching messengers
along the heights, which now swarmed with soldiers; and
at length Deadeye ordered out a boat to ascertain if the
shore was practicable for landing troops. The boats having
in due time returned without an accident, and the report
being favorable, the ships of our squadron, at nightfall, took
up their positions directly in front of the principal batteries,
so as to cover the landing of the soldiers, which it was then
agreed upon should take place in the bay, which, as before
mentioned, lay a little to the eastward.

The morning was beautiful; a lovelier one never dawned.
The sun rose in clear, unclouded majesty, upon many a man,
on either side, who was destined never to see him set. The
success we had hitherto had made us rather more confident
than perhaps we ought to have been, and we little anticipated a determined resistance. At an early hour the signals
were made for the action to commence, and we set to work
with a hearty good-will. The steamers stood well in, and
threw the troops on shore. Sir Hugh Gough landed with
the first column, and at once succeeded in carrying the principal height. In the meantime we were blazing away, without intermission. At this juncture a signal was made from
the Nemesis for every seaman and mariner who could be
spared from the respective ships, for the purpose of support-
ing the troops who were hotly engaged.

"Can we spare any of our men, Mr. Morris?" said the
captain.

"Why, not many. I think a boat's crew or so might
go; we've nearly silenced our batteries, and there's no
knowing—we never can calculate upon these mandarins."

I asked and obtained permission to accompany the boat's
crew, which was placed under the command of Hamilton, as
I thought I should see more of what was going on than if I

11

remained on board, where, in consequence of the smoke, little could be observed. It seemed Amoy over again, without variation.

Off we went ; and having succeeded in effecting a landing, we joined the left column, which was led by Sir Hugh Gough in person.

Our first object of attack was an intrenched fort, which we never doubted to take by a flank movement, under cover of the Sesostris, who was keeping up a pretty smart fire of shells.

On we went ; and then, for the first time, I stood face to face with the Chinese soldiers. We saluted them with a volley, which they returned with a precision that knocked over our leading files, and then we charged them with the bayonet, the men from the Ida flourishing their cutlasses, and shouting as if the devil was in them.

This was a species of attack the Chinese had no mind to encounter. We had scarcely closed, when off they went, pell-mell. The ground was broken and covered with bushes, by its nature retarding any very effective pursuit ; we were obliged therefore to separate. I kept with the seamen as well as I could, but it was soon found very much every man for himself.

We made right at a host of Chinese, who appeared determined to withstand our further progress, at the extremity of a narrow defile, where they took up a commanding position.

As we passed a tomb which lay in our way, there was one of their officers, apparently of rank, perfectly unmoved, and looking on as if he were the unconcerned spectator of a drama.

"Shall I cut him down ?" said Brown, one of our seamen, flourishing his cutlass.

"No, let him alone ; he looks as if he meant no one any

harm," replied Hamilton; and so it turned out. The Chinese, as we passed, instead of being grateful for his escape, began deliberately to cut his throat with a knife. I paused for an instant (curiosity getting the better of all my excitement) to see if he were really in earnest. He was, and he soon effected his purpose. "Well," thought I, "you are certainly a curious fellow. It would have been very much the same to yourself, had you let us knock you quietly on the head; you would then have died like a Christian and a gentleman."

Having come up with my party, I found them engaged in a hand-to-hand encounter with a party of the enemy, who were commanded by a Chinese mandarin on horseback. Hamilton made a dash at him; the mandarin rode furiously forward, making a lunge with his long sword at the assailant. My messmate dextrously warded it off with his cutlass, and catching the horse by the bridle, the animal reared up and threw his rider. The mandarin, however, was on his feet in a moment. The combat which then ensued reminded me of one of those described by old Homer. The mandarin was as active as a cat. The weapon he wielded was a formidable one, and he understood its use. The flash and glitter of the ringing steel was almost dazzling. I paused for a moment as each party watched the encounter. It did not last long. A thrust in the shoulder roused my companion's wrath. One sheer stroke from the English cutlass, breaking through the Chinaman's guard, felled him to the earth; and when he was down, we despoiled him of his peacock's feather and white button, both of which are badges of high rank

We now entered a deep gorge, in the centre of which was a large building surrounded by a dead wall, inside of which the fugitives had retreated, keeping up a smart fire from the embrasures and the windows of the house. We

summoned them to surrender, but the only reply was a rattling volley, which sent several of our party to their account; a temporary pause was the consequence. We had
not enough men to carry the place, we therefore waited
until we were rejoined by our companions. When they
came up, it was determined to pause until some of the guns
had arrived, as the place seemed strongly fortified. But
the excitement of the moment unfortunately prevailed over
the dictates of prudence; Colonel Tomlinson swore he
would take the place, and, throwing himself at the head
of a party of the Forty-ninth, advanced to the attack.
But the gallant leader had scarcely gained the entrance,
when he was shot dead, in the very act of waving his sword
and cheering his men on to the attack. We rushed on to
avenge his loss; the men were furious with excitement, but
a volley fired with deadly precision sent them staggering
back from the scene of conflict. It was at length found
prudent to sound a recall; the place could not be taken by
storm. We waited until the arrival of two pieces of artillery, which soon silenced the Chinese fire. When it had
ceased, we entered, and a scene of slaughter met my eyes
which I can never forget; out of three hundred men, by
whom the place was defended, only fifty were found alive,
and nearly all of these were terribly wounded. The unfortunate wretches were aggravating their deplorable condition
by attempting to commit suicide; we found them deliberately occupied in setting fire to their long cotton dresses,
with lighted matches, and many perished before we could
possibly prevent them. Inside one of the sheds was found
the body of a soldier of the Eighteenth Light Company,
whom the savages had mutilated horribly. They had cut
off his ears and nose with his own razor, which they had
taken for the purpose out of his knapsack—a singular proof

f cruelty, at a time when few of them could have anticipated an escape with their own lives.

With the destruction of this building, thus resolutely defended, terminated all attempt at resistance. The batteries
had been silenced by the fire of the ships, and the city was
now in our hands. Every possible care was taken of the
wounded, but all our efforts were unavailing to prevent repeated attempts at self-destruction on the part of our prisoners. We found women destroying their children, and afterwards putting an end to their own existence; husbands
poisoning their wives, and cutting their own throats, with
every other species of barbarism which it is possible to
imagine.

The Chinese force engaged in the defence of this city has
been estimated at considerably above seven thousand men,
of whom nearly one-fourth were Tartars. The number of
killed and wounded must have been immense; on our side
the loss was considerable, but it was for the most part confined to those who were engaged in the land service, the
ship's crews had scarcely suffered at all; and when we returned on board we found old Deadeye pacing to and fro
on the quarter-deck in the highest possible spirits. His joy
was, however, somewhat damped upon hearing the casual-
ties which had occurred on shore, especially in the loss of
Colonel Tomlinson, who was an old and valued friend. It
had been determined upon that the remains of this distinguished officer should not be interred on shore, lest the Chinese should avail themselves of our absence to dig them up,
and afterwards commit some of those horrible acts of mu-
tilation which one shudders to contemplate. Sir William
Parker having placed a steamer for the purpose at the disposal of his friends, on the 20th of May the body was removed on board of the Phlegethon, and taken out into deep
water. All our officers attended in full uniform, and the

scene was one of such touching solemnity that it can never
be effaced from my recollection. It was a beautiful spring
morning ; a light breeze swept the surface of the water, as it
sparkled in the sunshine. As we arrived on board of the
Phlegethon the officers and men were drawn up in full uniform upon deck. The bell began to toll about eleven
o'clock. It has a strange sound upon the ear, that tolling
of the funeral bell at sea, bringing with it associations and
memories of scenes of our earlier days, and subduing the
sternest hearts with softened emotions. The body of the
departed veteran, sewn up in a hammock with shot attached
to the feet, was brought up and laid upon a grating, which
was covered with a union-jack. The officers stood behind
the captain, on the quarter-deck, while the crew, and such
of the soldiers as had been directed to attend, assembled on
the gangways and by the sides of the grating. The bell
then ceased tolling, and an impressive silence ensued, unbroken save by the rippling of the waves against the ship's
sides, and the whistling of the breeze through her shrouds.
We all took off our hats, and the chaplain, in a clear and
solemn voice, began to read the burial service for the dead.
When he came to that portion beginning, "Forasmuch as
it hath pleased Almighty God," there was a slight pause,
while the men were engaged in getting the grating forward ;
at the words "we, therefore, commit his body to the deep,"
the grating, colors and all, were launched forward, and fell
with a deep and heavy splash into the sea. The blue water
swept above the remains of the gallant dead, its enlarging
circles alone indicating the spot where he had fallen ; seeming emblematic, I thought, as they widened and widened
into infinite space, of that eternity to which we had con-
signed him. It was a moment full of touching solemnity; a
deep stillness prevailed on board, broken only by the ripple
of the waves. I could see that the captain's eye was moist-

ened by the expression of an unwonted feeling, and I
thought that there were few of the spectators who did not
share an honorable sympathy with the old commander.

When we had separated, and returned to our respective
ships, the conversation of the gun-room mainly turned upon
the events of the morning.

"Did you never see a man hove overboard before, youngster?" inquired Staunton, with a want of feeling which, from
that time forth, by no means tended to elevate him in my
good opinion.

"No, I never saw a man buried at sea before. It seems
to me a much more inferior ceremony than any other description of funeral could be."

"Well," said Hamilton, "I would rather rest down
among the coral rocks, and the great old wrecks, at the
bottom of the sea, and have all kinds of quaint monsters of
the deep eyeing me cunningly as I lay in my hammock, than
have the snuggest monument in Westminster Abbey."

"Well, so would I."

"In a word," said Staunton, "you would rather be food
for the fishes than the worms. Well, perhaps you are nearly
about right; I shall not argue the subject with you."

"I think a common seaman's burial is the best of all."

"How does it differ from that which we saw this morning?"

"Why not? surely there's not so great a fuss made about
it; but only mind, it's more ship-shape and regular like."

"Give me some sort of notion, if you can, of what you
mean."

"Oh, if we are out here much longer, you may have an
opportunity of seeing it for yourself."

"But I should like to know—don't they heave them overboard just as they did our poor fellows who were killed in
action?"

"Why, yes, to be sure they do ; but afterwards all hands are piped to grog, and everything is as jolly as possible."

"And, therefore, you like it better. Well, you are a queer fish, that's all I can say on the matter."

"Then comes the sale of the defunct's effects, which are put up to auction."

"Well, that's easily disposed of, I should think."

"The men are then mustered at divisions. The clerk brings up the ship's books, and marks after his name the letters D. D."

"What does that mean?" I inquired.

"What a muff you are, to be sure—discharged dead, of course."

"You don't know what making a dead man chew more tobacco means, I suppose, neither?"

"No ; tell me, by all means."

"Why, you see, pursers are generally the most infernal villains on the face of the earth ; they are worse than hotel waiters or schoolmasters ; and the first thing the purser does, when his name is fairly disposed of, is to chalk up to his account an extra pound of tobacco or so, out of which he afterwards turns a little profit on his own account."

"Well, that surprises me, I must confess. Now that you mention it, I do remember poor Tom Pipes saying—"

"Yes, the villain did for poor Tom ; you may depend upon it, if he left you his executor, you'll have a Flemish account of his effects, that I can tell you," said Hamilton.

In conversation of this kind the evening passed away ; and when the master-at-arms came with the usual order for the removal of the lights, I was not sorry to be left alone, and to have an opportunity of pondering in silence over all that I had heard and seen that day.

Chapter IX.

The Cruise of the Ida draws to a Close.

As far as the war was concerned, it was looked upon as decided by the important conquest I have described in the last chapter. The tone of the government began consider- ably to moderate ; we had stricken terror into the heart of the nation, while the moderation with which we used our power inspired them with a feeling of confidence such as they had not previously entertained. After the action at Chapoo, overtures of a pacific nature were made, which were repeated with more earnestness as each subsequent success of our arms showed the Chinese the utter futility of further resistance.

Towards the commencement of June, the whole of the fleet bore up for the entrance of the Yangtze river, with a view to operations against the capital of Shanghai ; but our progress was considerably retarded by the tides, which were flowing against us with great velocity and strength. It was during this passage that one of those disastrous events occurred incident to a sailor's career, and against which no skill is of any avail.

"A man overboard !" was the cry which, caught from one of the crew to another, startled me as I was reading one morning in the gun-room. I was instantly upon deck, where I was soon informed of the cause of the accident. It appeared that about two o'clock some hands had been ordered to reef topsails ; the rigging was instantaneously crowded by the seamen, each vieing with the other who should be first. Meanwhile the weather topsails had been rounded in, and when the canvas filled to the wind,

11*

"Lower away the topsails !" sung out the first lieutenant through a trumpet.

The order was executed almost as soon as it had been given, and the braces having been belayed, again the word of command was uttered:

"Trice up—lay out !"

. The men were soon all on the yards ; the reef tackles were hauled out, and the order given to take in a single reef. It was just at this crisis, when the men were out on the yards, that a sudden gust of wind, filling the main-top-sail, carried away the brace. The yard, relieved from re-straint, flew fore and aft, and three men were flung over-board, two of whom never appeared again ; they were probably killed by the fall ; but the third, a lusty seaman, was soon observed to reappear, battling manfully with the waves. The ship had not much way on her at the time, and the deck was instantly crowded with men anxious to render all the assistance in their power to their messmate The cutters were unfortunately covered, in order to protect them from the burning rays of the sun ; but the launch was soon afloat. The men cheered lustily to the struggling swimmer, whose efforts to keep himself afloat seemed now to have nearly exhausted his strength.

"Give way, my lads, give way !" thundered the captain

The boat's crew plied their oars a few minutes, and they were at the spot just as the head of their messmate dissap-peared beneath the surface.

"He's gone, by G—d !" said old Deadeye.

"Hurrah ! no, he has him !" sung out the first lieutenant, and the whole of the ship's company gave three hearty cheers as the bowman; who had plunged neck and shoulders into the water, was observed drawing himself up : he had succeeded in getting the boat-hook into the clothes of the drowning man, who was soon safe on board ; but so com-

pletely exhausted was his condition that we were obliged to
call for the aid of the surgeon before he could be resuscitated.

"Well for you there were no sharks about," said Deadeye, when the man had recovered.

"Why, yes, your honor ; I should have been in kingdom
come by this time, as the ship's chaplain would say."

"You would have been in a shark's belly in the mean-.
time," said the first lieutenant, who, as I have already intimated, set up for being a wit in a small way. "You have
been saved, Bill Jones, from going to Davy Jones's locker,"
he added ; "you shall therefore have a double allowance of
grog if the doctor thinks it good for you, and now you may
turn in and take a snooze if you like."

I shall not pause in my narrative to do more than briefly
glance at the subsequent events, which followed in such
quick succession, that the war was speedily brought to a
close, after the fall of Woosung, in which we took our usual
prominent part. Shanghai was the scene of our next hostile
operations. At the latter place the conflict was maintained, on the part of the enemy, with a determination
which, considering the heavy losses they had sustained in
the former actions, was truly wonderful. The Tartars, in
particular, fought with a desperate valor. They were in
general men of fine athletic frames, and masters in the use
of their weapons ; had they been only armed with the British bayonet, the result of the conflict would, in all probability, have been very different ; but undisciplined valor,
however chivalrous, can avail but little against trained soldiers. Many of the Tartars rushed furiously upon the bayonets of their assailants. In some instances they even succeeded in penetrating the soldiers' guard, and, seizing them
by the body, would drag them over the walls. In sword
combats, or personal encounters of any kind, their prowess
was unrivalled ; and many a British soldier bears on his

person, to this day, memorable marks attesting the arduous nature of the encounter with these barbarian tribes. The attempt to open negotiations, on the part of the Chinese commissioners, had been repeatedly made, but, as we thought they had not been able to show that they had full authority from the Emperor to treat for peace, all overtures were positively declined. At length, as our forces lay before Nankin, and very formidable preparations had been made for the attack, only three days before it was to commence, the Chinese commissioners signified that they had full authority from the Emperor to treat for peace. The attack was therefore delayed until a meeting could take place, which was held at a temple on shore, in the southern suburbs of the city. The Emperor's commission being produced, was examined by competent persons, and pronounced to be satisfactory. A treaty, upon our part, was submitted to them, and, after considerable delay and much diplomatic acuteness, the Emperor's full assent was received, and the signature of the document took place, with considerable solemnity, on board of the Cornwallis—the venerable commissioner, Elepo, attending on behalf of his Imperial Majesty, and a number of officers of high rank being at the same time in waiting, to witness the signature of the British plenipotentiary. The war was now over, and, in the month of December, we took our departure, and soon afterwards bid a final adieu to China.

One of my favorite modes of killing time, during the long voyage which ensued, was by taking a book up to the top, and spreading the top-gallant sail into a canvas couch. I was occupied in this way one morning, when the captain of the top shouted out with the voice of a Stentor :

" Deck ahoy ! a sail on the weather-quarter."

On hearing this, the officer of the watch ordered the signal midshipman to the masthead, to ascertain of what size

and nature the stranger was. With the aid of a telescope, it was descried to be a squadron of five frigates, not English.

The news flew like wildfire throughout the ship, and I hastened down to glean further intelligence.

"Mr. Staunton," said the captain, "what do you take those vessels to be ?"

"They look most like French, I should say."

"Why, so they do. But their rigging is scarcely trim enough for Frenchmen."

"They may be Dutch or Portuguese."

"No, they are French hulls to a certainty. Who rigged them is another matter."

After some further discussion, it was decided that the ship should be cleared for action, in case the strange sails should prove to be an enemy—though what enemy, for we were then at peace with all the world, with the exception of a slave ship, old Deadeye expected to meet, was a question none of us could solve.

The decks having been cleared accordingly, and the men reported ready at their stations, old Deadeye took another long look through his glass, and when he had finished his inspection, his aspect looked more puzzled than ever.

"I can't, for the life of me, make them out," he said, turning to Morris, who stood near.

"I'm d—d if I can either," was the reply.

"I wish you would give up that profane habit of yours, sir ; it's blasphemy, positive blasphemy ; by the Lord it is !" growled Deadeye.

It was now nearly nine o'clock, and grew so dark that the vessels could scarcely be distinguished ; but enough light remained to display the rugged faces of the Ida's men as they thronged the quarter-deck. Deadeye stood on the skylight gratings, slightly elevated above the rest. Around him were piled shot of every description, muskets, cutlasses, pistols, and bayonets, with every other requisite for commencement of the fray.   He was in the highest possible spirits, and evidently itching to get at some one, no matter who it should be.   Towards eight o'clock, a thick fog came on, which shut out the enemy from all further observation. There was neither moon nor stars, and but little wind. We were going through the water at the rate of about five knots an hour.   So far, all was well.   Deadeye was still peering through his night-glass, when, with a sudden oath, he let it fall on the deck.

"A large press of sail close on the weather-beam !" he said.

To advance further in our present course would have been to show our stern to the enemy ; he therefore shortened sail, and prepared to heave to.   It was Hamilton's turn to be on deck, and I, as usual, was close beside him.

"Main deck there !" shouted Captain Deadeye through his trumpet.

" Sir ?"

"Take care that not a port is opened till I order. Every one but the captains of the guns to lie down, and keep silence."

Slowly the strange sails were seen looming through the mist ; they were now close to us ; yet nothing more than a huge towering mass of canvas could be seen, so thick was the fog ; he concluded it was a foreign frigate, though of what nation it would be hard to tell.

" Down with the main-deck ports, and stand by to fire Man the larboard fore and main braces.   Port your helm, and brace up !"

As the captain uttered these words, the ship's head was laid nearer to the wind, so as to intercept the frigate as she

advanced upon us. Another minute, and we should have been in a desirable position to open the ball.

Deadeye was walking to and fro, with rapid strides, on the quarter-deck, waiting for the proper time to pour in a broadside, and his empty sleeve was working to and fro with its accustomed alacrity when he had any business on hand.

"Now, then, by G—d! (he forgot his horror of swearing when any constraint was upon him,) ready on the main-deck.".

But before he could complete the order, or the men obey it, a voice exclaimed from the approaching enemy, in good round English—

"Ship ahoy, there!"

A mingled exclamation of surprise ran through our crew at the sound; in another instant our broadside would have been at them.

"What ship is that?" sung out Deadeye.

"His Majesty's ship Pluto, Captain Clewline."　.

"His Majesty's ship Ida, Captain Deadeye."

"My compliments to Captain Deadeye, and I shall be glad to see him on board," said the Pluto.

But Captain Deadeye was in no humor for paying visits that evening; he was too much disappointed at being baulked of his amusement, so he trundled down stairs in the worst of all possible tempers, saying, as he did so, "Let the first lieutenant go, and Mr. Staunton get my cabin bulk-heads up again; secure the guns; give me my supper, and pipe to grog." This was the last incident of any note which occurred during our cruise.

OLD ENGLAND.

I must pass over the greater portion of our homeward voyage, the monotony of which was unbroken by any inci-

dent worth recalling.   The fresh breezes carried us bravely
along over the laughing blue waves ; the foam flew from
our bows, and the sails strained like impatient couriers as
the good ship Ida proceeded on her way.   Early one fine
morning, as I was pacing the decks during the morning
watch, I was accosted by Hamilton, who, taking me to
leeward, asked me if I recognised the low blue line of coast
which was rising in the distance.

"It's not possible, cannot be England ?" I exclaimed, as
the tears started to my eyes.

"Yes, indeed, it is ; no mistake whatever about it."

We sped rapidly along under the influence of a favorable
breeze ; the long line of blue coast now became more distinctly visible, and at length we saw the Isle of Wight
looming through the sultry haze of a summer's morning :
we could clearly distinguish the white cottages scattered
over the pretty wooded coast.   We soon saw Portsmouth
once more—rising above the water's edge ; and towards
evening we cast anchor beside the battery.   My last night
on board was a jovial one ; but I cannot stay to describe
it, nor can I ·pause to linger over the parting with my old
messmates.   When it becomes necessary to leave those to
whom I ·am attached, or with whom I have been long associated, the farewell to me is always trying.   Hamilton
affectionately embraced me ; the rest of the officers shook
me cordially by the hand ; old Deadeye gave me a parting
gripe, prophesied that I should one day become a sailor,
and once more my feet were on *terra firma*.   I rested that
night at the small inn at Ashton, and on the following
·morning proceeded to Plymouth, where I arrived in due
time for the mail which was to convey me to Redburn
Hall.

As I proceeded rapidly along the well-remembered road,
my thoughts reverted to the day upon which I had travelled

upon it last. How feelingly did each incident of that melancholy journey arise to my recollection! How my heart
yearned to see the beloved inmates of the dear old Hall
once more! Towards evening, as we drew near Silverthorne,
I heard the distant sounds of a carriage which was fast
overtaking us. Turning round I recognized at a glance my
uncle's livery. My heart beat so rapidly that I almost lost
my breath. I could see, as the vehicle whirled by, an
elderly man of stately presence, and beside him a young
lady. It was without doubt my uncle and my cousin.
The cloud of dust which followed in the train of their
equipage had nearly subsided when the carriage seemed
to stop. We were following so rapidly that we soon came
up to the spot, and I then saw that an accident of some
sort had happened: one of the horses was down, my uncle
had jumped out, and was in the act of assisting the postilion as we drove up. I called to the coachman to stop,
and, getting down from the box-seat, hastened to render
any assistance which was in my power. I was anxious to
avail myself of so favorable an opportunity to see if I should
be recognised. The horse which had fallen was plunging
and kicking violently among the traces. I cut them with
a clasp knife I had in my pocket, and secured the horse's
head. I could see at a glance that I was unknown to
either of my relatives. It was growing dark, and I drew
my hat over my eyes as I asked if I could render any further assistance.

"Not any, thank you; we shall do very well now; we
will replace the fallen horse by one of the leaders, and get
on all in good time."

"You are a sailor, I see," said my cousin, bending forward
from the carriage, as they were engaged about the horses.

"Yis, marm," said I, in a gruff voice, touching my hat

"Where have you served?"

"In the Chinese war."

"Good Heavens!" replied Lucy, with a sudden start; "are the ships returned? We have had no intelligence about them as yet."

"Just come into port, ma'am," I replied.

"What was the name of your ship?"

But before I could reply, my uncle had resumed his seat, and ordered the postilion to drive on; not, however, before my cousin in a whisper had requested me to call at Silverthorne, which she said was quite close at hand, a fact I knew quite as well as she did.

The coach in the meantime having rolled away, I was left to pursue my way on foot, and in about half an hour's time I drew near the gate of the well-known park. It was open, and I passed on, reaching the door of the Hall without meeting any one by whom I could be recognised. I rang the bell, having previously muffled up my face as well as I could. The door was opened by a strange servant.

"I suppose you are the young man Miss Herbert is expecting?" the man said; and upon my answering in the affirmative, he added—

"Will you walk this way, and I'll fetch you to the housekeeper's room."

I walked after him, and was forthwith transferred to the care of my cousin's maid, who informed me that her mistress was waiting for me in the library, and that I must take care and wipe my feet before going in.

Thus warned, I was duly ushered into the old library, where I found my cousin seated by a table with a book in her hand, and occupied in gazing pensively into the fire. Her beauty exceeded all my expectations.

"I wished to see you," she said in a soft low voice, "that I might hear the latest news from China. When did you arrive?"

"Only yesterday, madam," I replied.

"What ship did you serve in?"

"The Ida," I replied.

"Gracious Heavens! then he must be come," she ex-claimed, as a sudden flush mantled her neck and brow.

"The Ida! did you know an officer called Charles Her-bert?"

"Yes, madam; very well."

"Do you know if he is safe and well?"

I had the cold-blooded cruelty to answer with great com-posure, that I believed he was very ill, and confined to his berth with fever; but I was soon punished for my wicked-ness by seeing the sudden pallor that overcame the lovely countenance before me.

"Not dangerously ill, not dangerously, I trust?" my cousin said in a tremulous tone.

"Why no, madam; I don't believe he is so very bad, neither."

There was something in the tone of the last sentence I uttered which caused my cousin to turn round. She had been sitting in an oblique direction, and I was keeping as much behind her as possible to escape observation. She gave me a penetrating look as she said in reply—

"Who are you?"

"Take a good look, and you will see," I replied, tearing away the covering which had concealed the lower part of my face.

In a moment we were in each other's arms, and our lips met in a long and ardent kiss. "But I must tell the others," she said, springing to the door of the dining-room, which I knew communicated with the library

"Papa! Uncle Herbert is come!—he is safe!—he is here!" she said.

"Come? who? what, my love, have you lost your senses?"

replied the measured accents of each known voice, and in another instant I was locked in my father's arms. He had been over to dine that day at Silverthorne, and the sudden surprise almost startled him out of his wonted equanimity.

"Good Heavens! who could have dreamt it?" he said, taking off his spectacles, and pausing to have a longer look at me. "How the boy is altered. How like his mother he is. She'll hardly know you, Charley. You have grown as brown as a berry, and your hair is a shade or two darker. Why, God bless me, my boy, but this is indeed an unexpected pleasure."

"Let me have a turn at him now," said my uncle; "but had you not better all come into the dining-room? there is a better light there, and we'll get up the dinner in a moment."

Once more I found myself seated at my uncle's table. Many and particular were the inquiries made as to my adventures, and that evening, I believe, I talked more than I had done during the whole time I was away. Nothing could satisfy my cousin's longing to hear every circumstance connected with the war and my experiences of seafaring life, and at any allusion I made to the dangers we had run— which I had the good fortune to escape—I saw a shudder creep over her frame, or a tear start to her eyes. We did not separate until it was long after midnight, and my father had finished another bottle of the favorite port with the yellow seal. When I turned in, I dreamt I was once more back in the old ship; and I wakened, I remember, wondering how the deuce I had got stowed away in so comfortable a berth.

I have now arrived at the last page of my log. It only remains for me to say that, within a year from the day of my arrival, I had received my commission as a lieutenant; but I have never been afloat since, for, shortly afterwards, I married my beautiful cousin, and once more the hearth of the old Hall burns with its wonted splendor.

HOMEWARD BOUND. .

"SIT ye down here, my lads," said Bill Sykes, the mate of the Juno, as he turned a quid of tobacco in his mouth, and hitched up his trousers. "Sit ye down here, while I twist you this 'ere yarn.

"We may be a-going into action, or we may not; that no mortal can tell—not even the skipper himself—and we may be licked, although that is far from likely; but one thing is certain—whenever sailors give up 'baccy and three-finger grog, and sing no more songs, we lose our superiority. We'll be swept off the face of the sea as clean as the deck at seven bells, that we shall, or my name aint Sykes;" and having uttered this oracular preamble, the veteran tar refreshed himself with some new tobacco, smote his thigh with one. brawny hand, by way of adding emphasis to his assertion, and looked to his auditors as if awaiting a reply.

"But where's the yarn you promised, Bill—that aint it, surely?" said one of them.

"By no manner of means. I was a comin' to it, presently. It is many a year ago now, since I sailed in the Semiramis on the East India station. She was French built, but had been captured in the war, and did duty as an English frigate—and a stunner she was, let me tell you. Well, there was in the enemy's squadron, a vessel as was well known. She was called the Victorieuse, or some such name. She measured fourteen hundred tons, and mounted fifty-two guns, or there-away. She was always at some

devilment or another, here, there, and everywhere she was
not wanted. Her captain was as big a devil as his ship. I
forget his name now—nor is it of any great matter, as regards the story.

"This here vessel, you see, my lads, was big enough to
have stowed the poor Semiramis away; and when one of
the officers of the Victorieuse, chancing to come on board,
heard we were going out to the Eastern station, he whistled,
and said something which the first lieutenant, who understood his lingo, said was very like he could eat us without
salt, or some chaff of the kind. Well, my lads, to sea we
went, when the time came, and we sailed for the Madras
roads, where we expected to find this wonderful Frenehman.
She had played the devil among the Indiamen, and generally, every Saturday night, we would get together and sing
the youngsters a song, and tell them what sort of work was
before them. When we got alongside this skyscraping son
of a wretch, the Victorieuse, which we were a-looking after,
then the boys would gather round about, and every mother's
son of them would cock up their ears like the mate of the
deck when grog-ahoy is the word. There is no doubt about
it, that these yarns, when they're not over long, keep up the
pluck of the service, and no mistake about it. As I was
saying, the night was dark, and the wind was rising; we
were on the larboard tack, standing under easy courses,
close hauled, looking a little to the south-west, when the
look-out reported some flashes, which, although they were
not unlike lightning, looked more like guns, I can tell you.
The fact being duly reported to our skipper,—it was then
about nine o'clock,—he says to the first lieutenant, 'Mr.
Clewline,' says he, 'I think it would be quite as well if we
were to put on a little more sail, and bear down in the direction of those queer looking lights, just for the fun of the
thing, to find out what they are, if we can.'

"'The lightning has come to an anchor. I don't see no more of it now,' said the signal-man from his station.

"'No matter; tear away in the direction it came from; put out every light; beat to quarters, and let everything be ready for action,' said the skipper, as he turned down the cabin stairs.

"We made as much sail as we could, passed round on the starboard tack with top-gallant sails flying, and went right smack for the spot where the lights had last been seen; and sure enough, we saw, looming large through the fog, a tremendous French man-of-war.

"'That's him, by jingo!' said the captain, who had returned to the main-deck, where he stood with the night-glass in his hand.

"'I'm d—d if there isn't another—two—three of them,' said the first lieutenant. 'Don't you see them bearing up to the leeward?'

"'Nothing of the kind—it's only the fog,' replied the skipper.

"'Three sails to the leeward,' sang out the signal-man.

"'By the powers of war, what you say is true! We're in for it now!' said the skipper.

"And in for it we were. To run away, if we had been disposed for such an amusement, was out of the question. It was too late for any such evolution. The three vessels, as they drew nearer, were evidently on the same tack as we were; and so, about midnight, when we ought to have been turning in, all hands stood at quarters—many a man of them never to turn in no more—but this talking is dry work. Hand me the can of grog, before I go any further. When I have wet my whistle you shall have the end of my yarn.

"If a single man on board the Semiramis had been disposed to show the white feather, then was the time for doing it," continued the old tar, wiping his mouth with the back of his hand, and biting off the end of a fresh quid. "Then was the time, I say; for the moon came out splendid, as if to show us whereabouts we were. Three spanking French men-of-war were close athwart our beam; the biggest of them, the far-famed Victorieuse, within a couple of musket shots off."

"'Now, my men, are you all ready?' said the skipper. 'Not a shot until I give the word.'

"'Ay, ay, sir,' said the captain of the nearest gun.

"'Man the fore-tops. Look sharp, then up with the helm.'

"The requisite manœuvre having been performed, we passed close under the enemy's stern, so near that we barely cleared her, and as we passed, the whole of our broadside went slap into her. We then came short round on the larboard tack, and gave them another stunner of grape. It was now nearly one o'clock. The moon was shining beautifully, and we went at it fairly, broadside to broadside, blazing away, as hard as we could, until the guns became too hot to load. The Victorieuse had evidently found she had caught a Tartar; her fire began to slacken, and one of her masts went by the board. The sea was now nearly calm. We were close alongside, and the skipper, putting his speaking-trumpet to his lips, summoned them to surrender.

"There was no answer, all was silent as the grave.

"'Why don't you speak, and be d—d to you?' sung out the skipper again.

"There was still no reply.

"'Give them another broadside, my lads, and see if that will find them any voice.'

"At it we went again, but they never returned a single shot.

"'Avast firing, and silence on the main-deck,' and again the skipper tried the speaking trumpet without the least effect. We could hear the men jabbering and chattering like a parcel of monkeys caught in a cocoa-nut tree ; but there was neither voice nor sound, until, all of a sudden, there was a rush aloft to set any sails that remained unhurt by our shot.

"'Loose top-sails, run the foreclew garnets, give them another broadside,' shouted the skipper, who had no intention in the world of letting such a prize out of his clutches.

"There was evidently great confusion on board of the Frenchman, while but few of our men had been hurt. We were quite steady, and had our sails out before the enemy could hoist a square yard of canvas.

"'Cast out the grappling irons—and ready with the boarders forward!' sung out the skipper.

"A few minutes more, and the vessels were in contact; the irons did their work, and fifty picked men, with the first lieutenant at their head, were thrown upon the Frenchman's deck. Ten minutes' stiff work did the business; three hearty cheers, and down went the tri-colored flag—the renowned Victorieuse was our prize. When morning broke, there were the dead and wounded lying about their decks. I won't for many a long day forget the sight. Some were moaning and crying for water, while many of their shipmates were found down below, stowing away all the money they could find in their pockets, and clapping two suits of rigging over their mast-heads. Victorieuse had lost two of his lower masts, the bowsprit was lopped clean off, and seldom, since the time when Admiral Noah went to sea in his ark, was there ever a ship afloat more like his own. On the topsails of the Frenchman, you might have counted hundreds of musket balls, for a detachment of an Irish regiment we had on board, had blazed away pretty cleverly, let me tell you. And now, my lads," continued the old tar, "my yarn is ended, I hope you will lay the story to heart; be-

12

fore this time to-morrow we may be in action ourselves, and if you only work the enemy as well as we did the old Victorieuse, there will be no end of prize-money."

"But what of the two other vessels that were bearing down upon you, Bill?" inquired a brother seaman who stood by, a not inattentive auditor.

"I'll tell you the rest another time; have you not had enough? Now I shall turn in," replied the old seaman, parrying the question, and moving off to his hammock.

"I'll tell you what it is, messmates," said the questioner, "if I believe one word of all that gammon, may I be a soured gurnet."

While this emanation was going on, during one of the night watches, the Juno was standing, with all sails set, in pursuit of two strange sails which had been signalled towards night-fall, bearing to the south-east. It was of course impossible to ascertain what progress had been made, until the approach of daylight, but nothing could exceed the anxiety both of officers and men to come to close quarters with the enemy, if enemies indeed they were. The watches were thus keeping themselves alive by spinning such yarns as the above, and were waiting with anxiety the approach of day. In the meantime, a scene somewhat similar was being enacted in the gun-room, where the younger portion of the officers were whiling away the tedious hours that must intervene before the appearance of daylight, by a narration of their own adventures. The scene was a curious one, and it would require the pen of a Marryat to do it any adequate justice. A small lamp suspended from the ceiling served to make the darkness visible, and threw out into strong relief the figures of the occupants of the apartment. These consisted of about half-a-dozen young officers, who were sitting in every imaginable species of dishabille at an oblong table, which was covered with the scattered frag ments of a frugal meal ; a huge bottle of rum, flanked by two decanters of water, stood in the middle of the board, but the consumption of the purer fluid bore apparently but a small proportion to that of the stimulating beverage, with which it was slightly diluted.   They were all talking at the top of their voices, and now and then a song would burst forth from some uproarious youngster, less remarkable for the musical intonation of its cadence, than for the vigorous melody with which it was given forth.

"Avast your squeaking there, we have had enough of it !" said Walter Long, striking the table with his fist, until the glasses rang again.

"You have no ear for music, Walter ! you never had from the time of your infancy—in short, you are little better than a savage."

"I hope to be one to-morrow if we get into action," was the professional reply.

"I shouldn't be surprised, if after the first shots are fired, you are found skulking in the after cabin."

"Shouldn't you, my boy?   I should."

"Well, then, if you object to singing, what shall we do to pass away the time ? sleeping is out of the question."

"Tell us a story, no matter whether it is true or not, that is of no importance," said Walter Long.

"Let me see—I think I have something that will just suit you ; it has, however, the disadvantage of being founded on fact, being the authentic account of how my old mess-mate, Tom Feather Vane, became acquainted with the Griffiths, into which family he afterwards married."

"Let us hear it by all means," said Walter Long.

"The introduction of Tom Feather Vane to the paternal mansion of Laura Griffiths, runs somewhat whimsical, and is not unworthy of recording, as forming a remarkable exception to the usual 'modus operandi,' by means of which

young gentlemen contrive to get their legs under respectable mahogany. The hall-door of Mr. Griffiths' abode was
of a gay pea-green color, and the knocker of brass, bur-
nished so brightly that to touch it was suggestive of burned
fingers. This ornament had attracted the notice of the er-
ratic Tom. He accordingly seized an early opportunity of
wrenching it off and conveying it home in his pocket, where
it formed a splendid addition to a collection of articles of a
similar kind he had for some time been engaged in forming.
But as Tom passed through this street the next day, he saw
the absent knocker replaced by one if possible of a still more
brilliant appearance. He made up his mind at once, that it
too should follow its predecessor ; and as night-fall came
on, he returned to the spot for the felonious object he had
in view. But as he was engaged in the very act, by some
unlucky coincidence, the door was opened by Mr. Griffiths,
who, as he emerged from his dwelling to inhale the freshness of the evening air, caught Tom, who had just succeeded
in his attempt, with the knocker in his hand. An exclamation of astonishment, followed by an oath and a blow so
well planted, that Tom rolled down the area steps, was the
immediate result of the discovery. Rolling from the area,
the culprit tumbled into the kitchen window, which chanced
to be open, greatly to the astonishment of Mrs. Nipper,
the cook, who was sitting *tête-à-tête* over a quiet dish of tea
with Tom Jones, her follower. The gentleman's arm was
round the lady's waist at the very moment when the intruder, holding the new brass knocker tightly grasped in
his hand, made his unwelcome *entrée.*

" 'Lor', good gracious me—fire ! robbery ! murder !'
screamed Mrs. Nipper, at the top of her voice.

" Thunder and turf !" shouted her companion, who was
a native of the Emerald Isle.

" But the astonishment of the lovers was as nothing to the

amazement of Tom Feather Vane. He had only recovered the use of his scattered faculties, when the voice of Mr. Griffiths was heard in the passage, and his heavy step sounded on the stairs.

"'You infernal young villain ! The second knocker in two days ! Punch his head with the kitchen poker, until I come, Mrs. Nipper, if you please, and then call the watch.' That functionary might have been called, but I question if the summons would have been attended with any beneficial result, as he was fast asleep in his watch-box round the corner.

"When Mrs. Nipper had in some degree recovered from her amazement, her thoughts ran less upon the detention of the robber than the concealment of the 'follower,' who was a contraband article in that establishment. 'Run !' she said, 'run ! Master will be here like winking ! Cut out of the back door—there's time yet !'

"But the gentleman thus affectionately appealed to was deaf to the voice of his charmer ; he had probably indulged in a larger potation of beer, before he dropped in to tea, than usual ; he stood stock still, staring attentively at Mr. Feather Vane, with the knocker in his hand, and at his mistress. The few minutes, therefore, that were left to him. for escape were thus irrevocably lost. Presence of mind, however, was not one of those qualities in which Tom Feather Vane was ever found deficient. He saw, at a glance, the precise posture of affairs, and that no time was to be lost. He sprang from the recumbent posture he had hitherto maintained, and hustling up to the bewildered Mr. Jones, thrust into his pocket the spoil of which he had become possessed, and passed at a bound out through the area window, at the very moment of Mr. Griffiths' entrance into the kitchen. 'You infernal robber ! Have you stunned him with the poker, Mrs. Nipper ?' shouted the angry house-

holder. 'You villain ! I'll have you transported for this, if
there's law to be found in Southsea. Where is my new
brass knocker ? Give it up this instant.'

" 'Knocker, your honor !' responded Jones. 'Bedad, sir,
nothing' to do with it ; I came to have a word with the
cook.'

" 'You brazen impostor, I caught you at the door. I'll
be bound you have it somewhere secreted about you. Give
up the knocker this moment, or I'll knock you to eternal
smash.'

" 'Hands off, old gentleman ; I'll stand none of that nonsense. I haven't your knocker, as I knows of—keep your
distance !'

"But the blood of Mr. Griffiths was now going at fever
heat. He squared up in pugilistic guise at the intruder,
who squared at him in return. A blow or two was interchanged, and in the midst of this skirmish the knocker dropped out of Mr. Jones's pocket upon the floor.

" 'I told you you had it ; surrender to the law !' shouted
Mr. Griffiths, springing vigorously on, and seizing his antagonist by the collar.

" 'Be aisy now, be aisy, and I'll akimpany you, since you
will have it so ; but, be Jabers ! I could knock ye to pieces
if I plaised——'

" 'Come on, you villain, none of your bad language. Push
him behind, Mrs. Nipper ! push him behind, will you, and
pick up the knocker—there it is, on the floor.' But Mrs.
Nipper seemed as one deprived alike of the power of speech
and motion. Her faculties had become paralyzed. She
stood with one hand pointing through the open window by
which the audacious intruder had effected his escape, and
with a dish-cloth in the other, in lieu, it is presumed, of a
pocket-handkerchief. She tried to speak, but could not
articulate a word. Meanwhile, old Griffiths swore, and

pulled, and shook his prisoner to and fro—without however
being able to prevail upon him to ascend a single step of
the stairs.

"Such was the crisis of affairs, when a violent ringing
was heard at the street door. 'Thank Heaven, there is the
watch !' said the old gentleman, wiping off the perspiration
which streamed profusely down his forehead.

"'Help! help! watch! watch! come along, you ruffian.
I'll teach you to steal knockers, that I will,' shouted Mr.
Griffiths, tugging energetically at his captive. Again a
precious peal sounded at the area bell.

"'Why the devil, Mrs. Nipper, don't you go and open
the door? what the deuce do you stand staring there for?
Is the woman a fool?'

"Thus objurgated, away went Mrs. Nipper. She sprang
up the stairs, and flinging open the door, saw Tom Feather
Vane, who, making a polite bow, inquired if her master was
at home.

"'Yes, sir, he is—but no! I rather think he is particularly engaged at present.'

"'Give him my card, if you please, and say I wish to
speak with him for a moment.'

"'Halloa! come here, whoever you are, come here!'
shouted Mr. Griffiths from the foot of the stairs.

"In obedience to this summons, Tom walked into the
passage; but no sooner had the light of the lamp fallen upon
his features, than Mrs. Nipper recognised the gentleman
who had interrupted her tête-à-tête in the kitchen a short
time ago.

"'Fire! robbery! murder! murder!' shouted Mrs. Nipper, accentuating the last syllable to give it greater force.

"'Thieves! halloo! let me at 'em! where are they?'
shouted Tom.

"'Here! this way! I have you now, you villain!' sung

out old Mr. Griffiths. Tom Feather Vane proceeded accordingly, without taking any further notice of Mrs. Nipper,
in the direction of the voice.

" ' Happy to see you, sir ; help me to hold this ruffian.
I'm quite blown——'

" ' Hold him—with pleasure. Has he been stealing the
spoons?' inquired Tom Feather Vane.

" ' Spoons ! no—my new brass knocker. We'll bring
him to the police. I caught him with it in his pocket.'

" ' That we will, by Jingo !' shouted Tom, seizing hold of
the innocent Jones by the collar.

" ' Now then, hold him tight until I fetch a light. Halloa ! Mrs. Nipper ! What are you about up there?—a candle—bring a candle.'

" ' You vagabond ! You come about gentlemen's houses
stealing their knockers ! I'll give you a lesson you won't
forget in a hurry—come in here, you shocking reprobate !'—
and opening the kitchen door, Mr. Feather Vane pushed in
his captive, while the enraptured Mr. Griffiths proceeded in
quest of a light.

" ' Punch his head with a poker if he attempts to stir,
shouted Mr. Griffiths from the top of the stairs.

" ' You nincompoop !' said Tom, shaking the bewildered
Jones ; ' why don't you make yourself scarce ? Do you see
that open window ? What is it there for, you idiot ? If
I were to let you go now, do you think you could jump
through it ?'

" ' I'll try,' said the man, scratching his head.

. " ' Be off, then, like a lamplighter, and keep your own
counsel,' said Tom, letting him loose.

" Thus released, Jones, the follower, without waiting to
thank his captor, sprang through the open window ; while
Tom shouted as loud as he could bawl, ' Stop him ! stop

him ! the villain has knocked me over. He's off ! Stop him ! stop him !'

" ' You don't mean to tell me you have let the rascal go !' inquired the old gentleman, as, candle in hand, he reappeared on the scene of action.

" ' Confound him !' replied Tom ; ' the devil couldn't hold such a fellow ; the very instant, sir, you left me alone with him, he gave me a thump on the head, which quite stunned me, and then he bolted like shot.'

" ' Blow on the head, my dear sir ?   I am really sincerely concerned you should have suffered in your anxiety to serve me.   But, bless me !   Why—yes, you are actually bleeding !'

" ' Oh, it is nothing of any consequence.'   (Tom had got the hurt in his previous rencontre at the street door.)

" ' It is of consequence—we must get it looked to at once. Here, Mrs. Nipper—deuce take the woman, where is she ? Mrs. Nipper, I say, some hot water and towels—be quick. If ever I find him on my premises again, I'll have him skinned alive.   The second knocker in a week.   Ugh ! the villain !   Now, pray, my dear sir, do let me look at your wound.'

" Tom having submitted his head to the inspection of Mr. Griffiths, endeavored to assume as solemn an expression of countenance as he could.   Mrs. Nipper entering with a basin of hot water, no sooner saw him, than she began to scream violently.

" ' Deuce take the woman, what is she at ?   Did you never see blood before ?   Run up-stairs and bring me some sticking-plaster.   Be quick, if you please, Mrs. Nipper,' said the energetic old gentleman.

" The cook departed, but soon returned to say that she could not find the article of which she had gone in quest.

" ' Stupid Nipper, you seem to have lost any little sense

you ever had ; give me the candle and I'll fetch it myself,
and off went Mr. Griffiths, to look for the plaster, leaving
his domestic face to face with the object which had inspired
her with such aversion and horror.

"'Now, don't look so frightened, my dear friend,' said
Tom Feather Vane, 'here's something to buy you a new
ribbon ;' and as he spoke he slipped a sovereign into the
lady's hand.

"'Lawk, my good gracious !'

"'Never mind your good gracious—I have let your lover
off, as you see—say nothing about it, and I'll make your fortune, you gipsy.'

"How this feat was to be accomplished, Tom Feather
Vane, who was always very ready, at any sudden emergen-
cy, with vague promises, never paused to determine. He
laid his finger on his lips—'Mum ! is the word, Mrs. Nipper,' he said ; 'you may trust me, my dear.'

"The approach of the master of the house rendered any
further conversation impossible, so Mrs. Nipper slipped the
coin into her bosom, and assisted her master in the surgical
operations which he proceeded to perform upon his interesting patient.

"When Tom Feather Vane was washed and brushed,
covered with sticking-plaster, and made as presentable as
under existing circumstances it was possible to make him, he
was invited to remain to supper as a matter of course, and
like a clever fellow as he was, he made so good a use of
this opportunity, that a very few weeks seemed to establish
him as a regular visitor of the family ; and it is somewhat
remarkable, that from the period of that occurrence, there
never was another knocker stolen from the hall-door of the
Griffiths' mansion ; a circumstance which Tom, with inimita-
ble *sang froid* and *nonchalance*, attributed to the personal
prowess of Mr. Griffiths, in his rencontre with the felonious

assailant of his premises. Such was the manner in which
the lieutenant obtained an introduction ; and it was at the
petit souper which succeeded to the affray, that his' eye was
most agreeably refreshed by the sight of a very charming
young lady, who, what with tittering and blushing at the
comical picture he presented with the right side of his head
covered with large stripes of sticking-plaster, and trembling
for the safety of her beloved parent, formed one of the most
enchanting pictures of youthful grace and loveliness he.
thought he had ever had the good fortune to behold. He
envied the old gentleman as his daughter threw her arm
round his pudgy neck with a loving pressure, and felt
inclined to defy him to mortal combat on the spot; but as
such a rencontre might have interfered with his future operations, Tom restrained his angry feelings at seeing a father
kissed by his daughter, and made himself so uncommonly
agreeable, that he produced a favorable impression upon
both ; so that in an unusually short time from this incident,
he had contrived to become the accepted suitor of the young
lady, whom he afterwards led to the hymeneal altar."

" Bravo ! capital !" resounded from all sides, when the
speaker had concluded. ◆

" And now, my boys, do you think we shall really catch
these fellows after all ?"

" Impossible to tell, until daylight doth appear."

" It's beginning to appear now, or I am mistaken."

" Douse the glim then, and let us have a look out."

The lamp being accordingly extinguished, the gray light
of dawning morning streamed in upon the assembled party,
who did not by any means appear to so much advantage
seen through its medium, as they did by lamp-light. But
they donned their various habiliments, and proceeded upon
deck—tumbling up, as the phrase is, one after another, the
companion ladder. The night watch was still on the look-

out, the men for the most part were asleep at their quarters. Neither the captain nor the first lieutenant had of course made their appearance, and the good ship was holding on under a heavy press of sail, the apparently solitary occupant of the vast expanse of sea.

"Blow ! blow, thou freshening breeze !" shouted Walter Long ; " blow us to the enemy !"

" There don't seem much probability of such a result, as far as I am able to judge," said Hamilton, who was sweeping the horizon with a glass. " No, none can tell what luck may be in store for us before the sun goes down."

" Whereabouts were they seen last ?"

" To the south-west," replied the captain of the watch.

"They have out-sailed us, then, and be d—d to them !"

" Shouldn't think that at all likely ; the fog is still heavy to leeward."

. "And when it clears off, you think they'll turn up, eh ?"

" I have no doubt of it, whatever," replied the man, touching his hat.

." How many of them were reported due ?"

" Only one sail, to any certainty."

"Well, one is enough, if we can only catch her."

"And so we shall with the blessing of Providence," said the captain of the watch.

But the daylight which they had all been so anxiously awaiting, although it had now fairly broken, and the rising sun had dispelled the floating mist, did not reveal to the anxious crew the enemy of whom they were in quest. But instead thereof, lay a long stripe, like a thin bank of cloud, floating on the surface of the water, far away in the distance, which was soon ascertained to be land, even before the man at the mast-head made the usual announcement. The disappointment was deep and universal. There could be no question that the strange sail had succeeded, under

cover of the night, in rejoining the remainder of the squadron in the harbor of Brest.   Deep and loud were the rail-
ings against the ill-fortune which had befallen the Juno in
allowing such a prize to escape; but there was apparently
no help for it, so all hands were piped to breakfast in an
exceedingly ill-humor, and the Juno held on upon her
course, the land of the French coast becoming every hour
more distinctly visible.   At length, towards evening, as the
ship passed close to the shore, a fine frigate was discovered
at anchor under the batteries of Carnantburg.   She rode
at her anchors, with top-gallants across, her large ensign
floating from the peak; she was evidently the object the
Juno had been so long pursuing, and there she was, to all
appearance secure from any hostile aggression.   The circumstance having been duly reported to the skipper, who
was not the man to be deterred from any course which
seemed to hold out a reasonable prospect of success, he
swore he would cut her out.   The news soon flew fore and
aft.   The men swarming at the quarters were not in a humor to be balked.   Then came all the preparations for this
desperate undertaking, for it was well known that the position of the frigate was such, that any attempt to cut her
out would be attended with a tremendous sacrifice of life.

"Well, my boy, which boat do you go in?" inquired
Walter Long of a messmate, who was selecting from a bun-
dle of cutlasses one which seemed the best adapted to his
length and strength of arm.

"I go in the cutter with Morris; we lead."

"The deuce you do! you may, too, if you can keep it."

"We'll do our best, my boy; who are you with?"

"Oh, I'm in the gig.   Brown is with us."

"I think Brown looks a little chalky about the gills,
hey, don't he, rather?   He is thinking of his little wife and
four small children at Gosport, most probably."

"Ah ! I didn't know he had any responsibilities of that kind."

"Yes, he has ; and serious ones they are when a fellow is going into such an action."

"Of course ! of course—I think this blade seems the stoutest: its temper shall be tried presently."

Towards nightfall everything was in readiness, and at a given signal, the boats, duly manned, in perfect silence left the ship. Such was the ardor of the men, that they strove, one division against the other, to near the frigate. In this effort to be first, there was displayed less discretion than enthusiasm—one would have thought they were rowing at a boat-race. And at length, the splashing of the oars in all probability had attracted the notice of the frigate ; for a blue-light was thrown up, and weighing anchor, she ran in close alongside of the batteries, where she moored. But the more the danger, the more sailors feel stimulated. The removal of the frigate did not cause the expedition for a moment to falter ; their hands and hearts were alike ready. There was not a sound heard save the measured dip of the muffled oars as they fell swiftly in the water.

The boats were now close together, and rapidly approaching the object of attack. The first halted for a moment, and the first lieutenant standing up, addressed his crew.

"Now, my lads," he said, "we have a stiff piece of work before us ; but the greater the danger, the greater the honor. To bring that frigate out from the teeth of them batteries will be no easy piece of work, I promise you. You, Bill Sykes, are a smart foretop man ; let us see how you can loosen the frigate's foretop sail, so as to catch any breath of wind, and we shall have a stiff one presently. You need not be particular in casting off the gasket ; a sharp knife and an easy conscience will do the work. Don't stand on stepping-stones, and in the meantime we'll see what

we can do with the fellows below. So now, my lads, one
single cheer, and then you'll follow me."

A hearty cheer, that seemed to ring from the very bosom
of the deep, was the immediate reply, and the boats dashed
on to the attack, the cutter leading the way.

But just at this moment a sheet of flame burst from the
frigate, followed by a crashing volley of grape and canister,
which taking effect upon the second boat, stove it into
atoms. This salutation, enough to have damped the courage of any men, however determined, was received with a
fresh cheer, and casting on their grappling irons, the assailants prepared to board. But this was no easy task. The
French, armed at all points, presented a bristling front of
boarding pikes and cutlasses, while a close and well-directed
fire of musketry was kept up from the poop.

Nothing could exceed the gallantry of the assailants, but
they were driven back with great loss, in spite of their
clinging cat-like to the ropes; while the enemy, seeing the
failure of the first attempt to gain a footing, shouted like
demons with rage and triumph. Never since man first engaged his fellow was there displayed on both sides more
desperate courage. The fire-arms of the British sailors
were now perfectly useless, and, armed with the cutlass and
boarding-pike only, they persevered in their attempt with
undaunted determination. The batteries had now opened,
and although the darkness of the night prevented them
from aiming with any certainty, the shot fell like hail in the
water. Undismayed by the furious fire from them and from
the frigate, undeterred by the forest of pikes which bristled
from her bows, and the loss of so many a gallant comrade,
the English sailors again and again rushed to the assault,
and at length succeeded in gaining a footing upon the forecastle.

"Hurrah for the first aloft!" shouted Sykes, who, clear

ing a path with his cutlass, sprang upon the rigging, and clambering aloft, was soon in the neighborhood of the fore-top-sail yard. But having made good his way, the gallant seaman found an unexpected obstacle : the gear was lashed close along the yard, but a clasp-knife, judiciously applied, soon set it free ; and so expeditiously was this accomplished, and so well did the seamen stationed to loose the sail per-form their part of the work, that in less than five minutes after the period of gaining the deck, the frigate had her three topsails and courses cut adrift, and the sails dropping down ready to be sheeted home. The sound of the falling sails was the first intimation of his danger to the enemy. So long as they continued under the batteries, they had lit-tle ground for apprehension ; but once drifting out to sea, with a desperate enemy on board, they felt their position would be hopeless. Everything now depended upon the wind.

Meanwhile the struggle upon deck proceeded. It was literally hand to hand and foot to foot ; the cutlass and the boarding-pike against the sabre and the bayonet. At first the French stood their ground with admirable determina-tion, and the assailants were repulsed with serious loss ; but the vigor of their attack at·last carried everything before it ; and although the deck, contested inch by inch as it was, continued swept by a heavy fire of musketry, it was soon in the possession of the British seamen. At this crisis a voice was heard to exclaim, " She goes ahead now !" The mo-tion of the ship was perceptible to all on board ; and then, high over the crashing of the shot, and the shrieks of the wounded, rose in tones of thunder the British cheer. But the firing from the ramparts still continued with unabated vigor, and it was quite evident that the soldiery, seeing the vessel had been taken, were determined if possible to destroy her, even at the sacrifice of all on board. The wind, however, increased—a few minutes more, and the vessel, with her crew and her gallant captors, would be beyond the reach of further injury. The crisis was one of intense excitement. On the forecastle stood Walter Long ; how he had contrived to escape destruction seemed miraculous, for he was in the first boat, which had been stove to pieces. He had fought his way to the post of eminence which he now occupied, surrounded by a few of his comrades. The acquisition of this position had been an achievement by no means easy of performance. As he led the way from the quarter-gallery, he found his progress impeded, in consequence of the door having been barricaded. All attempts to demolish this obstacle having proved in vain, he clambered up to the taffrail, and from thence succeeded in gaining the quarter-deck, where the fight was thickest. Sweeping his cutlass round his head, and cheering on his comrades, he had fought his way gallantly to the spot. And now the breeze springing up, the sails were trimmed, and the frigate drawing fast from the land, was soon out of the reach of any further mischief.

The exultation at the success of this gallant enterprise would be less difficult to imagine than to describe. The captured frigate was towed alongside, and taken into the nearest English port. The brilliant exploit we have thus recorded, found praise from every lip ; it was one of the most daring and well-executed naval attacks since the cutting out of the Hermione. The loss was, however, considerable ; fifteen men had been killed on the part of the assailants, and nearly thirty severely wounded. For some days after the engagement, the crew of the Juno were busily engaged in endeavoring to repair the damages which had been sustained from the shot of the batteries by the French vessel ; new sails had to be bent ; the gunwales, which were considerably torn by shot, to be replaced ; and many other repairs effected, before the vessel could with safety be pro· nounced fit for sea. Fitted for sea, however, in due time, she became ; and now, under another name, manned by another crew, and with a different ensign floating from her poop, she ploughs the waves, a very neat and unexceptionable English cruiser.

AQUATIC EXPEDITION

GIBRALTAR TO BARCELONA.

SOME years since—no matter how many, but it was in the month of May—I found myself (located, as the Yankees say) for four-and-twenty hours at the Ragged Staff Guard at Gibraltar, and, during my tour of duty, was visited by my friend B——, who mentioned his having obtained twelve months' leave of absence, and his intention of proceeding in his yacht to Carthagena, and thence through France to England, provided any officer would accompany, him to whom might be intrusted the charge of the craft on her homeward voyage. Yachting and boating are favorite pastimes with the military denizens of the Rock, and they who possess a taste for aquatic pursuits, have ample inducement to gratify their predilection, for the scene on a calm summer's evening, when the noble bay reflects on its unruffled surface the numerous vessels resting on its bosom, and the lofty Rock, with its batteries, houses, orange trees, geraniums and acacias, with the distant mountains of Spain and Africa, are bathed in the light of a brilliant sunset, is sufficient to win to exertion even the most indolent and apathetic. When, on the other hand, strong south-westerly breezes or the more dangerous "Levanter" prevail, gigs manned by adventurous spirits may be seen poised on the crests or descending into the trough of the accompanying heavy sea, whilst here and there trim little yachts, staggering under a press of canvas, the flag of England fluttering from their peaks, proclaim their owners sons of that nation whose

"March is on the mountain wave, whose home is on the deep."

Of that gallant and warm-hearted band who were then the chief promoters of boating parties, of pic-nics, and of fun and merriment of every kind, but few now remain. Some, chafing at a life of inactivity in our own service, joined the ranks of the British Legion, and at St. Sebastian "foremost fighting fell." Some have withered under the blasting influence of West Indian yellow fever; the bones of others are bleaching on the banks of the distant Sutlej; a few have achieved honors and renown; some still serve on, hoping for opportunities of distinguishing themselves which may never arrive; and others, passing into private life, have been absorbed and lost sight of in the great vortex of ever-changing society.

It may at the first moment seem strange that B—— should have expressed doubts as to any one joining him on the cruise he proposed, but a future description of the little "Midge" will somewhat account for his skepticism. Thinking this would be an excellent opportunity for seeing more of Spain than I had hitherto been enabled to accomplish, I immediately expressed my readiness for the trip—and there being, moreover, just sufficient risk in the business to render it what is termed a "*sporting undertaking*," served as an additional incentive to make the trial ; and on Lieut. R—— also agreeing to join the party, nothing remained but to apply for leave (which was granted) and to make the ne-

cessary preparations for the voyage. As none of us had
ever been eastward of Malaga, and were totally ignorant
of the coast, Admiral, then Captain S——, was consulted
us to the prudence of the undertaking, who thereupon informed us "we should all be drowned." This opinion (in
conformity with the perverseness of human nature) only
strengthened our determination to proceed ; but hearing
that the governor, the late Sir W. H——, had declared he
would not permit us to start upon so wild an expedition, we
procured bills of health for Cadiz as well as for Carthagena,
and thus in some degree blinded the authorities as to our
real intentions.   On the afternoon of Sunday, the second
of June, the anchor was weighed, and by the united assistance of the current and a strong south-westerly breeze, the
Rock was soon left far astern. The singular fact that while
at its upper extremity the Mediterranean receives a constant supply from the Black Sea by a current setting into it
from the Dardanelles, and at the lower by a current setting
through the straits of Gibraltar from the Atlantic, no perceptible influence is exercised upon it by this necessarily
vast accession of water, has been the subject of much consideration amongst the learned, and various theories have.
been propounded to account for this remarkable circumstance.   That the upper influx is counteracted by an under
efflux can scarcely be doubted, for that the superfluous
water could be carried off by evaporation *alone* bears upon
it the stamp of impossibility.   Behold us now fairly afloat,
and a description of the boat, destined for several weeks to
be our home, which gallantly weathered many a gale and
bore us over some hundreds of miles, may not here be out
of place.   Of about five tons burthen, and cutter-rigged
with a mizen, her capabilities of steerage were for her size
considerable.   Aft was an open space in the deck for the
helmsman, which could be closed at pleasure.   Round this

(in lockers for the purpose) were wines and provisions. The cabin contained two sleeping berths for ourselves, and opening from it was accommodation for the crew. Ledges of about five inches in height ran fore and aft of the berths, to keep the mattresses in their places, and a plank resting upon them, served as a bench when taking our meals, our heads when thus seated being within a few inches of the deck. In calm weather the frames of the hatches were raised upon iron stanchions, which added much to our comfort. A small table slung with cords from the deck could be unshipped at pleasure; drawers for knives, forks, and plates, a copper washing basin, a kettle, a coffee pot, a couple of saucepans, a frying-pan, and two "braseros" formed our list of indispensables. The commissariat consisted of seven days' water, salt provisions, a portion of the common red wine of the country, biscuits, tea, sugar, coffee, cheese, &c. The stores were three anchors, one chain, and two hempen cables, iron ballast, spare sails, &c. Two small guns forward, and two aft, for signals, working upon pivots, were, when at sea, usually placed below. This cargo, added to our three selves and the crew, (two men and a boy, the latter working his way to Santa Pola,) brought the yacht so low in the water that by leaning over the side we could reach it with our hands. The party was divided into three watches, one of ourselves being always in charge, and such other arrangements were made as were considered most conducive to our safety and comfort.

The fresh breeze with which we had commenced our voyage gradually deserted us, and we had the extreme *felicity* (?) of tumbling about in a heavy short sea during the greater part of the night; but the following morning the friendly south-wester again came to our aid, and after speaking H. M. ten-gun brig Philomel, (with the officers of which we were well acquainted, owing to her being on the Gibraltar station,) cruising under easy canvas, anchored in Malaga Bay about half-past twelve o' clock. The health-boat coming alongside and the officer in charge admitting us to pratique, a shore-boat was put in requisition to land us, the " Midge" not being sufficiently large to carry even a "dingy" for our own use.

We first paid our respects to Mr. Mark, the consul, and then proceeded to the authorities, whose duty it was to examine and sign the cutter's papers. The town of Malaga, situated in the province of Granada, and divided by the river Guadelmedina into two parts, presents, with the ruins of its ancient Moorish castle, a fine appearance from the sea ; the mountains which surround it forming a splendid background to the picture. The Cathedral was the first point of attention ; one of its towers only was completed, but from the other is a magnificent view of the adjacent country. The roof, supported by lofty pillars, has but little beauty to recommend it, but the choir is curiously carved and contains a number of stalls. Of the tone of the organs, two in number, we had no opportunity of judging. Great efforts were made to impress us with a sense of the *unrivalled* magnificence of the building, but our expectations in this particular were grievously disappointed. The Alameda is a beautiful promenade, planted with trees and surrounded with handsome houses. It is the favorite resort of the fair sex, and the Malagenas, equalling if not excelling their sisters of Cadiz in those attractions which captivate the sterner sex, here make sad havoc with the hearts of their attendant caballeros. Several parties of them were slowly pacing up and down, and certes the magnificent eyes and voluptuous forms of some among them were amply sufficient to have roused the passions of far colder blooded mortals than are the inhabitants of this fiery clime. The streets were narrow and crowded with people, some sitting, some standing, some

stretched at full length on the ground, some slowly sauntering, but all apparently revelling in idleness, and affording
by their picturesque costumes and lazy attitudes interesting
studies to the observant artist.

"Torijos" and his companions, some fifty in number, and
amongst them an Irish gentleman named Boyd, were shot
on the beach in December, 1831, by General Moreno, for
having endeavored to procure a rising in favor of the "Constitution," their capture being effected by a system of treach-
ery seldom heard of amongst civilized nations.   It is a matter of surprise, that, about to embark on a perilous service,
and as Spaniards well acquainted with the proverbial deceit-
fulness of their fellow-countrymen, they so easily fell into
the trap prepared for them—" Quos Deus vult perdere prius
dementat."   With Mr. Boyd some of us had been slightly
acquainted, and this circumstance added to the interest we
took in the scene of the catastrophe.   Having been deluded
by false representations on the part of the *government authorities* that the soldiery at Malaga were disaffected, and
that two *guarda costas* would join and escort the party on
their voyage, Torijos and his companions were, in an evil
hour, induced to start on their ill-starred expedition.   The
government cruisers, instead of proving friendly, drove them
on shore at a point where troops were prepared for their
hostile reception ; when taking refuge in a house, they were
compelled to surrender, and soon after shot without trial.
A letter was sent, by Mr. Boyd, to a friend at Gibraltar,
composed a few hours before his execution, expressing calm
and manly resignation to his fate, stating that a priest had
endeavored to make him abjure his religion, and requesting
the person to whom the communication was addressed, to
declare publicly, in case doubts should be expressed on the
subject, that he died a firm adherent to the Protestant faith.

Embarking in the evening, we sailed with the rising of

the land wind, the night being very dark, save when vivid
lightning shed its momentary blaze over the far horizon.
During the middle watch the storm was in all its grandeur,
and the scene was awfully impressive. The electric fluid
leaped from cloud to cloud, the thunder crashed above our
heads, while the phosphoric light which gleamed from the
water, as with a steady breeze the cutter ploughed her way
through the swelling billows, cast a ghastly hue upon her
canvas during the intervals of pitchy darkness. This turmoil of the elements gradually ceased, and morning at length
shed its cold gray light upon the restless waves. There is
something inexpressibly cheerful in the advent of approaching day; to behold it dispelling night, and lifting itself, as
it were, from out the ever moving waters. Objects hitherto
indistinct become gradually more and more visible, a golden
tinge irradiates the sky, and clouds of brilliant coloring herald the approach of the great luminary who diffuses light
and life o'er all created nature. During the early part of
the day we anchored abreast of a small village called Nerja,
and going ashore, paid our respects to the Padre, with a
view of obtaining from him any information that might
prove useful. He received us with politeness, and sent for
some fishermen to give us directions as to our future navigation along the coast. There being nothing worthy of observation at Nerja, and finding ourselves objects of unpleasant curiosity to the inhabitants, who appeared imbued with
eastern distrust of strangers, we returned on board the
yacht. The heat was intense; not a cloud obscured the
midday sun, whose rays were reflected as by a mirror from
the surface of a sea unruffled by the slightest breeze. A
white mist, floating over the summits of the mountains,
blended earth and sky in indistinct confusion. The "Midge"
riding lazily at her anchor, floating quietly upon the long
undulations of a heavy ground swell, combined with the

monotonous roar of the surf breaking upon the adjacent
rocks, superinduced a most overpowering feeling of lassitude
and distaste for exertion.   The hatches being removed, and
their frames elevated upon the stanchions, (previously
spoken of,) wet sails were laid over all, and a trifling degree
of coolness being thus obtained, we followed the example of
the natives and resigned ourselves to repose.   About 7 P.
M. we were again under weigh, a light air just filling the
sails, and soon had a fine view of the Apuljarras mountains
which extend many miles along the coast.   The morning of
the fifth brought with it an increasing breeze from the old
quarter, the south-west, and our gallant little craft dashed
through the water in first rate style.   Numerous vessels
were sighted during the day, one of which we spoke, and
found to be the "Rambler," from Leghorn, bound to London.   Towards night, the wind freshening almost to a gale,
with a heavy sea, the topmast was struck, the mainsail
double reefed, the mizen brailed, jibs were shifted, and the
hatches battened down, all hands remaining on deck whilst
we doubled Cape de Gata, a gigantic rock some twenty
miles in circumference.   Whether arising from any peculiar
formation of the coast, I cannot pretend to decide, but certain it is that at this particular spot storms are almost invariably encountered, and the native sailors have a great dislike to its unpleasant neighborhood.   Dark clouds driving
swiftly across the sky permitted a waning moon to shed its
sickly light at intervals upon the waste of waters ; occa-
sional flashes of lightning increased the wildness of the prospect, while far away to leeward the dreaded Cape loomed
spectrally in the misty distance.   The "Midge," with the
wind nearly a-beam, flew merrily over the heaving waves,
and quite satisfied us that happen what might, she, at all
events, would do her duty.

Continuing our course till we judged a sufficient offing

had been obtained to fetch Carthagena, the helm was put up, and the wind drawing right aft, the mainsail was furled, the square-sail hoisted in its place, and we had every prospect (if the breeze remained steady) of a fine run to our desired haven. Great care was requisite in steering the cutter, so as to avoid mischief from the huge seas that came thundering astern, as if determined to overwhelm her; but the buoyant little craft rose gallantly upon them, and they passed harmlessly by, hissing and roaring under the bows in impotent malice. The regular watch was now set, and the remainder of us sought the shelter of our diminutive cabin. On looking out from the hatchway on the morning of the 6th all was changed. It was a perfect calm; the bright blue heaven uncheckered · by a single cloud, and not a breath of air existed to fill the sails, which flapped and rattled as we gently rolled upon the heavy swells; a light air springing up about midday enabled us, assisted by our sweeps, to reach the "Puerto de las Aguilas," in the harbor of which we anchored for the night. It is very secure for small craft, protected by a hill jutting out into the sea, on the summit of which is a fort. We passed the night on board, and four o'clock on the morning of the 7th saw us again under weigh, with a more moderate south-westerly breeze.

A large *guarda costa*, carrying a heavy gun amidships, and full of men, bore down upon us about ten, evidently not understanding who or what we were, but upon our hoisting the English flag, and, in reply to a question from her captain, stating whence we were come and whither we were going, she went about and left us to pursue our voyage. The harbor of Carthagena is, from the narrowness of its entrance, very difficult of access to strangers, and it was with some little trouble, owing to our total ignorance of the coast, that we at length discovered it, when, standing in, we an chored about three o'clock in the afternoon. Having arrived at a place of such importance, it was determined to make as smart an appearance as circumstances would permit. The cutter's sails were furled with unusual care, the yard was squared with the utmost exactness, ropes were neatly coiled down, swivels mounted, and ourselves arrayed in blue undress uniforms, awaited the arrival of the healthboat, which, pulling twelve oars, and large enough to have taken the "Midge" on board, soon after came alongside and demanded our papers, the officers and crew using sundry exclamations of surprise at the smallness of the yacht.

Our credentials being delivered, we fully expected permission to land at once, when, to our amazement and indignation, the officials informed us we must perform six days' quarantine, that being the time fixed for all vessels coming from Gibraltar. In vain we remonstrated, stating we were *last* from Malaga, and *not* from Gibraltar as was declared, when the Governor's Secretary, who happened to be present, settled the matter by a direct falsehood, viz: that it mattered not *where* vessels *might* have touched at, but that if they were from the Rock *at all*, into quarantine they must go. As civility had failed in mollifying these worthies, we tried what effect a little bluster would produce, and vowed that every Spanish vessel should, upon reaching Gibraltar, perform the same number of days' quarantine they might inflict upon us, stating in addition, we should forthwith lay a complaint before our ambassador at Madrid. The Dons, evidently a little bothered, pulled away, leaving a health guard in a boat a short distance off to prevent any communication with the shore. A few pecetas rendered the man excessively obliging, and he procured for us a supply of water, fresh provisions and vegetables, and undertook to send a letter from us to the Consul, informing him of our situation, and requesting he would use his influence to ob

tain our release, as we were satisfied some knavery was at
the bottom of the transaction.

The whole proceeding, however, was most vexatious, and
the prospect of a long beat to windward of between two
and three hundred miles back to the Rock against the pre-
vailing westerly winds, without accomplishing the object of
our voyage, at the first moment entirely destroyed our equanimity ; but after hoisting the yellow flag, and consigning
Spaniards in general, and the Carthagena gentry in particular, to the tender mercies of a certain person who shall
be nameless, we lighted the pipe of resignation and patiently submitted to our fate.   Our arrival had evidently
excited some little interest ; first one boat, then another,
then two and three together, hovered round us, their occupants making remarks upon the size, rig, and appearance
of the yacht.   Some declared we belonged to the Navy,
others that we were spies ; in short no supposition, however
ridiculous, was too extravagant for their fertile imaginations.

The magnificent harbor of Carthagena, in which a navy
might ride at anchor, is situated on the coast of Murcia,
and, land-locked on all sides, save at its entrance defended
by an island, is secure from every storm.   A few coasting
vessels only were in port at the time of our visit, and trade
appeared almost to have deserted a locality once famous in
history for its commerce.   The shades of a lovely evening
at length stole over us, the hum of voices in the town had
ceased, and we retired to our berths speculating as to the
course that would be adopted towards us by the *great men*
on shore.   Advantage was taken of the fineness of the following morning to bring all our bedding, wet clothes, &c.,
on deck, and such little repairs were made in the rigging,
as upon examination were found requisite.

Whilst at breakfast, being hailed vociferously by some

person in a boat close to us, we showed ourselves above the hatchway, when a gentleman, taking off his hat and bowing politely, informed us in *Spanish* he was the *English* Vice-Consul—rather an Irishism—but though a Spaniard, he was the *locum tenens* of the Consul, who was absent from Carthagena. He had received our note, and had waited upon the governor, who promised that in a short time we should receive permission to land. After some little conversation, and leaving his address, he took his departure. The success of our diplomacy of the previous afternoon put us all in high spirits, and in about an hour the tub of a health boat with its numerous rowers was seen slowly approaching, two "heroes" in cocked hats being seated in the stern sheets. On coming alongside, one of them proved to be our friend the secretary, who, with much courtesy, *this time*, regretted the inconvenience we had been put to, declared the detention to have been a mistake, that we might go on shore whenever we liked, and that we should have admission to the arsenal, dockyard, &c. Many compliments having passed between us, the tub moved off, and we were at liberty.

A very short time elapsed ere we were once more on terra firma, and making our way through wide and well-paved streets to the residence of the vice-consul, who had procured for us the promised order. It was with feelings of regret that we viewed the deserted quays, rope walks, and foundries, and saw that everything was going to decay. Here it was, in more prosperous times, the Spanish fleets were equipped—fleets that, in alliance with those of France, contested with us the sovereignty of the seas. Then all was life and activity, now silence and solitude. In the year 1804, we were told, 4000 workmen had been employed in the various departments; the names of *forty* only were at this time on the superintendent's books, and a small

schooner and a gun-boat were the only government vessels
in the docks! The fortifications are strong, and the garrison numbered about 2000 men. The little trade remaining
is principally in "barilla," an impure carbonate of soda,
produced by burning marine plants, and "almagra," a red
earth used for polishing mirrors. There is likewise a manu-
facture of sail-cloth and of ropes and cable, made of "es-
parto," a species of rush. The costume of the peasantry
whom we met in the streets differed from that we had previously seen. A handkerchief tied round the head took the
place of the sugarloaf-shaped hat. The jacket of velvet,
round the waist a colored sash, white linen kilt instead of
breeches, bare legs, hempen sandals, and a gorgeous plaid
thrown over the shoulder ; the *tout ensemble* putting us in
mind of the Highlanders of Scotland. For the mantilla
the women had substituted white woollen shawls, and wore
blue petticoats with yellow bodices. Learning that allegiance was to be sworn to the young Queen of Spain at
Barcelona on or about the 20th of the month, in consequence of the abrogation of the Salic law, and that the
ceremonies would be upon a grand scale, we wrote to Gibraltar for a fortnight's extension of leave, to enable us to
proceed to the former city, stating, at the same time, we
should proceed to Valencia, and that if on our arrival there
we heard nothing to the contrary, should conclude it had
been granted, and continue our voyage. Having ascended
some hills in the neighborhood of the town to enjoy the
view, we afterwards returned to the yacht to dine, taking
with us the vice-consul. A strong breeze blowing into the
bay rendered the "Midge" rather uneasy, and we had not
long sat down to our meal when the unfortunate "vice"
was completely upset by "*mal de mer*," and as some time
elapsed before a boat could be procured to set him ashore,

he remained the intervening period in a state of pitiable discomfort.

We accepted an invitation to pass the evening at his house, and remained on board till the hour arrived for fulfilling the engagement. At the residence of the vice-consul we found several caballeros and señoritas (and very pretty señoritas too) assembled to meet us. There was singing to guitar accompaniments, and no lack of conversation, our broken Spanish affording vast amusement to our fair acquaintances, who whenever we got into difficulties assisted us out of them with marvellous dexterity.

In the course of the evening our host inquired if we had ever felt the shock of an earthquake. R—— replied in the affirmative, but B—— and myself never having been so fortunate, it was proposed we should touch at Torre-vieja, a village on the coast between Carthagena and Alicante, where it was affirmed "temblores de tierra" took place constantly with more or less violence, and that, as the mother of the vice-consul resided there, he should proceed thither by land, and give us the meeting.

This plan being agreed to, we naturally made inquiries concerning the country we were about to visit, when it appeared that in the year 1829 some ten or a dozen villages, Torre-vieja amongst the number, had been destroyed and many of their inhabitants swallowed up by one of these convulsions of nature, and since that occurrence "tremblings of the earth" had continued almost without intermission. Having passed a very pleasant evening we took our departure, the "house being placed at our disposal," and we in return for the civility "kissing (metaphorically) the ladies' feet," it not being etiquette on any occasion to follow the English custom of shaking hands. It was with some little curiosity we looked forward to that which it was said we should experience on the morrow, for though to "sea shaking " we were tolerably well inured, we could form but little idea of what would be our sensations when subjected to that of the earth. Early the following morning we got under weigh, meeting sharp squalls in beating out of the harbor, after which however it fell nearly calm. Having doubled Cape Palos, a low sandy point with a watch-tower at its extremity, near which are three small islands, called the "Hormigas," we anchored at Torré-vieja about three o'clock in the afternoon, finding several of the inhabitants on the look-out for us—as the Consul's arrival had by a considerable time preceded our own. On going ashore our friend received us, and led the way to his mother's house, where we were hospitably entreated ; and after remaining a short time there, started to examine the village, which stands upon the site of the former one. The streets were very wide, enabling the natives to assemble in them in time of danger, and the houses (*one story* in height) built of wood and cane, these materials yielding to the motion of the earth, without falling, which such as are composed of brick or stone invariably do. We were assured that scarcely a day passed without their owners being reminded upon what unstable ground they dwell ; that animals, such as horses, oxen, mules, &c., were the first to give warning of an approaching shock, stopping if in motion, and placing their legs apart to obtain a firmer footing, and that those who were accustomed to the locality were more sensitive than strangers. Familiarity with danger blunts the apprehension of it ; festive groups were assembled in front of the houses, enjoying the coolness of the evening ; the song and the merry laugh resounded on every side, and it might have been imagined from the conduct of the actors in the scene, that a recurrence of an event similar to that which had destroyed some hundreds of their countrymen a short time previous was beyond the bounds of possibility.

13*

Not long before our visit an eminent geologist had been sent from Madrid to investigate the cause of this phenomenon, which is confined to a comparatively small district The day succeeding his arrival shocks were felt, which con tinued with more or less violence during the remainder of the week. The philosopher at first bore them patiently, but at length he fairly took to his heels, vowing an infinite number of candles to the Virgin, and declaring that for all the riches of the world he would not live in so horrid a place.

Salt is exported in large quantities from this place, chiefly to the north of Europe, and three Swedish brigs were at anchor waiting for cargoes of this article.

Lingering on shore till between eleven and twelve at night, trusting that what we anxiously hoped for might take place, we were nevertheless compelled to embark without our wishes being gratified, but comforted with the assurance that so long a cessation of "quakings" had not been known for a considerable period. After returning to the "Midge," we remained long on deck both to enjoy the beauty of the evening, and that in case of a shock taking place, we might be on the alert, the sensation when on the water resembling that of striking on a rock.

The morning of the 10th broke gloriously, and with a pleasant breeze, and merely a ripple on the sea, we set sail for Alicante. The wind, however, drew ahead, and soon after deserted us altogether. Between nine and ten o'clock we could see, with the aid of a glass, the ruins of two villages, demolished by the same earthquake which had so grievously maltreated "Torra-vieja." Off Santa Pola we hove to, in order to land the boy who had accompanied us from Gibraltar at his native village, and the breeze having again freshened, we had to beat the whole distance to Alicante, in the roadstead of which we anchored, between four and five in the afternoon, and being admitted to pratique, lost no time in landing. The custom-house officials acted with unusual incivility, opening our carpet bags and strewing the contents on the pier. This conduct secured for them the " gain of a loss," as we in consequence withheld the fee usually presented to these jacks-in-office. Receiving every attention from the consul (Mr. Waring), we put up at an hotel in the Plaza del Mar, and passed the night (I cannot say slept) ashore for the first time since leaving Gibraltar. Whether this state of unrest was caused by the attacks of certain active little tormentors, by the closeness of the house, by missing the accustomed motion of the vessel, or by all three combined, it matters not, but our anticipations of unbroken repose were cruelly disappointed.

The town of Alicante, in the province of Valencia, stands close to the sea shore, overhung by a lofty rock some thousand feet in height, crowned at its summit by a castle. The streets were clean, and houses good, the flooring of the rooms (if it may be so expressed) being composed of a kind of porcelain, painted with various devices, well adapted to the sultry climate. The fortifications appeared strong, but an application on our part for permission to visit the castle was refused, on the plea of state prisoners being confined there. Part of the rock was blown up by the French in the year 1707, at the conclusion of a siege of long duration, in which the English were the defenders. The country in the neighborhood is very fertile, and the olive trees are remarkably fine. Salt is also made in the vicinity, and exported from Torre-vieja.

Being in the habit of wearing our usual boating-dress, (white jackets, white pantaloons, and straw hats,) when landing at the different towns where we touched, we became in consequence marked objects, and were frequently saluted with the title of "locos Ingleses," (mad English·

men,) and the anxiety of the female part of the community to get a sight of persons thus honorably designated, was very ludicrous.

While sauntering through the streets towards the close of the afternoon, we encountered a rush of persons running furiously in a direction opposite to that in which we were moving, and on inquiring the reason, found they were retiring from the unwelcome proximity of a bull, who, with a long rope tied round his horns, held by a number of men at some distance behind, was thus permitted to take his headlong course. The unfortunate animal, maddened by the blows and shouts of the pursuing population, tore franticly along, and before we well knew what we were about, two of us were forced into a shop by the crowd, I being left at the door in such a position that escape was out of the question. On came the bull, stopping in front of the very place at which I was posted, my comfort being in no degree added to by the information (conveyed to me by some *kind friend* inside) that the "toro" was a remarkably savage one, and having already killed two *real* men, had become so fastidious as utterly to scout the sham representations of the "genus homo," frequently lowered from the windows of houses for his own especial amusement. Taking off my hat, the only offensive weapon I possessed, I was prepared to strike him over the nose, when a native (a short distance off) threw his cloak across the ground, and the bull darting off in hot pursuit, I found myself extricated from this unpleasant predicament. A pilot being engaged for the voyage from Alicante to Barcelona, and to return with us to the former town, we proceeded on our cruise between ten and eleven at night, with a light north-westerly breeze, and the following morning doubled Cape San Antonio, the wind blowing strong from the south. A gale from the eastward with a heavy sea (both of which moderated towards evening) compelled us to put back to Denia, the access to the anchorage being through a narrow channel with sandbanks on either side, covered with a trifling depth of water. Upon one of these the pilot ran us aground, and had the weather continued as boisterous as during the early part of the day, the cutter must inevitably have gone to pieces; even as it was she struck hard, and we much feared she would have sustained serious damage, but after an hour's labor she was fortunately got off with only trifling injury. On the first semblance of danger our "Palinurus" commenced praying to his patron saint, a proceeding soon put a stop to by our threatening to throw him overboard if he did not instantly cease and assist the crew. By ten o'clock we were safely anchored, and though the night was dark, had a good view of the town and of the few vessels in the roads by the glare of continued flashes of lightning. The 13th dawned cloudlessly upon us, but the weather being stormy we remained in *statu quo*, and R—— and B—— went ashore, and paid their respects to the commandant, who received them in bed, and upon being informed of the nature of their expedition exclaimed, "None but Englishmen could have undertaken it."

Denia, in the province of Valencia, lies under a rock or mountain of great height. The town is a poor one, for the sea having receded has almost destroyed the trade. In the neighborhood, olive trees and vines flourish in profusion. About two o'clock in the afternoon a sudden shift of wind to the south-west caused us to lose no time in getting under weigh, passing in the course of the day the towns or rather villages of Almandrave, Olivas, Pilas, and Gandia. The breeze continued in the same quarter all night, but a head sea much impeded our progress, causing the cutter to pitch heavily. The pilot expressed great anxiety lest a north-east gale should come on, in which case he declared we must

run back to Alicante, as he would not venture upon a second
attempt to make Denia.   The native sailors dread the whole
of, this part of the coast, as when the wind blows strong
from the quarter alluded to, a tremendous sea breaks with
unmitigated fury upon a long tract of sandy shore almost
destitute of any refuge.

Between twelve and one o'clock the following day, we
anchored at the Grao or port of Valencia, during a gale
from the south-west, to the force of which it is much exposed, and the yacht for a short time was in some little
jeopardy.   Two strands of the cable parted soon after the
anchor took the ground, when a second was let go and cable veered upon each.   The topmast was struck, bowsprit
run in upon deck, and hatches battened down.   Finding
the cutter dragging, we had recourse to our third and
largest anchor, which fortunately brought us up within a
short distance of the breakers.   To have worked out to sea
in the teeth of the gale would have been impossible, and
had we gone ashore, not much would have been left of the
poor little " Midge."

"A miss is as good as a mile," saith the proverb, and
the weather becoming moderate towards evening we took
up a more favorable berth, and landed between six and
seven o'clock.   A " tartana," a kind of van without springs,
drawn by one horse, (the common conveyance of the country,) was put in requisition to take us to Valencia, distant
about two miles, the road the whole way being planted on
either side with fine trees, producing a most delightful and
refreshing shade.   Numbers of persons of both sexes, and
" tartanas* innumerable, were passing and repassing along
this agreeable drive.   Being ignorant of the topography,
our " Jehu" was ordered to take us to the best hotel in the
town, upon which we found ourselves at the " Fonda de la

Paz," which he declared to be unequalled, though whether such was the case or not, we had no time to discover.

Having refreshed the inner man, we sallied forth into the streets, which were narrow, crooked, unpaved, and gloomy, still retaining the character given by their Moorish possessors, and the appearance of the natives at this day bears a strong resemblance to that of the inhabitants of the opposite coast. Numbers of women (whose complexion was less swarthy than that of the men) were seated in the open air pursuing their several avocations ; their heads uncovered, and their hair fastened at the back with huge gilt pins. It being too late in the day to visit the cathedral, we made our way to the river Guadalaviar, at this time an insignificant stream, and so nearly dried up, that a market was held in its bed. When swollen, however, by winter rains, it becomes an impetuous torrent, and the length of some of the bridges (five in number) testifies its width, under these circumstances, to be very considerable. We much admired the prospect from the Puente del Mar. Close at hand were the walls of the town following the course of the river, the bridges, ever picturesque objects, diverting the eye from its uninteresting condition. Beyond were various roads leading to the " huerta," the latter clothed in perpetual verdure, and brought by the marvellously perfect system of irrigation, introduced by its ancient and maintained by its present possessors, into a state of fertility entitling it to the appellation of the " Garden of Spain."

We proceeded thence to the " Glorieta," the fashionable promenade of Valencia, planted and provided with fountains ; numbers of persons were here congregated, and the " señoritas " present appeared in no way inferior to those of their countrywomen whom we had already met with, either in personal charms or in their knowledge of displaying them

to the best advantage. Here we remained a considerable
time, admiring the varied dress of the passing groups, our
own unsophisticated apparel contrasting strangely with the
butterfly costumes of the light-hearted crowd surrounding
us, to whom we in our turn were evidently objects of much
curiosity. It was late at night ere we sought repose, giving strict injunctions before doing so, that we should be
roused early in the morning, in order to waste as little as
possible of the short time we had it in our power to devote
to the inspection of this famous city.

By seven o'clock we were ready to commence our pere-
grinations, and, as a matter of course, bent our steps in the
first instance to the cathedral, the tower of which, standing separate from the main building, between one hundred
and sixty and one hundred and seventy feet in height, was ascended. From its summit was a splendid view of the adjacent plains, teeming with fertility, and producing in the
greatest profusion, corn, rice, and every description of food
for man and beast. Mulberry, orange, and palm trees, are
thickly spread throughout its whole extent, and we gazed,
and gazed, and gazed again upon the unsurpassable beauty
of the prospect, heightened and increased by the lustrous
brightness of a cloudless summer sky. The architecture of
the cathedral is partly Gothic; on the back of the choir
(worked in alabaster) are representations of scriptural subjects. The seats are handsomely carved; behind the altar
are some curiously painted doors, and the church possesses
fine pictures by different artists. Hiring horses, we made
the circuit of the town, (the walls and some of the towers
of which are in excellent preservation,) and subsequently
effected a short excursion into the country, which fully real-
ized the expectations we had formed of its beauty from the
view obtained in the morning from the tower of the cathedral.

On returning from our ride, visited the "Plaza Santa Catalina," El Mercado, the "Calle de Caballeros," and entered a shop in which were sold that peculiar species of tile, bearing the name of the town, which have been already alluded to, as being used instead of flooring. The blue and purple colors were very rich, and the tile is expensive, owing to the difficulty of bringing out a perfect article. Patios surrounded by colonnades appeared almost as common to the houses here as to those of Andalusia. The number and importunity of the beggars of Valencia exceeded anything we had met with, (even in this land of beggars,) for no sooner was one set disposed of, than another swarm were always ready to take their places.

Whilst reposing in our inn after the fatigues of the day, a commotion in the street induced us to move towards the window, to discover the cause of the uproar, when it appeared that two men having quarrelled were proceeding to settle their differences with the knife, when the bystanders (among whom were some women) thought fit to interfere. The violent gesticulations, flashing eyes, and bronzed countenances of the parties concerned, reminded me strongly of a *fracas* of a similar nature I had witnessed in Barbary, swords being substituted for the weapons now used, and females being left out of the question. The combatants were not easily pacified, and furious attempts at stabbing, parried by the left arm wrapped in the "manta," had already been made, when two or three of the softer sex threw themselves upon the antagonists, completely frustrating their attempts at mischief. The chattering that ensued (totally unintelligible to us, the conversation being carried on in the *patois* of the country) was perfectly deafening; but at length the principals, scowling, and muttering, as we were told, threats of future vengeance, were led away in opposite directions, by their respective friends; the affair ending for the present, at all events, without bloodshed, but it afforded a fine specimen of the temperament of this excitable people, and the insecurity and little value placed by them upon human life.

In the evening we repaired to the café to eat ices and amuse ourselves with watching the manners of the persons there assembled. Gaiety and good humor were in the ascendant, and music occasionally lent its aid towards increasing the harmony of the entertainment. Entering into conversation with some well-dressed persons near us, we found that they supposed that all Englishmen came from London, having an idea that London and England were synonymous, while of the geography of many of the principal towns of their own country, they possessed but little knowledge. They were, however, extremely polite, insisting upon liquidating the expense of our refreshment, (which compliment we returned,) and after remaining till rather a late hour, we parted with mutual expressions of good-will.

On the 16th of the month, no letters having arrived for us from Gibraltar, we determined on proceeding to Barcelona. Hiring a tartana we returned to the Grao, embarked on board the cutter about eleven o'clock, and got under weigh at one, with a slight north-easterly breeze. Murviedro, the ancient Saguntum, was sighted during the afternoon, and as the wind freshened considerably towards night, with a heavy swell from the eastward, and much lightning, we reduced our canvas and struck the topmast.

The next morning, finding ourselves almost becalmed, with what little air there was drawing to the south-west, all sail was again made; the heat was intense; an universal white glare overspread the sky, the wind had scarcely strength to fill the sails, or ruffle the surface of the long swells which heaved noiselessly around, and the general appearance of the atmosphere betokened an approaching change. This unsatisfactory state of affairs continued till

towards evening, when the breeze gradually freshening, and
heavy, lurid clouds rising in masses to windward, gave warning that our anticipations were likely to be verified.   The
gaft topsail was taken in, topmast struck, mainsail and fore-
sail close reefed, jibs shifted, mizen furled, hatches battened
down, and every preparation made to resist the fury of the
storm.

About six o'clock, gusts of wind, accompanied with vivid
lightning, and peals of thunder, announced that the war of
elements was about to commence.   For about half an hour
after, it blew a steady gale, when in a short time a violent
squall compelled us to furl our mainsail, and scud under
bare poles.   The sea was whirled aloft in foam and spray,
the air was one continued blaze of quivering, blinding lightning, the thunder rattled amid the blast, the wind whistled
through the rigging, the rain poured down in torrents, and
it seemed as if the demon of the tempest had exhausted all
its fury upon our devoted heads.   Onwards flew the
" Midge," almost rivalling its namesake in the vivacity of
its motions, and whilst passing Peniscola, (a conical rock,
surmounted with a castle,) during the height of the squall,
a schooner anchored close in shore hoisted a small English
ensign.   The well-known color was hailed by us with delight, not that in case of mishap any assistance could have
been rendered, but it was cheering amidst the surrounding
turmoil to see our country's flag so proudly floating in the
howling storm.   The fury of the wind abated as suddenly as
it had arisen, and sail being again made, we reached Vinaroz
between nine and ten, and anchored there for the night.

By three o'clock on the morning of the 18th, we were
again under weigh, with a moderate easterly breeze.   The
river Ebro empties itself into the Mediterranean at the port
of Alfaques, about five-and-twenty miles from Vinaroz,
sand-banks rendering the coast in this neighborhood excess-

ively dangerous.   Towards evening the wind again changed
to the southwest, and soon after fell calm.

The pleasure of navigating the Mediterranean is frequently the theme of discourse, and the climate is certainly delicious, but the winds are baffling, the sea short and broken
when blowing fresh, and the sudden alternations of calm
and storm, and storm and cálm, must be experienced to be
thoroughly comprehended.   From the dawn of the following
day till evening, light airs from the eastward prevailed, and
at intervals we toiled hard at the sweeps.   Sunset was magnificent.   Sea and sky sparkled like gold, and as the orb of
day sunk into the western waves, columns of light (fit emblems of its departing glory) shot brilliantly across the
arch of heaven.   When darkness closed around us, the
stars looked calmly down, veiling their modest beauty, when
with refulgent splendor a glorious moon rose solemnly o'er
the tranquil sea.   Between eleven and twelve at night we
reached Barcelona, and as soon as the sails were furled and
everything made snug, all hands turned in, and in a few
minutes were lost in the regions of oblivion, for we had had
a hard day's work, and were much fatigued with the labor
of continual sweeping.   Our slumbers, though profound,
were not destined to be of long duration, for soon after
dawn on the 20th, the thunder of a salute from a brig of
war, close to which we had anchored the night before,
roused us from repose.   Landing about seven, we put up at
the Fonda de la Constancia, a second-rate house, but so
crowded was the town, from the numbers of people flocking
into it from the country to participate in the approaching
festivities, that we were fortunate in obtaining accommodation anywhere, and its situation moreover possessed the
advantage of being at no great distance from the harbor.

Starting very soon after breakfast upon an exploration
of this, the chief town of Cataluna, the change in the cos-

tume of the peasantry immediately attracted our attention.
Long red woollen caps, one end hanging down the back of
the neck, (giving the appearance of bags,) very wide trousers of dark-colored material reaching almost to the arm-
pits, a jacket (very short in the waist) generally thrown
over the shoulder, and a gorgeous sash, composed the dress
of the men.   With the women, mantillas were at a discount,
handkerchiefs generally superseding them, and huge ear-
rings, some of them apparently of great value, seemed everywhere much in vogue.   Of a fairer complexion than the
Andaluzas, they were as little to be compared to them in
grace and elegance of figure, as the cart-horse to the high-
bred, fine-limbed racer.   The streets are narrow, but the
public promenades particularly fine.   The principal one, the
Rambla, planted with trees, is the centre and great
thoroughfare of the town, and there are likewise Pascos
both on the land and sea sides, the latter being the resort
of the beauty and fashion of the place, who here congregate
to enjoy the freshness of the evening breeze ; and as the
northern stranger paces backward and forward, charmed
with the picturesque effect of the many-colored costumes, his
eye involuntarily wanders to the brilliant sky, the deep-blue
sea, and the indented coast, whose distant points are by the
clearness of the atmosphere brought as it were close within
his reach, and the conviction unwittingly forces itself upon
his mind, how far inferior is the climate of his own land of mist
and rain, to that of the sunny and beauteous south.   The
walk round the ramparts abounds in beautiful views, em-
bracing mountains, highly cultivated plains, the fortification
of Monjuich, and the Mediterranean sea.   In addition to
those already named, there are several others equally pleasant, and the superiority of Spanish over English towns
in this particular is very remarkable.   The providing of
places of recreation, entirely open to the public, is a custom

worthy of imitation, for did such exist in our own large
cities, the artisan population could resort thither when the
toil of the day was over, instead (as is too frequently the
case) of being compelled to seek for amusement in dens of
vice and infamy. The cathedral has two towers, from the
top of which is a splendid view of the neighboring country.
The painted glass in the windows is rich in the extreme,
and the screen (ornamented with purple and gold, with a
column of red marble on either side, crowned with an angel
holding a torch) has a fine effect. Some sculptured figures
with large scissors and boots attracting our attention, we
were informed that in days of yore the tailors and shoe-
makers had been of great service to the cathedral, and that
these images had been put up in honor of them. There are
several other churches, but we did not visit them.

After wandering about all day, we proceeded on board
the cutter, giving orders that she should be hove down, her
bottom examined, and her rigging thoroughly set up. Bar-
celoneta is an ugly suburb, inhabited by an amphibious race
of beings, of every genus connected with the sea. The
harbor is large, protected from storms by a mole of considerable length, and from hostile aggression by the citadel
and a smaller fort, both of which are commanded by Monjuich. A few coasting and other vessels, with two Spanish
brigs of war, and three or four *guarda costas*, comprised the
whole of the shipping then anchored there. Having (in the
evening) passed an hour on the " Muralla del Mar," we adjourned to a café, and spent a short time there very agreeably, making acquaintance with some officers of a regiment
of Royal Guards stationed at Barcelona, whom we found
gentlemanly and well-informed. The hill of Monjuich,
about a mile from the town, crowned with the fort of that
name, is approached by a zig-zag road, and though the
ascent is steep, the magnificent view of the Mediterranean,

and of the city beneath, amply repays the trouble. The
fortifications are very strong, and if well provisioned, adequately garrisoned, and firmly defended, are from their position almost impregnable.   Our request to examine the
works was civilly refused, so retracing our steps, we made
a detour to visit what is supposed to have been the Jews'
burying-ground, but found nothing to reward our curiosity,
save some large stones, with unintelligible inscriptions.

An early opportunity was taken of seeing the guards under arms ; and a fine-looking corps they were, well dressed,
and well appointed, but their movements wanted the regu-
larity and steadiness of those of English troops.   Individu-
ally, they were stalwart men, containing the raw material
of excellent soldiers, and were smarter in their appearance
off duty than any infantry we had hitherto met with in the
country.   The undress of the officers, blue coatees, and
cocked hats bound with silver lace, had an exceedingly neat
effect.   The principal public buildings.are the Exchange,
the Foundry, the Captain-General's Palace, and the Casa
de Caridad.   The language spoken by the natives is a
patois, in which villainously pronounced French is discerni-
ble, and falls harshly and unpleasantly on the ear.

On the morning of the 22d,. B—— started, per diligence,
for Perpignan, *en route* for England, and in the evening,
R—— and I attended the theatre, and found the acting
and dancing very indifferent.   The expected order for com-
mencing the ceremonies in honor of the young Queen having arrived, the festivities commenced on the 24th by
figures of the King, Queen, and the little Isabella, ele-
gantly attired, being placed on a highly decorated platform
in front of the Captain-General's residence, and were welcomed by thousands of spectators with loud "vivas,"
though at the same time many present were of opinion that
Don Carlos had been hardly dealt with, the repeal of the

Salic law having been obtained by the artifices of Christina.
A strong guard of soldiers was present to keep order, and
add importance to the pageant. Troops of maskers, representing dragons, horses, bears, and outlandish figures of
every description, accompanied with bands of music, paraded
the streets, and afforded much amusement by their grotesque
appearance. In the evening a salute was fired from all the
batteries, from Monjuich, and from the ships of war ; the
cafés were thronged, and hundreds were abroad till a late
hour. The following day the captain-general and the authorities proceeded to the cathedral to take the oath of
allegiance to the young Queen, presents of clothes being
afterwards distributed to numerous indigent persons, the
town presenting a most animated appearance, from the
numbers of the peasantry in holiday garb, moving in every
direction, and the active preparations going forward on all
sides for a general illumination, which was to commence at
ten at night. At the appointed hour a glare of light blazed
forth, and much taste was displayed in the arrangements, the
devices in several instances being very beautiful. Amongst
the most remarkable was a triumphal arch at the barracks
of the guards, composed of variegated lamps, and allegorical representations similarly formed were placed in front of
the Exchange and the "Real Palacio." The trees in the
public walks glittered with tiny lamps suspended amid their
branches, the fronts of the houses were covered with white
linen festooned with flowers, arches composed of evergreens
spanned the streets, temporary fountains played at short
intervals, songs were chanted in honor of the occasion,
music sent forth its dulcet strains, pleasure was depicted in
every face, and what with the brilliant moon and stars
above, and the glittering scene below, the sight accorded
more with the representation of a fairy tale than with the
sober reality of real life. Fun and merriment lasted all

night, and early morning had arrived ere we could make up
our minds to retire to our hotel. A sham fight taking
place the ensuing evening, the consul procured for us tick-
ets of admission to the Mole, which was set apart for the
convenience of respectable spectators.   A fort mounting
three guns was attacked by a division of boats, covered by
the fire of two large *guarda costas.* The assailants made
good their landing, but after a short conflict were supposed
to be repulsed, and retreated to their boats, the *guarda
costas* standing close in to protect them whilst retiring.   It
was but a paltry exhibition, and little merited the applause
bestowed upon it by the admiring natives.   I had a long
conversation with the French consul, who, upon my pointing out the boat in which we had come from the Rock, expressed great surprise, and said that officers of the French
army would never have attempted anything of the kind ;
but, added he, " Englishmen are born half sailors."

On the 27th, at ten o'clock, was a miserable performance
ycleped a regatta, and at four in the afternoon a tourna-
ment.   A large wooden amphitheatre was erected for the
purpose, and was crowded from the lowest to the highest
seats.   The knights clad in armor (which some persons
near us declared was tin) tilted at each other, but their
efforts to unhorse their adversaries (if such was their intention) were very ridiculous.   By some regulation unknown
to us, one of the performers was declared the victor, and
was conducted to a lady personating the "Queen of Beauty," who crowned him with laurel.   Courses were then run
at the figure of a man working on a pivot, holding a large
sand-bag in one of its hands.   If struck fairly with the
lance, it spun round, and the attacking party escaped untouched ; if otherwise, he received a tremendous buffet—
which last one or two only escaped.   This caused great
diversion, and the unfortunate ones were greeted with roars

14

of laughter and every imaginable epithet of ridicule. This closed the rejoicings in honor of an ordinance which has since caused rivers of blood to flow in unhappy Spain. But three weeks of our leave remained, and anticipating a long voyage back to Gibraltar, on account of the prevalence of westerly winds, on the 28th we put to sea on our return home, and, after successive alternations of head winds, fair winds, strong breezes and calms, during the former of which we sustained a trifling damage, anchored at Alicante, on the afternoon of the 2d of July, the only incident worthy of record being that, while scudding before a smart gale off Cape San Antonio, R—— roused me from my watch below to say that, although no clouds were to be seen, the moon had gradually disappeared, and that he could not account for it. Of the reason I was equally ignorant, when, soon after discovering the fair "Luna" again making her appearance from behind the shadow that had concealed her, the conviction at once flashed upon our minds that an eclipse (totally unexpected by us) must necessarily have taken place.

On the 3d, we were again under weigh with a fresh north-easterly breeze, and having every prospect of weathering Cape de Gat without difficulty; but on the 5th, when within a short distance of the desired point, we encountered a gale from the west, which drove us back between thirty and forty miles to Aguillas, which we reached at night. Dŭring the 6th, and greater part of the 7th, it blew so strong that we could not venture from our shelter, but in the evening of the latter day, a light easterly breeze induced us once more to put to sea, for we were anxious not to over-stay our leave, and determined to make every effort to double the troublesome Cape. Soon after we sailed, the wind again chopped round to the westward, but after beating till the morning of the 9th, a gale from the east sent us past the Cape, the cutter plunging bows under on meeting the heavy sea caused by the previous westerly breeze. Our mast being sprung, it was fished with one of the sweeps, and when clear of the land, a square sail was hoisted, and we scudded till night, when the weather gradually became calm; but, owing to contrary winds, we did not reach Malaga till the night of the 11th. Strong westerly gales compelled us to remain at anchor during the 12th and 13th, but on the evening of the 14th we got under weigh with a light easterly breeze, which changed to the west ere morning, when we beat up for the anchorage of Fuengirola. Sailed on the 16th, and on the 18th of July we rounded Europe Point, the band of our own regiment (at drill on the Flats) sounding sweetly far above us in the morning air. On standing out into the bay, a gun was fired to draw attention to the cutter, and anchoring at the " Old Mole," about eight A. M., we recieved pratique, and went ashore on the twentieth day after sailing from Barcelona. Thus ended the "cruise of the Midge." That whilst at sea we were in a constant state of watchfulness and some little anxiety, can hardly be doubted. But we were young, active and light-hearted, careless of the present and reckless of the future. Those were joyous days, to which memory fondly recurs, regarding them with the eye of retrospection as green oases in the desert of life's weary pilgrimage.

MR. SNIGSBY'S YACHT

BY THE AUTHOR OF "SINGLETON FONTENOY," ETC.

CHAPTER I.

WELL, my dear," said Mr. Snigsby, "what do you propose to do ?" This was asked with the sweetest com-
placency, for Mr. Snigsby was well aware that his wife had
no possible suggestion to make.

"I think we must just stop on board—that's all," said
his wife, with sharpness.

"Why that, my dear, seems pretty obvious. I am informed that in trespassing on shore when in quarantine, you
are liable to be shot."

"I wish I was," ejaculated Alfred, gloomily.

Mr. Snigsby paced the deck with his hands in his pockets,
jingling his loose cash, according to custom. The yacht
was moored at a buoy, not very far from the *Parlatorio*.
That establishment will be long remembered by all who
have been in quarantine in Malta. The tabooed human
beings lean against a bar—a quarantine officer marches in
the centre—on the other side mankind at large are permitted to hold converse with you. If you want refreshments,
as of course you do, you pop the money into a little tub of
water held to you for the purpose. It was a great spectacle to see the Snigsbys lounging about there in the mornings, or playing quoits in the quarantine ground. To be

sure it was preposterously hot, but at it father and son
regularly went, while Mrs. Snigsby stood by and watched
them.

Meanwhile, Mr. Blobb the skipper's frame of mind was
something which induced him to compare himself—and
surely he knew best—to "a bear with a sore head." This
is a favorite illustration among nautical men. He slept a
good deal, and also swore a little, and continually complained of the heat. No wonder—Mr. Snigsby's bottled
stout kept bursting faster than ever, from that very cause.
It happened, as might have been expected, about the hot-
test time of the day—and, as has previously been hinted,
usually about the hour of Blobb's lunch. Mr. Snigsby had
his misgivings, but he was considerably in awe of the skipper. That awe had gradually increased during the voyage ;
for Mr. Blobb, having very soon discovered that they "was
not regular swells," had taken measures for making himself
of immense importance on board. He was an old yachts-
man, and had sailed under most specimens of the yachting
tribe—in the Sylph, for instance, with a sturdy old yachting dowager, who was a better sailor than many post captains—who would ring her bell in the night to know why
the gaff-topsail was not taken off her, (the yacht I mean,)
and who always made Blobb pay for the spars he lost.
His cruise with *that* "old *woman* of the sea" (who would
have made a good wife for the famous persecutor of Sinbad)
dwelt in his memory long. She was the widow of Admiral
Slumton, K.K.B., and had lived many a year on board her
Majesty's ships and vessels of war, pleasantly enjoying the
cream of naval life on the various stations where Slumton
had had commands. Blobb suffered terribly on board her
vessel, and finally had a desperate quarrel with her—having
lost overboard her wig, which she had sent on deck to be
dressed by her very ugly domestic. Then he had sailed the

Whelp for a young gentleman who took it into his head to take all the charge on himself, and superseded Blobb, till they were caught in the Gulf of Lyons by a tremendous gale, and the young gentleman was found on his knees in among his patent leather boots. Accordingly, he was a regular old stager, and often, when the Snigsbys sat down to a more delicate fowl than usual, the villain would *set the big jib*—as he expressed it—with motives so disgraceful that I decline to expatiate on them. A pretty thing indeed—fowls to dinner—to a person of his station of life! Such was the reflection of Mrs. Snigsby to her husband one day after Blobb had requested permission to kill a couple of chickens—for, of course, the Snigsbys now felt inclined to look down on the "lower orders." Everybody who rises in this country cuts and snubs the class he came from. We are all seemingly becoming "higher orders" together, so that by and by, society will be like the giant's castle, built on the top of a bean-stalk—a structure that must, of course, get more shaky the loftier and more pretentous it becomes.

Well, days wore on, and the quarantine people gave the yacht some grace, and allowed them to haul down the yellow flag before the time. The fact was, this was suggested to the authorities by little Grigg, the busybody of the island, who discovered, with considerable tact, that the Snigsbys were people with money, and took care to be introduced, and to let them know to whose interference they owed their premature escape. The family now established themselves in very nice rooms in Strada Reale,—that imposing street where the pavement looks so white and hot in the summer—where the Maltese girls go tripping along with their mantillas flowing—and his Excellency the Cardinal rolls by in a hideously ugly carriage—and military men saunter, and naval men walk, and Turks stroll, and priests glide monotonously in a pace different from all. Malta is the great olla podrida of

mankind. All varieties of races get mixed in that dish
Some ingenuity would be required to determine the proportions of the social mess ;—but the English mercantile classes
represent the beef—wandering artists the more tender and
luxuriant fowl—naval and military men the game, (a *little*
high, sometimes,)—the natives the malodorous garlic—and
Jesuits the titillating pepper! On the whole it is an agreeable compound—if your appetite is vigorous.

The Snigsbys, I say, perched themselves comfortably in
Strada Reale, and there they looked round about, and then
at each other in an inquiring way. They were now abroad,
there could be no doubt of that, and—why, now they must
begin to enjoy it. But the first stare some English people
give under these simple circumstances is odd enough ; they
seem to peer round with a sort of idea that they ought
to be somehow or other inspired. There is a disagreeable
air of "Is this all?" about them, made still more ludicrous
by their assumption of a contrary style of language. How
often must we preach the *cœlum non animum?* My dear
Mr. Snigsby, how could you expect to be touched by the
tombs of the Knights of St. John's, when nothing but your
pocket (on the demand of 6d.) was ever touched by the
tombs in your own Westminster Abbey? However, they
began at all events to get into "society" in time. For to
begin with, they secured the good graces of the little fat
pompous parson of St. Kilderkin. The card of the Reverend Mr. Fatton was sent up one morning, and the reverend
gentleman himself followed it, bowed, took a chair, crossed
his legs, and holding his hat on his knees, kept himself with
one eye on Mr. and one on Mrs. Snigsby, so as to secure
both, while "My son, sir,'' Alfred, sat uneasily on the sofa,
fumbling the "Racing Calendar." Mr. Fatton's business
was ushered in by a "hem," and "doubtless Mr. Snigsby
was acquainted with the depressed state of the Protestant

Church in the island?"   Our friend had certainly never become acquainted with anything of the sort, and glancing
with the eye of a man of business at the prosperous appearance of Mr. Fatton, could not at first imagine the possibility
of it.   But he felt he was very likely to expose his ignorance if he demurred, so he bowed blandly and rubbed his
hands with an air of acquiescence.   Mr. Fatton bowed also,
and went on to talk of the "abomination of desolation,"
and the machinations of the Jesuits, and, in fact, the sub-
scription list for the new Protestant Church of Malta, now
being built on the " Rock of Ages," as he expressed it, and
at a considerable expense.   (Indeed, Malta had recently
been blessed with a bishop who had been received with
"manned yards," and a salute—with considerably more
honor indeed than St. Paul was in the same island.)   Mr.
Snigsby heard the orator with attention, glanced at his
wife, went to his desk and subscribed with munificence.   Mr.
Fatton was charmed, begged to make Mr. and Mrs. Snigsby
acquainted with some of his friends.   Cards dropped in, and
the Snigsbys went out a good deal, and attended the fashionable movements ; saw the sailors landed to drill in the mornings, which was a freak of the new admiral's, which gave a
few gentlemen in the squadron an opportunity of galloping
about like dragoons; attended Florian gardens, and "stopped
the way" at the opera in the evening.   Then, there were
quiet solid dinners, at which Mr. Snigsby chatted over the
"currency" with mercantile men, the reduction of the dollar, the rise of the dollar, and so forth—for Malta is a mini-
ature England in business as in pleasure, has its own currency, and gets into commercial convulsions about two pence.
So, the Snigsbæan existence went on very pleasantly for a
while, scarcely jarred even by the singular conduct of a private in the Tralee Raffs, who, being comfortably drunk, and
seeing Mr. Snigsby's door open, tumbled up stairs unper-

ceived, and coolly turned into bed in the connubial chamber.
That misguided man was discovered by the astonished Mr.
Snigsby, in the evening, and subsequently duly punished.

One regrets to reflect, however, that all this time Mr.
Alfred Snigsby was finding things very "slow." How
could he be expected to relish the discussions on the "currency"—a word which simply suggested laughter to a disciple of the school of Brickles. He had come out to the
Mediterranean with the feeling of those who, as Punch said
the other day, think "the Mediterranean is not to be made
a French lake—its proper vocation being that of English
pond." He thought all enthusiasm about antiquities, and
so forth, "humbug." Indeed Brickles, his idol, had travelled, and published a work, pooh-poohing the Pyramids,
and snubbing the Acropolis, and conveying much such a
notion of the East as one would be likely to get of the
North from an alert inmate of that department of the
Zoological Gardens where the Simiæ dwelt. Alfred had,
accordingly, no sympathy with anything but such amusement as the island could afford to a man of London tastes ;
and all such people must have remarked how miserably inferior foreigners are to us in civilization. You may range
Constantinople or Smyrna for nights without ever finding a
place where you can get a chop and hear a "comic song ;"
at Athens, a friend of mine "out on the loose" at night,
was nearly eaten alive by the dogs that howl dismally there.
It was melancholy to see Alfred "mooning," as he called it,
about the streets in the forenoon, sometimes peering in at
the churches, and then slinking away "bored," afraid to go
home, lest Mr. Fatton should be prosing there, and sick of
the yacht, which was lying, looking trim and empty, near
the Dockyard Creek. Blobb's conversation (even had Mrs.
Snigsby not warned her son against being too familiar *with
his inferiors*) was somewhat monotonous, and Blobb now

14*

usually spent great part of the day in playing skittles at a
homely pastoral public-house called the "Shepherd and
Shepherdess," on the Burmola side of the harbor. Alfred,
in a word, was hipped.

But fortune had something in store for the youth,—an
excitement for that noble heart and brain. One morning
he had just " toiled" (the reader must pardon one more of
his expressions) out to saunter as usual, when he saw in the
distance a lady, at the sight of whom he involuntarily plucked
up his collar, and thought of his studs. She was, as regarded looks, apparently too dark for an English woman,
and too light for a Southern ; she walked with an easy, perfectly self-possessed manner, looking in at the shop windows
every now and then. Mr. Alfred involuntarily exclaimed
to himself—(for there is such a process, though I agree
with Theodore Hook in thinking "mentally ejaculated"
ridiculous,) "What a stunner !" He carelessly crossed the
street and strutted after her. . She paused at a shop.
Alfred paused. She glanced towards him, and met his eye.
Hers was a clear straight look, not likely to be startled by
the amount of expression which nature had bestowed on
Alfred's, but he fancied he saw something encouraging in it.
Accordingly, he followed her once more, saw her turn down
one of the streets leading from Strada Reale in the direction of the Quarantine Harbor, and enter a house. We
may be sure he booked the number. I suppose all men
have experienced what a relief anything in the shape of an
attachment is, if one is at one's wit's end for something to
do ; really it is quite a luxury, if one has something to think
about, but Alfred in this case was transported. Here was
a chance for him at last. He felt that he might do something now really " fast." Should she only be the new singer
expected at the Opera ! Your gentlemen of the Brickles

and Alfred Snigsby school, we may remark, have always
the most extraordinary interest in theatrical women in pre-
ference to others. They are moths that will hover round
the foot-lights. This is vice, doubtless; but it is a pitiable
vice that has a dash of snobbery in it. A few names that
disgrace the aristocracy, are associated with a few names'
that disgrace the stage. Now, Brickles & Co.—like *Trip*
in the *School for Scandal*, their type—must imitate their
superiors' vice. Hence their follies and their intrigues.
Our friend Alfred, for instance, when in London, would
have made as much hubbub about a little pug-nosed girl—
in the Covent Garden *ballet*—as if she had been a Font-
anges. But to return. He loitered about the house in the
Strada Sotta, glancing at the windows—saw the lady appear at one—looked up—met her look again. There were
no signs of anybody else about the establishment. It was
a dull, quiet street, a long narrow one, at the end of which
the water gleamed in a patch, as if seen through a telescope. He moved away presently, and went home, where
he was sadly *distrait* during dinner-time. His father essayed
to brighten him up, by asking him what curiosities of the
island he had yet visited—for Mr. Snigsby, though sadly
bored by "interesting" remains, faithfully visited them, and
Mrs. Snigsby went further, and earnestly tried to like them,
though both of them affected an edifying indifference to the
splendors of the "idolatrous" churches. Alfred had little to
say. That same evening he sought the enchanted street
again; the lady was seated at the same window, which was
half open, to let in the cool air during that delicious Mediterranean hour when the weight of the heat being lifted off
the earth, all the freshness and the sweetness rise up everywhere, like perfume from a vase of rose-leaves when the lid
is removed. Alfred sauntered past, mildly humming an

operatic reminiscence. The figure moved, and what was his
delight when he heard a piano, and a rich brilliant voice
begin !

Days passed, and to the best of Alfred's belief, he was a
favored man. At last it struck him, that he would make
.an experiment, which, if successful, would rank him among
the most accomplished men of his school. The magic window was open, apparently, *so* late; it was not *very* high.
Other figures, than that of the beauty, he had never seen
there. The street was silence itself. What a fine thing it
would be to scale the window by a ladder ! He had seen
Miss Deloraine (*née* Snogg) do it, in blue silk trousers and
a doublet, in Brickles' burlesque of *Jonah's Gourd; or Cut
and Come Again.* It would be tedious to narrate all his
musings on this project. He made up his mind to try it,
and having, by a judicious use of cash, procured two faithful Maltese, who were to bring a ladder at eleven P. M., or
so, to the neighboring corner, he fixed his evening, and
awaited the hour. About nine he rose from the sofa, where
he had been affecting to doze after dinner.

" Where are you going, Alf. ?" said his mamma.

" Just for a walk in the cool. It is too hot here. Good
night."

He gained the street, and marched along—just a little
cold about the heart, as if there was an ice-poultice there,
drawing the "pluck" away from it. It was not his time
yet, (but how could he have gone out with propriety much
later ?) and so he turned into a *café.* In the billiard-room
there, a company of seedy, bearded individuals were playing the Russian game. He sat on the benches at the side,
drinking negus and watching them ; there was a novelty in
the color of the balls and the mode of play which interested
him ; and then, you know, to be up to the Russian game
would look very well, by and by, at Pott's billiard-rooms.

in the Strand. He finished the negus ; he took some brandy
and water ; he began to feel rather like a Lovelace, and to
be somewhat proud of his meditated exploit. He sallied
forth—though to be sure he had a little qualm, partly fear,
partly something else, as having to pass the family lodgings
he saw a light in his mother's bed-room, where, I suppose,
Mrs. Snigsby was putting on her night-cap before the looking glass. This emotion, however, was very temporary. On
he went. He passed one *café*, just closing, and could not
resist a final little dose of brandy. At last he was in the
street. The window was open ; there was a faint light in
the room. He found his ladder in its place. He thought
for an instant of everything that had encouraged him to his
resolution, and slowly moved the instrument—a decently
light one—from the ground. At the very first start he
nearly run it through a parlor window, but he moved with
more caution. A moment, and it was in its destined place.
His foot was on the lowest step.

At this moment who should arrive at the end of the
street but the "Infant Phenomenon," Mr. Herbert Flower,
of the "Intolerable!" He was accompanied by an acquaintance, Velourby, of the "Bustard!" These two
young gentlemen, after having been riding out all the
afternoon, had been dining at the Clarendon, had played
billiards, and supped on quails, and were now open to any
amusement that anybody might have to offer them. Flower's eye caught the ladder in an instant. ·

" I say, Velourby, look there ! Stop a minute, the fellow's getting up. Let us stick at the corner and watch !"

Alfred mounted—his long legs looking ludicrous enough—
and commenced the ascent. When he reached the window
there was nobody in the room. He felt very like a burglar
However, he quietly got in. There was a small lamp burning on the table, and near it lay a sheet of music.

But by this time Mr. Flower had reached the spot.
" Gad," he said to Velourby, " here's a lark."

" Let's take away the ladder," said Velourby, "and he
won't be able to get down again."

Flower laughed, but the ladder looked quite tempting,
and he immediately began ascending it himself. Mr. Alfred's astonishment was immense when his head appeared at
the open window. Open flew the door, however, and in
rushed a stout old gentleman armed with a large stick, and
followed by two or three servants. Alfred involuntarily
assumed the attitude of the Chelsea Snob. The old gentleman flew towards the window, catching Mr. Flower just
within a step or two of the top.

" Good evening, sir," said Mr. Flower, taking off his hat
with immense coolness. " You seem to keep open house !"

Two servants rushed at Alfred, who gave the first of
them what he subsequently described as " a mouse under
the left eye." The stick wildly flourished over the " Phenomenon," but he ran down two steps, turned inside the
ladder, and came down " hand over hand." The police
were beginning to assemble, and the " Phenomenon" and his
friend disappeared. But Mr. Alfred, after prodigies of
valor, was taken prisoner, and locked up.

" His mother looked from her lattice high"

in vain for him the next morning, but Mr. Snigsby was
summoned by a forlorn note to the Court, and purchased
the youth's freedom on payment of a fine.

Mrs. Snigsby did not quite understand the affair. " Fun
is fun, my dear boy," said the excellent woman, " but what
did you expect to find in the house ?"

Alfred looked foolish. Mr. Snigsby pulled up his neck-
cloth with a significant "hem." " My dear," he said, " let
us be very glad that the affair is settled as it is."

"Yes, but it seems so odd, such a strange kind of whim——"

"My dear," said Mr. Snigsby, "your innocent mind———"

Mrs. Snigsby felt that there was patronage in the tone of the observation. "Innocent! Mr. Snigsby; I don't know that I'm more innocent than my neighbors, and——"

Her husband gave a hearty city laugh. "Neither, madam, is your son and heir!" And Snigsby, for once, had the best of it.

Chapter II.

Alfred in his agitation had not recognised Herbert Flower as the young gentleman to whose hoax the yacht owed her quarantine. Herbert Flower had recognised *him*, however, for that officer was not likely to be disturbed in his vision by circumstances of danger. In fact, he was a fellow of great pluck, and had distinguished himself on the coast, from no wish to distinguish himself to be sure, but there was a sort of excitement about capturing slavers, which he rather liked. When he returned, he had taken lodgings in London, drawn his prize money, and started a brougham. It is supposed that he meant to go down to the parental abode in the country by-and-by, but his father visited London in the interim, and found out his whereabouts in the oddest manner. The old gentleman was returning to his hotel from the theatre, when he passed through a street apparently in a high state of animation. A building flaring with lamps, and from which the wild clamor of a polka resounded, was the focus of attraction. Among many cabs was a small row of broughams, with their drivers nodding on the boxes, and one old yellow family carriage, which some youth had disgracefully brought while the family were out of town, and which stood there a forlorn protest of respectability against the surrounding scene. Mr. Flower was somewhat hustled and almost pushed against the broughams, when his eye caught, on decidedly the newest of them, a well-known symbol: He gazed on the panels and saw nothing more nor less than a shield, *argent*, *semée* of roses *barbed* and *seeded, ppr:* crest, a lion *sejant*, holding in its mouth a *fleur-de-lis* motto, *Olet, ut solet*. Mr. Flower well knew that no one dared assume that brilliant coat but a Flower of Flory. He woke the coachman, who answered to his question that his master's name was Mr. Herbert Flower. The youth appeared shortly afterwards, delighted to see him, of course, and next day was taken down to the country in triumph. Mr. Flower has since learned that the place was called the *Casino*, but has not yet been able to find the word in any dictionary. Is it generally known, I wonder?

A few days after Alfred's adventure in Strada Sotta, he was strutting out, keeping very clear of the scene of the ladder feat, when he entered a billiard-room. The usual party were playing pool there; the Italian count with the white beard, that fine old man, with a bevy of youngsters round him (a scene which my friend Fontenoy used to say could be excellently described by one line from *Don Juan*:

"A band of children round an aged ram!")

a mate or two, and Ludder of the Marines. Poor Ludder! To be without fortune and to be unable to live without luxuries—to make billiards help one's poverty, and games *of amusement* pay one's washerwoman—to be sneered at by men who never note any want in a man but a want of money— to have a dubious civility from the very marker, who has heard the whispers of the smokers, and esteems the poor gentleman, who plays so well, as little beter than himself!— what a destiny yours was! There are no tragedies like

those of civilization ; no lot so bitter as to have to make
both ends meet, by helping them with a little bit of the
heartstrings.

There Ludder was, as usual, with his pale, half-anxious
face, as Alfred came in, just resting the cue. Click. A
" life " is gone. Jenner bites his lips ; he had lost at several
successive games.

" Oh, I can't do anything," he muttered, looking sulky.

" Why play, then ?" said Ludder, quietly.

" Why do you ?" asked Jenner, with a sneer.

Ludder looked up for a moment, but his face was calm ;
he chalked his cue, and hummed. The markers exchanged
glances—the game went on quietly. Both Alfred and Herbert Flower, who was sitting on the side sofa, watching the
tables, with a cigar in his mouth, looked up at the same moment. Their eyes met ; Alfred began to recognise him
slowly, but Flower had heard rumors of the Snigsbæan hospitality. He went over to Alfred at once, and said :

" I made a sad mistake, t'other day, about that brigan-
tine ! Hem,—you see, the fact is, these brigantines are
the devil !"

Alfred had all a " knowing " man's misgivings that he was
being humbugged, but there was a good-natured look in
Flower's face, and Flower was a naval man, and Alfred
wanted to know naval men, and military men ; Brickles
himself had a turn that way, and sang funny songs, and told
anecdotes at the Guards' mess, and took a vacant seat in a
drag, when they asked him, &c.—so he accepted Herbert's
overtures with civility, and Herbert took him off to Joe
Micallef's to supper, and introduced him, as " my friend
Snigsby," to a few other luminaries.

There they sat and " chaffed " the fat and jovial Joe, and
made him cook some quails, and soon got very friendly.
Alfred asked three of them to dinner, and they came very

punctually indeed, and were very splendidly entertained.
Mr. Snigsby even apologized for his uncourteousness on the
occasion of Mr. Flower's official visit, and Flower begged
him not to mention it—with perfect sincerity, for the fact
was he dreaded bursting into a roar of laughter at the
thought of his subsequent exploits, which had raised him
amongst the youngsters of the squadron to the highest point
of popularity.

. All this was very agreeable. Alfred came on board the
" Intolerable " very frequently. They used to retire after
dinner to the bow-port on the main deck, and smoke there.
One evening, a thought struck Alfred,—"Would they
come and breakfast with him next morning on board the
' Paragon ?' " " Of course they would—of course. Nothing could be more agreeable, if old —— would give leave."
" Old —— has been sulky lately," a midshipman remarks ;
"fact is, we don't come up to see the hammocks stowed,
you know." " What kind of a man is old —— ?" Alfred
asks. " Oh ! an old muff." " Is he anything of a sailor ?"
asks Alfred, looking nautical. "Why—hem ! he may be
something of a sailor, it's true," says Flower, lazily assent-
ing to what he considered an unimportant merit. " However, old —— must be asked for leave, sailor or no sailor."
" You must put up with these things if you stay in the profession," says Jigger, philosophically. They make up their
minds to ask him at once, for he is just at dessert now, and,
to use his own favorite expression, " a child might play with ·
him now !" Lo ! off goes Flower to the ward room, steals
alongside the said old ——, and asks him, just as he has
taken a sip of his favorite wine—for Flower is an artist in
these matters—manages a commander as Wombwell would
a bear. Out he comes again, looking joyous. Old —— is not
such a bad fellow after all. " That's it ! you see," adds

Jigger, " he's not without his good points, Snigsby, mind you." And they arranged to meet next morning.

Morning came. Flower and Jigger had vanished early, for old —— might be bilious, and repent. "Too knowing to risk that, you see," says Jigger.· Alfred felt a justifiable pride as he showed them into the main cabin, with splendid furniture and hangings everywhere, breakfast laid out, game, fruit, wine, &c., on a table radiant with silver and china. " These people do it," thought Flower, and Flower wondered mentally " what things were coming to." Flory itself was a little seedy now-a-days, and his second sister had married somebody for money—somebody, alas ! who. had been obliged to get a grant of arms at old Flower's request, or she could not have transmitted their twenty-four quarterings to her children, in case Herbert (who was the only son) left his sisters co-heiresses of the name. Whereas—but, " Coffee or tea, Flower ?" broke the moment's reverie. I don't say Flower was envious of the wealthy broker ; I said he had had an English education and thought accordingly.

But a case of preserved grouse had been ripped with the sharp steel in a moment; in another, Jigger had helped everybody to Moselle, as an excuse for beginning himself, and the party began to get jolly.

" Call Blobb," said Flower. Blobb came down. Flower poured out a glass of wine for him. The tall skipper said "my respects," as his custom was, and drank it.

" And now," said Flower, slapping Alfred on the back, " let's run outside the harbor for an hour."

Alfred hesitated. Blobb looked at him inquiringly.

" There's a goodish breeze," said Blobb. " I should le᷇ these gentlemen see what the Paragon can do, sir—(Alfred knew one thing, that the Paragon could do for him in rough weather only too well)—When I sailed the Dream for Lord Blory——"

"She won the Cup," said Flower.

"So she did, sir.' Do you remember that? That was a wessel! Well, shall I weigh, sir?"

"I'll bet you the Lotos would lick you all to fits," said Jigger, to stimulate affairs.

"There ain't a vessel in the squadron as can touch us," said Mr. Blobb.

".We'll show them, eh, Blobb?" said Alfred, with desperate gaiety. "Get up the anchor." He felt that he was in for it—now or never must Alfred Snigsby be a nautical man! "Try a *paté!*" he said, with a magnificent air, and he further dived into the recesses of the yacht's resources by producing some *curaçoa*. If Herbert Flower had a weakness, (and it must be admitted he had a few,) his peculiar weakness was *curaçoa*. They pledged each other with all conceivable jollity; Flower had lighted a cigar, Jigger was just attempting one more slice of melon, when the yacht heeled, a plate on the edge of the table, all white and gold, shot off, spun like a catherine-wheel, and died out into sparkles of china-dust on the deck. In rushed the servant to clear the table.

"Come on deck," said Flower.

A goodish breeze! It was a stiff breeze, Blobb! The yacht paid off, and swept away towards the harbor's mouth. The red fair-way buoy bobbed ahead in the distance, like a cherry one moment, the next they were flying past it. The island seemed sinking into the sea as they shot away from it, gathering itself up with its forts and spires and its white stony rocks, before settling into the deep green waters. Every now and then the shadow of a huge cloud swept over the sea, which seemed to shrink under it as it hurried along.

"Well, how do you like her?" said Alfred.

"Oh, capital!" said Flower. He began walking about the deck with the old "Cowslip," air.

"How do you feel, Jigger?" said Alfred, suddenly

"Let's go back!" muttered the youth, making for the cabin.

"My dear fellow!" said Flower, "stuff! Now, do what I tell you," and he and Jigger seized their host, and led him in an attentive manner to the side. "Boy, some brandy!"

Alfred had one wild glance at the heaving, pitiless sea to leeward, and to the long hissing line of thin foam beneath him. Flower's hand was on his forehead. There was a pause, and Jigger came with the cognac.

"Now, old boy—there! off with it!" said Jigger.

"That's a man!" said Flower, patting him. "Never give in to this kind of thing."

Alfred was better. He took a little more brandy. He stuck to the deck. The yacht was still jumping about, and it was getting darker over head.

"We'll make a sailor of you, old fellow!" said Jigger. "Now, do you know how to put her about man-of-war fashion? Ready about!"

Mr. Blobb came running aft. "What's the matter, sir?"

"You're the proprietor, you know," whispered Flower to Alfred; "you put her about yourself."

"I'll put her about, Blobb," said Alfred.

"As you please, sir," said Blobb, quietly. There was a calm satire about that man's manner which Alfred stood in dread of. "Mr. Blobb," he said, "take some brandy."

"Thank you, sir, I ain't sick."

"Go forward, sir," said Alfred, majestically.

"Now then, 'ready, oh ready, cry,'" said Flower.

"Ready, oh ready," cried Alfred, to the inexpressible delight of the cook's boy, who was watching the proceedings from the bows.

"Helm down," said Jigger. Down flew the helm, and round came the shivering schooner, flapping in the wind, over glided the boom. Really, Alfred thought, it was the easiest thing imaginable. Accordingly—lunch, more brandy !

By this time Malta was lying far away ; the wind kept still rising. Blobb came and reported that the " glass was falling." •Oh, they would stand on a little longer, and Alfred was going to tack her again. This time he cried out "Ready, all ready," in a voice that would have done for a three-decker. Everything went right—except—whew ! a squall came, and carried away the foretop-mast !

" Mr. Blobb !" Alfred cried out, with a pitiable yell.

" Hush, man," said Flower, laughing, " it's no great matter !" Blobb came forward, and set the men to work to clear the wreck, which was struggling in a mass of confusion. Flower bounded down to the cabin for a moment, and came up again, looking a little graver. He then went and looked at the compass, and to windward, and towards Malta, now a cloud almost—Alfred's eyes all the time watching him with eagerness.

" Well ?" said Alfred, a little pale.

." Why, it's coming on to blow," Flower said.

" Coming on ! Don't you call this blowing ?"

Flower gave a little laugh, light, but ominous—like a funeral note on a silver hand-bell.

" Look at these clouds, my boy ; we call them horse-tails." And he glanced upwards at a group of long, black strips of clouds flying across the sky. " The fact is, we are in for a gale, and we shan't get back to-night."

The yacht was too far to leeward to get back in her disabled state, indeed, and Mr. Alfred had to watch the process of her being made "all snug." Snug, indeed ! Never did word appear to him such a misnomer as that.

And then he lay on the cabin-lockers, looking out on the place with ghastly eyes, tossed about till he scarcely knew

whether his head belonged to him. He saw, as in a vision,
Flower descend and huddle himself up in the corner, with
a cold chicken and a crust; and then Jigger came down in
his turn, and overhead there was an eternal rattling of
ropes, and a long night of dreams followed, till suddenly he
woke, and found everything very still. In the gray light
of the morning he saw Flower and Jigger asleep on the
cabin-floor, like the babes in the wood, heaped over with
cloaks. He went on deck; the yacht was at anchor in
harbor, but not the harbor of Malta. To the right lay a
quaint old town, which seemed to sprawl along the coast,
and end on a narrow neck of rocks. A long, low shore
spread far away to the left, vague and marshy, with patches
of water gleaming here and there, like fragments of a broken
mirror, on the flats. The herbage was of watery origin;
green flags were grouped together, near the shore. But
the distance showed a fine pastoral country, and the trees
near the town were mulberry trees. It was Sicily, the Idyl
of the World. The yacht was in the harbor of Syracuse.

It was the nature of Herbert Flower to accommodate
himself to circumstances. Circumstances having driven the
yacht into Syracuse, kept himself and Mr. Jigger away beyond their leave, and Alfred Snigsby away from his family,
why, what was to be done? Clearly to make the most of
the occasion, and see all that was to be seen in the town.

Behold the three young gentlemen, then, mounted on
mules, and trotting away into the country—ambling, I
should say—for ambling is the mule's true pace. The
mule is a classical animal, an ecclesiastical animal, a literary animal; he remindeth you of the ancients, of the Jesuits, of Cervantes. Lightly fall the cudgel on the beast
which ambles through the pages of Don Quixote!

Away they amble, and now they reach, passing through
light groves of pale green trees, on a road where here and

there the country café offers hard red wine—a kind of gleu.
There has been an amphitheatre here once; those long
brown stones, half covered by the grass, were the seats of
the audience; but what is that huge carved rock, that lofty
fissure in yon hill of stone, crowned by the scarred brow of
grass? 'Tis the famous prison—the Ear of Dionysius. It
is tall—long, ah! with what propriety it is long—eternal
type in stone of the long ear of its builder, who has left no
monument but the one that proves his infamy!

Well, of course, the prison has become vulgarized now-a-
days. There is a chair suspended from the top—dangling
ludicrously across the mouth of the sonorous cavern—
wherein you may be hoisted, for a small remuneration, to
the private hole in the rock, some eighty feet up. In that
hole, says tradition, the tyrant sat.

Now, Mr. Alfred Snigsby mounted in the chair, the
guides began their task of hoisting, and slowly he ascended
towards the place. Nothing could be more delightful than
the motion. As you rise the little scene around seems to
expand, the little picture unrolls itself, and beauty overflows
the boundary ring of the sight.

But hillo! here Alfred had stopped in air. The hole is
still above, the earth below; no motion is made either way.
He holloaed loudly; the melancholy echoes rolled round
the cavern, answering, but without sympathy. He pain-
fully peered down, but saw nobody. And so he must hang
till our next chapter.

Chapter III.

To be perched in an undulating, cane-bottomed chair, sixty feet above the level of the earth, before the cavern of an ancient tyrant, cannot be said to be a pleasant situation for a Cockney. There is something in London life which unfits one for adventure. You are so thoroughly secured by the protection of the law, so entirely reliant on the police, and so walled in by the tranquil homeliness of commerce, that you lose some natural manliness. You have not the vigor of the ancient life, when a man held his tenure of safety direct from Nature, and not from the joint-stock assurance company of society. One's ancestors, who had a Black Douglas in his castle a few miles off, must have felt more vividly, I imagine, than we do; their blood was a stronger brew. To be sure, we now-a-days are more *comfortable*—but we know how much the capon loses to qualify him for getting fat !

Mr. Alfred Snigsby peered round more anxiously than ever, when he heard no answer to his shout. His legs dangled absurdly, and a slight breeze arising, he began to turn uncommonly like a spitted goose. But here Mr. Flower came running down the glen at full speed.

" Snigsby !"

" Yes. What's the matter ?" shouted Alfred, anxiously.

" All right.. Lower away there."

Alfred felt himself descending, and was delighted to reach *terra firma*.

" What *has* been up, old fellow ?" he asked.

" Up ! A covey of partridges, to be sure. Why, Jigger and I have been across these fields after the red-legged villains, saw them down alongside a kind of fence, put them

15

up—missed. The fact is, you can't do anything without dogs. It's no go."

"Yes, that may be true," said Alfred ; "but I've been dangling all the time."

"I beg your pardon, old fellow ; these confounded guides *would* bolt after us, to see the fun."

Alfred stretched himself, considerably relieved, for he had begun to have a faint suspicion that something had happened serious. Perhaps he thought that Dionysius had seized his friends for trespassing. One might study a long time in the school of Brickles without having much more knowledge than the fear would imply.

There was now, to use the Snigsbæan phrase, which generally made its appearance at all places they visited, "nothing more to see." What we see, my dear Snigsby, will depend on the eyes we bring to it. I can testify, from personal observation, that the prison of Socrates consists of three small caves, with a round hole in the top of the middle one. It would not occupy four lines of the inventory of a broker, but I found no want of something to see there. The Brickles school of travellers and writers always count the items like shopboys, as, indeed, they some of them have been. They tell you that the Parthenon only consists of a moderate number of defaced columns. Very true ; and Man is a two-legged animal, with a round head, only that he is *plus* a soul, as people will one day find out.

The guides were paid. Flower stood for a moment before the cavern, moralizing. His laugh rolled all around the strange walls, as he turned away. The sound might suggest moralizing to others; it was the laugh typical of the youth and the satire of modern Europe, and in *all* the caverns of the past that laugh is raising, and will raise—thunder !

They mounted their mules and ambled towards the town

again. At the shore they saw a fine mulberry tree ; under
the deep, dark green leaves, the rich black berries were
sweltering, ripe, pouting at you, like the lips of a young
Æthiop. Flower's eye fell on it. He gave a wild exclamation as he approached, and then he bargained with the
proprietor to be allowed to perch himself there "like a cor-
morant," and devour *ad libitum* for a shilling. Neither
Alfred nor Jigger felt inclined to join. So the youth
mounted the tree with the aid of a "back" from Alfred,
and there he sat, perfectly happy, for three quarters of an
hour, and came down with a mouth as bloody as a cannibal's.
The others, indeed, accelerated his descent, by shouting to
him—they were lying on the grass, (smoking, of course,)
hard by—that there was a fair wind. Indeed, it was high
time to take advantage of that circumstance, and be off
again to Malta. So they left shore without calling on the
consul, even, which was a strange omission, for Herbert
Flower usually exacted the official attention paid to people
of mature years. He would have liked to have gone to dinner at the consulate in full dress—to have talked politics
with the functionary, to have finished a bottle of port at
dessert, and to have gone up-stairs to tea and flirtation with
the family.

Once more they gained the Paragon's deck. Blobb !
Where was Blobb ?

"I shouldn't wonder if he's gone to see the antiquities !"
said Jigger, with a laugh. (And why not, my dear Jigger ?)

"Ha, ha," laughed Alfred—"that's a good idea."

Mr. Blobb made his appearance just at dusk. He was
somewhat red in the face and confused in his ideas. Indeed,
he spoke of the vessel as the Dream, and appeared to fancy
that he was still sailing that remarkable yacht for Lord
Blory. Blobb cherished the memory of his lordship with

real affection. Lord Blory lived half his life afloat, luxu
riously enjoying himself all over the world. He was the
last of a long line, desperately impoverished, and too proud
(bless him for that!) to marry for money. How he managed to go on as he did, made those who envied his fortune
wonder. But some people do with their ancestors as the
papists do with their saints—work miracles with their relics.
And Blory did go on very comfortably, till the skull over
his hatchment in Grosvenor-street informed the connoisseurs
in heraldry that the race was extinct ; and the family vault
in ——shire opened for the last time.

"Weigh, Mr. Blobb," said Alfred, with a calm air of
command. Mr. Blobb gave the needful orders, going about,
shaking his head, with a maudlin expression. The anchor
was raised, and the yacht glided away in the twilight.
Luckily, there was a good fresh breeze right on the quarter,
and so she held on straight for Malta. They passed nothing that night but a few *speronari*, beating back to Sicily
from Valetta harbor. As they neared Malta, they fell in
with the Roarer, Captain Bulrush, hovering about with
apparently no distinct object. Bulrush was the comic Van-
derdecken of the ocean. His brig the Roarer was the comic
Phantom Ship. Destiny had apparently decreed that he
should expiate his sins by cruising about with too much sail
on—in a state of beer. He was sometimes hovering about
for days, when he ought to have been in harbor. One of
the most touching things in story is the fate of the Flying
Dutchman—but only think of the fate of the Flying Dutchman's creditors ! The Bulrush hailed the yacht, but Flower
sternly "stood on," and in an hour they were at the harbor's mouth.

So in the yacht swam, hauling down the gaff topsail and
swimming along slowly. Before them the harbor stretched
away gleaming—glittering like a sword sheathed in the

stone scabbard of the white island. The *marina* was fringed with vessels with their sails loosed. The men-of-war, too, had loosed their sails to have the thin night dew on them, burned up by the scorching sun of the noon. And such a noon ! It made the almond trees languid, and put fever in the blood of the blood-oranges.

The Paragon glided almost close under the stern of the Intolerable ; and on the poop was visible the gleam of a green parasol—a parasol green as the veil of a houri, if Mrs. Snigsby, its possessor, will permit me the rather "improper" comparison. Alfred saw at once that she was anxiously awaiting him, and had been suffering what is called "great mental uneasiness." If one could calculate the number of relatives who are suffering that well-known pain from similar causes at this moment, one would have an odd statistical return ; and next, one would like to know the aggregate cost of their luncheons.

The Paragon anchored—a great deal nearer the Intolerable than Mr. Flower liked. The commander was now to be faced, and two nights' absence accounted for. It was no use now to get up a story about sudden illness at the house of the Blocklys, who would not let you go. No, no. The yacht's return had been duly reported by the signal officer at the commander's particular request. So on board Mr. Flower walked, with as much coolness as was consistent with his visions of "stopped leave" and a "wigging." Commander —— was a perfect artist at wigging. If you argued with him during the operation, it made him worse. If you said openly, with the most polite submissiveness, "Well, sir, it shan't happen again," he came down on you like a shot with—"Not with impunity, sir !"

But the commander was not on deck, and some very extraordinary operations were going on there—operations of a character not very nautical. Let us fancy that Alfred

has been embraced by his mamma on the poop, to his unutterable confusion, publicly, and look round us. The quar
ter-deck guns were rolled forward (by-the-by, a certain captain once capsized them to teach the marines to *march over
rough ground !*) and the ropes all coiled up and off the deck ;
and beds—new beds from the purser's stores—were strewn
about, among an infinite variety of flags. I regret to add
that a number of little lamps, such as one usually associates
with the idea of Vauxhall, were lying in a row on the poop
. " Why, hallo !" said Flower, seeing the confusion around,
" is there an execution in the ship ?"

There was a loud laugh at this notion from a group of
officers who were standing by the gangway ; and, indeed,
there was a certain Titanic jocosity in the notion of anybody's " putting a man" in a three-decker ! It showed a
cheerful disposition in a youth who had " broken his leave"
by forty-eight hours.

" Hillo, Phenomenon !—Ah, Flower of Flory ! how are
you ?" were the various salutations which greeted him.

" All right. Where's old —— ?"

Old —— approached a moment afterwards.

" Come on board, sir," said Flower. " I regret ex——"

" Of course, of course," interrupted the commander, " you
are always regretting something. You could not get back
before the gale, of course not. You were obliged to help
a ship in distress—"

" I beg your pardon, sir—"

" Of course, you beg my pardon—but why incur the necessity of doing so ? No. You were enjoying your *cura-
coa*," said the commander, awfully imitating what he fancied a dandy tone of voice—" *ongtre vose, amee !*" he added—
and really he burlesqued French perfectly !

The Phenomenon looked very demure.

"Well, go away," said the commander, "go away, Mr Flower."

Lucky Herbert Flower! ` For an approaching event had cast something pleasanter than a shadow before. The Intolerable in fact—but this is the proper moment to invoke the shade of Benbow. Shade of Benbow—then—the Intolerable was going to give a ball!

This was why the guns were rolled forward, and the very capstan unshipped; why the flags were dragged from below, &c. The beds and flags were to be made into ottomans on the hatchways, duly shut up with gratings. The officers were "on hospitable thoughts intent." The ship was expecting her orders to come home soon, and they resolved to leave behind them the fragrance of a hospitable memory. The Snigsbys were invited, and accepted, very cordially, the invitation. It was extraordinary to see how good, solid Mr. Snigsby pardoned by this time the playful extravagances of naval life. Often had he, in full vestry, indignantly denounced an idle navy! Often had he fiercely inquired—backed, too, by the luminous Snogg—why the Mediterranean fleet was not sent to sea? Not unfrequently he had hinted that the service was kept up to support an oligarchy. But now he found these monsters— "fattening on the vitals of the people"—to be just a good-natured, gentlemanly, off-handed set of fellows, ready to give dinners, or eat them, with anybody thrown in their way. Mr. Snigsby could not hate them—no, he gladly accepted the present invitation.

The preparations proceeded on board the Intolerable. The little lamps gradually assumed the form of the letters V. R. The main-deck was prepared for the supper, everybody declaring it the proper place, always excepting Bob Ruggles, the second master, whose wishes not running in

the ball way, led him to condemn the proceeding as contrary to all discipline. And there was still a wound rank-
ling in the breast of Bob. When the Intolerable was at
Naples, some time before this, the officers were asked to a
royal ball. But the second master and master's assistants—
indeed the *genus* Bung (to use the naval name) were *not*
included. Bob went about the ship, indignantly inquiring
" why ?" to the inextinguishable delight of Herbert Flower
and the other youngsters. Herbert caused great amusement by the refined impertinence with which he consoled
Bob on the occasion.

" It's all part of a confounded system, Bob," he said ; " I
myself don't approve of those social distinctions, you know,
(here he shrugged his little shoulders inimitably,) a mere
antiquated affair, but somehow things are all based on 'em.
Eh, Rivers ?"

" But what do you mean, Flower, hey ? Aint I aboard
of this ship as an officer and a gentleman, and equal to anybody ?"

It was glorious to see the little villains gazing seriously
on Bob.

" Why, of course, you're an officer and a gentleman, Bob.
I suppose you know it is some confounded consideration of
family. I say nothing, Bob, only you know the nature of
aristocracy, Bob."

And so poor Ruggles went away with a burning heart
from his affectionate sympathizers, who roared jovially over
the incident, as they smoked the evening cigar. Of course
Bob Ruggles could not be expected to love balls or the sort
of people who frequent them.

Everybody was asked to this ball, that was one comfort.
The captain's cabin was abundantly supplied with refreshments for the benefit of quiet old fellows ; fellows whose
dancing days are over, and who just talk about professional

points and sporting, over sherry, and leave their daughters
to "amuse themselves." The dusk came on, and then boat
after boat began to leave the shore and the ships. Luckily
it was a beautiful night. So, thankfully ejaculated Mrs.
Snigsby, as she wrapped herself in an immense shawl, and
leant back in a shore boat. So, thankfully ejaculated
Alfred, putting on his gloves in *ditto*. Mr. Snigsby said
nothing ; he had a notion that it was chilly, but how could
he venture to say that a *Mediterranean* night was chilly before Mrs. S.?

"Bless me !" exclaimed Mrs. Snigsby, as they gained the
deck, shrouded in with awnings, brilliant with flags, and
glittering with lights. "Bless me, you would never think
it was a man-of-war."

"Never, *at any time*, my dear madam !" said Herbert
Flower, politely offering his arm, and looking like a pigmy
by the side of her majestic form.

Two or three people within hearing of the Phenomenon
chuckled. The commander, who guessed that it was a sarcasm, from the distance, summoned Mr. Flower to him.

"Not quite so conspicuous, Mr. Flower. Not quite so
conspicuous, sir !" he said, with his loftiest manner.

Herbert was annoyed, he did not like to be snubbed, and
that, too, just as little Lucy Beddoes was passing by.
Lucy Beddoes was a "nice little girl," according to Flower's phraseology.

"Isn't it a shame ?" he said to her, when he got her arm.
"That's the way *we're* treated, you see, in this profession."

"I hope he has not hurt your feelings ?" said Lucy,
simply.

"Hurt the—— (he was almost saying, hurt *the devil*)
Hurt my feelings ! No. He bores me, though, by his confounded impertinence. Ah, Snigsby ! Let me introduce
my friend, Mr. Alfred Snigsby."

15*

Alfred was superbly dressed. Lucy Beddoes knew they
had a yacht. Alfred had a very gracious little bow. She
could not help respecting a youth of "expectations." Not
that she was an atom mercenary, only helpless, poor thing !
You observe that girls *must*, many of them, put love out of
the question, now-a-days. Political economy demands it—
and is not that an answer to everything ?

Alfred's mamma called him away at this moment.

"Well, how do you like my friend Snigsby ?" said Flower,
chuckling.

"He is very nicely dressed," said Lucy demurely.

"A great deal of money, I assure you," Flower said,
"and he is the only child. What say you ? Let's go
halves !"

"For shame !" said the girl, laughing, and blushing a
little.

"I'm serious !—We'll divide him between us. You shall
have half the money and him into the bargain !"

But here began the music, and interrupted the pure playfulness of this child of nature. The company were crowding the deck. You were sheltered by a high awning, and
by flags of all hues. The effect was a bright lightness—the
temperature delicious. Nature helped the artificial to perfection. You just got enough air to keep you pleasantly
cool. If there happened to be a rent in the spacious trembling roof, you saw a star through it—and the champagne
must have been bad, if you could not say something pretty
to your partner *apropos* of that ! Unless, to be sure, she
was the daughter of a captain in command, and too conscious of her high rank to encourage any playfulness of
observation.

Flirtation, were the subject treated (not by a cockney
parvenu of course) by some gentleman and scholar with
humor, sentiment, and sense, would afford matter for a

delightful essay. Willis would be a dash too flippant; Sir
Edward is becoming a little too grave; and Thackeray
would tinge it with the melancholy of his deep reflection.
But, really, Flirtation deserves a commentator. It bears
the same relation to love that a belief in fairies does to religion. One might compare it to the old tournaments—
mimicries of real war—but not only mimicries—dangerous
wounds have been received at many a "gentle passage of
arms"—as the old writers called them. Flirtation is distinctly to be commended. Is it not a recognition—though
but in sportiveness—of the existence of that divine sentiment
which relates the sexes to each other? 'Tis an escape from
the too solid realities of "fortunes" and "expectations," a
playful butterfly flight over their iron walls. And Flirtation
will reveal to you, perhaps, the higher sentiment in time.
Franklin discovered the relation between lightning and
electricity by a simple schoolboy kite. Much has been
learnt about love's heaven by the playful idling of Flirtation.

But to return: for the band on the poop is playing away
merrily. The quadrilles are crowded. The "youngsters"
are enjoying themselves immensely—excepting those of the
"Borderer," for Captain Plebbe makes them dance with his
plain daughters—"to a man, sir, every one of us," says little
Jogg, protesting that it is disgraceful. The quarter-deck is
walled in from the ship's crew, but they peer through inter-
stices—the grave boatswain looking at the flying damsels
with the mingled awe and merriment of Tam o' Shanter at
the Kirk of Alloway. "Stand back, there," says Toadyley
to a sailor or two who are inclined to obtrude on the hal-
lowed ground. Toadyley wants to know "what things are
coming to," when the aristocracy can be subjected to this
kind of thing? Indeed, the poor fellow had plenty to do,
for Toadyley began by disposing of all the shawls with the

carefulness of a counter-jumper; then he had to set down
a snug sherry-and-loo party in a quiet cabin; then he had to
blow up the mess stewards who were preparing for the supper; to find partners (which was not easy) for the Commander's maiden aunt; to take care that nobody under the
rank of a lieutenant presumed to ask the Baronet's wife to
dance; and to keep the edtior of the *Popgun* from premature intoxication. And Toadyley did the work of a waiter
so well, you would never have thought he was a gentleman,
I assure you!

A polka—there was some rapture about a polka in those
early days!—had just concluded. Alfred had been dancing
with Lucy Beddoes, and really she could be very agreeable
if she liked. Herbert and one or two youths were moving
about near them. They approached.

" Well, and have you enjoyed yourself, Alfred?" asked
Mr. Flower, paternally.

" Yes," said Alfred.

" And you, Miss Beddoes, eh?"

" Oh yes; very much," Lucy answered; "where is papa?"

" Playing at your namesake—loo!—Alfred, I must introduce you to Captain Beddoes." Alfred said he would be
very happy, though he was a little frightened.

But at this time Jigger mysteriously withdrew his friend
Herbert from the group.

" Come along," he said, "there are a few of us going to
have a snug glass of bitter beer in the gun room. I'm hot
and bothered."

Herbert was just going to assent, but his eye caught the
figure of a lady on the poop. It is so delightfully cool there
on these occasions when the night is lovely! Herbert
quietly glided away. The lady was sitting on a chair by
herself—Mrs. Plumer her name was; a widow—travelling to
"forget"—and succeeding!

Mrs. Plumer was a very clever woman and decidedly good-looking—well-shaped, decisive features she had. She liked Flower as a "character," and motioned to him to sit down beside her.

"Ah, good evening," said Flower. "I did not know you were on board. I have not seen you for a long time."

"My father has not been well."

"I hope he's getting better. I am just come to have a chat with you. This is the place for flirting, you know, Mrs. Plumer. I can flirt with perfect safety. Flory is desperately mortgaged, and nobody would, could, or should accept me, unless they had plenty of money. I should like to water our ancestral roses with a shower of gold !"

"That's a romantic sentiment, I am sure, Mr. Herbert Flower."

"It is a perfectly truthful one, believe me. Now if I had the wealth of my friend Snigsby"—and Herbert gave a pompous burlesque accent to the three words.

"Snigsby—what a curious name ! Are they new arrivals here?"

"Not particularly new, but they are very rich. C'me in their own yacht."

"Is there not a Miss Snigsby ?" asked the lady.

"No. By-the-by, he ought to have a sister ! But I wonder you have never met them."

"Why, we have not been out much lately. You know we moved from our old place."

"I didn't know that."

"Yes, to *Strada Sotta*."

Flower gave a little srart. "Let me see—leads out of the Strada Reale towards the Quarantine harbor, don't it ?"

"Just so. And by-the-by, now I think of it," said Mrs. Plumer, laughing slightly and coloring a little, "an odd thing happened there a week or two ago." She paused and

laughed again. "One night after I had been playing—but
I must tell you, first, that a day or two before that, I had
once or twice met an English youth in the street——"

There was an exquisite gravity about Flower at that
moment.

"What manner of youth ?" he asked.

"Rather tall and what you call 'loud' in his dress. He
might be a gentleman who was silly, or a bagman who was
ambitious."

Flower covered his face with his pocket-handkerchief, as
if his nose had begun to bleed. Suddenly he jumped up
with a "pray excuse me," and ran down the poop ladder !
A dance was just over, and the group breaking up. He
met Jigger.

"Where is young Snigsby ?" he asked.

"Saw him just this moment. There he is !"

Flower went in the direction indicated, and found Alfred
sitting on one of the ottomans arranged on the hatchway
gratings, next a comfortable old lady, who occupied the
entire double-headed eagle of Russia with her portly person.
He was glad to get away. Flower was wanting to introduce him to a most agreeable person. He must come. Mrs.
Snigsby, who watched him from a distance, and who, by-
the-by, was very gloomy herself—while Snigsby, *père*, had
doomed an elderly gentleman to a dose of the currency—
felt quite glad to see her son receive so much attention.

"This way, old fellow," said Herbert, leading him to Mrs
Plumer.

Alfred stopped short, and turned deadly pale. Mrs.
Plumer saw the whole case in a moment, and bowed most
simply.

"I see, Mr. Flower," Alfred said. "I see it all. I'm a
gentleman—although—" he stuttered and gasped horribly
"It's too bad——"

Flower took hold of his wrist, and pulled him round.

"Hush, man, for God's sake mind what you are about !— It's the change of air from the quarter-deck, Mrs. Plumer, that affects him."

"Pray sit down, Mr. Snigsby," she said, kindly. "What a beautiful night it is."

Her manner was exquisitely contrived to make him fancy she was utterly ignorant of the cause of his agitation. How Flower admired her for it !

Alfred stammered out, "I *have* been a little ill." And sitting down, he began to feel quieter, and to feel attracted as he had felt when he first saw her. He thought, "Well, she does not remember me, really."

For Mr. Alfred (Brickles and Co. behold your pupil !) had no great opinion of the female intellect, poor fellow. And then, with the most innocent folly, he began babbling away quite freely to the lady, who laughed—not at his jokes, but at his sad mistake. Herbert Flower, who had been afraid of a scene at first, enjoyed the present phase immensely. And at that moment a sensation began on deck, like the commotion in the theatre at Pompeii, in Bulwer's novel, when Arbaces pointed to the smoke issuing from Vesuvius, for everybody heard the word "Supper."

Chapter IV.

Mr. Herbert Flower bounded away to take down little Lucy Beddoes. Mr. Alfred Snigsby offered his arm to Mrs. Plumer, and off they went together. He was in a pleasurable tumult of excitement, poor fellow, what in a merrier mood he would have called "spoony." It is observable, that the school of Brickles, who see nothing holy in any sentiment, are always made greater fools by what elevates

the rest of the world. The gods are just, and avenge them
selves on the proper. occasion. When the Bricklesarian
writers, for example, give up pertness for pathos, the dogs
become as common-place as mutes. When they try poetry
or love-matters, they describe like auctioneers, and introduce
us to dowdies. It is their consummate misfortune that they
cannot get out of their own offensive briskness without
becoming bores.

Alfred really became the very thing he most emphatically
contemned, a muff, on this occasion. He had not the incli-.
nation to try his favorite lively style of conversation. Mrs.
Plumer, too, saw farther into everything he started as a
subject than himself, and bewildered him immensely. All
he knew was that he admired her very much ; that he had
a great anxiety to keep talking to her, without knowing
what to talk about ; and that he was helpless. Somehow
he did not seem to advance at all with his attachment. She
resisted him by some unseen influence, like that which one
has read of as keeping off intruders from particular rooms
in enchanted castles. He would have liked just to be able
to say, " I love you. *I shall have an immense deal of money,*
much more than those nobs there. Be mine and marry
me !" I am far from supposing, by-the-by, that such a
straightforward course would not please many lovely beings ;
nay, I am not certain that it would not be a much more
respectable way of doing business than the ordinary one.
But we could not expect Alfred to set such an example of
originality. No. There he stood (a good deal in the way
of some of the guests) the Tantalus of the banquet.

Meanwhile, the said banquet was going on very bravely.
A few sturdy revellers whom nobody had seen till it began,
were mauling the architecture of jellies and raised pies, like
Turks among the Acropolis. Captain Plebbe of the Borderer kept his youngsters pretty busily employed supplying

the before-mentioned plain daughters with all "the delica-
cies of the season," as the *Popgun* of course called the
dishes. The poor boys attracted a good deal of attention
among observant people in consequence, and Herbert Flower
made an immense sensation· by calling out "waiter" to one
of them in a marked manner. The youngster was in a
furious rage of course ; several people laughed. As for
Plebbe, he was perfectly savage, and glared on Mr. Flower
like a demon.

"Really, you ought to be more careful about the opinion
of your superiors," said Miss Beddoes to Herbert.

"My superiors," said Herbert, "indeed."

"Now you know he is your superior, Herbert," said the
sensible Lucy, whose papa was a very worthy captain of
artillery.

"He is a captain, if you mean that, of course. But his
rank as Plebbe is not equal to my rank as Flower," said the
youth majestically. "Plebbe is who-knows-who, somewhere
about Portsmouth ; I am Flower of Flory ! I quarter the
shields of peers, and I date from Edward the First !" and
so saying, Mr. Flower tossed off a glass of champagne with
the air of an Emperor.

After all, the sentiment embodied in the young gentleman's speech has an existence afloat, nor is the said existence favorable to discipline. When the service *does* go to
the devil, as we are told by so many worthy officers that
it will, depend on it, it will be at its most aristocratic stage.

Lucy smiled and shook her head. She knew Flory well.
Her father had once been stationed at the heighboring
county town. Flower *senior* had twice written to Herbert,
to tell him to be very civil to the Beddoeses, and not to fall
in love with Lucy, whatever he did.

"Look at your friend Snigsby," she said, smiling. Flower
glanced along the table. Alfred was the picture of spoon·

iness, as his school call it, and the fair widow was talking
with uncommon animation to a group round her.   One often
wonders how some survivors must tremble at the word
RESURGAM on a hatchment !   To-be sure, it now-a-days
generally passes for meaning nothing.

One more polka ! The supper table was a splendid
wreck, and the deck strewed with crushed flowers here and
there.   There was a dim feeling of chilliness coming on on
deck too.   The daylight came faintly over the island, and a
stray breeze came freshly in, cool from miles of sea.   The
awning had fallen in at one part, and the flags shifted from
their places into disorderly gaudiness.   There was a general
murmur about shawls, and the necessity of getting boats
ready.   " Ship's boats, indeed, ha !—to land dancers, ha !"
Such was the growl of the Bung, from his hammock in the
cock-pit, as he heard the "pipe" sound.   Herbert Flower
put on his friend Lucy's shawl, playfully and fraternally.   I
am afraid he never thought, as the youths who lead Herbert
Flower-ish lives ought to think, of the sad contrast between
themselves and pure, fine-hearted girls.   Flower escorted
her to a boat, in company with her father, who had just
emerged from the sung cabin.   The old gentleman was very
red and silent, and apparently firmly brooding over something which employed his whole faculties.   He leaned rather
heavily on the arm, considering what a light little arm it
was, which Lucy held to him as he stepped into the boat.
So far Herbert saw ; half-an-hour afterwards you might
have seen a little figure, like a happy ghost, gliding away
with papa's candle—leaving papa snoring in safety—and
putting papa's Seltzer water within easy reach—and then
retiring to its own place of rest—the happy beautiful
ghost !

The Intolerable's deck was a scene of confusion, and pale
faces, and limp curls.   Boat after boat was sent away full,

and the ship's boats being insufficient in number, shore boats were summoned.

"Paragon's boat !" shouted Alfred from the gangway, with the air of a naval captain. That villain Blobb had sent the dingy, only ! How could that boat take on shore the family—*plus* Mrs. Plumer, and a female friend, to whom the gallant Alfred offered a passage ? At last Blobb sent —nothing excited Blobb to unseemly haste—the large boat.

In they all got, and off went the boat, keeping alongside another one loaded with merry guests. A young gentleman of the Rifles gaily threw off an operatic burst of song. Alfred was in the highest spirits, burning with conceit, and with that liquid embodied conceit—champagne.

"Boat there ; out of the way, that boat !"

A green and red shore boat came heavily steering— apparently right at the Paragon's boat.

"Yes," resumed Alfred—and off he went with a *youp, youp youp, tra la la, la la !* So I presume to attempt the notation of a remarkable chorus at all events.

"*Meester Sneegsby,*" cried a Maltese voice from the strange boat ; "*Meester Sneegsby,* pay me, *signor !*"

If the reader has never heard the peculiar shrill "pay" or "poy" me of a Maltese—I hope he never may ! There is an unearthly mingled with a Hebraic twang in it, impossible to describe—and equally impossible to tolerate.

Both boats of guests were astonished. "Keep that fellow off. Break his head !" cried somebody.

"I owe no man a shilling, sir," cried Mr. Snigsby.

"No, sar—de tall young gentleman, sir ! *Meester Sneegsby!*"

Alfred rose up in the boat. His face grew ghastly in the daylight—the fresh Mediterranean daylight.

"*Pay me for bring de ladder to Strada Sotta, Meestor Sneegsby !*"

What a catastrophe ! Alfred distinctly remembered that

there was a balance—a balance due the Maltese from that night of humiliation. He was sobered and shivered; stammered out something—flung some money into the terrible boat—more money by far than he even needed to have paid.

There was a silence as they passed on. Poor Mrs. Snigsby! Alfred's heart bled—to do him justice—as he saw her white handkerchief employed. Mrs. Plumer's veil was down. She said nothing—appeared to hear nothing. Mr. Snigsby leaned back in his seat, and looked like a condemned criminal.

There was not much jollity after this event. Some rumor about the ladder story had oozed out. The hero was now revealed. However amused the gentlemen were, they could not laugh. The ladies of course were "shocked." But soon the boats reached the landing place.

There they separated into parties, and the time came to bid Mrs. Plumer good night She was a strong-minded woman; she found two minutes in which to say to Mr. Alfred "two words."

"I shall not, I suppose," Alfred said, ruefully, "see you—see you—again, Mrs. Plumer."

"Candidly," said Mrs. Plumer, "I fear not—under the circumstances. My father—"

Alfred's jaw fell. He remembered the stout old gentleman !

"Then I shall not, I suppose, accompany you to the door ?"

"No," said Mrs. Plumer, "nor the window, I hope."

For the life of her Mrs. Plumer could not resist that parting shot. The groups separated. And off went the Snigsbys home.

"I wish I was dead," Alfred broke silence with as they strolled home.

. " You're in a fair way to obtain your wishes, sir," said his father.

" Don't be cruel to him, Mr. Snigsby," said his mother. " Poor Alf!"

"I don't want to be called Alf. I'm too old for these absurdities."

"And ought to be, sir, for your other ones," said his father, again. Mr. Snigsby once more had the best of it.

This last event decided Mr. Snigsby, who reflected on the matter, that they ought to take a cruise. He was getting tired of Malta. Those who remember his late exertions in the great "Papal aggression" question will know how often he alluded to his own "personal observation of the effects of a debasing superstition." The fact is, Mr. Snigsby was bored by the bells of Malta and sick of the sight of shovel hats. Mr. Fatton, of St. Kilderkin, though courteous, was not now cordial altogether. "No man respected Mr. Snigsby more," he said, it is true—and nobody can deny that he received his donation to the church in a friendly spirit! But still the Snigsbys were only "good worldly people," in the Reverend Mr. Fatton's parlance. "Well meaning people, undoubtedly," little Fatton added, "but—!" Somehow they wanted that sable bloom which distinguished the Fatton clique. And the little fat-headed man, though most polite when they met, came not to the hospitable rooms in Strada Reale so often as before. Possibly Mr. Fatton had doubts about the state of Mr. Snigsby's soul: possibly he was too much occupied with taking care of his own—though there was not *so very much* of it.

Then the squadron were going to sea for a cruise. And some people thought it was quite time. The youngsters were sadly dunned. Alfred was on board the "Intolerable" one morning, when an unhappy Maltese was pelted in the cockpit with clothes brushes.

Accordingly orders were sent on board to Blobb—Blobb
the stately—to prepare for sea. "They never knows their
own minds," said the sulky veteran, "never for a hinstant!"
But he went growling about and doing whatever was needful.

The squadron were all lying with top-gallant yards
crossed, and the studding-sail gear rove—to speak nautical-
ly. The admiral issued a long un-readable general order
about discipline—and sent the fleet to sea under the senior
captain—remaining on shore himself. There was a fine scene
of activity one morning. The "Intolerable" bumped
against the "Regina;" the "Bustard" let a top-gallant
yard tumble down, and it went bang through the deck;
the "Lotos" got aground; the "Struldbrug" split a sail.
Out they all got, however, ultimately, and commenced sailing in columns, which order they maintained by the aid of
the senior captain perpetually signalling certain ships to
"keep their station"—which with ships as with families is
just the most difficult thing to get done with accuracy. As
often as the signal was made, so often the captain "wigged"
the lieutenant, the lieutenant the midshipman—"the cat
began to worry the rat, the rat began to—" &c., according
to the well known process among cats, rats, and men.

Mr. Blobb made the necessary preparations, and the
Snigsbys once more embarked on the sea. It was evening
when they went on board the yacht. Mr. Blobb had
mounted the "green patch" again over his eye. There
was something mysterious about that patch, and it seemed
to bode no good.

They were to start next morning, after "a good night's
sleep." But what was Mr. Snigsby's astonishment when
waking in the middle of the night, he heard—not "the
night fowl crow," as Tennyson's Mariana did about that
time, but a louder and more disagreeable hubbub. There

was a shuffling noise indeed audible. Mr. Snigsby shuffled on some clothes, crawled up stairs, (to use his own phrase,) and found the vessel under sail. His first impression was, that Mr. Blobb was going to take them all off, and sell them for slaves.

"Mr. Blobb!" It was pitch dark.

Snigsby listened. "Mr. Blobb!"

"Hush! Oh, it's you, sir."

"Why, what the devil are you about, Mr. Blobb? I told you we didn't want to sail till the morning."

"Mr. S*h*nigsby," said Blobb, speaking thick, while the perfume of rum hovered in the night air; "you are a man and a brother."

Mr. Snigsby's heart sank within him at this commencement.

"I wash left an orphan, Mr. S*h*nigsby," maundered on the skipper, "and brought up to sea-faring, as my father before me. First of all, I s*h*erved along with——"

"Never mind, Mr. Blobb," said Mr. Snigsby, feeling his utter dependence on the terrible skipper. "But why are we a-weigh now?"

"S*h*top—all in good time, Mr. S*h*nigsby. I s*h*erved many' years in revenue cutters and gentlemen's yachts. When I sailed the 'Dream' for Lord Blory—oh, Mr. S*h*nigsby, that was a man." Here Blobb's feelings induced a hiccup, which accompanied him from that point. "De-s*h*ended of noble ancestors, Mr. S*h*nigsby, his lordship was a hindividual of the aristocracy."

"Of course, Mr. Blobb," said his hearer, shivering a little in the night air.

"And aboard of that yacht, Mr. S*h*nigsby, I contracted an unfortunate alliansh with a young 'ooman. We was very appy for a while, though belonging to the lower orders, Mr S*h*nigsby."

"Why not?" said Mr. Snigsby, philosophically. "But go on, Mr. Blobb."

"That female," said Blobb, with solemnity, "is now in Malta; come from Gozo, where she resides."

"Well."

"Yes, sir; and there's a very good reason in England," said Blobb lowering his voice, "why I can't have much to say to her."

Mr. Snigsby saw how the case was, and why Mr. Blobb preferred sailing in the dead of night. This was very unfortunate, but what was to be done? How could he get rid of him, and get a new skipper?"

He paced about the deck, musing. The yacht was right out at sea, floating lightly on over long blue waves. It was a clear moonlight night; all was still in the cabins below, where Mrs. Snigsby was forgetting her troubles, and Alfred his cares. Mr. Blobb was perched at the weather gangway gigantically calm.

Suddenly, Mr. Snigsby looking to windward saw a large object glaring through the night. He strained his eyes. The moon glided out of some thick clouds at the moment. The light revealed a sail. It was a brig with all sail set; her white canvas gleamed through the dusk. But there was no sign of life visible on board her; she held on calm, silent, and relentless as fate. Was she the doomed vessel whose hell is the eternal sea, in which the mariners' hair groweth gray at the wheel, as they beat on evermore in storm and calm with a life as restless as the water that bears them, till they are too weary to speak to one another any more—and their garb is antiquated, and the casual mariner crosseth himself as he sees the relics of a long dead generation moving gloomily on their deck? Was she that mournful spectre of the ocean, the Phantom Ship? Mr. Snigsby paused and stared. And the vessel neared them.

'Twas the "Roarer," Captain Bulrush. Yea, 'twas the Phantom Ship of the Mediterranean. The captain slumbered in the cot, and the lieutenant in the berth, and the officer of the watch in the hammock nettings, and the quarter-master on the gun-slide, and the mariner at the wheel! Steadily holdeth she on, without reference to the laws of place, or the decisions of the Admiralty Court.

"H—ll!" roared out Mr. Blobb, suddenly. "Port the helm! What are they at!"

Mr. Snigsby seemed to see a monster looming out of the darkness to swallow up his yacht. He shut his eyes; he heard a crash forward. The brig had carried away their jib-boom. The "Paragon's" crew came running up, and poor Mr. Snigsby heard a voice cry out in his cabin. The phantom had glided on into the darkness. Mr. Blobb was howling over the wreck and invoking horrid vengeance on the captain of the brig.

Mr. Snigsby ran down the companion, tumbling over Alfred at the bottom of the ladder. He found Mrs. Snigsby in high alarm. They deplored their unhappy position they bewailed their dependence on Blobb.

Meanwhile that officer, who was a very good sailor, was getting things put to rights again. When the family finally emerged in the morning, after breakfast, they found all square. It was a beautiful day, and the squadron were lying on the green water in a gigantic line, with glittering sails—looking like a row of castles on the border of an immense prairire.

Chapter V.

About this time the "affairs of Europe" had, as their
custom is, got into some phase of embarrassment which
required the presence of a squadron in the eastern parts of
the Mediterranean. I don't exactly remember the circumstances. I believe that an infringement of the Treaty of
Adrianople, joined to the marauding propensities of Grivas,
completed by the Porte's withdrawal of its approval from
the Pasha of Snobkali, were the leading causes of the disturbance. How these influenced each other, or, indeed,
what they meant, was not easy to discover. At all events,
a squadron had to be sent eastward. A *verbosa et grandis
epistola* came from the admiral to the senior captains of the
cruising ships. It was just the subject for Sir Booby Booing to expatiate upon. Sir Booby had a decided talent for
writing long dispatches. The duller the dispatch, too, the
longer, it always was—like a deep-sea lead—in proportion
as the lead was heavy, the line was long !

Accordingly the Intolerable, 110, the Struldbrug, 90, the
Verdant, frigate, and brig Lotos separated from the fleet,
and made away towards the Archipelago. What more
natural than that the Paragon should go with them ? Blobb
being asked whether he knew that part of the Mediterranean, replied, "like—Alcibiades !" That name was a rem-
nant of a small store of classical information which the
eccentric skipper had acquired while sailing the " Symbol"
for a little clique of Oxford men, who cruised about the
Mediterranean bewailing the Dead Past. They were a sect
of little bilious pietists, who wore sham hair-shirts, were
always blaming the Greek Church for separating from
Rome, and had some odd theory about the " Seven Candle-
sticks." They came home, wrote little poems, journals, and

pamphlets, dedicating to each other all round, and dating
"Feast of the Holy Block," or "Eve of St. Kilderkin."
Harmless little sect !—but I am digressing.

Mr. Snigsby, of course, was highly anxious to see those
classic scenes, the history of which had touched him so
sharply (as the birch of his school could have testified) in
his youth.   Alfred was ready to go; anything rather than
be bored by Malta, he said. , His mother was delighted to
think, as she said, that he would *recover a' free fancy* in a
still softer clime.   The dear, conventional old lady ! She
was always chewing the cud of some melancholy or other.
She wrote home long letters to her relatives the Bibbs,
informing them of her state of mind, and containing the
placidest conventional nonsense about what they saw and
did.   She was, too, always in extremes.   She would write
of "the great kindness of the Fattons," because Mrs. F.
had been kind enough to come and eat her lunch with her ;
and that "dear.Christian," Mr. F., on the strength of Mr.
F.'s sermons, which were produced as a newspaper writer
produces "leaders," because it was his profession.   She
now dipped a little into Lord Byron's works, of which she
had been wont to fight rather shy, and prepared for the
romance of the East.   So away went the "Paragon," in
company with the squadron ; and whenever there was a
calm or light wind, Mr. Snigsby had the honor of receiving
distinguished company to dinner—for the Admiral had not
allowed the squadron to come into harbor before starting,
under pretence of the urgency of the case, and the captains
of the Intolerable and Struldbrug had fallen short of fowls
and vegetables.   In consequence of this, old ——, of the
Intolerable—a very knowing card—sent one of his boats
one morning to the Paragon, with his compliments and a
melon.   Mr. Snigsby had at least ten melons hanging up on
board, but "how kind of Captain —— !" exclaimed Mrs S ;

so the captain was asked to come and partake of his melon,
and he did partake of it, and of two bottles of Lafitte into
the bargain. We may be sure that Blobb did not approve
of these visits, and he not unfrequently took advantage of
night to get five miles to windward of the squadron.

"They're as hinnocent as lambs," he said to the crew of
the Snigsbys, "as hinnocent as a Paskill lamb."

Whatever that phrase might mean, he acted a parental
part towards them, with a gigantic compassion; pointed
out the various parts of the coast as they came in sight of
the Morea; and showed Alfred how the never-to-be-forgot-
ten Lord Blory was wont to wear his fez. Of course Alfred
had now begun a beard and moustache, and assumed a kind
of oriental appearance, generally. He also cherished a
secret intention of going, in his fez, to the Cyder Cellars,
when he returned to London. That would rather astonish
Blow, he thought, and little Buck, the raffish actor, and all
the odd hangers on of Vauxhall, the theatres, the casinos,
the betting-rooms, &c. "Rather!" he thought. It was
just the kind of reflection to be full of as you saw the columns of Sunium, with the sunlight clinging to them at noon,
like a parasite !

The squadron—passing Ægina with its veil of blue haze
(you will find some ruins there, and partridges)—arrived off
the Piræus. The Intolerable and Struldbrug anchored in
the Bay of Salamis, dropping their best bowers among the
bones of the followers of Xerxes; the Verdant and Lotos
entered the Piræus, and so did the Paragon, dodging neatly
in between the two little lamp-posts in the mouth of it, with
a slanting wind. The captain of the Intolerable went on
shore to consult the authorities of the Embassy, and returned
to his ship with a serious expression on his face, and an increased air of self-importance. He was observed to nod his

head gravely to the commander, who nodded his to the lieutenant of the watch by and by, in his turn.   Toadyley—
who had a talent for getting hold of news like the scent of
a truffledog, though he occasionally got hold of a toadstool
instead of the luxurious fungus—came down to the gun-room
with the mysterious self-importance of old —— at third
hand.   There now began a discourse about "British interests," and danger to Otho's crown.

"It's all part of a general movement of the European
democracy, sir," Toadyley said.   "It will leave us no institutions, by and by!"

On this, Herbert Flower remarked very gravely, that
"nothing could be more annoying to a member of the aristocracy"—with a subdued grin as he coupled the last words
with a glance at Toadyley.   For Toadyley's reverence for
aristocracy was undoubtedly the result of a pure and disinterested (and snobbish) attachment.   Happy aristocracy,
which, however blind it may be, always has a cur to lead
it; to carry the basket, eat the fragments, and put up with
the kicks!   Toadyley saw Mr. Flower's intention, but said
nothing.   He found that the best plan of revenging himself
on his enemies, was to jog the memory of the commander
about their faults and misdoings.

Some days passed; it was very fine weather, and there
was nothing particular to do.   Mr. Slides, the gunnery lieutenant, peering from the poop, became gradually aware that
there was a fine clear range for firing down the bay.   Mr.
Slides was an officer from the "Excellent," a capital cannon
shot, and a great authority on shells.   He was said to have
once gone on board a hulk while the "Excellent" was firing
shells at her, to watch the effect on the spot.   Stories were
told of his seeing tenpenny nails spin like tops on that occasion—stories which were only believed by a faction, which

thought Mr. Slides "cracked." He hovered between two
strange reputations accordingly · Such is the fortune of the
brave !

Mr. Slides stood on the poop, gazing on the bay and
occasionally glancing up at the rock called "Xerxes' Seat,"
and wondering what "elevation" would fling up a shot on
it. Presently he went to the commander. I have hitherto
disguised that officer under a ———; let me withdraw the
veil. His name was Bilboes. Mr. Slides observed that
there was now an excellent opportunity of having a little
shell practice. Bilboes screwed up his mouth. He was
one of the old shool ; knew very little of the science of gunnery, and was rather afraid of shells. Mr. Slides urged him.
He wanted to make some experiments—was not quite sure
of the length of his fuzes. Now they could fire alternately
at two points—and have somebody near them with a watch,
to mark the moment of falling and bursting.

"But bless me, Mr. Slides!" said the commander, "what's
somebody to do when the shells fall near him ?"

"Get behind a rock to be sure !" said Slides with a superb
air. "Get behind a rock !" he cried out, "unless he wants
his 'ed knocked off."

"One of the midshipmen," suggested little Bloaker the
marine officer, with a quiet smile.

Toadyley, who had been within hearing all this time,
wriggled up to the commander.

"I beg pardon sir," he said to him, "Mr.—ah ! Mr.
Flower, sir, has not been doing much lately !" Artful Toadyley.

"By Jove ! no ; call Mr. Flower," said old Bilboes,
briskly. "Yes—we ought to find out the shells—all about
the shells—you're right, Slides." Bilboes was wonderfully
interested in the matter suddenly.

Mr. Herbert Flower came running up, bolting the last fragment of a lump of plum cake. "Want me, sir?" There was a sort of grin in the circle round Bilboes. There was a particular little imbecile grin about Bloaker; poor little Bloaker, who was what Thackeray calls "a feeble wag," and was called "wicked," by one or two old women. The commander told Mr. Flower what he wanted him for. The Phenomenon nodded, and held his tongue.

"Go and get ready, then," concluded Bilboes.

"I've no preparations to make, thank you sir," said Flowers, quietly. "The estate's entailed sir."

"What—what do you mean?" said old Bilboes.

"No need of a will, sir; goes to the Flowers of Herbham after our line. Branched off in Anne's time."

"Call away the cutter, sir," said Bilboes, "and look sharp about it."

Mr. Flower bounded off for the purpose, and the commander ejaculated, "Well, I'm d—d."

Meanwhile, Mr. Slides had gone down below to get one of the main-deck guns ready for firing. The gunner had had the keys of the magazine given him, and presently began marching with a dignified pace up the hatchway, carrying a shell. It is quite a picture to see a gunner carrying a shell—the reverence and affection with which he regards the deadly object are most interesting to observe. A young woman carrying her baby; a fast man bearing a pot of porter, are not more genially interested in their respective charges. A beautiful attachment—and surely a disinterested one; since occasionally now-a-days, the shell explodes "unexpectedly," (as the subsequent dispatch pathetically remarks,) and clears the neighborhood in a summary manner.

"Cutter's manned, sir," Mr. Flower said to the commander.

"Very well; now pull, sir, and land at that point to the right. We are going to fire alternately at that point, and yon other one to the left."

Flower was a picture of respectful attention.

"When we hoist the red flag, we are going to fire at you—I mean at the point on the right," he said, correcting himself, quickly.

"Same thing, sir," struck in the Phenomenon.

"Silence, and receive your orders, Mr. Flower. When we hoist the yellow flag, we fire at the point on the left. . You attend with your watch, and time the sounds of the falling and the bursting."

Mr. Flower ran down the side. "Shove off," he cried.

The oars flashed, the wake shivered, and away went Mr. Flower on his scientific mission. He occupied himself in looking at his watch, and ascertaining that it went properly, and the boat slashed along through the water—leaving the old Intolerable towering out of the sea in the distance.

"We had better warn that boat, sir," said the coxswain, suddenly. Flower looked up. "What's the matter?" he asked.

They saw one of the common Greek boats, with a dirty sail, creeping along some way from them. A fez just gleamed over the quarter, and a light curl of blue smoke hovered over it.

"Starboard, and near her," said Herbert.

"Boat ahoy, there!" The fez started. "Hillo, 'Erbert!"

"What—Snigsby!"

Mr. Alfred Snigsby jumped up. "O—this is jolly Flower, by Jove. I was just going for a little cruise—beautiful day!" He stretched his long figure with a most joyful air "I'll join you—are you going to land?"

"You may if you like," said Herbert. . "Follow us."

The boats moved away—Alfred's following the cutter,

and they soon reached the "point to the right," of which
Bilboes had spoken. It was a fine, long, rocky strip of
land, with shingle on both sides down to the sea.

"Now, shove off, coxswain," said Flower. "Take the
shore boat with you—out of the range."

Alfred and Herbert Flower were left alone on the point.
Alfred began to peer about with a curious look. If you
ever saw a long bird of the stork *genus*, observing external
nature in the strange way they do, you have seen something
that resembles the tone of Alfred's walk. Of course, his
little box of "magic lights" came out in an instant, and he
offered Herbert a cigar.

"You fellows have an easy life of it," said Alfred,
"upon my word." Herbert was fiddling with his watch,
and observing the rocks about them. "Here you are—you
come ashore—you—" So he was going on, when—suddenly—

But we must glance at the main-deck of the Intolerable
for an instant. Slides was hovering round the gun, and
peering through the port with a telescope. "Hang the
fellow!—tell the people to hoist the red flag on deck,
Jones. Elevate!—well!—oh dear. What's that long colored thing moving? Is't alive?"

"Take a cigar, Herbert," said Alfred. "I'll just run
and pick one of those leaves." Alfred galloped off. Herbert's eye was on the Intolerable's mast-head. "Snigsby,
Snigsby," he roared out, "come back for God's sake."

"D—n it, it's running!" said Slides. "Is the flag broke
on deck?" "Yes, sir," was the answer. "Mr. Flower
must see the flag"—and jerk went Mr. Slides' wrist; he
could be tantalized no longer.

A flash of fire, and a white cloud, and a rolling thunder
burst from the Intolerable, and then a long thin hiss followed through the air. Down went Flower, like a pointer,

instanter, with a wild glance at Snigsby. Snigsby at that
moment was a picture. He stood for one instant like what
the vulgar call " a stuck pig"—legs frozen—mouth agape.
And then he dropped backwards—I regret to say—in
among some furze and stones. The long hiss passed over
their heads ; there was a tremendous splash in the sea some
hundred yards ahead of the point—a white cascade sprung
up from it for an instant, and all was still.

"Alfred ahoy !" cried Flower. "Very pleasant duty,
eh ?"

"Murder, by Jove," said Snigsby, who was quite pale.
"There's some brandy in the boat, old fellow. Let's
call it."

" Gad, I don't know whether the boat ought to cross the
range now. Come here by me." Herbert was dotting
down the minutes and seconds on a card with a pencil.
Always cool the youth was; indeed he had had a good
schooling in the " Cowslip," on the Coast, the commander
of which was an officer who occasionally threatened to run
his brig alongside a foreign line-of-battle ship, if anything
on the part of the line-of-battle ship had offended him.
This he called "bringing people to their senses," while other
authorities considered it a taking leave of his own !

"You are a cool card, Flower," said Snigsby, looking
with admiration at Herbert's pencil and notes.

Herbert shrugged his shoulders. " Oh, I'm paid for it ;
what do I get my £30 a year for ?"

"Ah but—hang it, you know," said Alfred, whom the
shell had made wonderfully earnest all of a sudden, "it's
honorable, old feller ; courage is a fine thing, and it's a
great profession to rise in."

" Oh, courage is just a habit—like smoking. The profession's a bore. It's all humbug," said the Phenomenon ;
" everything's humbug."

Up went the yellow flag. "Keep your eye on that point, Alfred," said Flower—dropping adroitly down again—while Alfred tumbled right over him, and sprawled all abroad in his anxiety to imitate the movement. "All right, man," Herbert said, half laughing. "It won't be so near us this time!" He laughed, but he did not sneer at young Snigsby's "funk." He thought no worse of him for it; would have thought no better of him for the opposite; he neither loved, reverenced, feared, or hated, or despised hardly at all. *Nil admirari* was the basis of his nature. *Nil admirari* is really the motto of hundreds of our youth. *Nil admirari* will have to be examined very closely by-and-by. *Nil admirari* will have to be put down by-and-by.

Again, the fire gleamed in the heart of the white smoke, and the air hissed like a living thing. They saw a black speck in the air for a second—then the "point on the left" glittered with momentary fire, and a whirlwind of stones and dust flew up.

One or two more shells were fired without any noticeable results. At last one of them began to hiss, prematurely—as one feels inclined to do at a Bricklesian drama—while it was lying apparently harmless on the sill of the port. Everybody started. It was instantly kicked off into the sea—where, luckily, it did not explode, but sunk peacefully into extinction. Slides, of course, was quite ready to "account for" the accident. "Something" was wrong with the "cap," and there was "something" odd about the fuze. He would undertake to show, he said, that it could not happen to another; but the captain would have no more shell-firing that day. The "boat's return" was hoisted to Mr. Flower's great delight. Alfred remarked that he was beginning to take an interest in the practice, but, upon the whole, he was not sorry—I believe—to find that it was over. Long afterwards, the memory of his first sight of a shell adhered

to him, and many a time he narrated the circumstance to a
select circle, beginning—" Flower, of the Intolerable, and
I," &c., and his excellent mother never flagged in her shuddering sympathy—nay, not even at the twentieth repetition.

Alfred now came on board the Intolerable with Flower.
The commander received Flower with a little more courtesy
than usual, when he read his notes. Of course, Herbert
seized the occasion to ask leave to go on shore.

" Shore, shore," said old Bilboes, " you youngsters think
of nothing but the shore. No sooner is the anchor in the
ground, than you want to be off."

Flower said nothing. He knew his man. Old B. had a
notion that his *forte* was sarcasm—so, if you rather seemed
to wince, the harmless old gentleman thought you were hurt
by his harmless old jocosity, and ultimately relented from
his harmless old sternness.

" Ah, you want to see the ruins of ancient art," said Bilboes, feeling that his irony hit Flower very hard ; " well,
you may go."

Flower went off very quickly, indeed, we may be sure.
The apparently good-natured mood of old Bilboes induced
another young gentleman to try his hand likewise, but the
fatal inquiry, " whether his log was written up ?" put a stop-
per—as he afterwards expressed it—on his expedition.
That unhappy log ! How that log has tormented us naval
men ! How often have we had occasion to join with Ho-
RACE in imprecations on

Te triste LIGNUM te caducum
In domini caput immerentis!

Chapter VI.

The modern inhabitants of Athens—perched as they are beside the ruins—irresistibly suggest to one a camp of gypsies among the remains at Stonehenge. The contrast is just about as great, and the relation of modern to ancient there quite as respectable ; or, if you prefer a commercial illustration, I would compare the town to an insolvent establishment, into which Europe has put King Otho as a kind of "man in possession." There is a sort of tawdry, semi-Turkish, semi-French seediness about those narrow streets, which inspires one with profound melancholy and disgust. There is a muddy palm-tree growing at the entrance of the main street in a consumptive manner—a false life, like the life round about ; and there stand for ever and ever, brown and ghostly, the temples of the old time, beside which this said life, with its noise, falsity, and pettiness, goes bustling on : a kind of *wake* that life seems round the noble death there—a wretched wake over a dead queen.

They were stirring times at Athens in 184-. But, first of all, let us see our friends, the Snigsbys, safely deposited at the *Hotel d' Orient*. The Paragon, as I have said, anchored in the Piræus, where there is quite a gay little white town. Two Russian brigs, with gilt stars on their gun-tompions—that foreign dandyism—were in the harbor. They exercised their guns constantly, the crew hallooing when they loaded, as they drove the rammers in ; they always loosed sails, and then furled them just as the Lotos did so ; and used to beat the Lotos too, which was their ambition.

Mr. Blobb and a party from the yacht here employed themselves in landing Mr. Snigsby's luggage. Mr. Snigsby was surprised to see a regular cab-stand, and a fellow in a

red cap and white petticoats, with a sash round him, come
trotting up with a hackney coach, •directly he landed.
Blobb settled with him to go to Athens, for so many
drachmas. "Athens sir, yes sir,"—fancy that! and off the
coach rolled, along over a good highway road—flat, marshy
plains stretching away on each side—pale, thin woods of
light-green trees springing from them—barren Hymettus on
one side—distant Pentelicus, looking misty. "The cabman"
stopped presently, and Mr. Snigsby half expected, as he put
his head out of the window, to find himself blockaded by a
row of omnibuses ahead. They had reached the "half-way
house"—a bright, gaudy little *café* on the borders of the
wood, by the road-side. "The Socrates' Arms, I suppose!"
said Alfred, who was in high spirits, making a joke in the
style of Brickles. Mrs. Snigsby laughed, but her husband
looked grave.

"The name of Socrates is too sacred for these jests,"
said Mr. Snigsby, pompously.

"Oh," said Alfred, sulkily, "there's a great deal of cant
talked about these old fellows!"

"Possibly, sir," said his father with sternness, "but the
cant of the Cyder Cellars is worse!"

Mr. Snigsby was in a rhadamanthine mood, as was proved
by this speech. Whenever that sarcasm about the C. C.
(as Alfred would have said) came out, Mr. S. was indubi-
tably sulky. "Humph," growled his heir, but I am afraid
the old gentleman had the best of it! Meanwhile the driver
was getting himself refreshed, and taking some red wine
among the babbling, gaudy, thin-waisted groups who basked
in the sun, on the benches outside, kicking out their red-
buskined legs, twisting their moustachios, and gabbling
three at a time. Crack went the whip, and on the coach
moved. At last, the road turned and they approached the
town; the Temple of Theseus lying just on the right. They

rattled up *the* street (for Athens can only be said to have
one street) and went straight to the hotel. They were to
begin "sight-seeing" (a sadly vulgar word that is) next
day. The Snigsbys always "did" the curiosities of a place
on system, and regulated their sublime interest in antiquity
by the almanac. As these poor sketches of mine are not
wholly buffooneries, but claim some slight "purpose," I
think I ought to subjoin a "Memorandum" of Mr. Snigsby's, prepared that evening. It may, who knows, serve as
a hint to some future traveller of lofty aims. It will, at all
events, illustrate the character of various ditto dittoes.

MEMORANDUM.

"—*th instant.* Breakfast. Inquire price of tent. See
ACROPOLIS, old columns, ruins Greek worship, graceful Temple of Winds. Dinner at 6. Write Hugg and Bloaker.

"—*th instant.* Early breakfast (*qy.* why salt so dear at
Athens?) See ruins, temple Jupiter Olympius. Emperor
Hadrian, arch of. Not to forget Umbrella, heat so great.
Polytheism, reflections on. Dinner at 6½.

"—*th instant.* Breakfast. Honey at ditto, from Hymettus. (Odd story about Plato and bees in cradle; fabu-
lous.) See Pnyx. Prison of Socrates. Tomb of ditto!
Great man; opposed popular superstitions. Resemblance
of to passers of Reform Bill. P.M. Ride out in carriage.
Letters.

"—*th instant.* Old stream of Ilyssus. Groves of Acad.
Home early to see tailor. Evening—roam about St. Paul's
Hill:—"unknown God." Home to tea.

"—*th instant.* Off to Phalarum Bay. Any snipes in
marsh? P.M. Wander among ruins; reflections on.
DINNER AT EMBASSY. LETTERS."

The last sentence Mr. Snigsby has put in capitals, for
reasons which he does not explain.

The Snigsbys clearly made the most of their time, if the above document is to be relied upon. And, indeed, they seem to have enjoyed themselves. The autograph-book of the hotel still retains their names and their testimony to that effect, along with all the miscellaneous names and testimonies of that volume; in which you read, how Jones liked Attica, and Brown liked the hotel,—and the execrable joke made by Higgs on the words "fare and fowl," to which is subjoined with due signatures the announcement that "three English gentlemen voted the writer of the above, an ass." The English leave the oddest possible relics of themselves, in these parts of the world. The French leave their cookery and their prints; the Venetians have left architecture; our travellers leave their autographs and petty jokes. Well, every one to his taste, as the proverb says! Alfred favored the very tomb of Socrates with his autograph, and other names had been before him.

"Antiquities" being pretty well exhausted, what attraction had the capital to offer? There was a court; to be sure, it was a little one; with a little standing army, and little ceremonies and snug little despotic ways of its own— scarcely rivalling a European one in anything but its debt— which was highly respectable in amount. There was a large flat white palace, which I defy any one to look at without wishing to stick bills on it. The whole affair was worthy of the city which once boasted the Tub of Diogenes. But see the fate of empires! Just as the city has become most ridiculous, it has got no wits!

This last was the remark at all events of a young English gentleman at the *table d'hôte* one day. There was usually a rather pleasant party there—a quiet old Russian patrician who interested himself in what everybody said and was very agreeable—a Greek gentleman who had been at college at Moscow—a travelling architect, and so on. Mr. Snigsby, to do him justice, was fond of conversation.   On this occasion he pricked up his ears.

"Have you been long in Athens, sir?" he said to the speaker, a perfectly self-possessed youth, who had every appearance of being a thorough-paced traveller.-

"Came from Trieste yesterday.   I should have been here before, but I was detained at Malta on my way from Algiers."

"Indeed!" said Mr. Snigsby.   The company generally glanced at the speaker, who was just pouring some wine into his soup, with some curiosity.

"And how, sir," said Mr. Snigsby, "does the French settlement there succeed?"

"They're getting on very well.   Bugeaud is not looking so well as he used to do.   All these old fellows are dropping off.   I saw Metternich in May; his voice had got quite shaky."

By this time the entire table began to confine its attention to the mysterious stranger.   Mr. Snigsby felt the necessity of continuing the conversation.   The youth was quite unconscious of anybody's attention apparently.

"Then, you seem to like Athens, as you—" Mr. Snigsby said.   .

"I like it?   I hate the little hole!   It's all very well when you come here as a boy you know, but it's keeping me away from an old chum that I was to meet at Odessa, and go home with."

"Hem," said Mr. Snigsby, looking perplexed and scarcely knowing what to ask next.   "And shall we have the pleasure of your company long?"

"I hope not.   It all depends on what turn affairs take. They say Katwinkski is to be recalled.   I don't feel sure about it myself.   Besides, who knows, I may have to take a passage to Trieste with King Otho!"

At this moment, Mr. Herbert Flower came in bearing a
. carpet bag, which (between ourselves) contained his plain
clothes. Room at the table was instantly made for that
youth. No sooner did his eye light on the mysterious one
than he nodded and said, "Why, hillo, Saunders, I have
not seen you since you were at Lisbon." Friendly recognition, and "wining" instantly followed. Mr. Saunders
talked away more briskly than ever, told innumerable anecdotes, all about public men of one class or another, many
of them bitter sarcasms of public men against each other.
The impression left by the whole was, that European politics were just a large selfish game played by men more or
less clever and unscrupulous, and none of whom excited any
particular reverence in Mr. Saunders. After dinner he took
a cigar out of his case, and announced that he was going
for " a stroll."

"Who is that?" inquired the Snigsbys, eagerly, after he
had left the room.

Flower laughed. "That's our own correspondent," he
said, and named the journal.

"Dear me," said Mr. Snigsby, reverently. " A most intelligent young man he seems."

" Oh yes ; smart fellow enough."

"I wonder," said Mr. Snigsby, musingly, " what can be
the matter here. Something, sir, you may depend !" he
added solemnly. " I wonder if the government are in a
crisis. Pray, my lord," here he turned to the Russian no-
bleman who was always so polite, " do you know anything
of the state of politics here ?"

The Russian made a bland and negative inclination.
Russians don't talk politics in coffee-rooms, Mr. Snigsby !
And indeed one reason that the English are such bad social
conversors is, that continual political talk spoils them. If
they were more literary they would be more elegant.

Just then a waiter summoned Alfred, who disappeared. Mrs. Snigsby had gone up stairs to their rooms ; Mr. Snigsby remained, musing over his claret. I rather fancy he was meditating some "speculation," and I know that he often thought that this mere travelling without making money was very absurd. He turned to Herbert Flower, who, in political matters, was but a sorry resource. "What think you, Flower ?"

Herbert shrugged the little shoulders. "I'm never interested in politics, my dear sir. Politics, I take to be the art of sending gentlemen into parliament, or promoting them in the army and navy. My father does *our* share of political business, for the present."

Mr. Snigsby smiled. "But have not you heard how things are going on here, for example ?"

"Well, I understand the king's dunned," said Herbert, laughing, "but, by gad, I'm dunned—only I'm not a king."

"Dunned, sir, indeed ?" said Mr. Snigsby, seriously.

"Yes, I made rather a good joke about it t'other day. I said his Court was an Insolvent Court." Mr. Snigsby grinned.

How beautiful was this romance of monarchy—how fine a thing to be a king under Otho's circumstances! But if, for him, we have no particular sympathy, let our chivalry give a sigh to the lady of the house of Oldenburg—with the head too fair for such a crown—sweet flower of beauty among the ruins of the beauty of old,—whose presence might compensate an Athenian for the loss of the marbles that charmed Pericles.

Just as they were sitting silent, in rushed the waiter, flourishing a napkin. "Come out and look, sir. Come out, sir !" And a distant sound of voices, and the hurrying hoofs of horses, were heard through the open doors of the hotel.

Mr. Snigsby, with true political curiosity, bounded to his

feet and rushed out accordingly. The hotel was in an uproar. The residents were running down stairs; everybody
asking his neighbor what was the matter. Nobody could
answer with certainty. Only it was quite clear in the fresh
and moonlight evening, that the people of the town were
all swarming in crowds—that the picturesque groups were
marching along towards the palace—that lights were gleaming now and then through its lofty windows.

Mr. Snigsby came running into the coffee-room again,
quite excited. " It's a REVOLUTION, Mr. Flower."

" Is it?" said Flower. " Then, waiter, bring another pint
of claret and a cigar."

" Won't you come and look at it?" said Mr. Snigsby in
surprise.

" I? bless you; no. Mind, waiter, the Lafitte."

While the waiter was attending to the order of Mr.
Flower, our friend Snigsby ran out again. The *Hotel
d'Orient* is situated near the palace, and the residents had
a capital view of the proceedings that night. The crowds
continued gathering, and now they gradually swelled into a
mass round the palace. And now began shouts—discord-
ant, tempestuous hubbub round these white marble walls.
Presently, a horseman leaves the palace portico at a gallop
—gallops down to the Artillery Barracks. Brief reply is
given to the message; " Artillery decline to act!" Increased hubbub follows, as the news is diffused through the
mob. And now begins a general yelling—indicative, as is
explained to Mr. Snigsby, (who is watching the proceedings
with high constitutional emotions from a balcony,) that the
people of Athens would like to see his Majesty at *his* balcony! You have heard the call for " author," raised by a
literary gentleman's acquaintances at the close of a new
play! Such was the yelling for his Majesty on the present

occasion ; they always call on kings, however, to have *their*
performances condemned.

And now the lights moved even more restlessly at the
windows of those wide white walls. Figures appear and
vanish there occasionally. Mr. Snigsby's emotions became
immense. He half knocked down a waiter, whom he met
carrying a lantern—as he rushed to summon Flower again.

"Come, Mr. Flower—come ! Listen to the roaring
there !"

" Capital Lafitte, my dear sir," said Herbert, never moving an inch.

" Come out and see it, man," said old Snigsby.

" Bah, my dear sir—leave my wine ?"

Snigsby hurried off again, and resumed his observation.

" Mr. Snigsby, sir," cried the waiter.

The old boy ran down once more. There was some hubbub going on at the door of the hotel. A lanky Albanian
—so he seemed—was hustled rudely in by an armed mob.
His cap fell off, and Mr. Snigsby recognised Alfred.

" Why—what the devil's up now ?" he roared out to that
youth.

" I just went out," stammered Alfred, who was deadly
pale.

" In that dress, sir ?" shouted his father. " Go to bed,
sir. Waiter, show him to bed !"

Once more, Mr. Snigsby gained his point of observation.
The tumult was decidedly increasing—nay, arms of various
kinds glittered more prominently in the moonlight. The
opening on the royal balcony began to move. Who shall
describe all the anxiety and terror going on within these
walls then ? Honor to the queenly heart, warm with the
blood of Gustavus—which is true to one at this hour—true
at once to the honor of its noble Northern birth, and the
Greek site of its Southern palace !

A figure appears on the balcony, and there is a dead hush
for a moment—and a low murmur. The king? No! A
burst of yelling follows. This is a grim Bavarian—most
unpopular man in Greece! The muskets gleamed still
more prominently. Dense roaring ensues.

"I wonder, sir, you dare show yourself!" roars stern old
——, who heads the multitude. The grim figure retires in
again—cursing rather deeply, we may imagine.

At last, the king appears. There is a shouting, and a
cry about "constitution," and the negotiation, and three
times three. And the mob slowly disperses and settles
down in its own dwellings.

"Well," said Mr. Snigsby, returning to the coffee-room,
"I call that a great spectacle! *Vox populi*, sir!"

"Now then ; sup," said Flower, finishing his second cigar.
"The Revolution has not spoiled my Lafitte."

"Here's the people!" said old Snigsby, joyously.

"*Vivat Regina!*" said Flower, with gallantry. Alfred
was already in bed. His first "lark" had terminated very
sadly in the classical city.

A few days afterwards, the Paragon slowly dropped out
of the harbor, bearing the Snigsbys for a slight cruise among
the islands.

Chapter VII.

Diplomacy is like a funeral. It invests everybody engaged in it with an air of sacred importance for the time.
Reflect on this, reader, and you will see that it is unusually
true for an epigram. Doth not poor Hobbins, slowly
marching with his black wand, look a loftier creature than
his brother plebeian? Even so our friends at embassies
seem great men from their occupation ; and naval captains

become so, of course, when diplomatic duties devolve on them. The captain of the "Intolerable," for example, was twice the man, at least, when visiting a consul in the Archipelago on political business. The captain of the "Verdant" landed an armed party to call the Pasha of Snobkali to account for an insult to the British flag, and made the Pasha apologize. Yet the captain of the "Verdant" was not personally an important man! Intrinsically, indeed, he was Adam Jones, R. N., with scarcely talent enough to manage a country post-office. Beautiful system, which "ennobles whatever it touches!" Were "British interests" injured by the revolution in my last chapter? Not at all; British interests remained perfectly safe, and dined together as comfortably as ever the day after. Of course the captain of the "Intolerable" felt that he, as senior officer of the squadron, was the cause of this happy state of things, and Toadyley, the mate, explained the same in the gun-room. Oddly enough, this disinterested admirer of his captain happened to do so in the hearing of the gun-room steward, who happened to tell it to the captain's steward, who happened to tell it to the captain. Toadyley was a man to "get on, sir," as old officers were wont to say. He rose by the possession of certain qualities, which irreverent fellows like his messmates did not appreciate. Short-sighted observers! What enableth the ape to maintain himself high up on trees? His prehensile tail! Nature is rich.

These preliminary observations will give the reader to understand that the scene of our story is still classic. The "Paragon," after cruising for a little while in the islands, returned to the Piræus. Mr. Snigsby, whose interest as a politician in the revolution had been naturally very great, was glad to learn that the king had accepted a constitution. It was pleasant to him to see the regular old political business going forward in the old way. The king not being fit

for a king, why, of course, he must have one or two more
imbecile people to help him, and so everything would come
right. Frequently Mr. Snigsby broached the cheerful subject at the *table d'hôte*, the Russian bowing silently in answer
to his remarks as usual. The "own correspondent" had
gone to Odessa, and was charming the subscribers from that
quarter. Little did these subscribers know that the active
fellow was the same man who (aided by the Mediterranean
papers) charmed them at the same time from Algiers and
Beyrout! Alfred had kept very quiet since his latest adventure, the particulars of which were indeed sufficiently
ludicrous. It seems that he had assumed the Albanian
dress on the evening of the revolution, and gone forth on an
Attic "lark." The partiality of the disciples of Brickles to
fancy dresses is well known; they are the male "Bloomers"
of the age in their tastes; and Alfred sallied forth on this
occasion in no ordinary spirits. Being addressed in the
Greek tongue in the *Café de l'Europe*, he rejoiced in the
opportunity of "chaffing" a nation in a language which,
though known about the "coal-hole," and other similar
neighborhoods, had not as yet (though I doubt not it will,
the "fast" schoolmaster being abroad) become familiar to
the inhabitants of the East. The result was a row, and
that hustling of the youth into his hotel, previously described. Perhaps the person who felt dullest about this
time, of the party, was Mrs. Snigsby, who had no society.
The English people abroad always assume brevet socia.
rank, and cut their proper equals if they get a chance. So
the Sempsters (Mrs. Sempster's father being a cadet of the
Highlow family, as Sempster's family know well)—the
Sempsters, of their own Bustle Square, went to the *Etran-
gers* when they heard the Snigsbys were at *L'Orient*—
picked out the same day to go to Eleusis, that the Snigbys
chose for going to Marathon, and somehow were always,

during their walks, on the *other* side of the Acropolis. One would have expected . the respective youths, Alfred and Highlow Sempster, to fraternize. But Highlow, though "fast," was that melancholy variety of the fast tribe—a fast Prig. Does the reader know this order of young fellows—solemn, conceited little sinners—grave, pompous reprobates—fellows, as Fontenoy once said to me in his savage way, who " voluntarily associate with the devil, and yet seem to feel that they are patronizing him !" Highlow was one of these, then, while Alfred was really a good fellow at bottom ; he loved to write to a prize-fighter, and seal with the Highlow shield, not knowing, as connoisseurs in heraldry do, that he had no right to use his mother's arms, his father not having any. Such was the youthful Sempster, who has since sat for a borough, and married into a government office under the auspices of old Riprigger, who gives young gentlemen situations, on condition of their taking one of his daughters into the bargain. A more determined aristocrat than Sempster does not of course exist now; for in our times Mammon is the most bigoted of all aristocrats. If you want to boast of your "blue blood," do it in the company of men of fortune, whose grandfathers were tradesmen.

Mr. Snigsby had made up his mind to leave Athens, and his final preparations for sea were being made on board the yacht, under the auspices of Blobb, when our friend had an opportunity of seeing a political spectacle. It must have been gratifying to a constitutional heart. In a word, the king's friends were leaving for Trieste in a steamer, escorted to the very water's edge by cavalry, to save them from "popular fury !" Popular fury, or the "rage of the rabble" (so described by Brigg the *attaché*—himself, of course, being sprung from emperors) accompanied the fugitives to the harbor. Rarely has a · more dignified spectacle been

17

presented to observation. That a king should be obliged to send away his companions, and to have them cheerfully pelted with mud by his loyal subjects! Why, one would rather *act* the king in a country barn! Indeed, being a king of Otho's class is very like following the theatrical profession, and doing the royal parts. The poor monarch was criticised in the newspapers like any stroller, hissed by the public, and short of money into the bargain! Mr. Snigsby pitied him heartily as the "Paragon" left the harbor in the Trieste steamer's wake, and he saw the sulky mustachioed gentlemen on the poop looking very fierce, yet not sorry to be out of harm's way. What became of these courtiers he never afterwards heard ; he supposed they went to some other court, and doubtless they are hanging about one to this hour, sneering at the "people"—and living on them.

The Squadron were still in the bay of Salamis. Mr. Snigsby's party went on board the "Intolerable" to bid them good bye there. We must fancy an affectionate parting between the commander and Mr. Snigsby, accompanied by a request from old Bilboes that he would take down a huge chest of drawers to Malta for him, and accompany Alfred, who is looking for Herbert Flower.

"Mr. Flower, sir?"—"On the poop," said the quartermaster.

Alfred ascended the ladder leading to that domain, and found Herbert pacing about there. There was an air of calm, yet satirical endurance about him.

"Well, 'Erbert, we're going to Malta. Come down and have a chat for a minute."

"Hem !" said Herbert.

"Why, what's the matter?"

"I can't exactly leave the poop at this minute. (Stand between me and old Bilboes a moment—there.) The fact is, I'm ordered to walk the poop by that old villain ; but there's a pocket-pistol in that fire-bucket."

Alfred gave a demonstration of sympathy.

"Pooh ! my dear fellow, the temporary triumph of the obscure ! no more ! A mere result of temporary supremacy. A similar thing happened to Sir Ralph Flower in Charles's time, when the Roundheads were uppermost." Herbert looked magnificently calm

" Really, I'm very sorry," said the affectionate Alfred.

" Never mind. Everything in this world fluctuates. The world, sir, as old Mehemet Ali loves to remark, is a wheel. And our world here is a cart-wheel."

They paced aft, and Herbert explained how this punishment had befallen him. Rarely do we meet with a more monstrous case. Herbert's dog having fallen overboard, Herbert had let go the life-buoy ; and for this Bilboes had doomed him for a time to walk the poop !

" So you are going to Malta ?" Here Herbert mused a minute, and then said, " Well, I heard you were likely to go ; so I have a letter for you to take, if you will."

" Delighted," said Alfred.

The quartermaster was privately dsipatched to the gunroom, and presently returned with a note, very neat in appearance, sealed with the magic roses, and addressed to Miss Beddoes.

Alfred looked so knowing when he saw the direction !

" Don't you remember the girl you danced with on board here ?"

" To be sure," Alfred said, digging him playfully in the ribs.

" Well, didn't you think she was jolly good-looking ?"

" I did, indeed," the youth replied, with the same knowing look. Herbert smiled in a queer, quiet way.

" Just call when you arrive, and give her that then," he

said. Alfred placed it most sacredly in his pocket, and felt quite proud of the mission. It was drawing near the time of departure now. Alfred, with all his "fastness," never could get rid of that softness of temperament, which, he affected to attribute reproachfully to that hateful abstraction—the "spoon." He grasped his friend's hand romantically. "Good-bye, old feller! I'm obliged for all your kindness."

"Stuff, my boy," said Flower; "that's the sort of thing one says to one's schoolmaster at the end of a half. I've not been kind to you. Pooh, pooh!" he continued, seeing that Alfred was about to protest, and putting his hand over his mouth.

"Yacht's boat's manned, sir," cried a voice from the gangway.

"Take care of yourself, and don't forget the letter."

"Ah! Flower," said Alfred, "you affect to hide those em—"

"Bless us, Snigsby," said Herbert, "you should leave '*hinc illæ lachrymæ*' to the Commons. You had better take some saltpetre to sea—a capital thing to cool wine when you can't get ice! And, I say, tell Muir to send up George Sand's *Consuelo* by the *Brickbat*, and make——"

"Walk the poop, sir!" was the stern and brief sentence from Bilboes, which cut short Herbert Flower's farewell. He turned away to pace backwards and forwards as pretentiously as did ever Sir Ralph Flower himself, and the Snigsbys got into their boat, the good lady of that name having given many thanks for his "kindness" to the captain of the "Intolerable," who had been kind enough to dine with them so often. Possibly we shall never be able to approximate to anything like a just admeasurement of obligations in this world. People's notions vary so! There was Jack Pitt of the *Lucifer*.—could mortal man have

been more cordially treated than Jack was, by the consul at
Snobkali? Yet the recollection of the dissolution of that
friendship is fresh in my memory. Jack's words yet occasionally haunt my ears : "He thinks," said the worthy
lieutenant, speaking of that consul's recent misconduct, and
red in the face—"he thinks, because I eat his dinners, and
dine at his house, and ride his horses—he thinks, sir, that
he is to call me *Jack!*"

The sails were loosed, the anchor up; the Paragon
dropped away to sea, glimmering like a star along the coast,
getting a "clean bill of health" at Cerigo, and moving on
towards Malta. The autumn was very fast departing by
this time, and Mr. Snigsby longed to return to England.
That that country was undoubtedly the best in the long run
he frequently asseverated now ; and reminded his family
that they had now seen a good deal of the world, and that,
as to Alfred in particular, it was time for him to be "settling
down"—a favorite phrase of his. And certainly it is a
happy phrase—though, of course, the value of anything in
the "settled-down" condition depends on the nature of the
mixture. Gooseberry and champagne both effervesce, but
the settling down leaves different results ; notwithstanding
the general notion that the wildness of youth is pretty
much the same thing in all youths. Alfred listened very
reasonably to the parental admonitions by this time, occupying himself in the afternoon, as the yacht drifted along,
in arranging his various purchases—his sabres and daggers,
and caps, and pipes, all which he destined to his future
"chambers ;" for a secret, dearly-cherished feeling lurked
in Alfred's breast—a determination to have "chambers"
when he returned to England, and to keep himself clear
from the parental control for the future. A hoary moralist
delights—and there is ground for the reflection—to comment
on the little sympathy that exists between fathers and sons

in the present age ; but if an old gentleman has no principles nor faith of his own, how can he expect his son to
value anything about him but his money ?   Show me a
youth who don't value that, and I will admit that our youth
are degenerate, as compared with their papas.

In due time, Malta gleamed along the surface of the water, white and low, like a dumpling in a pot. The Snigsbys
thought they would sail briskly in, in the fine part of the
day. But they did not know how it was—though Blobb
did—that the yacht reached in at night. It was too late
to go on shore then, and in the morning Mr. Blobb was absent. Snigsby remembered the mysterious sailing on the
occasion of their leaving for the Archipelago, and felt a dim
apprehension of some calamity ; but in the meantime they
established themselves once more at the old rooms in Strada
Reale. The island was dull at this time, and most of the
squadron away—those commanded by people of "interest"
dawdling about the Ionian islands—the working and obscure
ones, on the contrary, were at such places as Beyrout or
Tunis ; while the admiral, in command of all, was snug in
his house on shore, in a kind of seedy tranquillity,'if the
phrase be intelligible. Sir Booby Booing was a good judge
of value. He was lavish of his intellect—in dispatches and
orders—but very sparing with his table-money ! He knew
the worth of things—"he did," as Lieutenant Hireling
would say ; and he did not patronize society much, chiefly
that of wandering people of rank, who make a convenience
of the public authorities, getting passages in men-of-war from
them, and patronizing their families, and cutting them afterwards in England, in the regular hackneyed old way.

Mr. Alfred Snigsby arrayed himself, the next morning
after their arrival, in his most sumptuous style. He was
going to call at the quiet respectable lodgings of Captain
Beddoes, where dwelt the fair Lucy, and the captain's maiden

sister, an old lady of reading and sewing propensities. The captain was away at the club; and Alfred, who walked up stairs in some perturbation, found there Lucy by herself, looking fresh, white and trim as a camellia. The favorite ideal lady of a "Bricklesian" is a smart damsel, well acquainted with light literature, something of a flirt in her manners, and *tant soit peu* of a "snob" in her feelings. Lucy, however, was a quiet little girl, with just enough sentiment to sadden her, whose perception of fun was rather a matter of heart-sympathy than of acuteness, (and so more akin to genius,) and who, brought up always in the peculiar worldly atmosphere of garrison life, was worldly and orthodox from timidity somewhat. A spoiled high character, to meet which (as you do constantly) has an effect like dropping on a flower used as a marker in a heavy materialist volume!

How much depends on natural good feeling! Hireling, above mentioned, (formerly of H. M. Brig Snob,) Hireling, I say, deputed, once, to report to his commander the news of the death of his nearest relative, did it thus: putting his head inside the cabin door,—"Come on board, sir," said he, "your father's dead."

Alfred's obvious good feeling was in his favor. Lucy was up, and said she was glad to see him. Alfred envied Herbert Flower.

"Let me see," he began, after remarking that Malta was dull, "I've a note for you from Herbert Flower," and he produced it.

"Oh," said Lucy, "I hope he's well. Does he keep on good terms with his commander, now?"

She played with the note, and glanced at the seal, as if laughing at Mr. Flower's profusion of armorial wax. Alfred thought he ought to say good morning. How anxious she must be to read it! He rose up.

"Oh, don't hurry, Mr. Snigsby: I expect my father in every moment," said Lucy, putting down the still unopened note; and she began to talk about all the most lively subjects of the day. At last, however, Alfred felt—the captain still not having arrived—that he really ought to go; but he found he was wonderfully more at ease with the young lady than before. The chat was very lively, just as he was saying good morning.

"So, Herbert still occasionally excites the captain's wrath," Lucy said, laughing.

"Oh, yes; perhaps Commander Bilbocs is jealous of him," said Alfred, gallantly.

"Of his high-flown names of kinsmen, and his ancestral roses, as he calls them?" Lucy laughed again, and looked at the seal.

"Of *the* rose, perhaps," said Alfred, bowing, and inwardly wishing that he was dressed as Don Cæsar de Bazan—his favorite ideal.

Lucy blushed and looked demure. "Oh, Herbert's heart, like his shield, holds a whole *bouquet* of them. You're mistaken about him. I think you have been deluded by your own chivalry there, Mr. Snigsby."

Lucy giggled as she spoke, but her blush was earnest; and she meant it to be so.

"Well, I must bid you good morning. I shall hope to find the captain in, again."

"He will be very glad to see you," said Lucy.

"Good morning."

"Good bye, Mr. Snigsby."

The drawing-room door closed; Alfred's foot resounded on the stair; Lucy seized the letter, and listened: the street door resounded hollowly. The wax cracked in an instant, and she began to read.

Will our story be declared improbable for communicating

the purport of Mr. Herbert Flower's note? How Alfred's heart would have beat, if he had known that it was a kind of sentimental *letter of credit* for him, wherein Flower had favorably commended him to his young friend—the Lucy with whom he had flirted from childhood—as a very promis ing match.

"You see, Lucy dear," said the youth's note, "sentiment reminds me, sometimes, though I don't deal much in meta phors, of perfumes. People don't use perfumes, unless they can afford cambric ; and sentiment is a superfluity compared with fortune. Really, this strikes me as pretty ! I com mend you to a brilliant establishment ; and we part, don't we, luckily, if we can be torn away without bleeding ? Se riously, your papa would be delighted with the match, and so would our family. You have too much sense to call me bad-hearted, for saying all this, I know. I shall keep half a lock of your hair, for old acquaintance sake."

Lucy read this effusion with a shade *more* emotion than Herbert had written it with ; and laughed a good deal less than he had done : but neither of them suffered very deeply.

When Captain Beddoes came home to a quiet family din- ner, Lucy informed him that the Snigsbys had returned, and one of them called with a note from Flower.

"Hah, rich people, Rivers was saying," the captain said, carelessly ; "the old man was very civil to me at the Intoler- able's ball. We'll ask them here, if you like."

"Just as you please, papa," said Lucy, simply.

"Sure it wouldn't bore you ?"

"Oh no ; they seem kind, well-meaning people."

"Ah, we'll arrange about it."

At the same time, Alfred was narrating his visit to his family, and failed not to remark that Lucy was "jolly good looking."

17*

CHAPTER VIII.

THE ordinary notions of the requirements in an alliance might be summed up for general purposes as follows :— Money *and* birth—if possible—but, at all events, money ! Here and there a stray fellow plumes himself upon his ancestors, and declines to mix the paternal stream with blood which, like the Sacramento, brings mud along with the gold. But even such a stray fellow is found frequently to reflect that, while he has barely money enough for one, he has " blood" enough for two. This philosophical reflection once admitted, the mind wonderfully opens to the more liberal notions on these points. A pecuniary prospect dawns clearer and clearer. Some young lady of means is forthcoming, and the " prejudices of antiquity" glide gradually away. *She* has been born with a silver spoon in her mouth, and *he* puts his crest on it—what can be more delightfully harmonious ? In this way all ranks of us are gradually mingling in England, and intolerance in classes is becoming daily more hateful and ridiculous Now and then, to be sure, somebody exclaims—

" Leave us still our old nobility ;"

but, as a general rule, the length of a man's pedigree by no means atones for the length of his ears.

These highly philosophical remarks have been suggested by the circumstances mentioned in the last chapter. Alfred Snigsby left the *Strada* decidedly impressed with Miss Beddoes' beauty. We have seen how susceptible he was on a former occasion, and now the favorite vision of " chambers" lost its attraction, and he began to form a new ideal—that of his being the presiding spirit of a country house, and giving breakfasts on hunting mornings to the neighboring

'gentry. With regard to the consent of parents there was
no difficulty to be apprehended. Her Alf's happiness was
Mrs. Snigsby's only object; and his father, who knew that
he would have to make a settlement on him some time, had
philosophy enough to reflect that it might as well happen
now as at a future period. (And it required some philosophy to know this, at least, if we may judge by the irrational
prejudices of so many parents to whom instant disbursement
is so ridiculously awful.) We must therefore consider Alfred in the capacity of suitor; and sympathize with him in
his suit. We can fancy how one call led to another, and
the second to an excursion to Citta Vecchia; and how
their names were mentioned together in social gossip; and
how soon Miss Lucy contrived to inform him that never had
she thought of Herbert Flower except with the ordinary
affection of an old family friend. Alfred wrote to that
youth to say how happy he was; and received a most cordial reply, with a postcript respecting something he had ordered from a well-known firm in *Strada Pocco*, which had
not attended to him punctually as usual. The conduct of
the worthy Captain Beddoes was a model of quiet tact.
He first satisfied himself by corresponding with an old
friend, a "man of the world," in London, who ascertained
the Snigsbæan fortune with the accuracy of an accountant;
and then—to use a classical metaphor of no ordinary beauty—he lay down at leisure, and listened to the murmur of
the Pactolus which was to enrich his house. Never did
anybody manage to escape being bored with the prelimina-
ries better than he; and when an intimate or two, men of
the world likewise, asked any questions about the matter,
he shrugged his shoulders.—"People of fortune, sir," was
the phrase which, like the *Allah akhbar* of the Mussulman,
expressed the essence of his reflections on the subject. An
easy, experienced, loo-loving, sherry-consuming old gentle-

man, brought up in good old garrison traditions, he accepted
the piece of luck, just as he would have done a fluke at billiards—without particular comment—yet quietly making it
up. He showed Alfred a good deal of dignified attention,
and asked him to dinner at the mess, and when he had occasion to scrawl a note to Mr. Snigsby, senior, he impressed him considerably by the use of a ferocious-looking
but harmless old "wyvern," which adorned his seal. In
the meantime, the yacht was lying in the harbor, and Blobb
was passing his mornings—one may suppose—as usual, at
the "Shepherd and Shepherdess." Here he pursued the
classic game of skittles among his peers—occasionally giving snug little entertainments on board the "Paragon,"
when he entertained his guests with dry sarcastic observations on the Snigsbys, his employers. These, as we have
before seen, he had long since discerned not to be "regular
swells." Few things are more amusing and interesting than
the aristocratic tendencies of men like Mr. Blobb. It is a
real old piece of superstition that tendency which they have,
to respect a genuine "swell." For they are not to be im-
posed upon by mere money. Lord Blory—as his tradesmen
knew—was not rich. Nevertheless, Blobb respected him as
an ancient Briton did a Druid—and entertained a mystic
awe for his ancestors. It is common to speak of the present
as an "enlightened" age. But wherever there is stupidity
there is "darkness." The fact is the present age believes
in *ghosts*—to an extent which no previous age ever paral-
leled—in the *ghosts* of institutions, my dear reader—in the
ghosts of all sorts of mediæval figures, which have not the
reality people pretend to see in them at all. "Ancestors"
are very noble possessions to a man who is right worthy
and able himself ; but to my mind, the more ancestors a
blockhead has, of eminence, the worse it is for him. To
such a man the ashes of the dead, had he any feeling, would

be like coals of fire !   All this has only, however, an indi-
rect application to Mr. Blobb ; Mr. B.'s regard for Lord
Blory's ancestors was interesting and illustrative ; it was
something so darkly and mysteriously reverent !   I verily
believe that some people fancy the "lower orders" never
had any forefathers at all—but sprang out of clay in some
unexplained manner a few generations back.

We must however return to Alfred, who now assumes an
unusual importance, on account of the event which is supposed to be impending.   It is amusing to see the tender—
the rather melancholy—interest which invests a person in
his situation.   Though, to be sure, courtship, unless of the
high-flying, passionate, and poetic character, (we could do a
little in that way if we liked, reader !) is a very dull affair
to describe.   For after all there goes so much common-place
to make it up.   Like "swizzle," as was remarked by a naval
friend in a philosophic mood, it is two parts water !   It com-
prises so many ordinary every-day proceedings, such lunch-
ing, and dining, and walking when it will come on to rain,
such fluctuation of moods, and ebbing and flowing of tides
of fancy, that it is apt to be prosaic in detail.   Then, as
genius is more shown in making details interesting than in
anything else, it becomes a very hard thing to treat of in
fiction.   And one is driven to generalities, and to request
the reader to fancy Mr. Alfred Snigsby paying his addresses
to Miss Beddoes from day to day.   Lucy, who with all her
simplicity has a kind of tact—of which she is half conscious
—which gives her insight into character, has several times
arrived at the conclusion, and always deliberately shut her
eyes when face to face with the same, that Mr. Alfred is—
a fool, shall I say ?   Why, not exactly.   No.   She does not
like to say that, and she strives to reconcile matters, by saying to herself, that she has no right to judge harshly of anybody.   And this pleasant sophistry, which, I apprehend

everybody carries on more or less, is very like a habit of taking laudanum, which grows upon one, and at last becomes, instead of a pleasant variety, a most miserable necessity. It was all the more painful too, of course, for Lucy to observe that Alfred had no suspicion whatever of the same kind himself. The truth is, that the disciples of Brickles (and I am anxious to illustrate in this story the effect of the writings of that great man) mistake their superficial contempt for all that is serious in life, for a sort of Talleyrandish superiority to it. They think, poor fellows, that when they have grinned at "earnestness," and sneered at anything professing a·"purpose," they have risen into some lofty Machiavellian height from which they can look down. Hence—though the high Bricklesian, perhaps, can manage to keep the sneering worldly height with some success permanently, as a dog can stand on his hind legs after very much practice, the weaker Bricklesian becomes ten times more infatuated, *when* he gets what he calls "spoony," than anybody else. And so far was Alfred from knowing his weakness, that—to adopt a saying of Fontenoy's—one of those disgracefully acrid sayings which shock all right-minded people, "he carried his ears as if they were laurels." Encouraged by Lucy's encouragement, he began to blend with his "spooniness" a sort of semi-comic tone, and I dare say sometimes thought that the fact that he, the brilliant Alfred, should meditate matrimony, was a falling-off, and a joke. It was no joke to Lucy, however.

One morning Mr. Alfred Snigsby might have been observed seated at his desk in Strada Reale, with a very brilliant sheet of paper before him still untouched, though there were several blurred, blotted, and scribbled ones beside him. The fact is, he was about to make his formal-proposal! And though he had been virtually "accepted" for some time, yet there *is* a point in every courtship, my good reader, when sentimental generalities have to concentrate themselves and assume a practical form.

The Practical (with a big P) vindicates its right always in due time. There never was a religion yet which did not require bricks and morfar to build with ; that touching sen- timent, commercial confidence, *will* embody itself, every now and then, in an I O U. Courtship leads to settlements. So, Alfred had made up his mind to put the formal question to Miss Beddoes, and to pour out his expectations to her papa. He tried, poor fellow, while concocting the epistles, to persuade himself into a light, easy, comic view of the matter. But there was a fullness about the throat which did not exactly proceed from the effects of his *Joinville,* and a general sensation of his uneasiness, which belied his grin. At last he finished the notes, and sent them off. And then he emerged from the house into *Strada Reale.* I regret to say that he then went into "Joe Micallef's," for he wanted some "soda and curacóa" to "set him up."

"Morning, sar !" said Joe, in his affable way. Joe was presiding at his counter there, with the usual stump of a cigar in his mouth. There was also one naval youth there, (of course)—young Ricketts, of the Polypus—who had a nodding acquaintance with Alfred, and who nodded accord- ingly, and said—

"Queer this morning—out late. Supped at the Govern- or's—devilled kidneys—mulled port." Which sentences, Ricketts of the Polypus jerked out in a fragmentary man- ner, without adding a single phrase ; just as he had jerked them out to three different casual visitors of "Joe's" that morning.

Alfred stayed dawdling about "Joe's" in a wretched state of uncertainty. First of all he kept looking at the clock, and wondering whether his note for Lucy had reached ; whether his note to her parent had reached ;

when the answer would come, &c. "Now," thought Mr Alfred, "she is just writing."

In truth, Lucy *was* writing. And if the reader will permit me, we will peep into the drawing-room of her dwelling, and see her. I have her image before me at this moment—a slight delicate girl—what Mr. Herbert Flower was wont to call to his intimate friends, a Poppet—that is, with a certain innocent dollishness of prettiness, which to some people is peculiarly enchanting. There she sits radiant in a light morning dress ; the airy, beautiful coolness of which seems like a piece of English summer inside the Southern summer. Before her is a most brilliant ink-stand, and several sheets of creamy paper—and she has broken at least three flowers to pieces in musing over the subject which occupies her attention. At last she begins, and she looks up to her aunt, who is sitting beside her. Miss Beddoes, that maiden lady, is a most excellent person, not given to developing herself in talk, but who turns out, if you get friendly with her, to be considerably " up " in controversial theology.

" Well, aunt," Lucy said, " I suppose I must write ! I suppose I ought to—ought to be very happy—oughtn't I ?"

" My dear, you ought to know best. I would not undertake the responsibility of advising you on so serious a matter ! You are aware that in a worldly point of view—(how beautifully do these periphrases, my dear reader, avoid the unpleasantness of using the word ' money !')—in a worldly point of view—the match is one which would be quite satisfactory to your family. Perhaps, my dear, you would like to have me, in perfect confidence, consult Mr. Fatton ?"

(Our readers have not, I hope, forgotten the Rev. Mr. Fatton, of St. Kilderkin. The Rev. Mr. F., who openly denounces the " confessional " of the rival establishment, is yet given to a little private confession and absolution among his flock—in a quiet way.)

" No, thank you, dear," said Lucy, a little drily.

" You must then consult your own heart alone, my darling."

Lucy made a dash at the note.

" DEAR MR. SNIGSBY—(It's certainly a strange name.)"

" I dare say, as you are an heiress, he might be induced to take your name, my dear—if that is a serious objection."

"I have to thank you," resumed Lucy, " for the kind letter which you have sent me ; and I hope I am *not insensible* of the honor of the proposal which it conveys. I do not think you will find that I fail to appreciate the sentiments which have prompted it ; and I shall *be happy* to hear from my father, in such a spirit, as I expect him to treat the offer which you tell me you have made to him.

" Very sincerely,   L. B."

" There, aunt ! that's civil enough—and common-place enough—and un-romantic enough, I hope !"

And up started Lucy, in some agitation, and looked at herself in the glass, and bathed her forehead in *eau de Cologne.*

" For goodness sake, be calm, my darling," said her aunt, folding up the note gently, but promptly.

" You approve it, aunt ?" said Lucy, looking very much as if she were going to cry.

" It is quite correctly worded, my dear, I think."

In ten minutes more the note was sent off.

So far so good. Meanwhile Alfred's note to Captain Beddoes reached that officer at the club, and was handed to him just as he was playing billiards. He glanced at it—it was his turn—he made a very pretty winning hazard, and

then—leaving himself very safe—read it at his leisure. A
youth who had been watching the game, strolled out, leav
ing the Captain alone with his very old chum—a certain
old Colonel Bechamel—with whom he was playing.

" I suppose there's no harm in showing it to you," said
he, pitching it across.

" Hah !" said the Colonel resuming his cue, "that tall
young fellow—I know him. Plenty of money, I think you
said. Well, I'm glad to hear it. To be sure, Lucy's a girl
that ought to marry anybody she likes."

" You're kind always ; you good old Bechamel. But
you and I have lived long enough to know that money is
after all the great thing in these times."

" Yes," said Bechamel ; "you know what poor old Blory
used to say ? ' They use us old families,' said he, ' as they
do the ancient remains in Greece—patch brick walls with
us !' How like Blory that was !"

" Clever man to be sure. He might have done anything
he liked."

" So I told him ; and he said he preferred doing everything he liked. And he certainly did it !"

" We won't play any more, then."

" No."

. The two old veterans left the club, and crossed the square.
As they walked along, they chatted about the matter in
hand, and parted with more warmth than usual, as men who
care for each other do, when anything of consequence to
either of them has been the subject of conversation. The
captain moved on, musing on Mr. Alfred's letter—on the
advantage of having a rich son-in-law, and wondering
whether it would not be a good thing for the youth to go
into a dragoon regiment for a year or two. That would
polish him up, the captain very justly thought, reasoning
(without the aid of Rochefoucault, who has made the obser

vation) that *l'air bourgeois se perd quelquefois à l'armée.* But
by this time he was at home.

There were two gentlemen there, making a call on the
ladies ; but the captain caught his daughter's eye, and they
exchanged glances.

" Heard the news, Beddoes ?" said Captain Trivet.

" News ?" (the captain smiled inwardly ;) " what news ?"

" Oh ! the Alexandrian mail's come in—a great battle
in India."

" Ah ! bless me !"

" Of course, we've thrashed the fellows," said little Trivet,
(who has not been in action, that I am aware of,) complacently ; " but several of our fellows of high rank are killed.
You remember Philabeg Herbert ?"

" Major in the —th ?   I know."

" Most gallant charge—killed with a round shot."

" Poor fellow !" said the captain.   " Then, that young
midshipman in the Bustard comes in to the estates ?"

" There's the odd part of it.   I've just heard—in fact it's
come out—now that old Philabeg's killed—that—ahem !
You see, this young Herbert, or youth called Herbert, we'll
say—" Trivet grinned—" can't succeed.   The estates are
most rigidly entailed on—ah ! the real Herberts—most
awful thing for this poor boy in the Bustard to find out all
about his—his unfortunate position—now !"

The captain gave a low, strange whistle of an eccentric
and prolonged description. . " And who succeeds, then ?"
And here he rose and brought out the " Landed Gentry,"
which occasionally amused his long evenings, and turned to
the " Herberts of Cockrow Tower."   Of course, there was
a " Ranulphus de Herbert ;" and there was an " ancient
rhyme" which tradition had " preserved," (which Tradition,
by the way, too often " preserves" mere offal, as the Admi
ralty contractors do,) viz., this beautiful fragment—

"When ye De Herbert doth ride,
Woe doth ye churl betide."

And there was a De Herbert who was a "favorite" of some king ; and there was a "*from whom descended,*" (con- cerning which favorite, little, sly line, reader, you and I have our suspicions, perhaps, often ;) and, finally, you came upon firm substantial pepigree about Charles's time. You then saw—that is, our friend the captain did—how few Herberts there had been every generation ; and that, finally, the late Major not having left legitimate issue, the estates would revert to the issue of his great-grandfather's daugh- ter, Ada ——, married in 17—, to Charles Henry Flower of Flory.

" By Jove !" said Captain Beddoes, rising solemnly, like a Presbyterian about to say grace—" by Jove ! the Flow- ers get that splendid property !"

"" What, papa !" said Lucy, flushing all red with surprise, " our friends ?"

" To be sure ; won't young Herbert be delighted ? Now, Lucy, it will be a graceful thing, as we're old friends of the family, for you to write and tell Herbert the news. His ship's at·Athens, and he will have it from you first of all."

Lucy left the room ; and when she was snug in her own room, what with emotion and the excitement of the day, and looking at Herbert Flower's last letter to her, (which, in my private opinion, it was about time for her to have burned before this,) she cried ·bitterly. A water-lily in a shower of rain—oh, reader ! did you ever see that ? How the river is quivering all round it, and the broad leaves pat- ter and dip, and the whole white beauty of the flower is shivering and glancing in a fever of excitement ! Such-like was our friend·Lucy then. If you remark, it is only at a certain period, perhaps even by accident, that one finds out that one has a real heart   Circumstances, education, may

have made one feel worldly, and look worldly; but suddenly, by what you may call a conversion, an impulse—it
may be a death, it may be a pretty face—your whole emotions are awakened, and you seem a new man or woman.
For, under the thickest conventionalism, there lies plenty
of emotion, just as under solid old London and its founda-
tion of chalk there is plenty of the purest of water.

But Lucy had to come down in due time, and the three
Beddoeses dined together. And then there was a private
interview between Lucy and her father; and next morning
Captain Beddoes dressed himself elaborately, and visited
Mr. Alfred Snigsby, who, in spite of his "knowingness," in
spite of his acquaintance with the writings of Brickles, who
had sneered at matrimony, and other things holy, till his
whole moral nature (like his nose) had a sneering turn upwards towards heaven!—in spite of all this, was, to speak
his own beautiful language, in a "very great funk." Old
Beddoes, who was a gentleman, (not a manufactured gentleman, made out of the raw material, but a born one,) conducted the delicate matter with the greatest tact. Alfred
was an accepted suitor.

The reader is now requested to follow me to the "Intolerable." The Squadron is still in the Archipelago, putting
the Eastern question to rights. The affair is conducting
itself beautifully. Snogg at Lemnos has landed a party of
armed men, and bullied a Pasha into "apologizing" for
something—a great triumph for Snogg, who inherits a turn
for severe officiality from his grandfather the beadle. Snogg
has made a long dispatch about this. Snogg has become
more pompous than ever on account of this. Snogg now,
more successfully than ever, helps to spoil that climate, and
make miserable the brig "Lotos," for the two midshipmen
he most hates—MAXWELL ADAIR, who is a scholar, and

pleasant CHARLES HILDERSTONE, who quarters the arms of the Plantagenets. Meanwhile, at Athens, the squadron are enjoying the hospitalities of the Minister, including Bulbous, who keeps the entire Greek ministry waiting dinner at the embassy half an hour, comes in red and reeking, when everybody is disgusted with waiting, and then (mark this as a *trait* in vulgar people generally) is sulky with the company all day, *because he* has annoyed *them!* And so the affairs of the East arrange themselves, and Greece is put to rights in the orthodox manner.

It happened that the note of Lucy Beddoes found Mr. Herbert Flower, by an odd coincidence, where we left him, viz., walking the poop for punishment! I don't say that he has been there during the whole interval, but he had certainly been sent there that morning, by the worthy Bilboes, for some offence against discipline. Fancy his delight when the news came. It turned his head. He gently walked below without consulting the authorities. "Steward," he roared, "half-a-dozen of champagne!" Astonishment seized the mess.

"I thought you were on the poop, Mr. Flower," said Toadyley.

"Did you?" said Herbert, in reply. "We think many strange things. I once thought all officers were gentlemen, but I know better. The corkscrew!"

Toadyley turned pale, and eyed a cane which stood in a corner of the gun-room. He was wondering whether it would be "*safe*" to "*lick*" Mr. H. F.

"Pop" went the first bottle. But here the right-minded reader's mind suggests a question to him—was not this glee rather odd on Mr. Flower's part—glee on the strength of the slaugther of an old gentleman who was his father's cousin?

My dear reader, when the late Lord K——, my long

descended neighbor, who bore a title renowned in the history of our native land, received the unexpected news of his uncle's death, which placed him in the estate and title— "What !" cried he, "is the old fellow dead, *screwed down, and all safe?*" Let us proceed.

Bottle after bottle went "pop" likewise; and presently a loud cheer reached the ears of Commander Bilboes in the ward-room. Mr. Flower's friends were welcoming the news which he told them; and by this time Mr. Toadyley had conveyed the intelligence of Mr. Flower's desertion of his station to the commander's ear. The commander, in high indignation, sent for him; and the youth, first looking round to see that there was no witness within hearing, stole up to the commander, and spoke thus—(*horresco referens!*)— "Come, sir, you are talking like a tyrant! You *are* a tyrant, with the heart of a flunkey, and the manners of a boor! You delight to inflict petty annoyances on the gentlemen whom accident has put under your power—"

"Sen-try! Sentry!" roared old Bilboes, gasping for breath. "Come here, sentry!"—a cry which brought the marine running to his side. Mr. Flower declined, however, to repeat his vigorous sentence; but he was sent below "under arrest." "Under arrest" is a favorite mode of inspiring terror with some commanders, but is not always very successful. "D—n him," said Gunne of the Orson, of one of his midshipmen whom he had subjected to this restraint, and who took it philosophically, "*he gets fat.*" Herbert Flower, like Gunne's victim, showed a tendency to take the matter easily. So they sent him on to Malta to be dealt with by Sir Booby Booing. Sir Booby loved punishing. He loved to bite, though he hadn't a tooth in his head. He was in his second childhood; and, as in childhood, children smash toys, in second childhood admirals smash officers.

A youth who has health, pluck, and hope, and loves his
intellectual independence, feels no particular awe of an
imbecile old gent. in a seedy blue coat ; and Herbert
Flower's interview with Sir B. B., to whom he was introduced with awful ceremonies by flunkies and flag-lieutenants,
left no permanent impression on his mind. (I have heard
him regret that the admiral was not more particular in his
toilette.) The upshot was, that Mr. Herbert Flower was
discharged to the Kabob to await a passage to England,
and went on shore when he pleased from that vessel. Indeed, he may be said to have now become what naval men
call a " T. G."—a travelling gentleman. It was probably
this feeling which induced him to wear plain clothes always
when on shore. The affliction which he had suffered in the
loss of Major Herbert, at the battle of Blarianshillah, (the
major had been sent into a jungle with a company to attack
10,000 Ramshangs, heavily armed !) was proclaimed out-
wardly by the most elegant mourning—the appearance of
which of course naturally led to inquiries—which inquiries
led to the explanation of the luck which had befallen the
house of Flower. The excessive buoyancy and audacity the
news had produced in him was something wonderful ; he
openly proclaimed, in Ricardo's, his intention of "standing
for the county." He would then announce his contempt
for Sir Gruffin Ribs, who at present enjoyed that honor—
Sir Gruffin Ribs, the inventor of the Patent Potato-Crusher,
who had purchased huge estates there. " Fact is," Herbert
would say, " we were too poor to contest it, and the great
magnate, the Duke of——, wouldn't condescend to interfere—except, by-the-by, when that man, Creekles, tried it ;
d—n it, that was *going too far*, as the duke observed !"
All this, with the shrugging of the little shoulders, and
the ineffable precocity of our friend the Phenomenon, generally, was extremely amusing to the philosophic observer.

In the meantime Captain Beddoes had heard of Flower's arrival in Malta, and one day at dinner—Alfred being there —he said, " Oh, Lucy, I wonder why Herbert Flower has not called ?"

Lucy started slightly : people will start when particular names are abruptly mentioned. " I'm sure I can't guess." She seemed languid, and it had been a very oppressive summer that year. Alfred Snigsby felt a little pang of fear ; he liked Flower, but always stood in some little awe of him.

" We ought to see him," said Captain Beddoes, innocently. " I suppose you are too much occupied to look him out, Mr. Snigsby, eh ?"

" I will go and see about him this evening," said Alfred ; and, in the interval between dessert and tea, he and the captain strolled out together. " I have forgotten my hand-kerchief," said Alfred, abruptly, when they had got about a hundred yards from the door. He ran rather smartly back. The servant happened to be standing at the door, so he went in unannounced by a knock. Running up to the drawing-room, he passed in. Lucy was sitting near the window, in the twilight. Everybody has some little touch of poetic sentiment ; and the long Bricklesian paused to look at the girl, who did not hear him, and who was musing absently. Alfred entered softly and unperceived—and, as he gained the table, he saw a letter on it. He drew his breath suddenly. He knew the hand. It was the writing of Herbert Flower.

Alfred felt suddenly very much startled, and there was a sort of mistiness floating before his eyes. By a sudden impulse, he seized the letter, and backed tranquilly out of the room with it, still unperceived. He gained the open air. The captain was waiting for him at the corner of the street.

" Got it ?" he asked, carelessly.

" Eh ?" said Alfred.

" Your handkerchief ?"

Alfred had forgotten his handkerchief altogether; he
stared a little, and then said, hurriedly, "Oh, yes," and was
in a semi-somnambulist state; and feeling an intolerable
desire to be alone for a little, he informed the captain that
he must go and call to see his mother.   " All right," the
captain said, quietly.

Stupid Mr. Alfred Snigsby !—for the note which caused
him such excitement was nothing but the same note which
he himself had brought from Athens.   "She needn't have
kept it, though !" he thought, sulkily, after looking at it.
"Perhaps she don't care for me, after all," he muttered.
"Why the deuce was it on the table ?"   Oh, jealousy—thou
who art called "green-eyed"—thou art in thy element, with
a green subject to deal with !   But by this time Alfred was
at the paternal room.

He found them very much agitated and bothered.   Some
official, speaking execrable English, had been calling, and
had asked Mrs. Snigsby many *questions about Blobb:* "Who
was Blobb?—Where did they engage him?—What refer-
ences had they with him ?"   What did this portend ?

" I knew no good was in that abominable man," said Mrs.
S.   " I always feared him.   Now, Alfred, you must ascertain what all this is about."

" Oh, by Jove, ma—I can't undertake the bother !"

" What, sir !" roared old Snigsby from the sofa, where
he had been lying—"what ! why, what the devil will you
do—what the devil have you ever done ?   I have been
working all my life—[here poor Mrs. S. rose and ran out
of the room]—working all my life, sir, like a horse ; and
you—a fellow six feet—standing six feet in the boots which
I pay for," continued Mr. S., aiming at point ; "you'll do
nothing !   And you ain't ornamental either !"

Alfred rose up in a preternatural calm, and whistling loudly from the opera, Gustavus the Third, stalked majestically out of the house.

But there was one more interview to come off for this unhappy fellow this evening. How was he to face the adorable Lucy, having carried off the letter which indeed the poor girl had missed, and in extreme agitation had been wondering where it was. Off he must go to the house, and arrange *that* affair somehow. " I do like her ! She's a stunner," he muttered to himself, " and hang it, the governor must do something handsome when I'm married. He wants to see me settled. He'll like to see me so respectably married. He's afraid of these respectable people. He'll come down handsome !"

Once more he ascended the stairs, and there again was Lucy by herself.

" Oh, Lucy dear," began Mr. Alfred, " I found a letter of yours."

Lucy turned round quietly. " I did not lose a letter, Alfred," she said, with ever so little emphasis on the verb.

" Oh, I found it," said Alfred, hurriedly.

" It was on the table, I think," Lucy replied, with perfect simplicity. " A letter from a friend of my family, lying on the table. Did you take it away ?" she asked, looking inquiringly forth from her charming gray eye.

" Yes, I did," said Alfred, getting a little sulky. (Have you remarked how original vulgarity breaks out with most effect, then ?) " It's from 'Erbert Flower."

" Are you quite sure," said Lucy, who felt her cheeks growing hot and a little tremor, " that it was a gentlemanly thing to do ?"

Now Mr. Alfred dreaded the word "gentlemanly;" he had morbid sensibilities concerning the application of that word.

"I don't know, I'm sure. I'll think of it," he said.

" I hope so," said Lucy, going fluttering out of the room
with a motion like a falling blossom.

" Oh, a general crisis," remarked Mr. Alfred to himself,
moodily ; but he coolly went off for a walk, of course get
ting a cigar.

Well, it was now the evening of September 15th, 184–,
as I remember minutely ; for the subsequent adventures of
that night were singular, and often the subject of conversa
tion in the squadron.

It seems that Alfred went wandering about the least-fre
quented parts of the town, and it is conjectured (Jigger, of
the Bustard, swears to it) that he refreshed himself more
than once at *cafés*. Zarb, of *Strada St. Giovanni* (who, by
the by, would like Jigger's address, if convenient !) heard
him singing as he passed *his* shop ; and then it was noticed
that a suspicious-looking fellow was following him. Near
the *marina*, at all events about twelve, it would seem that
Alfred was seized from behind, and carried on board the
Paragon.

" When I awoke," said Alfred, at the C. C., afterwards,
" I heard a strange gurgling noise, and found myself in a
very narrow place. By Jove, Sir ! I was on board our
yacht : [look of admiration from Buck, the ruffish actor :]
and that fellow, Blobb, had carried me off to sea ! They
were going to have him up for bigamy, it seems ; his English wife had come out to Malta. And, by Jove ! he
wanted to be off cheap : so he, made up his mind to go to
Sicily—and he made me go, or they'd have seized him for
stealing the yacht. Gad ! I was obliged to do what he
pleased ; and glad I was to get rid of him at Naples, for he
went there."

The reader must fancy the astonishment of all parties
concerned next morning. Nothing was heard of the yacht

for ten days. Lucy Beddoes was in great terror, poor thing, and Herbert Flower (as an old friend of the family) was constantly at their house. At last, news came that the yacht was at Naples, and Alfred at the Victoria waiting for supplies from Mr. Snigsby. It was remarked, that his letters to Lucy were very cool. But one never knows the truth of these breaking-off cases. An "attachment," as a fanciful friend remarks, when it does break, smashes into so many bits, that you can never put them together, so as to get a notion of how it looked when it was whole!

At all events, the "attachment" did break off. Mrs. Cockatoo asserts, that Herbert Flower, one evening, kissed Lucy Beddoes, without being required to apologize; and Mrs. Flower, wife of the present Herbert Flower, Esq., of Flory, is a very pretty gray-eyed woman—and the only one of the "county people" who is properly civil to Lady Gruffin Ribs, as the excellent Sir G. R. assured my friend Fontenoy.

It was from Fontenoy that I heard the whole history, at the hospitable house of his brother-in-law, Alfred Welwyn, R. N. The Snigsbys are highly prosperous, and Alfred much improved since his father compelled him to work. Herbert Flower is extremely improved, likewise.

"There is always a chance for a gentleman," said my friend F., philosophically, "if he has an atom of *sentiment* in him. Much thumping is required to bring a disciple of the SIMIOUS SCHOOL into good order though."

THE DEATH SHOT·

A Tale of the Coast Guard.

WERE a man to go to Jericho, the reason for such a journey would be sufficiently palpable ; but did he cross the
Irish Channel, who is there who would not exclaim, "What
on earth could induce him ?" nor would the beauty of the
lakes, the picturesque sites of Wicklow, or the sublimity of
the Giant's Causeway, arise in the mind as a ready solution.
Say Paris, Rome, Naples, Venice, Vienna, Florence, Lau-
sanne, and all their multifarious attractions at once crowd
on the imagination, and readily account for the migration
of the most indolent gossiper who ever lounged in the bay-
window of White's.   I sin, therefore, with my eyes open, in
not setting forth an elaborate *exposé* of the causes which
moved me to visit

"The first flower of the ocean and gem of the sea ;"

but whatever I may purpose hereafter, it happens not to
enter into my present plan to communicate more than that
I not only found myself in Ireland, but in as black, bleak,
rugged, rocky, mountainous a spot as ever an Italian bandit
sought, or Messrs. Grieve & Co. delighted a London audience with.

From the turf-fire of the room in which I was located at
the village inn, a sufficient quantum of smoke intermingled

with the atmosphere to give it that peculiar high-dried odor so agreeable to the olfactory nerves of the Milesian. I will not deny that, on the crazy bed which stood in a corner of the room, I had often slept soundly enough—still it offered no temptation, and, like the good sauce of hunger, which makes the toughest steak delectable, you must be thoroughly knocked up before you sought the luxury of such repose as it offered. To be sure, two thirds of a bottle of whiskey on the table, and a steaming toddy-kettle on the fire, would have given a very comfortable sort of night-cap to any one who cared not to awake feverish in the morning.

From the windows, however, a far different scene presented itself: the sky was cloudless, the moon in the full, and every ray reflected by a boundless ocean-mirror—not a zephyr ruffling its glassy surface, save at its margin, where the ebbing tide receded from a blanched and almost impalpable sand.

It was the witching time of night. I raised the latch, and incontinently strode forth. Howard's picture of fairies disporting by moonlight rose on my imagination, and I looked wistfully for those light, tiny, aerial beings he loved to depict. The only living object, however, which revelled in the moonbeams and moved along the sands, was, though picturesque enough, as diametrically opposite to light, tiny, aerial beings, as a tall, square-shouldered, stalwart, heavy-bearded man could be—especially when, instead of butterfly wings and Arachne-wove gossamer robes, he was accoutred in a glazed nor'wester, a tarpaulin cloak and leggings, bore in his hand a formidable bludgeon, and belted round his waist were pistols, sword, ammunition, and port-fire; in place of fantastic gambols, his gait was slow and measured; in lieu of quirks and wiles, and wreathed smiles, he cast around cautious, scrutinizing glances. His was no merry sabaoth, but the lonely, dreary watch.

I addressed to one so described, some observations on the beauty of the night, fell into his step, and we proceeded together. The sands, baying with a bold sweep, were terminated by a precipitous ridge of black rocks running out far into the sea. Among these huge, black, chaotic fragments, a narrow, slippery and dangerous path was marked by white stones, a few feet apart on either side. Notwithstanding the brightness of the moon, it required all my attention, as we rounded the rugged, frowning point, lest by a false step I should be precipitated some thirty feet on the bristling bed of rocks that ranged beneath us. Over head hung a heavy mass, that occasionally left the path in the deepest shade.

In one of the most difficult and intricate passes my guide suddenly started, stopped, and with an agitated voice and manner, in a deep Connaught accent, asked : " Did you hear that, sir ?"

I had heard nothing but the monotonous washing of the waves.

" God rest his soul !" he continued, devoutly crossing himself. " Then it's a fearful thing to be cut off unshrived, and no holy man by to make God's peace with you !"

"Yet," I observed, " your calling often puts you in such peril !"

" Ah then ! when one's on duty, I take it to be quite a different thing. But what I mean is, when one's thoughts are upon life, and maybe about one's wife and children, to be suddenly murdered."

" Who ! How ! When did this happen ?"

" On the very spot where we stand. There ! did not your honor hear that ringing shot ? Every year, on the night and at the hour he received the ball that killed him, the report of the carbine is heard. The time was clean out of my head, or I would not have patrolled this spot, at this

hour; it always brings bad luck to him that hears it, as
what befell poor Mike Blaney, who was on this ground last
year, makes certain."

There was in the manner of the sailor such a solemn conviction of what he said, that whatever might have been my
own incredulity, I forbore making more expression of it
than uttering—

"It's strange!"

"Then indeed," he replied, "it is strange. Many of us
have heard it—and I was talking to your honor, and not a
bit thinking about the spot or time, when the report came,
sharp as though you had discharged a piece close under my
ear; and, what is not less strange, on the night of the murder, his wife—poor thing—was just getting into bed, when
the report of a musket, as exploded hard by, made her
scream to the servants to know what had happened; and
as they ran to inquire, they met the men on watch coming
to the house to know the cause. Nor could it be made out,
until the poor officer was picked up and carried stone dead,
and cold, into the house—though your honor sees it was
clean impossible for the report of a carbine to be heard from
this to the house. Nor did the men on watch, at either of
the next guards, hear a breath of noise that night."

Whether that emotions springing from mystery are infec-
tious, or that there is a latent tendency to superstition, never
so thoroughly eradicated as we are prone to believe, the
perfect credence the sailor had in these preternatural omens
affected me. The hour, the scene, the dreary spot, all lent
aid to the interest I felt to know the circumstances that
gave rise to these wondrous anniversary mementoes of a
deed of blood and crime.

"Neal Briant, your honor, was a regular man-o'-war's
man, and what's more rare—before father Mathew introduced the pledge—was very sober. He returned with a

18*

good sum of prize-money, obtained leave of absence, got spliced to a comely young woman, with a neat little fortune of a hundred or so; and as they loved each other, and soon had children enough, it was natural that they should like living together better than being separated for months or years from each other. He got, therefore, turned over to the coast guard. He bought a fishing-boat or two, and as soon as his boys could handle a tiller, or trim a sail, they became expert fishermen, and added to the family stock.

"Neal Briant, as well as being a handsome, smart fellow, could read and write well; so that it was no wonder that in a few years he became a commissioned, and then a chief-boatman. His sons, in the mean time, had become strapping, clever fellows, and thorough seamen. Not a pilot knew the coast better than Willy and Jemmy Briant. They were dare-devils, too. The one went mate some time to a West Indiaman; the other was master and part owner of a coasting vessel, running with general freight.

"Times weren't then as they are now, sir. There was plenty of money afloat. Gentlemen—and, indeed, all other classes of people—drank hard. Duties were high; home-made adulterations were not invented. The genuine foreign article must be had at any price, and at all risks. It was a glorious time for smugglers, and for the coast guard too, as far as that went. It was desperate work, it is true, but the rewards on both sides were great. A good run or two was a fortune to a man; and it was a bad winter for a coast guard's man if he did not share some hundreds prize-money. I say winter, for in the short, light nights of summer the risk to the smugglers was too great; not that they stood at trifles, or cared to sink the craft if they ran the cargo.

"An able, resolute young sailor, especially if he knew the coast well, need not beg for service, then. He had his own

terms, and all sorts of temptations were held out to him ;
and if we were not tried, more's the pity. Some of our
men made a thousand or two, though how it was made,
divil a soul could say.

"As you came down by the Lough, off to the right, you
may have remarked, sir, a high, white house ; it is nigh
ruinated now ; only a bit inhabited. The window-frames
are shattered, the door planked up—all is desertion. Well,
there was some good doings in that house, and many a
jovial night—whiskey galore, and the reek of the kitchen
could be winded a mile round. A hard-featured, grizzled-
headed old fellow lived there—one Captain M'Sweeny.
He was a cute old fox, with glimmering eyes half shut,
and a kind of grinning mouth half open, except when he
listened, and then it was wedged together, as if he feared
the breath would escape him.

"He was born a fisher-boy, and glad of a 'tato paring,
or the skin of a herring. But he built this house, had a
good holding of land, and none know what money. But
he is off to America, years ago ; God knows if dead or
alive now !

"More than by the guards, revenue cruisers, and customs-
officers, the smugglers were ruined by splits among themselves. Many hands must be employed, principals, agents,
crews, sea pilots, land pilots ; and it was a great difficulty
to find men true and silent, who never babbled over their
liquor, and could withstand the bribery and protection
government offered for informers ; besides, with temptation
without, envy, jealousy, hatred, revenge rankled within.

"Now here it was that M'Sweeny went beyond all men ;
he was known to be colleagued with the smugglers in two-
thirds of the ports of Europe ; he shrunk from no adventure,
however desperate ; yet so cute, wary, and cautious was he,
so hedged and fenced, that never once was he implicated,

much less anything brought home against him. The devil's
cure to him ! One thing was, he trusted as far as possible no
one—till the last minute, he kept everything dark ; and
those few in whom at last he must trust, he proved his keen-
ness and craft by the choice of, and endeavored to bind to
him, body, and soul, and estate. Well, sir, the lads—bad
luck to him !—his treacherous old eyes soon fell on were
Willy and Jemmy Briant ; and didn't that prove the daring,
as well as the craft of the old rogue? for while the lads
were clever, fearless, and faithful, warn't they the sons of the
most dauntless, intelligent, active man in the customs service, the most inveterate enemy to the smugglers, one they
most dreaded, and knew incorruptible ?

"Maybe M'Sweeny might not have been an ill-looking
fellow when young, for time changes all, especially one sub·
ject to weather and watches, but, above all, suspicion ;
evil doings—bad passions—cause deep furrows and dark
lines.

"Kate M'Sweeny, too, his wife, was a stout, well-built,
brave girl enough, and a good wife to him, one that did as he
bade her, and never had eyes to see further than he wished,
or ears to hear one bit more than he desired, with a ready
hand and nimble foot when requisite. Not but one often
sees a cross-grained couple with buxom children, but God's
truth is, a prettier girl than Kathleen M'Sweeny mortal
eyes never looked on ; she had large, loving, soft, blue eyes,
swimming amidst long dark lashes ; her light hair fell waving and curling in light golden ringlets ; her little rosebud
mouth showed rows of pearls. She was a lily, a snow-drop,
with a sweet tinge of carnation grafted on her cheeks. She
was tall and slight built, but each year added fresh beauties
to her form.

" If old M'Sweeny loved anything as money, it was Kath·
leen. You may depend she had suitors enough ; how any

pleased the girl it was difficult to say, for the heart of a young girl is a riddle that has perplexed many a wise head ; however, none received encouragement from M'Sweeny ; not that he turned the door on them, but now with a good word, now with a bad word, just kept them dangling on. So that, with his money, his cunning, and the beauty of Kathleen, there was not a young fellow he had not some hold of, and whose heart did not jump with joy when he bade them welcome, and Kathleen smiled. Then, among all these young fellows, there was none more tantalized than Willy Briant. Poor lad, one day he looked as though he would throw himself into the sea ; on another he was as joyous as the sunbeams dancing on it.

"Perhaps this was a courtship Briant himself might not altogether have approved of, but like all other things in this world, there was much to be said on both sides, and whatever one might think of old M'Sweeny, devil a word could be said in disparagement of Kathleen. If she were a bit of a coquette, as all the sex, and liked to be admired, there was something so coy, wild, and roguish about her, that not one of the lads could ever boast he had pressed her hand, or breathed five words of love together in her ear. Indeed the night work we have and other duties prevented Briant knowing much about the matter, and as Mrs. Briant would have liked well enough that Willy should have such a load of money as M'Sweeny, and such a wife as Kathleen, many a time at dinner she would say he was out laying his lobster pots in the Lough, when he was but just dangling about to catch a glimpse of Kathleen. Then, she was just like the rest of the world—mighty forgiving how a man made his money, provided he had plenty, and gold was never the worse in the children's hands, however the father might have come by it.

"The old fox's eyes glimmered as he saw his victim flutter about the money-jar; he gradually softened into pretended confidence, asked Willy's advice and opinion upon sundry little nautical matters, and whatever might have been his - ultimate views and ambition for Kathleen, filled Willy's heart and head with a thousand hopes built on those vague nothings, which to the young and sanguine are solid as the rocks we tread on.

"The vessel Willy had been mate of being in dock, M'Sweeny offered him his interest to get him appointed master of a large schooner trading to Flushing and other parts. This Willy leapt at, and Jemmy, who loved his brother, and believed he would ultimately win Kathleen, was induced to sell his share of the coaster, and embark as chief mate of the Atalanta.

"At first the trading seems regular, all above board, though there may be concealments for contraband goods, of which neither master nor mate knows anything. The lads once in the hands of those daring desperate gangs, are by degrees worked on, and led astray. First it might be but some lace for Kathleen, or a keg of brandy or a tub of bacca for M'Sweeny. Then without the young hands well knowing what they are about, they implicate them in some larger transactions, till what by example, what by love of adventure, cupidity, the impossibility of escape, all their good principles are debauched, they become bound soul and body in the perilous, but profitable traffic.

"Oh! the old sinners know well enough how to work round a spirited young fellow, and so the two lads, though as yet with characters untainted by suspicion, and being looked on as thriving, honest young fellows, became foremost in carrying on old M'Sweeney's nefarious plans.

"Then he was a real gentleman, a great scholar, and a good officer; there was something proud and haughty in his manner, yet he was the civilest man to speak to. I ever knew—the devil an oath ever came out of his lips. He was one Lieutenant Gascoine, and a smart seaman, strict and fond of discipline, and liking to see the duty done as it should be, yet he would spare any one else sooner than himself. He was never prying or bothering his men, now with this, now with that. He had been married to a pretty young woman, just long enough to have a little boy, who was the darling of both.

"In this service there are continual dispatches, because, do you see, we are a splice of all things, sailors, soldiers, police customs, conservators of the fisheries, quarantine officers, just something of everything, without being much of anything. Well, sir, as became known at the court-martial, one night the officer received a confidential dispatch from Flushing. It described the Atalanta by name, build and rig; the strongest suspicions were entertained that she belonged to wealthy adventurers, and was about to attempt a large run. The letter went on to say that the master and mate were supposed to be the sons of some chief-boatman of the coast guard. The officers were enjoined to keep a strict look-out for this vessel, secretly to inform themselves of the employment of the men's sons, and to report thereon, with such intelligence as they could collect respecting the Atalanta.

"Soon Lieutenant Gascoine learnt that it was Willy and Jemmy, the sons of Briant, who were the master and mate of the Atalanta. The lads were constantly writing home to their mother and sisters to have news of Kathleen, and of themselves, so that the whereabouts of the Atalanta, probable time of her sailing, where it was likely she would touch, where bound, when to return, were continually known to our officer, and reported; and thus every precaution taken for her capture in due time.

"Thus the affection of the boys for their parents betrayed

their employers, and the garrulity of the fond mother, and the pride of old Briant in his sons, betrayed the children.

"The sun was setting heavily among the gathering black clouds, when the man on duty reported that an unknown schooner was working in the offing: the officer took his glass and examined her movements. We were all standing by, when Briant taking up the glass from the man on watch, after an instant's sight of her, exclaimed joyfully—'She's the Atalanta, she's the Atalanta.'

"The officer turned on his heel without a word, and in a few minutes expresses were sent off to the commander of the district, and to the officers commanding our flanks right and left. Not long after that, Paddy Sullivan, a fisherman, who has a hut and a 'tato' field down by the bourne, wanted to have a speech with the Lieutenant.

"Now, whether it was Paddy Sullivan or not, God knows! only Paddy was known to change a ten-pound note not long after in the purchase of a cow, and he added a bit more to his potato garden ; however that may be, it seems that Mr. Gascoine got intelligence that Mike Magee, who had been absent some months, suddenly returned.

"Now, your honor must know, Mike had the reputation of being one of the cutest land-pilots of these parts—and as you may have heard more of sea-pilots than of land-pilots, I'll just tell you the nature of their business, which is this: when the run has been made, they direct the route, and the way in which it shall be passed up the country ; and there is not a cave or hole, or rabbit burrow, nor a crag, nor a glen, nor a pass, that they are not acquainted with better than your honor may be with the high road. There is not a hare that could double like Mike, nor a fox more cunning to cut off the scent when pursued.

"There is one McIvoy, a well-to-do man, that holds a large farm convenient to the sea. Now, all the world

knows that McIvoy is not over nice how he comes by a bit
of money, so long as he can but grab it. Well, he has a
few sheds and out-houses that are washed by the sea at
high tide, and since Mike's return, he had been employed
in making repairs, though not a rail had been driven in before, this many a day.

"Now, I have been out on many a dark night, but one
so black as that, in my life I never knew—not the twinkle
of a star; the sky was like a tarpaulin. I had patrolled
here, then, ten to fifteen years, but not a step could I take
till I got a glimpse of one of our marks to direct me.
Well, sir, our officer having as usual examined all our arms,
sent us out to the different guards, but between twelve and
one, when he came out to visit the guards, instead of ex-
changing us, he brought us in with him.

"We all thought that since all was so quiet, and it was
impossible to see a yard before one, it might be to dismiss
us to bed.

"Lieutenant Gascoine marched us beyond McIvoy's,
then whistled in the patrols at the extreme south. He
called Briant, and Bob Smith, a commissioned boatman,
aside, and gave orders to Briant to take three men, and
moving among the rocks to the water's edge, to lie in am-
bush close to McIvoy's sheds; while Bob Smith was to
take a file, go round by the north, and do the same. They
were to be silent as death, and not to move should any one
approach, till a landing had been effected, when they were
to rush out and secure the men.

"Mr. Gascoine and the rest moved down on the centre
We were to conceal ourselves standing, squatting, or lying
down, as best we might—but as I told you, it was pitch
dark, so that was not a matter of much difficulty.

"We laid there, may be half an hour, not the whistle of
a curlew to break the silence. Some fell asleep, and all

wondered what we were doing there, for as I before said,
Gascoine was not a man to have whims or caprices, as
some officers have.

"At length our attention was aroused by a slight splash
in the water, for ears become wonderfully acute by watching, when all around is silent. The leap of a fish would
have more disturbed the sea ; at long intervals another, and
another, followed.

"We strained our eyes, but could perceive nothing—we
somehow felt the approach of something, rather than saw
or heard it. There was a slight sound—then a rush, and
the crossing of swords ; and the low call and whistle of parties—the deep struggle—the shortened and panting breath—
and then the centre charged down.

"'Look out to the north,' roared Briant, 'I have grap-
pled one villain,' and striking his port-fire, the light glared
on his prisoner, whom he held by the throat. He gazed on
his son, William.!

"'Father !' exclaimed William.

The port-fire fell from Briant's hand, the prisoner from his
grasp, but Bob Smith, with the butt end of his carbine,
felled him to the ground.

"'Surrender, surrender ! or by heaven, I fire,' called
out Gascoine, holding a light in one hand, a pistol in another.

"The light fell on a youth, who, with a naked cutlass in
his hand, seemed irresolute to fight or fly. He rushed forward ; but the ball from Gascoine's pistol struck him, and
he rolled over. Oh ! then it was Jemmy Briant. The skirmish went on, though it was difficult to tell friend from foe.
Some of our men ran into the sea and shouted, 'We have
got the yawl ! they are shoving off! lend a hand here, my
lads.' Gascoine and some of us leaped into the sea : they
were desperate in the boat. I got this lash on the cheek

boarding her; but, however, we got on board—some we overpowered and manacled, some leaped into the sea.

"Our officer shouted to those on shore to look out for them.

"Daylight broke. We found two or three kegs of brandy on shore, ten more in the boat, and four or five tubs of tobacco; five men we had prisoners—two badly wounded, one of whom was Jem Briant.

"Some of us got a hurt or two, but lost neither life nor limb. From the intelligence Lieut. Gascoine had given, the Atalanta herself was captured by the Eclipse revenue cruiser. Well, sir, we shared a good lump of prize money; but one would think there was a curse on it, for, somehow or other, it seemed to bring misfortune to us all.

"It is a remark I have made, that, let a station be ever so happy, and officer and men and men with men ever so well together, the moment there is money to divide, instead of pleasure it brings discord, envy, hatred, bickering, discontent, and quarrels. They say the way to gain an action is, that each man should believe the victory depended on him. This may do in the fight, but when the prize comes to be divided, each thinks the whole or largest share should belong to him, and that every other division is unjust. Why should Tom have that? was it not I that——? Oh! there's no end of the bragging and backbiting. Well may they say money is the root of all evil; and yet we are glad to risk our lives to get it.

"It was an unlucky hour for the Briants. The prisoners were committed to jail. Jem Briant long suffered from his wound, and they were all transported for fourteen years.

"Lieut. Gascoine always appeared to have great confidence in Briant, nor do I think would willingly do him harm. But the authorities did not like the affair altogether.

" Briant was tried by a court-martial. It was a hard
case for him, after his long service and good conduct. But
the feeling of the court was unfavorable, and the evidence
of the lieutenant and Smith as to the release of William
bore against him, so that he was broke and mulcted of his
prize-money, while Robert Smith was promoted to chief-
boatman.

"From that hour Briant never held up his head. He and
his wife were broken-hearted at the fate of Willy and Jemmy, and his own disgrace. He became an altered man—
wan and slovenly. in his appearance, and at last took to
the drink—dispirited when sober, and quarrelsome when
half drunk. Faith, he was sorely tried! for his daughters—
buxom girls—it may be they dressed too much, held their
heads too high, and looked upon themselves as the best
matches in these parts—could not bear their fall, and that
the Miss Smiths should take the lead ; so one morning both
bolted, and, I have heard, took to bad courses—first in
Dublin, then in London. Altogether, Briant had desperate
fits of wrath, and looked on Lieut. Gascoine as the ruin of
himself, wife, and children. I often tried to talk him over,
and to show him the officer only did what was his duty, and
what indeed he could not help doing. But that only made
him outrageous, and with oaths he would say—

" 'Did he not make a catspaw of me to betray my own
boys? With his own hand did he not shoot Jemmy, and
command Black Bob Smith to fell the other when he had a
chance to make away? On the trial, what color did he
give to the shock I felt when I found I grasped my own
son by the throat ? I am no coward, or traitor, and have
always done my duty like a man, and fear nothing. But
was it not natural I should feel amazed and woe-struck?
And for this am I to be broke—mulcted even of my miserable prize-money ? The d—d villains ! I should like to

know how they would have acted! I would pitch the service to the devil; but at my age—now they have had all my youth and best blood out of me—what am I fit for? Was it not enough to lose my two boys—to have my poor girls' hearts turned—to have the poor old woman's heart broken!—but that here I am disgraced and degraded, the labor of my life lost! Mark me! 'I am d—d, but I will be avenged yet!'

"Now the truth was, the officer pitied him; and often, when his keen eyes must have detected that Briant was fuddled, though it was clean against his nature and principles, he would overlook it, and take opportunity privately to encourage Briant, and to warn him against taking to liquor. But all this only exasperated Briant the more against him.

"Then Mrs. Gascoine herself would walk over with her little boy, and call on Mrs. Briant, and try to cheer her, for the poor old soul would sit weeping and wringing her hands by the hour. It was sad to look on her, sure enough! and I believe the sight of Mrs. Gascoine and her son, seeing them look so blooming and happy, and Gascoine and her so doating on each other, only made Briant hate them the more.

"Now it was just such a lovely still night as this, and your honor may have noticed a clear spring of water that jets from a rock, and has worn itself a basin, into which it continually falls, while the rock whence it flows is covered with moss, sea pinks, and a thousand tiny rock flowers. Ah then! that was a favorite spot with Mrs. Gascoine, and often, with the wide ocean at their feet, she would sit there and work, while her husband read to, or conversed with, her, and the little boy would be filling her lap with, or twining in her hair, all kinds of wild flowers. Poor fellow! he called it after her, 'Jessie's Font,' and it goes by that name to this hour.

"It was anigh midnight, and Gascoine was about to
visit the guards, when she came out with him, and they
seated themselves at the font, and he clasped one of her
hands in his, while with another he was pointing out the
stars that were in full glory, shining sweetly on them. He
had thrown off his hat, and she was without a bonnet, and
as their eyes were cast up to heaven, I thought I never
looked on a more beautiful couple, for you see, as the moonlight fell on them, it was a picture. I had that guard, and
as I walked past them, I could hear them converse on the
soul and immortality—that was the last time I ever saw
him alive.

"Then it is an awful thing to condemn any one, more
especially when the laws have acquitted him, seeing there is
no dependence on circumstances, however suspicious they
may be.

"Neal Briant, the night before, had been making too
free with the whiskey. The officer sent him to bed, and in
the morning spoke kindly, but determined, to him. He
told him, with almost tears in his eyes, that, however it
would grieve him, he could never again overlook such conduct—that he must report him, and that Briant well knew
the consequence. This seemed to touch Briant for the moment. But his heart was all changed and altered, and instead of penitence, he was all vindictiveness. Gascoine
passed along the guards, changing the men, as is our
custom.

"Briant had the patrol we are now on, which is next to
the extreme south ; the man who had the guard below saw
them walking together, that is, the officer in advance,
Briant following some paces in the rear. Briant relieved
Blake at the extreme, who came in on this guard, but he
was alone, and no mention was made of the officer. Blake

took the sands, but as the tide was making, returned by the
path, and just here, in this dark nook, on the spot where I
heard the report of the carbine, he stumbled over something. He found it was a man—he shook him—no reply.
He dragged the body to the moonlight—to his horror it.
was Lieutènant Gascoine weltering in his blood, the back
part of his head blown off: he was lying on his face, quite
dead, but still warm.

"Blake whistled and called; he fired off his pistols, and
burnt his port-fire. Smith and the crew came rushing to
him; they bore the body to the station, where they found
us in consternation, for Mrs. Gascoine and all of us had
heard the shot that must have killed her husband; though
whence it came we knew not. The suspicion of Smith, then
in command, fell on Briant, but his carbine was clean and
loaded, and he had his regular charges of ammunition; the
muzzle of his tarpaulin carbine-case was, however, blown
off, but this he proved to have been done by accident several days before. All he knew was, that the lieutenant had
sent him on, to send in Blake. Smith had him taken before the magistrates, and he was committed.

"The ball that killed the officer was found, and sure
enough it was one of the regular carbine balls.

"Ah, then! it was a house of woe, and it would have
moved the heart of a flint to see Mrs. Gascoine and the
little boy throw themselves wailing on the corpse—our
wives and the fishermen filled the house, and there was not
a dry eye among us, for the bleeding body and the young
wife and child looked piteous, and all loved Gascoine, except perhaps M'Sweeny and his gang.

"Well, sir, Briant was tried, and, in spite of all, acquitted; but in our own minds he was never clear, and when
he returned from gaol, we resolved not to petition for his

removal, and that we would associate with him, if he would swear by his holy Saviour that he was innocent of the murder. However he might turn it, he never would swear direct that he did not commit this black deed."

"Would a man," I exclaimed, "who had committed a murder, hesitate about an oath?"

"I know not, sir; but Briant never would swear.

"He was discharged from this, but what became of him we never heard."

THE END

№ 661639

Thrilling scenes on
the ocean.